AS A GIRL, SHE DREAMED OF HIM. AS A WOMAN, SHE FOUGHT FOR HIS LOVE.

Earl Britton was the one person left in the world who cared for her. Jacintha was just seventeen when he became her guardian, but she had worshipped him, secretly, for as long as she could remember.

Now, as Jacintha's dreams became the desires of a woman, Earl was forced to admit feelings that he knew could lead only to disgrace and scandal. He was a married man—bound to a spoiled, selfish heiress—and, despite his aching need for Jacintha, he could not do the honorable thing by her. And Jacintha could never accept dishonor.

Somehow, Jacintha would survive on her own. And someday, whatever she had to do, she would find a way to have his love.

ALL FOR LOVE

Patricia Gallagher—bestselling author of *Castles in the Air* and *No Greater Love*—once again has created a captivating heroine, and an immortal love, in a sumptuous romance from America's past.

PATRICIA GALLAGHER

ALL FOR LOVE

AVON
PUBLISHERS OF BARD, CAMELOT, DISCUS AND FLARE BOOKS

To my brothers and sisters,
and in memory of my parents.

Fate, Time, Occasion, Chance, and Change? To these
All things are subject but eternal Love.

—Percy Bysshe Shelley
(1792–1822)

PART I

Chapter 1

FOG rolled in from the sea shortly before dawn, thickening as the day wore on, snarling traffic, paralyzing the harbor, and disrupting life in the crowded, narrow southern tip of Manhattan Island where, in 1858, most of New York City's eight hundred thousand people lived.

The carriage had just turned off Broadway on the way to Greenwich Village. The coachman, aided hardly at all by the flickering lamps flanking the perch, drove haltingly, cursing the fog, though never quite loudly enough to reach the ears of his master and the young lady who rode inside.

Jacintha Howard sat in pensive silence, gazing at the spectral mists, her stark black costume contrasting sharply with the luxurious interior of the coach, its sapphire velvet upholstery and silver embellishments. There were tufted footstools, plump cushions on which to rest the head and back, fringed swags decorating the windows, and a pair of mounted sterling vases holding sprigs of fern and fresh flowers.

"Are you all right?" the man beside her inquired solicitously, as he had frequently done all morning.

"Yes, thank you." Jacintha turned to him with a poignant smile. "You've been so kind and thoughtful, Mr. Britton. I don't know how I'd have managed without you."

"That's what friends—and executors—are for, my dear. But didn't we agree to be less formal?"

"I'm sorry, Earl. I keep forgetting."

"Is there anything you don't understand about the will, Jacintha? The lawyer wasn't very explicit."

"I understood him clearly enough. There wasn't much to explain, actually. Grandpa was bankrupt."

"You didn't seem much surprised."

"I had no illusions about my inheritance, Earl. I'm just glad the house isn't mortgaged. At least I'll have a roof over my head, even if it is a leaky one. Of course, the estate isn't settled yet, is it?"

"No, not until the creditors make their claims. The funeral, medical, and other outstanding debts must be paid first. I'm afraid there won't be much cash left, Jacintha. Possibly a thousand or so, which you will receive in monthly payments of fifty dollars. Do you think you can manage on that small amount?"

"I'll manage," she said determinedly. "If I take more, it will only deplete my funds sooner."

"You've been wonderfully brave, Jacintha."

"I've tried to be, Earl, but I must admit I don't feel very brave now. I don't feel much of anything, except loss and loneliness. It wasn't this hard when Grandmother died. I loved her just as much, but I was younger then, and I still had Grandpa. Now I have no blood kin." She shivered slightly.

"Are you afraid?"

"A little," she admitted timidly. "Maybe more than a little. I don't honestly know."

She looked so small and vulnerable, Earl wanted to take her in his arms and comfort her, as he would have comforted a bewildered child. The impulse was strong, but stronger still was the realization that she was no longer a child—and amazement that he had not realized it until now.

Yesterday, or so it seemed, she had been a chubby little thing in pinafores, hair ribbons, and high-topped shoes. Today, all he recognized of that delightful little girl were the dimples and lustrous dark curls. Even her eyes had changed. Once round and blue, they were now oblique and a clear, deep turquoise accented by long black lashes. Fascinating eyes, wistful and compelling, were easily her best feature.

Earl was touched by the schoolmarm simplicity of her black taffeta gown and prim poke bonnet, the likes of which he had not seen since his governess days. He suspected that her clothes were left from her grandmother's wardrobe and had been hastily altered for the occasion. The staid high neck and long sleeves were not relieved by the tacked-on white lace collar and cuffs. The buttoned bodice was designed for a fuller bosom, the gathered skirt for larger hips, and the matronly black lisle stockings were incongruous with the dainty, girlishly bowed slippers.

Her downcast lashes shadowed her cheeks, and Earl saw that her skin, though fair and flawless, was not as white as it appeared next to her glossy black hair, but actually a pale ivory with a soft pink translucence. She would blush easily, he thought, and exquisitely.

His gray eyes, narrowed in guarded scrutiny, were as critical as a jeweler's appraising a gem, a connoisseur's studying a work of art. Was she beautiful? The tilt of her nose was perhaps a bit too retroussé, and her mouth a shade too full and sensuously curved for patrician beauty. But it was an extraordinary face, at once arresting and provocative, with a sweetness and purity that made it seem uniquely beautiful.

A fringed black cashmere shawl, surely another relic of her grandmother's, fell over her shoulders in soft folds, and her small black-gloved hands were clasped demurely in her lap. Lovely creature, even in those grotesque rags! What then would she be like in appropriate adornment—a jewel in a proper setting?

The desire to embrace her persisted until Earl was forced

to discipline himself. "Don't look so forlorn, Jacintha. I know this is difficult for you and things seem bleak now. But you will survive. It just takes time and adjustment."

"Time and adjustment," she repeated, as lessons to be learned. "I only hope Grandpa didn't impose on friendship, Earl, appointing you executor of his will. You're so busy at the bank and all."

"Nonsense! He honored me with his confidence. I was quite fond of your grandfather, Jacintha. He and my father were good friends, you know."

She nodded, sighing. "That was long ago, wasn't it? Before my family's many misfortunes. It was dreadful for them all these lean years—and one reason for their seclusion. And having me to raise on top of everything else—"

"You mustn't feel that way, Jacintha. Your grandparents loved you deeply. You brought them great joy. Without you, they might have given up completely."

"But I was a burden, too, and a constant worry. Grandpa's business was gone. Then my mother died in the cholera epidemic and my father was killed in that terrible steamboat explosion, and poor Grandma was ill most of the time. The housekeeper had to care for me in addition to her other chores, which is why I can't think of Lollie as a servant. She was more of a mother to me, and still is. I owe her so much, I'll never be able to repay her."

"I'm sure she doesn't want to be repaid, Jacintha. Try not to worry."

Slowly the fog was lifting. Foghorns and steamer whistles announced that the port was busy again. They were approaching Washington Square. Jacintha could distinguish the Gothic stone towers of the university, the row of stately mansions facing the park, and the autumn-turning trees. Soon they would arrive at Riverview, once an imposing estate, now merely an old manor in disrepair, most of its land long since sold.

As the carriage jolted over the cobblestones, their bodies touched on the narrow springing seat, and Jacintha retreated farther into her corner. Earl had performed the executor's duties most graciously, but they could hardly be pleasant for him. She imagined that he was embarrassed by her poverty. She assumed that he had been offered a choice in the matter of her guardianship and could have declined. Had he simply lacked the heart to refuse a sick old man's request? Now, suddenly, he had a ward, whom his wife had never even met and might regard as a nuisance.

Mulling over this unwelcome prospect, she told him, "Please assure Mrs. Britton that I intend to live in my home, sir. I'm not a child, after all, and don't really need a guardian. I suppose, according to the law, someone must control the estate until I come of age. But I don't want you to feel responsible for me."

"Your grandfather did not intend you to live alone at Riverview, Jacintha."

"I won't be alone. Lollie will be with me."

"A housekeeper is not a proper chaperone for a young maiden, my dear."

"Not in formal society, perhaps, but that's not my situation. Lollie and I will manage, somehow."

"You can't confine yourself in that old brick tomb and wither away," Earl argued. "Seclusion was all right for your grandparents. They preferred it. But you're young and healthy—you need friends and entertainment. You're old enough for marriage, Jacintha."

She averted her eyes. "Girls get married in Greenwich Village, don't they?"

"Certainly—but how many eligible bachelors do you know? You've been immured in that ruin since childhood, except for a few years in boarding school. It's time you ventured out into the world, Jacintha. Mrs. Britton and I could sponsor a debut for you, introduce you to some worthy marital prospects."

"Put me on the block? To be scrutinized and then auctioned to the highest bidder?"

He smiled. "Is that your idea of a debut?"

"Yes, essentially. Anyway, I don't wish to put your wife to all that trouble. Why should she bother?"

His silence spoke eloquently. Earl knew that Laurette would not care to sponsor a lovely young lady. She was accustomed to being the center of attention and had never even wanted children for that very reason.

Not long after their honeymoon, Laurette discovered that she was pregnant. Her fury was boundless, and their first serious quarrel resulted.

"I told you to be careful!"

"I tried to be," Earl replied reasonably.

"You didn't try hard enough, then! How could you do this to me?"

"We're married, Laurette," he pleaded, astonished at the outburst. "And I'm not at all unhappy about this."

"Well, I am, damn you!" she cried, running from the room.

Ignoring his pleas and the doctor's orders, she continued to ride daily, jumping fences and hedges, until the premature birth of a baby girl too weak to survive. Two years later, discovering herself pregnant again, the lithe nymph suddenly became clumsy, tripping over carpets and slipping on stairs. Finally, she disappeared for a day, announcing some time later that she had suffered a miscarriage. Earl's suspicions about this second "mishap" estranged them temporarily, and Laurette went home to Philadelphia for a long recuperation. Reconciliation did not help the marriage, and there were frequent separations, during which Laurette visited Philadelphia, and elsewhere, for long periods.

To Earl's knowledge, Laurette never conceived again. She refused to consider adoption, insisting that parenthood should rest in the hands of God and nature. After two years of unsuccessful persuasion, Earl had given up all attempts to change his wife's mind.

Jacintha glanced at him furtively, puzzled by his grim silence. It occurred to her then that, while she had known Earl all her life, she did not really know him at all. His visits to Riverview had been infrequent and her vivid childhood memory of him was due to the fact that there had been so few visitors at all, and no one else who called her "Curly Locks" and treated her to candy and trinkets.

From his mother, a Carolina aristocrat, he had taken his thick dark hair and smooth, regular features, while the sturdy New England stock of his father showed in his lean, hard jaw and granite-gray eyes. It was a handsome face from every angle, but especially so in profile, and Jacintha wondered how old he was. Suddenly, she was curious, acutely aware of everything about him: the magnificent breadth of his shoulders in the finely tailed gray broadcloth frock coat, the firm, muscular thighs in tight-legged trousers, the slender, long-fingered hand holding the high beaver hat on one knee. Did she dare intrude on his thoughts?

"How is Mrs. Britton?" she asked softly.

"Which one?" he drawled, still preoccupied. "There are two, you know. My wife is visiting her family in Philadelphia. My mother lives in Charleston and was well, the last I heard."

"And your brother?"

"Larry has just returned to Harvard for the fall semester. He's a senior this year and quite a scholar."

"Really? I haven't seen him in so long, I doubt I'd know him anymore. Has he changed much?"

"Not much. The Carolina summers haven't improved his health as much as we hoped. He's still too thin and pale," said Earl in a worried tone. "Poor Mother. She was so sure a few sabbaticals in the sunny South would transform Larry into a bronzed giant."

"Is the Southern climate so much better?"

"To a true Southerner, my dear, everything is better there than here. And my mother, bless her, is a devout Dixielander despite all the years she spent in Yankee territory. She returned to South Carolina shortly after my marriage, and one would think she had never been away from it."

"It's only natural to love one's birthplace," Jacintha said. "Does your brother like the South?"

"He likes what he has seen of it."

"But Larry will live in New York after graduation, won't he, and go into the bank with you? Grandpa used to say the Brittons were bankers by tradition."

"Only for the past three generations," he said. "I'm not positive about my Great-Grandfather Britton's business—that chapter of the paternal family history is somewhat obscure. Father said he was a privateer during the Revolution, and a merchant prince afterwards—but he may have really been a pirate, for all I know. As for Larry," he continued, "I hope he will join the bank. That's what Father would have wanted and Uncle Peter is expecting, but he may decide to please Mother instead and be a gentleman planter. If so, the Evanston plantation will be waiting for him."

"In South Carolina?"

"Yes, on the Ashley River, not far from Charleston. The region is known as the Low Country. Mother and her sister divide their time between the plantation and a town house in Charleston. Aunt Evelyn is a spinster. She and Mother would love to see Larry become master of Rosewood."

"What a pretty name for a plantation! Do they have many slaves at Rosewood?"

"A hundred or so."

"It must be enormous!"

"As large as any in those parts. The original grant dates back to the seventeenth century, and the first Evanstons arrived with the colonists of the Lords Proprietors."

Jacintha wished she knew more about the history of the South, and resolved to do some research. "What do they raise?"

"Rice, mostly. Cotton has been profitable since the Whitney gin invention, and they are experimenting with tobacco. But these crops are more widely grown in other areas of the Carolinas. Rice is king in the Low Country because it thrives along the fresh water rivers and tidal basins."

Jacintha plied him with questions and listened raptly to his obliging description of Rosewood, the splendid gardens, the grand magnolias, the picturesque knobby-kneed cypress in the dark-mirrored swamps, the long, wide colonnades of moss-draped live oaks forming the traditional canopy over the entrance driveway, the scenic woods.

"Rosewood sounds enchanting," Jacintha murmured wistfully. "I'd like to see it."

"I'd like to show it to you."

Their eyes met briefly, Jacintha glancing away when she realized that he meant it. "Will—will your mother stay there if there is a civil war?"

Earl hesitated. "I don't know. I just hope she never has to make that decision."

"When will Mrs. Britton return from Philadelphia?" Jacintha digressed, disliking talk of war.

His response was wryly succinct. "In time for the first important ball of the season."

His mood turned somber again, and his gray eyes became distant. She was mystified by these intermittent preoccupations. Had her emergency kept him in New York, when he would rather have been with his wife? She could hardly apologize because her grandfather had died at an inopportune time.

She was relieved to see the chimneys of Riverview just ahead. Wisps of fog clung like cobwebs to the garnet brick walls. Weeds and brambles had long since overrun the grounds and sprouted between the cracks in the walks. Rank shrubbery, touching the eaves and gables, had to be periodically whacked away and the shutters left open to admit light. On dark days the interior was dim and gloomy, and because of the many unpruned trees, Jacintha had to climb to a cupola to see the Hudson River.

Despite its present appearance, Riverview was home to Jacintha, and she loved it with the simple binding love of a child. She never wanted to leave it and would do anything in her power to keep it.

"You're very quiet, Jacintha."

"I might say the same about you."

"Just brooding," he explained. "It's a habit with me. Do I puzzle you?"

"A little."

The coachman drew rein beside the carriage block, and the liveried footman leaped down to open the door. The fence gate was ajar, the iron pickets twisted and rusting.

After escorting her to the house, Earl asked, "Shall I come in? Is there anything you would like to discuss?"

"No, thank you. I'm sure you have other appointments."

"None more important, Jacintha. Your first allotment will be due soon. I'll bring it or send a messenger. Do you have enough cash for necessities?"

"I think so. And it's settled, then? I can stay at Riverview?"

"For the present," he agreed. "But remember, if I consider it in your best interests to take you away from here, I'll have to do it. Understand?"

She nodded reluctantly. "Goodbye, Mr. Britton."

He took the hand she offered, smiling. "Mr. Britton again, is it? Very well, Miss Howard. If you have any questions or need anything, let me know."

"Thank you," she answered, hammering with the knocker. Earl turned and left her there.

The door opened and the housekeeper asked anxiously, "Was it as bad as you expected?"

Jacintha's gaze trailed after the elegant carriage. "What?"

"The will."

"Worse, Lollie. Much worse. There's hardly anything left. A few hundred dollars and this property, that's about all—and the creditors still have to be paid." She brushed away threatening tears. "We're poor, Lollie."

"Baby," the elder woman soothed, drawing Jacintha to her large soft bosom, "didn't you know? We've been poor for a long, long time."

Chapter 2

AFTER a week of dreary days and dismal nights, Jacintha woke to find patches of sunlight in her room. The cherrywood furniture had a warm, mellow glow, like Burgundy wine. The faded flowers in the old carpet appeared brighter, the dull blue walls and limp lace curtains fresher.

She had not slept so late in months, not since the exhausting vigils in the master bedroom. Nor had she been so hungry recently, and as she lay drowsily in bed, yawning and stretching like a kitten, she thought wistfully how nice it would be just to ring for her breakfast. This had been the routine at Riverview once, before the financial crises. Jacintha listened raptly when Lollie talked about the good old days, the many servants and luxuries, when Jacintha's mother was the adored only child of Ronald and Penelope Hartford, born in Penelope's fortieth year and cherished above all else on earth.

Jacintha knew her mother had been exceptionally beautiful. Madeline's portrait, painted when she was sixteen, wearing a bouffant white ball gown and pearls, hung in the drawing room. Unable to recover from Madeline's death, Penelope had become an invalid, living on memories, while her husband gazed somberly every day at the great river where ships from all over the world docked with cargoes for Hartford Imports & Exports. Perhaps one of those foreign ships had carried the plague that had taken their daughter's life. One of the company's steamboats, bound for Albany, had killed their son-in-law, exploding and sinking rapidly.

Too young to remember much of either tragedy, Jacintha knew only that life at Riverview was never the same after a certain point. No parties, teas, balls, and very few visitors. Talk and laughter were subdued, smiles rare and fleeting. Her governess was dismissed. She attended a nearby day school for several years and was then sent to Miss Austin's Female Academy in Brooklyn, because the board and tuition were reasonable. Of what use was that education to her now?

Jacintha sat up, hugging her knees to her chest and pondering her future. The elms outside her windows were shedding their golden leaves, baring the boughs enough to afford a glimpse of the wide blue Hudson rolling toward the sea. She should hate that river for orphaning her, but she loved it as much as her ancestors had, and enjoyed watching the water traffic from the cupola. She had passed many lonely hours up there, pretending in childhood, daydreaming in adolescence. Woolgathering, her elders had called it.

Between the boat whistles and horns, she could hear the Village vendors chanting in the streets. Should she give the ragmen her grandfather's clothes? Lollie had made good use of her grandmother's wardrobe, and indeed Jacintha was wearing some of it herself. But Grandpa had been buried in his best black suit, and it was doubtful that even the secondhand dealers would be interested in his other garments.

As hunger began to gnaw at her, Jacintha forced herself out of bed. Her billowing white cotton nightgown swallowed her small figure, concealing the mature breasts and curves. Modesty had been inculcated in her early, and Jacintha had only a vague idea of how lovely her body really was. She ignored it most of the time, as she tried to ignore the curious sensations she occasionally felt, most recently when her person had touched Earl Britton's in the carriage. Lollie had confided the necessary biological facts when she had reached puberty, and Miss Austin's hygiene class had provided a few more—but sex was never discussed, even euphemistically. Presumably all the deep dark secrets of the human anatomy would be revealed in marriage—one reason, Jacintha imagined, why adolescents looked forward to it.

She was trying to decide which of her few morning dresses to wear, when Lollie knocked and entered, grinning. "Someone to see you, Missy," she said, using Grandpa's pet name for her.

"Is it someone I can meet on an empty stomach?"

Lollie laughed. She was a short, sturdy woman of English-Irish descent, with pale-lashed hazel eyes and braids of ash-colored hair wound neatly about her head. "I think so."

"Don't be so mysterious, Lollie. Tell me."

"It's him."

Always spare of speech, the older woman was sometimes prone to maddening monosyllables. "Him?"

"Mr. Britton. With your allowance, I suppose."

"He could have sent a messenger for that," Jacintha said. "I'll bet he has bad news. Hundreds of unpaid bills, and he has to sell the house, or worse."

"What could be worse?"

"Going to live in his home," Jacintha replied, frowning. "That's what could be worse!" She opened the armoire, distressed by the small, drab selection. "If only I had something new and pretty to wear!"

"Well, you don't, and you couldn't, anyway," Lollie reminded her. "You're in mourning, remember."

Jacintha disliked black, and she knew that weeds were not really required for young maidens, but in her case they served a dual purpose, substituting for the lack of other garments while showing respect for her late grandfather.

"All right, help me dress."

Jacintha descended the stairway several minutes later. Hoping she appeared as starved as she felt, she entered the parlor, smiling faintly.

"Good morning, Mr. Britton. How are you?"

"Fine, thanks. And you?"

Jacintha sighed and touched a hand delicately to her forehead—a gesture remembered from Miss Austin, a frail middle-aged spinster given to periodic attacks of the vapors. "A bit weak, I'm afraid, but otherwise—"

"Have you had breakfast?" he asked solicitously.

"Not yet."

"I'm sorry. I came too early. Go ahead, please. I'll walk outside."

"Oh, no. I'm not really hungry—not much appetite lately. Sit down, sir," she invited demurely, easing herself onto the faded velvet settee.

Earl chose a worn tapestry chair opposite her, reached inside his coat, and removed an envelope, which he placed on the marble-topped table at his elbow. "Your allotment for next month, my dear. The creditors are filing their claims."

"Is there enough money to pay them?"

He glanced away, afraid his expression might betray him. "I think so. Your grandfather had some extra cash in his safe at the bank, and I've persuaded them to settle for a percentage of the debts. There's one obstinate fellow, however, who refuses to compromise."

Her heart sank. "Oh? Who is he?"

"It doesn't matter, Jacintha. You won't have to deal with him, I will."

"How much is his claim?" she insisted.

Earl hesitated. "Five thousand."

"Dollars?"

"Well, not pennies."

"Five thousand dollars," Jacintha murmured in awe. "It might as well be five million! Can't you talk to him, explain the situation?"

"It's a gambling debt, Jacintha."

"Gambling?" she cried in astonishment. "Why, that's ridiculous! Grandpa never gambled in his life!"

"Only once, apparently, and that's the trouble. He didn't know anything about the game and foolishly tried to win the money he desperately needed. The casino owner holds the promissory note, which he could easily destroy, but gamblers don't usually operate that way. I asked him to cancel or at least reduce Mr. Hartford's I.O.U. as a special favor to me, considering the thousands I've lost at his tricky tables, but he laughed."

"Perhaps if I spoke with him?"

"No, Jacintha." His tone was final.

"But if it's a debt of honor?"

Her innocence was really quite pathetic. "Gambling debts at casinos are usually incurred through dishonest dealers, marked cards, and loaded dice. I doubt your grandfather lost half that amount at faro, and a fourth would probably be more accurate. It's a racket, Jacintha."

"Well"—she sighed disconsolately—"where does that leave me? If he insists on being paid . . ." Her voice was fairly calm, despite her internal quivers. "Surely you can do something?"

Earl shook his head. "I'm a banker, not a magician. I'll try again to persuade him to sell the note at discount, but it's still a goodly sum, Jacintha."

She stood, holding her chin proudly high. "You want my permission to sell Riverview?"

"I don't need your permission for that," he replied, to her shocked dismay. "As executor, I can dispose of any assets necessary to satisfy legal claims. That's the law, Jacintha, but I don't want to act without your consent."

"Then you'll never have it!"

"Jacintha." Earl rose and moved toward her. "You need not decide anything now. But you must realize it's only a matter of time. You can't possibly continue living here on your meager income. The sooner you accept the fact, the better for you and Lollie. You can bring her with you to my home, as your personal attendant. There's an entire floor not in use now. You'd be in a proper environment and meeting the right people. Unless the eligible bachelors in this town are totally blind, you'd be a bride within a year."

"You said I didn't have to decide now," she reminded him.

"That's right," he agreed. "Let's forget it for now and go for a ride. Have luncheon somewhere. Things will look brighter in the sunshine, Jacintha. It's dismally dim in here."

"The shrubbery needs trimming."

"I'll send a handyman tomorrow."

"Lollie and I can do it."

"Jacintha, for heaven's sake, don't bicker over trifles! I'll charge it to your account, if you insist." He took her arm. "Come along, now. I hope you don't mind riding with me at the reins. I'm an experienced driver, really quite good."

Jacintha did not doubt that, for she had read that he raced his English sulky and thoroughbred horses in Harlem Lane and elsewhere, competing against other wealthy men who favored the sport. "I don't mind," she told him.

It was the most striking phaeton Jacintha had ever seen —bright yellow, with a black-fringed calash. "Pray step into my glorified pumpkin-shell, Miss Howard," he invited, offering gallant assistance.

She laughed, glad to be abroad on this glorious day. As they neared Washington Square, she cried, "I love autumn! It's my favorite season, next to spring. Isn't the park pretty, with the changing trees?"

"You'd never guess it was once a wretched potter's field and hanging ground, would you?" asked Earl. "Many a criminal's neck was stretched from those colorful trees, and many paupers' bones lie beneath them."

"Did you ever see any executions?"

"Hardly. That was before the turn of the century." He grinned at her. "Just how old do you think I am?"

She shrugged, embarrassed. "I don't know."

"I'll give you a hint. I'm not quite as ancient as the Pyramids, and I didn't help finance the Coliseum."

"Don't tease me, Earl. Shall I guess?"

"Maybe I'd better tell you, in case you imagine sixty. I was twenty-eight last month."

"Twenty-eight," she repeated, apparently considering even that a venerable age. "You don't look it."

He glanced at her, then laughed softly, low resonant laughter as pleasant as his baritone voice. "I expect to grow a long white beard and buy a fine mahogany cane any day now."

Abashed, Jacintha turned her attention to the white stone buildings of New York University which, modeled after King's College in England, rose like a medieval fortress on the east side of the square. Students strolled nearby, nattily dressed young men with books under their arms, and Jacintha eyed them with interest.

"Under thirty," Earl remarked, "every one of them."

"Oh, hush," she murmured petulantly.

"You should pout more often, Miss Howard. It becomes you."

Jacintha knew he shouldn't compliment her so liberally. Nor should she be out alone with him in this conspicuous contraption of his. Even betrothed couples had to be discreet in public, and here she was riding unchaperoned with a married man.

Just then her mind was diverted by a smartly dressed lady crossing the street, and Earl did not miss the longing on her face.

"Stunning gown, isn't it?"

"I've never seen a prettier one."

"And that, my dear, is what I call an attractive bonnet."

"Isn't it a bit frivolous?" It was little more than a puff of feathers and wisp of veiling.

"Not on her. She's young and pretty enough to get by with it, and so are you."

"You think so? Well, perhaps when I stop wearing mourning—" Reality and common sense intervened. "I could never afford anything that expensive."

Absorbed, morose, she barely realized that they were passing through Chelsea, a small village of Irish immigrants who had fled the great potato famines. Chickens and geese scattered out of their path, pigs ran squealing into the underbrush. Several women in shoddy dresses and old bonnets, baskets in hand on the way to market, paused to stare at the sporty carriage.

"Where are we going?" she asked.

"To an inn in the country which serves excellent food and wine."

"So far out?"

"Would you have preferred Delmonico's?"

She would indeed! She had never been to that famous restaurant, or to the Astor House, the Brevoort, or the fabulous new white marble St. Nickolas Hotel on Broadway.

"It doesn't matter," she said. "But we mustn't be gone long. Lollie will be worried."

"We're almost there."

He put the horse to a faster gait, and soon they arrived at a secluded stone building almost hidden by trees. Appetizing aromas wafted from the kitchen chimney. The delicious beef Wellington was a welcome treat after the economical stews, meat pies, and fish chowders that comprised most of the fare at Riverview. Jacintha ate heartily, enjoying everything, especially the marvelous pastries. She even succumbed to a small glass of Madeira from the wicker-encased bottle Earl ordered.

A candle glowed in a hurricane lamp on the table, and Earl gazed at it pensively as he sipped his wine. What caused these sudden silent moods? Jacintha wondered.

"Thank you for the luncheon," she said quietly. "It was most enjoyable, and I'm ready to leave now."

"Are you in a hurry, Jacintha?"

"Don't you have to get back to the bank?"

"Not necessarily. I don't manage it alone."

"Do any ladies work there?"

"None. The only thing most women know about money is how to spend it." He paused, peering at her intently. "You weren't thinking of applying for a job?"

She nodded.

"Doing what, Jacintha? Banking is a complicated business, and you have no training. You're a child!"

"I'm seventeen, and last week you said I was old enough to get married."

"That's different."

"Why? If I'm not too young to marry and have children, why can't I work?"

"You weren't reared to support yourself," he reasoned. "Your grandparents never intended you to work and you're not qualified for anything. Be sensible, Jacintha. There's nothing for a girl like you except marriage."

She gritted her teeth. "So we're back to that again? Sell Riverview!"

"A minor needs a guardian," he patiently explained. "We can do this amicably, or legally in Surrogate Court."

In the phaeton again, Jacintha became defiant. "I won't do it, Earl! I won't sell Riverview or live in your home. I'll run away."

"I'll send the law and bloodhounds after you."

"And lock me in the attic?"

"If necessary." He sounded uncompromising.

She stood up. "Stop here, now! I want to get out. I can walk home."

"Sit down, you little ninny!" His voice roughened with the scare she had given him and he yanked so forcibly on her skirts that her bottom smacked the seat resoundingly. "You can't jump from a moving vehicle! You'll break a leg."

"I don't care what I break! Stop or I'll scream."

Realizing she meant it, Earl hauled on the lines, keeping one hand firmly on her quivering arm. "Whoa! Whoa, there!"

"Let me go!" she demanded furiously.

"You're behaving like a shrew."

"A shrew? Oh, take your hands off me!" Her spine arched like a hostile cat's, and she clawed at his restraining grip. "I think you're horrid, Earl Britton!"

"I think you're delightful, Miss Howard, and I'm really quite fond of you."

"A fine way you have of showing it."

"I promised your grandfather—"

Jacintha interrupted. "I can take care of myself!"

"Can you?" He clinched her tighter, and his narrowed gray eyes had an odd, intense glow. "Can you, my dear?"

"Mr. Britton, you wouldn't—?"

"Rape you? Certainly not. But any ruthless man could, Jacintha. You don't know anything about the world."

"I can learn."

"The hard way? From some brutal sweatshop boss? Some greedy gorilla who would demand a part of your pitiful wages, a part of your body, or both, in order for you to keep your job?"

"They can't all be like that," she argued, relaxing as he released her. "Lots of girls work in factories."

"And the ugly ones are fairly safe. But you're young and beautiful, Jacintha. My God, don't you believe your mirror? A man would have to be gelt not to want you."

"What does gelt mean?"

"Castrated—and you don't know what *that* means, either, do you? You don't know the difference between a stallion and a gelding, or why eunuchs are the only males allowed in harems. And you want to enter the commercial jungle and earn your living? Jacintha! You'd end up in white slavery and never even realize how it happened!"

Her wide-eyed innocence told him just how little of this she understood.

"You are not going to work, Jacintha, and that's final!" He picked up the reins and headed back to town. "Did you hear me?"

"Yes, Master."

"Don't be sarcastic."

She was quiet for a mile or so, looking out over her side of the road, along which ran a meadow of ripening goldenrod. Then she turned to him with an apologetic smile.

"I'm sorry, Earl. Let's not quarrel anymore. I want to be friends. I need you so much—why, I couldn't get along without you. Grandpa knew that, or else he wouldn't have put me in your care. I'll do whatever you say, whatever you think best for me."

"Except leave Riverview?"

Jacintha smiled again, dimpling, and Earl was caught by those enchanting eyes. Those turquoise eyes could mesmerize the devil himself. He wanted her even more than he had realized. He could not bring her into his house to live. It would be a mistake for her and sheer hell for him. Yet giving her in marriage to another man would be the worst torture of all!

"Jacintha—"

"Yes?"

Earl hesitated, shrugged, then drove the horses as fast as he dared.

Chapter 3

JACINTHA had long been aware that Riverview was in disrepair, but not until she made a full inspection did she realize the extent of the deterioration. Cracked plaster, sloughing paint, sagging wallpaper, water-ringed ceilings, dingy woodwork, dilapidated outbuildings, unkempt grounds—the sad signs of poverty and neglect were everywhere. How much longer could repairs be postponed before the place became uninhabitable?

Indian summer was over, replaced by a rainy autumn. Earl had sent a handyman to trim the shrubbery and prune the trees, but the house was still dark and gloomy inside. Candles were cheaper than gaslight or kerosene lamps, so the rooms were bright only on sunny days. To save on fuel, Jacintha and Lollie shared a bedroom. They stopped buying from the street vendors, shopping instead at Washington Market, where Jacintha learned to barter for bargains. A soft voice, a sweet smile, a flutter of long dark eyelashes, and the stall-men fought for her patronage. Lollie guarded her, a stern duenna, assuring that even the bold fishmongers of Fulton Market took no liberties.

A messenger delivered her December allotment, and Jacintha was disappointed to find only the exact stipend. "Fifty dollars exactly," she complained. "Scrooge didn't even include a little extra for Christmas shopping!"

"But you told him—"

"What difference does that make? He could use his own judgment. He's unreasonable!" Jacintha declared, ignoring her own capriciousness. "The roof must be fixed, Lollie. All the upstairs ceilings are being ruined, and the loose windows are letting in more cold air. But why should King Midas care, snug in his Fifth Avenue palace? He doesn't even come here anymore, just sends an errand boy."

Jacintha had not seen Earl Britton since the day he had taken her to the country inn. She imagined he was greatly relieved, now, that her obstinacy had kept her at Riverview. She doubted that he had ever mentioned the will to his wife, much less his ward. The New York social season was in full swing, and the Brittons were an important part of it. Balls, musicales, dinners, teas, the theater and opera, coaching and sleighing parties—there seemed no end to the pleasures of the merry and idle rich. The Brittons also had houseguests for the holidays, including Laurette's parents and other relatives, and Earl's family and friends.

Lollie baked a plum pudding for Christmas, and they feasted for several days on a nice fat goose, stuffed and roasted, which Jacintha had charmed out of a jolly, generous butcher for a fraction of its worth. But she neither sent nor received any season's greetings, and the most exciting thing she had to do for New Year's was to hang up the calendar from Britton Bank, delivered with her January allotment. She wept as the jubilant bells pealed and whistles blew, and all New York celebrated the arrival of 1859.

The housekeeper, kneading a batch of dough for the weekly baking, prayed fervently, "Dear Lord, give us this day our daily bread and a better year ahead."

"I hope He's listening," Jacintha said skeptically.

"Seems to be, Missy. We're getting by."

"We're surviving, Lollie. I want to live! Go places and do things, dance, wear pretty clothes—"

"And have beaux?"

"What's wrong with that?"

"Nothing, honey. It's perfectly natural. But you'll never meet proper escorts on the street, you know, or in public markets. Maybe you should reconsider and let the Brittons sponsor you."

"I think that was just claptrap, Lollie. Mr. Britton's mind is elsewhere now."

"Well, never fear, someone will discover you."

"Like a pearl in an oyster? The odds of that must be a million to one."

Her grandmother's precious jewels had long ago been sold, along with the best silver and the paintings. But her grandfather must have had some hidden assets to satisfy his creditors, for she was not dunned by bill collectors, thank heaven. Not even the casino owner.

Snuggled in her featherbed on the long, cold, dark nights, Jacintha longed for spring, promising God that she would never again complain of summer heat. In the trundle, Lollie snored the deep sleep of exhaustion, oblivious to the sleet hissing against the windows and the banshee wailing of the fierce wind under the eaves. But Jacintha slept lightly, disturbed by the eerie sounds. During her menses she was especially tense and nervous, her breasts swollen and sore, her abdominal cramps only slightly alleviated by Lollie's herb tisanes and the hot-water canteen. Occasionally she experienced intensely vivid dreams, once with a phantom lover so realistic that she woke embracing her pillow, but his identity escaped her. Did this feeling happen when people made love together? If so, then marriage must be utterly marvelous.

One morning in March she glimpsed crocuses blooming in the yard, vying with the lustily sprouting weeds, and in April the hardy perennials struggled into bud. Birds nested in the burgeoning trees, and at night Jacintha could hear their gentle cooing. But the nocturnal caterwauling from the vacant carriage house, where the wanton tabby entertained her amorous toms, was not so pleasant. It's certainly spring! Jacintha thought. More kittens! Feeding them would be no problem, however, for rats and mice were plentiful at Riverview—another fact she planned to keep from Earl.

Her eighteenth birthday passed in June, uneventful except for the angel-food cake Lollie baked and frosted in white spun-sugar swirls like ruffles. Traditionally this was the age for debutantes to be formally presented to society, in the most lavish "coming out" ceremonies the relatives could afford, indicating the young lady's availability for marriage and her potential dowry. What were Jacintha Howard's prospects? She'd probably be a spinster, like Lollie Fairgale.

"Why didn't you ever marry?" she asked Lollie, as they munched on the cake, savoring even the crumbs.

"Nobody asked me," came the honest reply. "Poor folks, mine, and ignorant. All we could be were servants. Papa was a coachman and my brother was a stable-groom. Papa died of a cough, and a horse kicked Kevin in the head and killed him. Mama just went to bed one night and never woke up. I don't know what happened to my two sisters. Last I heard, Molly married a Dutch farmer and went to live in Pennsylvania, and Maggie took up with an Irishman given to drink and wanderlust. All the stories about immigrants striking it rich in America don't apply to the Fairgales. For us, the streets were paved with manure, not gold."

"And here you are, fifty and stuck with me!"

"I'm not complaining, Missy."

"I know, Lollie, but I can't even pay you. What about your old age?"

Lollie shrugged. "No sense fretting about that. Mama did, and she never reached it. Besides, you'll marry a fine, rich fellow someday. He'll restore Riverview, and I'll be your housekeeper, with a whole staff of servants."

"Cheer up, the prince is on his way? Well, if he doesn't hurry up, it's going to be too late!"

"Faith, honey. Courage."

"Of course," Jacintha said with a sigh. Lollie would be saying that when the furniture was auctioned and a "For Sale" sign tacked to the house.

It occurred to her that she might meet some college students by strolling in Washington Square or sitting on a bench and pretending to read a book. But boys had little respect for girls encountered so casually, and such desperation could lead to trouble.

But of one thing Jacintha was certain: a start must be made to repair Riverview, even on borrowed money.

Hoping to find Earl Britton in a tractable mood, she donned her mourning garments and rode a horsecar to Broadway, where she transferred to an omnibus bound for Wall Street.

Britton Bank stood opposite the New York branch of the United States Treasury. It was a square, solid building of Vermont granite with a pillared portico, bronze portals, and tessellated marble lobby. Men in dark suits and conservative cravats stood in the brass tellers' cages or sat at desks behind low wood partitions. A wide marble staircase led to the executive offices on the second floor, where the president occupied a large suite of oak-paneled walls, leather furniture, Persian carpets, bronze gas chandeliers, onyx ashtrays, and polished brass cuspidors. It was an unmistakably masculine domain and permeated with the aromas of tobacco, bay rum, and money.

Arriving without an appointment, Jacintha was obliged to wait until Mr. Britton finished a board meeting. This she did in the luxuriously appointed reception room, where someone else was also waiting whom Jacintha immediately recognized, although she had not seen him for several years. They had been a pair of awkward adolescents then, fourteen and seventeen. Peering around a potted palm, Jacintha saw that Lawrence Britton had not changed much.

Shaving did not apparently present much of a problem, and he was still plagued with eruptions about the chin and forehead. He was tall but rather frail, as if a strong breeze might rattle him. His long pale face, lusterless eyes, sandy hair, and slightly receding jaw bore no resemblance whatever to his brother's. Sensing her observation, he glanced up from his book and coughed nervously.

"It's Miss Howard, isn't it?"

Jacintha nodded, smiling. "I wasn't sure you'd remember me, Mr. Britton."

"Oh, but I do! I was so sorry to learn of your grandfather's passing and meant to convey my sympathy in a note, but somehow my studies took every spare moment. I was preparing for final examinations."

"Congratulations, sir! I understand you graduated from Harvard with honors. Summa cum laude, in fact."

"Thank you, Miss Howard—and now Earl expects me to take my place in the family institution." He smiled, embarrassed.

"I'm not certain about it. There's no pressing need for my services, anyway. I'd like to spend more time in the South before deciding. I enjoy the leisurely pace there. Life in New York is rather hectic, don't you agree?"

Not at Riverview, Jacintha thought. "I wouldn't know, Mr. Britton. I live in virtual seclusion."

"Yes, I remember your grandparents, Miss Howard."

What else did he know about her? Did anything interest him beyond books? It was difficult to visualize him as a banker in the fierce, competitive financial world. Maybe he was better suited to plantation life, with hundreds of slaves to do his bidding.

"I suppose you'll be leaving for Charleston soon?"

"Next week. Perhaps we'll see each other before I go, Miss Howard?"

"Perhaps," Jacintha replied.

"Do you like poetry, Miss Howard?"

"Some poetry, Mr. Britton. The Brownings, Tennyson, Sir Walter Scott. I enjoy novels, too. Jane Austen, the Bronte sisters, Dickens." The Riverview library included all of these, plus some heavy tomes with which she was unfamiliar. Her grandmother could quote Shakespeare and the Bible, often confusing them. Her grandfather had studied the great philosophers, particularly in later life. Her own literary tastes were not broad enough, she feared, to interest this erudite young man. "I imagine everyone reads those authors."

Before he could answer, the door to the president's office opened and a male secretary spoke to Lawrence Britton. "You may go in now, sir."

"Let Miss Howard go first," he offered.

"Oh, no!" Jacintha protested. "You were here before me."

Finally Jacintha was coaxed into preceding Larry into the inner sanctum, where Earl welcomed her warmly.

"What a pleasant surprise, Miss Howard! Rather like the mountain coming to Mohamet. Is anything wrong?"

"Not exactly, sir. That is, Lollie and I are all right. But the house—"

"Yes, what about it?"

"The roof leaks terribly! The spring rains almost flooded us out. I—I want to borrow some money to fix it."

"That won't be necessary, my dear. I'll hire a carpenter. Is the roof tile? Slate? I've forgotten."

"Slate."

"Then I'll hire someone in that business."

"Thank you." She paused, reluctant. Finally she asked, "Is the estate still solvent?"

"Fairly, and there's also a piece of property on the Battery I can sell."

Jacintha didn't know whether to believe this or not. He might be inventing assets, to keep her at Riverview instead of being burdened with her. "Did the gambler settle for a percentage of Grandpa's debt?"

"No, I played him for it. Double or nothing."

"I don't understand."

"Poker, Jacintha. Using a new deck of cards. And I won, compensating in bluff for what I lack in skill."

Was this the truth? "Suppose you had lost? I'd have owed twice as much!"

"Ah, but I didn't lose, little girl! I usually win, when

something is important enough to me, such as your security and happiness."

"Indeed? Is that why you no longer visit Riverview?"

He gazed at her intently. "Why are you still wearing mourning, Jacintha? Your grandfather wouldn't approve, and those matronly weeds would frighten off any timid youth."

She longed to tell him that one shy young fellow had seemed attracted enough. "Your brother and I renewed our acquaintance this morning," she said. "He gallantly insisted that I take his appointment time."

Earl laughed. "Larry doesn't need an appointment to see me, Jacintha, and neither do you." His hand under her elbow urged her toward the door. "There'll be an increase in your next allotment for some new clothes."

Larry rose quickly as Jacintha emerged, jocularly accusing his brother, "You didn't tell me that Miss Howard had grown up, Earl. And so charmingly, too. I'm tempted to delay my departure."

A barely perceptible frown creased Earl's brow. "Mother is expecting you, Larry," he said evenly.

"I'll write her," he said, smiling at Jacintha.

"She'll be disappointed, Larry. Aunt Evelyn, too. And all the lovely young belles of the Low Country." And to Jacintha, somewhat impatiently, "Good day, Miss Howard."

"Good day, gentlemen." Jacintha's gracious nod included both brothers, but her eyes lingered ever so slightly on the younger.

"So you find Miss Howard attractive?" Earl said, without the teasing tone Larry had anticipated.

"Very. Don't you?"

"Any man would, Larry, even in that ghastly outfit."

"I'd like to call on her."

"It wouldn't be proper, Larry. She's still in mourning."

"But she's a granddaughter, Earl, not a widow! And such a pretty young thing . . . she must be dreadfully lonely and bored in that old house."

"Isn't there someone in Charleston you fancy?" Earl asked.

Larry shook his head. In his three summers there his mother and her sister had forced him to meet the eligible daughters of their peers, but he preferred reading in the library to sipping tea with giggling young ladies in the parlor. He would decline a ball to attend a lecture or sit alone in the family box at the Dock Street Theater, and leave a barbecue to meditate on the Battery. He cared little for riding or shooting, but he enjoyed concerts, musicales, and poetry recitals, too absorbed in the programs to notice the curious glances of nearby maidens. And the lusty young men wondered about him. No drinking, gambling, or whoring, and he considered dueling barbarous. They all wore tucked and ruffled dress-shirts, but perhaps Larry Britton wore lacy drawers as well? His contemporaries at Harvard, most of whom frequented the Boston bars and brothels and raised whatever hell they could, at the risk of expulsion, had entertained similar suspicions. The most doddering old professor was hardly duller than Larry.

"No one," Larry replied to his brother.

"Jacintha Howard is my ward," Earl said. "I'm responsible for her until she's twenty-one. As you know, Father's will puts you in the same position until your majority."

"Well, if I need your permission to visit her—?"

"I'd rather you didn't, Larry."

"Why not? She seems to be a fine person."

"But hardly in your class, Larry."

His jaw dropped. "You can't mean that, Earl? You've never been a snob. We've both criticized the caste system of the South. Even so, I daresay Miss Howard's ancestry is adequate, though her finances may not be. Her grandfather was quite wealthy once, and he and Father were good friends, weren't they? I intend calling on Miss Howard, with or without your consent, Elder Brother."

His defiance surprised Earl, who had never encountered much resistance in his brother before. He told himself he should be pleased that the docile boy was finally showing some manly spirit. "Just remember, Jacintha is naive and vulnerable. Don't trifle with her."

"That's the sort of advice—or was it warning?—I used to hear Father give you," Larry reflected wryly. "And with good reason, his firstborn son being something of a rascal. But I'm not, Earl, so rest easy about your pretty little ward. . . ."

Chapter 4

DESPITE his show of bravery, Larry invited his sister-in-law to accompany him to Riverview.

Flattered, Laurette agreed. But she was also curious to meet the girl who could capture Larry's attention. Certainly none of the young ladies in their coterie seemed to interest him.

"Who is this Jacintha Howard that Larry talks about?" she asked her husband that evening as they were dressing to attend a dinner party in Gramercy Park.

"The granddaughter of one of Father's friends," Earl explained. "Didn't Larry tell you?"

"Yes, but I didn't know she was your ward."

"I'm executor of Ronald Hartford's will, and Jacintha is under age. That's the gist of it."

"How old is she?"

"Eighteen this month."

At twenty-seven, Laurette suddenly felt old. "Pretty?"

"Beautiful."

Her personal maid, Polly, was helping Laurette into a new chartreuse moire gown. The deep décolletage exposed her smooth fair shoulders and much of her bosom. The intricately draped skirt over enormous crinolines enhanced her slender waist. She would carry an ostrich fan tinted to match. Her wardrobe included various shades of green to complement her eyes and red-gold hair, and though she loved all jewelry, emeralds and jade were her favorites. She hoped someday to acquire the Britton collection, but the old lady seemed to think the family jewels should go to her granddaughters, if there ever were any.

"Why didn't you tell me about Miss Howard?"

"Nothing to tell," Earl said, tying his white cravat, motioning aside his valet's attempts to assist.

Damn her feminine curiosity! He should have stayed in his own rooms, with the connecting door closed. But Laurette liked conversation while preparing to go out, while at other times Earl could scarcely buy a word from her. Apparently she felt safe from his amorous advances in the servants' presence. At night, alone in bed, when he tried desperately to reach her, she was all but mute. Did she really love him? Did she enjoy making love? What could he do to give her happiness? His pleas were answered with faint murmurs, vague sighs. Did she realize that he sometimes had other partners? Did she care?

"She must be quite spectacular, if Larry has noticed her."

"Why? He's twenty, Laurette. It's not difficult to notice a pretty girl at that age."

"Or any age, from what I have seen of men." She cast him an accusing glance. "You certainly notice them, don't you?"

"We're going to be late to the Barclays," Earl muttered.

Laurette shrugged. "They expect it. We're never on time."

Polly was arranging her mistress's coiffure while Edwards held the black broadcloth tails for his master, both pretending, as proper servants should, to be deaf and dumb.

"And whose fault is that? I'm ready, Laurette."

"Open my jewel box, Polly. I'll wear the three-stranded emeralds . . . and you must have the clasp fixed on the bracelet, Earl. I nearly lost it at the theater the other evening." Laurette adorned herself with the fabulous jewels, allowing her husband to fasten the necklace while she slipped on the pendant earrings, and then stood back to admire herself in the mirror. "Am I beautiful, Earl? Have I aged?"

How often must he affirm her beauty and youthfulness, deny any imperfections? "Yes, and no," he answered mechanically.

"What does that mean?"

"Precisely what you want it to mean."

"It's deliberately ambiguous."

"Laurette, we'll miss the first course."

"I hope so. Mona serves such dreadful soups, one would think they came from a witch's caldron. I wish she'd hire a decent cook, change her recipes, or give her dinners at Delmonico's. The French chef there is a marvel."

In the carriage, moving down Fifth Avenue and across Broadway, Earl was silent. The bawdy nightlife of the city was just beginning in the saloons, casinos, dance halls, and brothels. There were many people on the streets—some of whom seemed to emerge from underground with the rats. Prostitutes plying the main thoroughfare did not lack for customers.

Laurette knew that whores were a necessary evil. Her mother had explained that marriages were not made in heaven, because there was some devil in every man. Some of the best gentlemen, including a few of her friends' husbands, patronized the elegant parlorhouses, where references and appointments were required. Others kept mistresses. Some wives had secret lovers, and one prominent lady of their acquaintance actually supported a young gigolo, pampering him as her husband did his paramour.

Why was Earl so quiet? Brooding again! She hated these dark, private, impenetrable moods. Was he worried about Larry now, afraid he would fall in love with an impoverished nobody and want to wed her? Was he disenchanted with his own marriage? What did he want of his wife, his brother, his life?

She was relieved when they arrived at the Barclay residence in Gramercy Park. It would be easier with people around. They were no longer comfortable alone together. Ironically, there was a time when they would not accept many invitations, or would invent excuses to leave early, so as to be alone. But no matter how boring the company now, it was preferable to being alone.

Laurette decided they should visit Miss Howard in the landau. She sat in billows of green organdy, holding a matching parasol over her charmingly bonneted head, feeling as pert and vivacious as in her girlhood, when her popularity was at its peak. There had been much competition for her hand, which Earl Britton had eventually won, not because he was the most physically desirable of his rivals, but because he was a New Yorker whose exciting reputation made her proper Philadelphia suitors seem stuffy by comparison.

Having met Earl Britton through mutual friends at an Astor charity ball, Laurette was fascinated by the idea of marrying him and living in Manhattan, which many people regarded as Babylon on the Hudson. Quakerism still lingered strongly in her own family, whose patriarch had arrived with William Penn and helped to build the first ship to sail from the colony to England for more religious refugees. Eventually they owned the shipyard and a fleet that included whalers, freighters, privateers, clippers, yachts, and steamboats. Lancaster ships had fought in the Revolution, the War of 1812, in the Spanish and French Wars, against the Barbary pirates, and would fight the South, if necessary. Lancaster-built craft could be seen on every navigable American waterway and all the seven seas.

A marital alliance between the Lancasters and the Brittons would, it was hoped, preserve the dynasties. None of the Lancaster sons had reached manhood, and Laurette was the last surviving daughter. Her elder sister, Helene, a spinster Quaker missionary, had died of a fever in a distant foreign jungle several years ago. The Brittons were in a slightly less pressing predicament, with two sons of direct descent.

Her childless state had never bothered Laurette, however, and no longer seemed to concern her husband very much either, except that it deprived his mother of the joy of grandchildren. Laurette consoled her disappointed parents with unfulfilled promises and the fact that any future progeny would be only half-Lancaster anyway.

Larry, sitting across from her, admired his sister-in-law, pleased that Earl had such a chic and lovely wife. And how kind she was, agreeing to assist his courtship of Miss Howard, whom he did indeed wish to court. The realization had occupied his mind from the moment they had met at the bank. His humble note, composed under Laurette's guidance and requesting permission to call at Riverview, was answered promptly with an invitation to tea on Friday, for which they arrived punctually at four o'clock only because Laurette feared the anxious boy would leave without her if she delayed her toilette too long.

Riverview, now a mere remnant of what it had been, did not impress Laurette. She exclaimed, "Heavens, what a decrepit old place! I hope it isn't haunted."

Larry suppressed his own surprise at the condition of the house. "It's just sadly neglected, Laurette. The family were victims of the panic."

"Which one?" Laurette mused. "Riverview appears to have undergone a long, hard siege."

"Be kind to Miss Howard," Larry pleaded before hammering with the tarnished brass knocker.

"But of course, dear," she murmured. Just then, Lollie, in a mended calico dress, opened the door.

Smiling, Larry presented their cards. "We're expected."

"Yes, sir. Come in, please."

The parlor had been thoroughly cleaned and brightened with fresh flowers bought from a street vendor, but there was no disguising the worn upholstery and faded carpet. The only new item in the room was Jacintha's hastily purchased turquoise voile gown, fetchingly flounced, and the ribbon bow perched like a bright butterfly in her glossy black curls.

Expecting staid black garb, Larry stared appreciatively until Laurette reminded him to introduce her. He obliged, speaking with a slight stammer that irritated her. "This is my—my sister-in-law, Mrs. Earl Britton."

Jacintha said, "I'm happy to know you, Mrs. Britton."

Laurette smiled, taking her hand. "Oh, let's not be formal, Jacintha. Call me Laurette, or Laurie. I can't think of a diminutive for your name. It's lovely, however, and different. Your mother used her imagination, as did mine. I loathe common names, don't you? And common people."

"Do sit down, please," Jacintha said invitingly. "We'll have tea shortly. I rather expected your husband would join us."

Laurette's plucked brows arched. "Really? I'm afraid your guardian doesn't care much for tea parties, Jacintha. He prefers stronger beverages and often tarries at one of his clubs before coming home from business."

It was apparent to Jacintha that Laurette intended to do most of the talking. Perhaps Larry had brought her along because of her facile tongue, his own being frequently tied. He looked bewildered now, sitting stiffly in the wing chair, as if he had just discovered a treasure in a ruin and was wondering what to do with it. His tan suit was wrong for his sandy hair and sallow skin, making him look drab, and it was absurd for him to torture himself by wearing a vest in warm weather. But Laurette knew exactly how to dress, and could have posed for the summer issue of *Godey's Lady's Book* or *Demorest's Fashion Magazine*. And why not, when she was married to the Beau Brummell of Wall Street!

Lollie wheeled in the rickety teacart, which held the best of the remaining china service and silver flatware. Jacintha poured, hoping her guests would not notice the chipped pot, praying that the cream was still fresh. Ice was too costly for her budget. She offered a tray of finger-sandwiches and cookies. Laurette sampled both gingerly, finishing neither, but Larry obligingly ate a couple of everything.

Serving her guests occupied Jacintha's nervous hands,

and conversation busied her mind. But how would she entertain them once the tea ceremony was over? She could play the spinet fairly well but the heirloom needed tuning, and her voice would probably quiver if she tried to sing.

Her fretting proved unnecessary, however, for Laurette was quite ready to leave. Afternoon tea, not designed for long visits, was never prolonged into the dinner hour in America, although English tea often continued well into the evening. As if on cue, Larry stood and expressed his pleasure and appreciation for Jacintha's gracious hospitality. Obviously reluctant to depart, he glanced helplessly at his mentor.

"Perhaps Jacintha would like to come to dinner Sunday," Laurette suggested tentatively, gathering her accessories.

Jacintha hesitated, wishing not to appear anxious, and hoping that Larry would persuade her. "Well . . ."

"Please do us the honor, Miss Howard," he entreated.

"I'd be delighted, Mr. Britton," Jacintha agreed, accompanying them to the door.

"Miss Howard, Mr. Britton," Laurette mimicked. "My word! One would think you were students in an etiquette class." She smoothed on her gloves, finger by finger. "We dine promptly at two o'clock, Jacintha, and will send a carriage for you. Naturally, we attend church in the morning."

"Naturally." Jacintha nodded. "Good afternoon!"

When they had gone, Jacintha walked into the kitchen with a worried frown. "What do you think, Lollie? Did they like me?"

"Him, yes. Her, no."

"Oh? I thought she was . . . nice."

"Hypocrite," the older woman appraised. "Wouldn't trust her as far as I could throw an elephant. Hoity-toity! Didn't you see her taste the food like it was poisoned? You really going to dinner in her house?"

"Yes, though I don't know what I'll wear. This is the only new dress I have, and no doubt she has hundreds of the latest fashions. Anything I could afford would seem cheap by comparison."

"Mister Larry wouldn't notice, honey. He couldn't take his eyes off your face."

"Maybe," Jacintha sighed dubiously. "But he was at least partially aware of his surroundings, Lollie. I saw him covertly looking over the parlor. I hope he doesn't think I'm only interested in his money, because I like him. I really do."

"More's the pity."

"Why do you say that?"

"Because they probably have other plans for him."

"They?"

"His family."

"A girl with money and position, you mean?"

"It's only natural for folks to want the best for their loved ones," Lollie reasoned. "Your grandparents felt the same way about you—especially Mister Ronald. I think he always secretly hoped that Mr. Earl Britton would wait for you to grow up, and was mighty disappointed when he married that rich Philadelphia snob."

"I doubt that. Look at the difference in our ages. Anyway, it must have been a love match, since neither of them had to marry for convenience. Not many people are so fortunate."

"Not many," the servant agreed. "But you can be sure of one thing—Mister Larry likes you for yourself."

"I hope so, Lollie! Because I have nothing to offer him except myself."

"Which is a lot, Missy, and maybe too much for that boy. He's not half the man his brother is. I fear Mister Larry is a bit of a milksop."

"He's just young," Jacintha said defensively. "And who asked you, anyway? You had no business snooping on my guests! Oh, I noticed you peeking from the hall, Miss Fairgale, and no doubt Mrs. Britton did, too. I bet her servants don't eavesdrop. I bet they wouldn't *dare*!"

Lollie grinned. Their tiffs were always more suggestive

of mother and daughter than servant and employer. "I wasn't spying, baby. I was just curious about that woman, and I don't think my judgment of her character is far wrong."

Jacintha was pondering the wilted watercress sandwiches. "Mr. Britton promised to send some tilers to repair the roof," she reflected woefully. "Let's hope they come before it rains again."

Chapter 5

DETERMINED to look her best on Sunday, Jacintha went on a shopping spree at A. T. Stewart's Department Store, charging the bills to the Ronald Hartford Estate in care of Britton Bank. "Mister Earl won't like this," Lollie had warned. But Jacintha was convinced that the admiration in Larry's eyes, when she appeared in the imported pink India muslin gown and stylish bonnet of pink silk roses and malines, would compensate for any unpleasantness with her guardian.

It was impossible, however, to gauge Laurette's reaction as she welcomed Jacintha to the Britton home—one of the finest in New York, elegantly decorated and more than adequately staffed with liveried servants, including a stately butler and his housekeeper wife, several maids, footmen, and errand boys.

The building's baroque exterior seemed to have been designed by the same architect who had designed the rest of Fifth Avenue, but the interior was uniquely its owners', and Jacintha did not think any of the social reporters had done it justice. The columns, foyer, and great central stairway were of Genoese marble. Some of the walls were paneled in rare woods, while others were brocaded, tapestried, or muraled. Jacintha could not begin to calculate the value of the magnificent furniture and art treasures. It made her wistful to realize that she had been invited to live here.

Absorbed in reverie, she was only vaguely conscious of Larry's naked adulation. He stood near her, boyishly awkward, wishing he could conceive an original compliment. How beautiful Miss Howard had grown in the years he had been away, oblivious of her existence! If only he possessed a little of his elder brother's urbanity, eloquence, and charm!

Larry knew nothing about the fair sex except that they were supposedly delicate creatures, complex as a Chinese puzzle and mysterious as the Holy Trinity—impressions gained from his proper Southern mother and her sister. He held females in awe, put them on pedestals—and left them there. This was the first time Larry had ever wanted to examine a lady closely. His face flushed and he felt a sudden alarming tightness in his throat and chest. Oh, God, not another wheezing attack!

Laurette rescued him, as she so often did, chatting graciously as she led the way to one of the drawing rooms. She showed Jacintha her collection of miniature *objets d'art*. "My favorite hobby," she proudly announced, indicating a large ornate gilt-and-glass curio cabinet containing the precious diminutives, each one perfect in every detail. "It began on our honeymoon abroad, when my doting husband indulged my every whim. Now dealers everywhere contact us about unusual pieces. I never buy indiscriminately, however, and always have the authenticity of the offerings verified by reliable appraisers. One must be very careful about antiques, you know."

Jacintha was convinced that Larry had the utmost respect for his sister-in-law and every confidence in her judgment. To please him, she would have to please Laurette—and probably his other relatives as well.

"This tiny crystal stag belonged to Napoleon Bonaparte," Laurette was saying. "That darling marble knife-grinder was uncovered in the ashes of Pompeii. I like to think the adorable gold violin belonged to Nero," Laurette joked. "After all, he was a fiddler, wasn't he?"

"Isn't she witty?" Larry smiled admiringly.

"Exceptionally," Jacintha acknowledged, feeling rather wilted. "I wonder if I might freshen up a bit before dinner?"

Her hostess smiled. "Certainly, dear. Come with me. Larry will excuse us, won't you?"

He bowed gallantly and sat down to wait for his brother, hoping Earl would not be late. His brother had not accompanied them to church, and Laurette complained lately that he was behaving more like a pagan than a Christian. Larry did consider it improper for Earl to be exercising his horses rather than worshiping on Sunday.

The second-floor suite consisted of several rooms, and the exquisite decor was primarily French. The colors were complimentary to Laurette's hair and complexion. The bedchamber, patently a lady's boudoir, was too feminine for male comfort, suggesting that the Brittons occupied separate sleeping quarters. Jacintha's grandparents had shared the same great testered bed throughout their wedded life. Perhaps this arrangement was now outmoded?

"Did you know the Britton family well?" Laurette inquired, preening herself before the queenly vanity table.

"No, I've never met Mrs. Alicia Britton and scarcely remember her husband. I was quite young when he died."

"Oh? I understood that he and your grandfather were close friends. Was it only a business relationship?"

"Possibly."

After too long a silence, Laurette invited her guest: "Take off your bonnet and gloves, Jacintha, and make yourself comfortable. If you need powder or rouge—"

"Thank you, but I don't use them." Immediate qualification was necessary, lest she offend her hostess, who had a smorgasbord of cosmetics spread before her. "Not that I disapprove. I simply don't know how to use them."

"Poor child, you are so pathetically naïve! I don't equate naïveté with innocence, however. A girl can have one without the other. Virginity and ignorance are no more synonymous than chastity and intelligence." She smiled, amused by her guest's discomfort. "And so your color is the natural glow of youth? How nice! But you do need some pins for your hair, my dear."

"They don't help much, I'm afraid."

"Unruly curls? If you cut your hair short, you'd resemble a pixie. Not a cherub, however. One rarely sees a darkheaded one in the famous religious paintings, although I believe Raphael and Michelangelo made some exceptions." A cupid-encrusted Bavarian clock ticked away on the Breche rose-marble mantel. "It's time for dinner, and Larry will have to be our host. My husband is out with his animals again today."

Avoiding me? Jacintha wondered.

They were having demitasse when Earl strolled in, crop in hand, casually debonair in tan riding breeches and brown cordovan boots, the open collar of his linen shirt exposing a triangle of thick black hair. Jacintha's heart thumped and a prickling sensation assaulted her, but he smiled easily and his greeting was cordial.

"Good afternoon, Miss Howard. Laurette. Larry."

His wife frowned. "You've had dinner?"

"Yes, at a tavern." No apology for his tardiness, no explanation for dining at a public inn when a feast had been spread for him at home.

"What detained you?" Larry questioned. "One of your steeds break a leg?"

Earl laughed. "Great heavens, no! That pair of pacers I bought last week are the fastest things on hooves. They'll make Commodore Vanderbilt's team seem like spavined nags."

"One of these days my beloved husband is going to break his neck!" Laurette commented coolly.

"It's my neck," Earl reminded.

"So it is, darling, and how recklessly you expose it! No cravat, or ascot even. You look half-dressed."

"It's summer, and damnably hot in the sun." He turned to Jacintha, lazily flicking the crop, which assumed the shape of a cat-o'-nine-tails in her mind. "But you look refreshing, Miss Howard. Is that charming costume the result of thrift, or talent?"

Her delicate blush delighted him. "A little of both, sir. Thank you for the extra clothes allowance."

"Money well spent," he declared, his slate-gray eyes lingering on her.

"I—I didn't have quite enough, however," she stammered, "and had to charge a few items to the estate. Stewart's were quite nice about sending the bills to the bank."

"Why not? I get a sheaf of them almost every day. My wife's purchases help keep the ladies' stores in business."

"A worthy boost to the economy, which Wall Street is always so concerned about," Laurette quipped, grinning impishly at him. "We must shop together soon, Jacintha. Larry can come along and treat us to lunch."

Earl addressed his brother. "I assume you've written to Mother, telling her not to expect you for a while?"

"Yes, I posted the letter yesterday, with a suggestion that she and Aunt Evelyn come north on holiday. Perhaps we should urge them to move here permanently, Earl. If Abraham Lincoln is elected president—well, we know where his sympathies lie on the slavery issue. There could be grave trouble."

"The election is still a long time away, Larry. There'll be time enough to try to persuade them, and you know it won't be easy."

Larry nodded, sighing. "Mother can be obstinate."

"A feminine trait," Earl stated laconically. "You should have ridden with me this morning, Brother. A swift horse is never quite as dangerous as a cunning woman."

Larry did not appreciate the jest. "Come, now, Earl. These lovely ladies are perfectly harmless."

"Mere kittens, eh? Cats have claws, Larry. Wait until you get scratched a few times."

Laurette smiled wryly. "Pay no attention, Jacintha. They

frequently engage in fraternal debate. I'd rather hear some music, wouldn't you? Play the piano for us, Larry."

"Why me, Laurette? My brother is far better. Maybe a duet?"

Earl shook his head. "The honor is all yours, Larry. This way, ladies, to the Music Room."

As they stepped into a long wide hall hung with ancestral portraits, Larry said humorously, "Don't let the gallery frighten you, Miss Howard. They're all family. This is Father. He was in a serious mood."

"Father was always in a serious mood," Earl said.

"Gilbert Stuart did Grandfather Britton, there on the far right," Larry continued, indicating a grim face protruding from a high, stiff collar and impeccable stock. "He had a stony countenance but a heart of gold."

"Which he used to found Britton Bank," Earl drawled, "thereby rendering himself heartless, some thought. The gent partially hidden in the extreme left corner is Great-Grandfather Britton, the one who wasn't a banker."

"He was a merchant prince," Larry put in.

"Ah, yes! But first a privateer. Roguish looking chap, wasn't he? Seems very amused by it all. I've been told I resemble him. Do you agree, Miss Howard?"

Jacintha studied the painting of the dark, handsome man. The resemblance was quite strong, especially in the brooding eyes and cynical mouth. "Definitely, sir. Did he have the temperament to match?"

"Identical, I should imagine," Laurette declared before her spouse could answer. "You'll discover his descendant's true personality in due course, Jacintha, if you haven't already."

Larry paused before a lovely gray-haired lady in sapphire velvet, whose serene blue eyes and pensive smile seemed as lifelike as the dewy-petaled white rose in her delicate hands. "This is Mother, and one of Henry Inman's best works."

"With such an inspiration," Earl reverently agreed, "almost any artist could execute a masterpiece."

"Earl and I will be up there one day," Larry murmured. "Laurette, too." His tentative gaze included Jacintha in the future gallery, and she demurely dropped her lashes.

Earl suppressed a scowl, saying, "Enough of this! On to the entertainment!"

They entered a white-and-gold salon—with fleur-de-lis satin walls, frescoed ceiling, and ornate frieze—so large and elegant that Jacintha supposed this was also the ballroom. Thick gold cords looped back the white satin draperies along tall corniced windows, and many gilt chairs and settees circled the polished parquet dance-floor. She visualized myriad candles and gaslights glowing in the elaborate crystal chandeliers and sconces, a blazing fire on the massive Carrara marble hearth, and festive reflections in the gold-leaf mirrors.

A white grand piano, draped with cloth-of-gold and holding an alabaster urn of gilded fronds, dominated the orchestra platform. Beside it stood an exquisite golden harp, prompting Jacintha to ask who was the harpist.

"My wife," Earl replied. "You see, she has the appearance and all the attributes of an angel."

"Why, darling, how sweet!" Laurette responded to his veiled sarcasm. "Some Mozart, please, Larry."

"If you wish, and I'd be honored if you'd accompany me on the harp, Laurette."

"Not today, dear. I pricked a finger on a rose thorn yesterday, and it's sore. But I'll turn the pages for you."

Earl sat near Jacintha, his booted legs crossed, looking uncomfortable and incongruous on the delicate gilt chair. Now and then she sensed his eyes on her but kept her own on the stage, applauding at the conclusion of the long, dreary composition. Her hopes for a happier encore faded when Earl requested Beethoven's *Appassionata*. Why should this tragic music appeal to him—or the moody Mozart to his wife? They were an enigmatic couple.

Striking the final chords of Beethoven, Larry declared, "Enough grandioso! Jacintha may prefer something lighter. A waltz, perhaps? Schubert, Strauss, Gungl?"

"Yes," she cried eagerly. "A waltz, Larry. Anything, please. I like them all!"

Larry resumed playing, with considerably more confidence now. Laurette hummed in her rich, smooth contralto, and Jacintha lapsed into reverie.

How wonderful it would be to attend a ball in this palatial atmosphere, meet bright and charming people, and be a part of all the enchantment! The mock cotillions at the Brooklyn boarding school, in which the girls danced with one another to learn the proper ballroom etiquette, had not been much pleasure—especially when stuck with a clumsy partner. And when Jacintha wanted to practice at Riverview, her grandfather had been inclined to march militarily and try to teach her the minuet, now long passé.

Her face, beautiful in wistful repose, stirred Larry whenever he glanced up from the keyboard. Earl was equally aroused by Jacintha's beauty, but he looked impassive.

The sweet, romantic strains of Strauss ended all too soon for Jacintha, who complimented sincerely, "That was enchanting, Larry. I was completely carried away."

Earl bravoed his brother. "Take a bow, Maestro! Your music transported our guest to another plane. A sublime one, I presume, Miss Howard?"

"Yes," she murmured, standing. "I could listen to you play for hours, Larry—but I must be leaving now."

He left the stage, disappointed. "So soon? I had hoped we might drive in Central Park."

"A marvelous idea," Laurette quickly agreed, "since we must take Jacintha home, anyway. Do join us, Earl."

"And ride in that fatuous carriage parade? No, thanks. It's an exhibition, Jacintha, imported from London's Hyde Park and Paris's Bois de Boulogne—to display clothes, carriages, and escorts. Laurette likes it, of course. Go ahead, the three of you. Enjoy yourselves."

Laurette spoke to Larry. "Order the carriage, dear. I'll run up and fetch Jacintha's things."

"I'll go with you," Jacintha said hastily.

"Oh, don't bother! Your guardian may like a few words in private with you."

Left alone with Earl, she tensed. He growled, "Get back on your budget, young lady! You'll be broke soon enough, without all this extra spending."

"You told me to stop wearing black, sir. You even sent extra money."

"But you can't afford a new outfit every time you see my brother! And you'd need a gold mine to keep up with my wife's wardrobe. Do you expect me to gamble Mr. Stewart for the price of those clothes?"

Tears surfaced, shimmering in her turquoise eyes. "I—I just wanted something new and nice, Earl."

"Don't cry, Jacintha. It's all right. Just don't go overboard. Understand?"

She nodded, sniffing.

"Jacintha, please." He turned swiftly away. "You realize that Larry is infatuated with you?"

"And you don't approve."

"I didn't say that."

Defiance took the place of humility. "But it's true, isn't it?" she accused. "You think I'm not good enough for him?"

"Oh, Lord! No, that's not true, Jacintha." He ground the words out.

Voices sounded in the hall, and soon they had company again. Laurette, wearing a large Milan straw hat with jade-green ribbon ties, handed Jacintha her tiny bonnet, gloves, reticule, and frilly pink parasol.

"Poor dear," she sympathized, sensing that Earl had been scolding his ward. "Did the brute chastise you severely—employ the whip?"

Larry frowned, embarrassed for Jacintha, who was busy with her accessories. "Don't jest, Laurette."

His sister-in-law smiled coyly, patting his downy cheek. "You don't think your wonderful big brother is capable of cruelty?"

"Well, not toward a female. Now, if we don't hurry, we'll miss the best part of the procession, Laurette."

"And get caught among the intruding riffraff." She

nodded disdainfully. "I know it's a public park, but there should be *some* restrictions."

"You have a choice, madam." Earl's tone was harsh. "Stay at home."

"And let the riffraff and the foreigners take over? Perhaps pushing their filthy pushcarts? No, indeed! They have gained too much ground already, while the real Americans do nothing to stop them."

"The real Americans are the Indians," Earl drawled. "All the rest of us are immigrants."

Laurette glared at him. "Will you be here this evening?"

His shrug irritated her as much as the nonchalant wave of his hand. "Come again, Miss Howard."

"She will"—Larry beamed—"if I can persuade her."

Chapter 6

ALTHOUGH preoccupied with Jacintha, Larry realized that all was not well in his brother's household. The couple did not often flare into open conflict, at least not in Larry's presence, but they seemed to live under an armed truce. It troubled him.

No marriage was perfect, he knew that, but Earl and Laurette were constantly at odds, and Larry wished they would reconcile before the breech became permanent. Earl seemed to be the worse offender, deliberately vexing his wife by being late for meals or missing them altogether without apology, spending long hours at his clubs, and venturing out alone at night.

His evenings at home were restless. He would read for a while, then pace the library floor, cigar or drink in hand. When Earl turned to the piano, his music varied in mood. It might be cynical, careless, trenchant as his wit, or profound, full of passion and despair. Enigmatical music, as puzzling as his heavy smoking and drinking and his unexplained absences from home. Larry couldn't help wondering what happened when his brother and Laurette retired together. Did Earl abuse his wife in bed or merely use her as a sexual convenience?

Meanwhile Laurette concentrated on supervising her timid brother-in-law's courtship of Miss Howard, planning entertainments: a picnic in New Jersey's rustic Elysian Fields and another on Long Island's popular Rockaway Beach; drives in the country; river excursions; an evening concert at the Academy of Music and a matinee performance of the great Edwin Booth's *Hamlet* at the Park Theater.

The simplest events were exciting to Jacintha. Everything was delightful. But always they were a trio, never a duo. Didn't Larry want to be alone with her? Or was it his brother's wish—possibly his command—that they be constantly chaperoned?

Yards of white linen and lace covered the dining table, always set as if for a banquet, with the best china and crystal and silver, fresh flowers, and flickering candles. Uneasy in the host's chair—which Laurette insisted that he occupy in Earl's absence—Larry was furious with his brother for missing dinner again this evening. Treating his wife so badly, and she so patient! Earl deserved a shrew.

"Would you care for some backgammon later?" he asked, to boost Laurette's morale.

"Fine, although I never win, which is probably why Earl avoids playing with me. He prefers winners, Larry. If his stocks and bonds don't perform well in the market, he unloads them. And if his horses lose in the races too often, he sells or trades them."

"How long has he been behaving this way with you, Laurette?"

"Several years. Since I lost our second child, in fact. Unfortunately, I lose in that respect as well."

Larry looked puzzled. "I can't believe he'd neglect you because of that, Laurette. You couldn't help it if you miscarried. There must be some other reason."

"Oh, Larry! Men don't need reasons for neglecting their wives. It's as natural as breathing, and infidelity is a part of it."

"You think Earl is unfaithful to you?"

Laurette hesitated, as though reluctant to accuse her spouse. It had the effect of implanting the suspicion in the boy's mind. "Well, I daresay more husbands than bachelors have mistresses, Larry. A wife learns to cope with infidelity. Some may retaliate, but most simply accept it as a fact of life. In the South, didn't you learn about plantation masters and their female slaves? The cities are full of convenient brothels, and even the smallest hamlets have harlots."

The conversation embarrassed Larry, as much as Laurette's candor surprised him. He changed the subject.

"Did you hear Earl playing last night? God, how he can render the masters—especially Chopin!"

"I thought he insulted Chopin," Laurette said. "He was either furious or frustrated or both. Music is only an escape for him. We play because we love music, but Earl plays only for release. It makes a mockery of good music."

"Perhaps it's just as well," Larry sighed, running his hands nervously through his hair. "Something keeps my brother strong and sure of himself at all times. "Earl's an iron man. I'm a weakling, and I'm not making much impression on Jacintha, I'm afraid."

"You're quite smitten with her, aren't you?"

"More than that," he admitted sheepishly. "Tell me the truth, Laurette. Have I a chance of winning her hand?"

"You'd like to marry Miss Howard?"

He nodded emphatically. "Will you please help me, Laurette? You've done so much already, and I'm very grateful."

A faint smile curled her patrician mouth, now theatrically rouged. "You want me to act the role of Miles Standish in this little drama, Larry?"

"Are you advising me to speak for myself?"

"I think that's what Jacintha would wish," she responded. "Besides, I can't risk Earl's wrath by promoting a match that may displease him. He considers you too young for marriage, Larry, and in that respect I agree with him. Why, you haven't even taken your Grand Tour yet! Furthermore, you couldn't propose to anyone without his

permission until your twenty-first birthday, which is still
months away. And there's a clause in your father's will
extending Earl's control over you even longer, if he deems
it advisable."

"I know, but with you on my side, Laurette—"

She interrupted. "You overestimate my influence, Larry.
I assure you it's not enough to overcome whatever objections Earl may have to Jacintha Howard. Apparently she's
a nice girl, but she has neither position nor wealth to
recommend her. Besides, I suspect Earl has designs on
Jacintha himself."

Larry shook his head vehemently. "No, you're wrong
about that, Laurette. Whatever Earl's faults, he wouldn't
betray her grandfather's trust in him, or his own integrity.
He'd never take advantage of his ward, or any other helpless female."

"I've shocked you, haven't I? Forgive me, Larry. Yes, of
course, I'm mistaken. A jealous wife's fantasies! Still interested in some backgammon?"

"If you are."

"We may as well, dear. I doubt we'll have your urbane
brother's stimulating company this evening. . . ."

The next day they went to a Coney Island carnival and
Jacintha enjoyed riding the carousel, eating popcorn, and
drinking pink lemonade—joys she had missed in childhood. Larry won a prize for her by guessing the number of
peas (give or take fifty) in a bottle, and Laurette insisted
that the painted doll should be hers, because it had reddish-
blond hair. Jacintha conceded. But Laurette left it behind
in the puppet-show tent.

She didn't want that cheap little souvenir, Jacintha realized. She just didn't want *me* to have it.

Gradually Laurette revealed other facets of her nature—
selfishness, envy, inordinate vanity, deceitfulness, subtle
cruelty; and Jacintha realized what astute Lollie had
understood from the start. There was much hypocrisy
about Mrs. Britton's friendship. Laurette liked being
squired about by her young brother-in-law, and tolerated

Jacintha's presence as a necessary expedient. She was never going to allow them any privacy, and Larry was too timid to advance on his own. His boldest gesture so far had been to squeeze Jacintha's hand furtively while their chaperone's back was turned.

Jacintha knew that he longed for more intimacy. Once, as he was helping her into the carriage, her arms filled with wild flowers and both of them laughing, his hand accidently slipped from her elbow and came up under her breast. He caught his breath and began to cough. Laurette gave him a piece of rock candy, which was preferable to the smelly horehound lozenges his physician had prescribed.

One afternoon Jacintha entertained them at Riverview, with tea and a few songs at the spinet. In a dainty blue-sprigged dimity frock, with the candlelight casting soft shadows over her beribboned hair and sparkling in her brilliant eyes, she sang a pert and comical ditty about a Dutch boy and girl, and two tender ballads, "Flowers in the Rain" and "The Flame Burns Low." Larry praised her sweet soprano, comparing it to Jenny Lind's, and pretended not to notice the few sour notes she struck on the faulty spinet. Laurette, fiddling with the tuning fork and metronome, chided him for his gallantry.

"You sound like a Southern cavalier, Larry. Don't be beguiled, Jacintha. He pays me the same extravagant compliments when I sing and play the harp."

Afterwards she was cross with him. "You're overdoing the chivalry, dear. Jacintha has a passable voice, but she's all thumbs at the keyboard. And that relic of an instrument belongs in Barnum's Museum!"

"Aren't you feeling well, Laurette?"

"Quite well, Larry. Why?"

"You seem touchy today. Perhaps you are tiring of being with us so much, and I should start calling on Jacintha alone?"

"That isn't done in polite society, Lawrence Britton! It simply isn't done!"

"Were you and Earl always chaperoned?"

"Not always, no. My parents allowed us some privacy in the parlor and garden. But we were both older than you and Jacintha, and we never appeared in public alone until after the betrothal. I assume Jacintha has sufficient breeding to know what is proper. Do you want to offend her?"

Certainly the proprieties must be observed. Larry had learned this in the South, where a maiden's reputation was closely guarded, not only by her family, but by the servants as well. Chaperoning unwed girls was the chief occupation of spinster aunts and mammies, and to ignore the principles of courting was to risk the code duello.

"I'm a gauche fool, Laurette, and you've spared me another rash blunder." He reined the horse, which was pacing too rapidly. "I suppose Earl is leaving for Saratoga next week?"

"Yes. He has already shipped his rigs, horses, and grooms."

"You could still change your mind, Laurette, and go with him," Larry suggested, anxious to mend the apparent breach between the couple.

"Only if you come along, dear."

"Perhaps later on, Laurie."

"Then I'll wait and accompany you." She touched his arm, pleased that he had used her nickname. "I couldn't possibly get ready on such short notice, anyway. I've so much shopping to do. Jacintha can help, although she's hardly an authority on fashion or quality. She has so few clothes, and none very chic or expensive."

"But all becoming," Larry mused.

"Even that rag she wore today? It must have been purchased at The Red Store, on the Bowery."

"I doubt that, Laurette. Anyway, I thought her gown was quite charming," he insisted defensively.

"Well, at her age, I suppose pinafores and rompers would seem sweet," Laurette said sulkily. "And hair bows, too! Sometimes those curls look positively unbrushed."

Larry smiled. "She doesn't mind the wind, sun, or rain. She actually enjoyed that shower we were caught in the other day. I think she'd like to wade in the brooks and surf, and run barefoot through the meadows. She's the most vivacious girl I've ever known, and I envy her her vitality."

Laurette smothered a yawn. "It's growing late, Larry. Drive a little faster."

"You expect Earl this evening?"

"I never expect him any time, Larry. But he may just surprise me by coming home early, for once!"

Chapter 7

SINCE Laurette preferred the first meal of the day in bed, Larry knew he could manage some private conversation with Earl at breakfast and was waiting in the dining room when his brother came down.

"Good morning, Big Brother."

Earl smiled, glad for the company. "Hello, Larry. Up a bit early, aren't you?"

"I didn't sleep very well last night." He looked tired, and paler than usual, the circles under his eyes darker today.

"Take your medicine?"

"That wasn't my problem," Larry said, choosing from the large selection of food on the buffet.

Earl noticed the small portions on Larry's plate and his nervous toying with the damask napkin. His finicky appetite had always worried the family as much as his respiratory ailments. "Was Jacintha Howard the cause of your insomnia?"

"More or less."

"Which, Larry? More, or less?"

"More," he admitted nervously. "I think of her all the time, Earl. She's so beautiful and gentle and appreciative of every little thing. I want to give her so much—the world, if I could—and ask nothing in return."

"Most women expect the world, Larry, and give nothing in return."

"She's not like that, Earl."

"They're all like that, Larry."

"Not Jacintha," he insisted.

"All right. So she's different, unique. Does she reciprocate your feelings?"

Larry shrugged. "I don't know. We've never been alone long enough for me to find out. Laurette's very diligent about the proprieties. I keep hoping—"

"She'll go to Saratoga with me?"

"Well, yes. But she told me she wasn't going this season."

"Exercising her feminine prerogative, Larry, which she does rather frequently."

"Changes her mind?"

Earl nodded, buttering his toast.

"Then she may still go with you?"

"Possibly, but don't expect it. Is that all you're going to eat? No ham or eggs? Courting is strenuous activity, Larry. Juice, coffee, and a roll don't provide much energy."

"And Jacintha has such an abundance of it!"

"You should, too, at your age."

Larry sighed disconsolately. "We're not well matched, I'm afraid."

Earl finished his coffee. "I have to get to the bank. Why don't you come along? Work is usually an effective antidote for the poison of love."

"Poison?"

"You've heard of love sickness, dying of a broken heart, drunk with love, crazy in love, et cetera? A little farfetched, perhaps, but love can have adverse effects, Larry. Sometimes it can even be fatal, indirectly. You're not eating or resting properly, and anxiety could agitate your asthma. But all that aside, it's time you reached some decision about your future. Uncle Peter would like to have you on the staff before he retires."

"I'm not a banker, Earl."

"Neither was I, Larry, when Father died."

"But you were the firstborn son, and family responsibilities always devolve on the crown prince," Larry said wryly. "Besides, you have the brains for it, plus the stamina and fortitude. I'd be more of a liability than an asset." His eyes focused on the centerpiece of yellow roses. "I guess Dad turned over in his grave at that. Grandpa Britton, too."

"Well, you know Mother's preference for you."

"Yes, but I'm not sure I want to be a planter, either."

"I see, and that narrows the field, doesn't it? But you can't just drift, Larry."

"Why not? You did for two years."

"I was traveling," Earl reminded him. "But you don't seem to be interested in the Grand Tour."

"Maybe later, I don't know. I'm so restless and confused."

"The entire country is restless and confused."

"Prelude to revolution, and I'll probably end up in the military. It seems that people must fight periodically, even among themselves, like those Kansas fools who started the Border War in 1856. John Brown and his Free Soilers simply went wild at the Potawatomie Creek massacre. A dangerous firebrand, that fellow."

"Abolitionist fanatic," Earl agreed, "and the Dred Scott Decision just gave him additional ammunition. Some flammable dust was kicked up on those wheat prairies which may ultimately have to be settled with blood, sweat, and tears."

"The possibility makes Europe seem more inviting," Larry mused. "Most of my college friends have already sailed."

"Well, think about it, Brother, and don't worry about Uncle Peter. I can talk to him."

Larry smiled reflectively. "You always could, even as a boy. I think he regards you as a son."

"He feels the same affection for you, Larry." They stood

together, and Earl embraced him briefly. "I suppose Laurette has plans for the day?"

"We're going shopping."

"You enjoy toting her bundles?"

"Not particularly, but I can see Jacintha."

"A lady finds little pleasure in watching another one spend money, Larry. It's subtle torture, and Laurette's an expert at it. Spare Jacintha those humiliating expeditions, please. She can't afford them."

Arriving at the bank, Earl went directly to his uncle's office. The old gentleman, usually most punctual, had not yet come in—a relief to Earl, who was reluctant to tell him that Larry's future plans were still in abeyance. Peter's interest in Britton Bank was primarily sentimental. Having no sons to succeed him, he had sold his share to his brother, Jerome, in order to keep the bank exclusively in family hands as long as possible.

Peter had then purchased a country estate in Yorkshire, on Manhattan Island, only to have his retirement interrupted by Jerome's sudden death from apoplexy. Jerome's elder son was then in his early twenties, a few years out of Harvard and a few months off his Grand Tour, and Peter felt that the boy would need advice and assistance. Earl had been something of a prodigal in his youth, and Peter had seen family fortunes squandered by reckless young scions suddenly given control. To his pleasant surprise, this did not happen with Earl, who took over with little difficulty, and Peter hoped that Larry would prove himself equally capable when the time came.

When Peter entered, Earl was standing at a window, watching an attractive young blond alighting rather ungracefully from a carriage in the street below.

Characteristic of the clan, Peter was tall and had once been an imposing, heavy-shouldered man. But a delicate stomach, developed in middle age, had reduced his stature to boniness, and subsequent bouts with gout and lumbago caused him to stoop and even occasionally limp. His hair was now iron-gray, his flinty eyes perpetually squinted behind square-lensed spectacles, and his curly beard resembled moss. Peter dreaded senility, but, at seventy, his wit and acumen were not in the least diminished. Clearing his throat noisily, he inquired laconically, "Anything worth seeing down there?"

Earl turned, grinning. Their fondness for each other was obvious. "Good morning, sir. I didn't hear you come in. Wearing moccasins?"

"I was trying to sneak in. Thirty minutes late, but I have a plausible excuse. Our new cook couldn't seem to find the kitchen stove to prepare breakfast, and burned it when she did. Don't mind me, son. Continue your observation. Never gaze at an old fossil if there's a shapely young female in sight. Is there?"

"Look for yourself," Earl invited.

"Wouldn't do me any good," Peter muttered.

"Couldn't do you any harm, either. Why so grumpy, Uncle? Your gout acting up?"

"My dyspepsia, Nephew."

"I thought your doctor had a cure."

"Doctor Morris has a cure for everything," Peter grumbled, popping a peppermint tablet into his mouth. "Trouble is, none of them works."

"Maybe you're taking the wrong prescription. Try a dose of this tonic, sir. Might pep you up."

"I'm trying to cure indigestion, boy, not impotency. I've already discovered that's incurable. There's no restorative for lost manhood."

"No? I presume you've investigated all the aphrodisiacs and remedies advertised in the *Herald?*"

"Enough to know they're quackery."

"Well, then a pretty young wench might be just the cure! They say that's how Commodore Vanderbilt retains his youth and vigor."

"I have a few years on Old Corneel, remember, and my wife is not as lenient or gullible as his. Unlike Mrs. Vanderbilt, your aunt Ida Mae doesn't hire tempting housemaids to accommodate me, and I'm too decrepit to go out chasing crinolines. That's a young man's game."

"On the contrary, sir. Some of the old brokers on the Street seem to have the flesh market cornered. Won't hurt you to consider this attractive commodity, anyway. I think she has some interesting collateral to offer."

"Airing her assets for your benefit, is she?"

"She's not even aware of me yet. Milady is crossing the street now, coming toward the bank. I wonder who she is? I've never seen her before."

"There must be a few women in town who've escaped your notice," Peter said, his curiosity finally piqued enough to approach the window. He hummed, stroking his grizzly whiskers appreciatively. "You're right, that's a neat column. You always did know your figures. Aha! She glimpsed you and is frisking her tantalizing tail. I reckon you could get a lien on her handily."

Earl laughed. "Just appraising and speculating, Uncle. But her reaction is typical of her sex. Leer at a lady from a garbage wagon, and she'd probably have you arrested. Ogle the same creature from a coach-and-four or a Wall Street window, and she'll smile."

"Which proves?"

"My old theory that money, or at least the appearance of it, is a man's most potent charm. Ah, yes! I have no fear of growing old and ugly, only of being poor."

"Now that we've wasted a valuable half-hour, tell me the real reason for your early visit. We rarely meet before noon, and this is the longest nonmonetary conversation we've had since the last board meeting. It's Larry, isn't it? Can't decide if he wants to be a banker or planter, right?"

"Partially."

"Partially?"

"He's in love, Uncle Pete, or thinks he is."

"At twenty? Poppycock! Send him abroad. The Continental cocottes will sever any romantic attachments here, and Larry would soon overcome his timidity in Paris."

"He's postponed his trip South."

"Can't much blame him," Peter said. "It's a hotbed of seditionists now, preaching secession and violence. Your mother should come home."

"She feels she is at home."

"Once a Southerner, always a Southerner," Peter reflected. "I remember the ball where your parents met. Miss Alicia Evanston was the prettiest belle there, and Jerome was immediately determined to win her—which wasn't easy, because he had stiff competition, and her folks naturally preferred a native son-in-law. But Jerome was persistent, courting her by correspondence when the Evanstons and their slave entourage returned to South Carolina—and somehow wrangling an invitation to visit their Low Country plantation, where they lived like feudal lords.

"The wedding took place at Rosewood, with hundreds of prominent guests, including President Jackson and many of his Cabinet. I was best man. Oh, Jerome's marriage had an illustrious beginning, and no doubt Alicia hoped at least one of their progeny would follow the Evanston way of life. I rather imagined she and her sister, Evelyn, had a bride in mind for Larry. Has he met someone in Boston, perhaps? The Britton men seem to have a penchant for ladies from localities other than their own. My Ida Mae was born in Hartford, you know. And you chose a Philadelphian."

Earl was pacing the Tabriz carpet. "Miss Howard is a native New Yorker."

"Jacintha Howard, your little ward? Well, that explains it! Delectable child, natural curls, not the kind tortured in wires and crimps, and those gorgeous eyes could set fire to a damp stick. Quite a luscious armful too—or haven't you noticed?"

"You did, at your age, didn't you?" Earl quipped. "Well, my vision's as good as yours."

Peter grinned at his favorite nephew. "Not jealous of Larry, are you?"

"Don't be senile!"

"Then what's the trouble?"

"They're both too young, that's all."

"Too young for what?"

"Marriage, damn it!"

"Has Larry proposed?"

"Not to my knowledge." Earl paused before the fireplace, pondering the dark hearth. "Neither of them could marry without my permission, and Laurette's vigilance would discourage elopement. But none of this need concern you, sir, or affect your retirement. Regardless of what Larry does, I can manage the bank."

"Certainly. You've got a competent staff and can hire sharper brains than mine, if necessary. But they wouldn't be Britton brains, Earl, in keeping with what your father wanted. Blast Ida Mae! If only she'd given me a couple of sensible sons, instead of those silly, frivolous daughters."

"Now, Uncle Pete, you know you wouldn't trade Jane and Louise for a dozen boys."

"Even so, that's not the issue now, is it? I'll stay on until Larry gets his bearings or the grim reaper gets me. Nothing much to do in the country, anyway, might as well make myself useful here. And you leave Larry's romance alone, Earl. He couldn't go wrong with Jacintha Howard. I think she'd be a fine mate for him and bear healthy children, which the Brittons desperately need now. Otherwise they may disappear from the face of the earth—this branch of the Britton tree, anyway. It's Larry's life, so let him choose his options—North or South, bank or plantation, Grand Tour or wedding." His tone was emphatic. "Don't try to be your brother's keeper."

Earl had been drumming his fingers restlessly on the mantelpiece. Now he turned and peered at his uncle. "Do I give that impression?"

"Sometimes." The elder man nodded. "Slack your reins on that pretty little filly, too. You're only her guardian, remember, not her master."

Earl frowned. "She's broke, Peter. Ronald Hartford's estate is bankrupt."

"I know that, son. I'm treasurer and auditor of this outfit, and I know that you've been paying her bills out of your personal account."

"What else can I do? Let her starve?"

"Help her find a husband. Not necessarily Larry, if you feel he's too immature, but someone worthy of her charms. It shouldn't take more than a couple of soirees, or one grand ball, to make some appropriate contacts. I can think of several suitable swains right here on the Street."

"Yes—well, I'll consider it. Couldn't be before autumn, however. Most of the best prospects are on vacation."

"What if Larry proposes?"

Earl smiled cynically. "Not much danger of that, with my wife chaperoning. She's not going to Saratoga this year."

"Larry's too old for a nanny." Peter's brow furrowed over his shrewd eyes and craggy nose. "Maybe Laurette has good reason to stay here. She hinted to Ida Mae that the Springs are not much pleasure anymore, because you ignore her to pursue your own diversions. Now I realize that many husbands do so, but not many have wives comparable to yours. And if you're tomcatting on the sly, as I suspect, you'd better never let your house pussy catch you. Her temper wouldn't be easy to control. You might get mauled."

"I already have," Earl muttered.

"What?"

"Never mind, Uncle. We'd better get to work. Cole Danvers is on my calendar this morning."

"Borrowing to expand his enterprises again? Just don't haggle with him on interest rates. Danvers is a tough, greedy bastard and doesn't deserve any discounts."

"Or any concessions," Earl agreed.

Chapter 8

THE short, robust man who strode into Earl's office with outstretched hand would not have been offended by Peter Britton's harsh evaluation of him. He would have been flattered, because the description accurately fit many of the most successful businessmen of the century. John Jacob Astor had been Cole Danvers's boyhood hero. And Cornelius Vanderbilt, now considered the nation's top titan, was his current inspiration. He admired men of humble origins who had triumphed over adversity through ambition, vision, and ruthless determination.

To Cole Danvers, success was the supreme goal, the methods of achievement irrelevant. It was an age of loose principles and confused morals, of malleable integrities and of wheeling and dealing. He was convinced that his contemporaries shared his convictions.

Earl had no personal feelings whatever for Cole Danvers. Since they were in different social realms, theirs was strictly a business relationship. Danvers's genealogy was of far less importance to Earl Britton than his character and ethics. A person could not help the circumstances of his birth, but he could exercise some control over his own conduct—and the choices that Cole Danvers had made were hardly admirable.

"Hello, Cole," Earl greeted him, shaking hands. "It's good to see you again. Have a seat. Care for a drink?"

"A little hair of the dog later, perhaps," Danvers said, taking a leather armchair before the massive desk. "Celebrated a mite too much when I hit town yesterday. King Cole was indeed a merry old soul!"

His expensive clothes were rumpled, and a grease spot shone on the loud silk cravat, alongside a great diamond stickpin. Jeweled seals dangled from the heavy gold watchchain spanning his embroidered satin vest, and a fabulous ruby ring adorned one stubby-fingered hand.

Earl surmised, correctly, that Danvers had passed the interim in one of the better parlor houses, where a rich man could revel without being robbed, cheated, doped, or murdered.

"You look every inch the sated monarch this morning, including the 'crown jewels.' But a king should have a queen, Cole."

Danvers laughed raucously, revealing large stained teeth. "I got lots of queens, Earl, in many places."

"Those aren't queens. They're ladies-in-waiting, and you'll never get a legitimate heir that way. Don't you want an heir for your kingdom?"

"Doesn't every sire worthy of his sperm? The trick is finding the right dam. She'd have to be young, pretty, a perfect lady—and that's a treasure I've not yet discovered. I'm forty, you know, and not such a handsome stallion as yourself. Oh, I could have my pick of widows with broods, sour old maids, and factory drudges, but I have higher hopes for a wife." He selected a Havana cigar from the teakwood box Earl offered, and fired it with a match struck on his boot sole. "If you know someone who meets the qualifications I just mentioned, I'd be much obliged for an introduction."

Earl shook his head. "Sorry, old boy."

"Ah, come, now! There must be a bevy of such prospects in your fancy society, which I've never been able to crash. Some lovely little lady whose family needs money and would be willing to barter position for assistance?"

"There are obstacles en route the higher elevations," Earl said.

"Of course, and fortunes acquired by inheritance are the most desirable, eh? But there are such things as expedient mergers. I'd be mighty generous with an attractive offer. Unfortunately, I'm not exactly overburdened with bids to debut balls, even though I'm a damned eligible bachelor. You could do me a big favor and earn my eternal gratitude."

"I'm not a marriage broker or auctioneer, Cole, and I assume this is a business call."

Danvers nodded, puffing on the cigar. "A million-dollar one, actually. I need at least that much for construction and equipment to enlarge and improve my textile mills and leather-goods factory. And I want the expansions completed before war comes, as it most certainly will. There'll be great demand for my products. I expect to double, triple, and more, my investments on government contracts. Give me your best interest rate."

"Twelve percent."

"That's extortion!"

"Have you tried Daniel Drew or August Belmont?"

Danvers hawked and spat, narrowly missing the polished brass cuspidor at his feet. "Those pirates want fifteen."

"How about Jay Cooke in Philadelphia, or the Bank of Boston?"

"Shylocks, all of 'em," Cole declared. "Would take mortgages on their own grandmothers' homes, and demand arms and legs for security."

"Financiers must live too, you know. Hundreds went under in the last panic, when they were left holding worthless scraps of paper for hard cash loaned without sufficient collateral. Our loan officers are not that careless."

"All right, I realize this isn't a charitable institution, Britton. Let's get down to facts. You'll want a substantial mortgage on my property and equipment. Have your sharks draw up the notes and I'll sign 'em in blood, if necessary. Twelve percent is usury, criminal, but I'll agree to it."

Earl glanced up from the memo he was writing with a gold-tipped raven's quill. "Only because you can't do better elsewhere, Danvers. How long will you be in town?"

"Long as it takes to get the loan," he replied succinctly. "I'm registered at the Astor House."

"Our attorneys should have the papers ready in a day or two. You may want yours to look over them."

"Damned right! And I'd like that drink now. Your finest liquor. The kind you serve your intimate friends and preferred customers."

"It's all private stock in this office, Cole. But when did you get so particular? You used to brag about the red-eye whiskey and lye gin you drank in waterfront saloons and two-bit bordellos."

"Of course, when I couldn't afford anything else. But I'm accustomed to better stuff in both categories now. I like my spirits old and my females young. Virgins, if possible. There's a first time even for whores, and a couple of Manhattan madams specialize in innocents."

Earl laughed. "That's the oldest trick in the oldest profession, Cole. A credible actress and a capsule of chicken blood! Those clever madams have sold the same 'virgin' to scores of gullible lechers. Don't tell me a smart fellow like you can be so easily fooled?"

"Naw, I can tell when they're faking. I had a tight one last night, only fourteen, and fresh off the farm. Cost me plenty, but it's worth it to avoid the clap."

"A mistress would be safer."

"But not cheaper. A friend of mine spends thousands on his. House, servants, clothes, jewelry. Any woman I buy that much for will be my missus."

Earl opened the cellaret. "Your pleasure?"

"Some of the superb cognac you import from that French monastery."

"I suppose good brandy is one of the few enjoyments of monkhood," Earl surmised, partially filling two crystal snifters and handing Cole one.

"Poor devils. Can you imagine living without female companionship?"

"Not very well. Still, there must be some happiness in celibacy, considering the number of priests and nuns in the world."

"But more satyrs and nymphs, I'll wager. Could be the sheikhs and Mormons have the best idea."

"Polygamy? One wife is difficult enough, man. A harem only compounds the trouble."

"And the misery? Maybe the wise man settles for whores. And bastards. Most of us are bastards anyway, nameless or not."

The son of penniless immigrants of Irish and Welsh ancestry with a soupçon of Scotch blood, he had risen from the gutter to the pinnacles of prosperity. With little formal education and a family constantly on the move in search of better opportunities, he had worked at various trades in numerous locations, saving his meager earnings and purloining whatever he could from his employers— food, merchandise, tools, and money when he could dip his hand in the till.

In his early twenties he was already acquiring failing enterprises at auctions for a fraction of their worth, some with warehouses full of salable stock, and real estate for delinquent taxes. His industries were highly competitive, and he accorded his employees no more mercy than his family had received in the factories, foundries, mines, and mills where they had slaved. He owned tenements in the same Boston and New York slums where his people had once lived, and charged the same exorbitant rents they had been forced to pay. Like many other landlords, he expediently denied ownership of his saloons, gambling houses, and brothels, while collecting their lucrative revenues.

"Sold your fleshpots yet?" Earl interrupted, inhaling the excellent Benedictine cognac.

"Long ago. A respectable businessman can't maintain an unrespectable business, you know. The preachers and reformers would condemn him to hell—and bankruptcy."

"You're lying, Cole. I know damned well you still own

your Bowery dens! Next you'll tell me you've become religious."

"Not yet, but I do go to church occasionally, when it suits my purpose."

"Which church?"

"Don't matter. There were many creeds in my clan." A negligent shrug. "They all preach fire and brimstone, sin and repentance. I do plenty of one, little of the other. Was never a choirboy—and I bet you weren't, either."

"Wrong. I sang at Grace Episcopal Church until my voice changed from tenor to baritone in the middle of a Sunday service. The horrified instructor said I sounded like a frog, and I had to turn in my robe. Terribly embarrassing, because I was only eleven years old. Early puberty."

"Me too. Had my first tail at twelve. You?"

"Fourteen, and seduced by an older woman. She was twenty. Quite an experience."

Earl was silent, visualizing Larry's pretty young English governess, who had elected to educate his precocious older brother. Great fun, until the day Miss Winfield was suddenly dismissed sans reference. Five-year-old Larry had missed his charming governess after an older, austere, and homely replacement was hired, but not nearly as much as Earl had missed Sally Winfield.

"I guess every boy remembers his sexual initiation," he reflected.

"Yeah, even if she was only a common bitch, like mine was."

"More cognac?"

"No, thanks. Got some other places to go." Danvers stood. "I'll be waiting for those papers, and if you could find it in your flinty heart to reduce that interest rate . . ."

"Would you, in my position?"

"Hell, no!"

"Well?"

"You know something, Britton? You might have better blood and breeding than some of your competitors, but in business matters you rank with the biggest bastards."

"Not quite, Danvers, or you wouldn't be here. You already approached the worst wolves on Wall Street. I'm tame by comparison."

"Sure, and God help the widows and orphans."

"Especially in your sweatshops," Earl countered. "We don't employ women or children here, and only the executives work more than ten hours a day. How many hours do your factory slaves work? From dawn to dusk? If child labor is ever abolished, the manufacturers will do the loudest howling."

"True, because they'd have the most to lose." Danvers grinned, offering his hand. "One of the main differences between us, my fine friend, is that I've got fewer illusions about myself. . . ."

Chapter 9

LARRY was in his room writing a letter when the door opened quietly and Laurette entered in a clinging emerald satin wrapper, her long burnished-gold hair cascading down her shoulders. He had never before seen her in such intimate attire, which belonged only in a lady's boudoir, and he thought again how lucky his brother was to have such a desirable wife.

"Busy?" she whispered in her low, soft contralto.

He gazed at her curiously, wondering why he had not heard her knock. "Just taking care of overdue correspondence. I owe letters to Mother and Aunt Evelyn. Have you had breakfast?"

"Tea and muffins. I never eat much, which is why I don't go to the dining room. Heavy food early in the morning—or any time, for that matter—doesn't suit me. Did you and Earl have a nice chat?"

Larry put the quill down and closed the leather stationery portfolio. "We discussed many things."

"Including Jacintha Howard?"

"Yes."

"And?" Laurette moved slowly toward him, her lithe body seeming to slither under the shimmering fabric, and

Larry felt a sudden tension in his chest and loins. She shouldn't be in his room in a negligee!

"Nothing was decided about anything. But he mentioned Uncle Peter's retirement again."

"Don't feel bad about that, Larry. Uncle Peter enjoys working at the bank. He would be bored without it. Besides, Aunt Ida Mae prefers their town house in Union Square to that lonely old estate in Yorkshire, as do Jane and Louise. Of course, they've given up on marriage for the girls. Past thirty now, both of them, and confirmed old maids. And no wonder! Plump frumps, stuffing themselves on sweets. Stringy hair and bad teeth. Who would have them?"

Larry's shrug dismissed the subject. "If you still plan to shop today, Laurette, I'd rather not invite Jacintha along."

"Why not?"

"Well, she's on a strict budget, you know."

"You're parroting Elder Brother now. Why is Earl so concerned about Miss Howard? She's not a child, and that stupid will making her Earl's responsibility should be revoked in court! Her grandfather must have been a simpleton to put the poor girl at the mercy of a man."

"Not just any man, Laurette, but his friend's son. And one of the purposes of a bank is to administer trusts."

"Oh, Larry! You still regard Earl as some kind of paragon, don't you? Over two months in this house, and you still haven't discovered the tarnish on your knight's armor. Your loyalty is touching, Larry, but also pathetic, because Earl is not worthy of your adulation. And now you look as if I'd stuck a knife in your heart! Is it so difficult to believe, seeing how shabbily he treats me? It's not an easy job being mistress of a great house, Larry, and I do my best to please Earl. But—" She broke off, as if unable to continue.

"You manage wonderfully, Laurette, and I'm sure Earl appreciates everything you do."

"No, Larry. He gives the credit to the servants."

"But you hired them, Laurette! Gaston and his wife are the best butler and housekeeper in New York. The entire household staff is the finest money can buy."

Laurette frowned. "Earl says I couldn't manage a three-room flat without hired help. He takes every opportunity to wound me." She glided about the chamber, pausing to examine the toilet articles on the bureau, sniffing the cologne, fondling the silver-backed military brushes, touching the cravat draped over a chair back. "And he'll never forgive my sterility. I think he finds a barren woman useless. He's bitter, cynical, often cruel, and his vices far outnumber his virtues. He's too fond of liquor and gambling, and—well, where do you think he spends his nights away from home? I can't help wondering how many bastards he has sired around this town!"

Larry listened helplessly, intimidated by the tirade. He felt like a little boy hearing that Santa Claus did not exist. Before, Laurette had only implied Earl's faults.

"Laurie, please! Don't tell me these things. Even if they're true, I'd rather not hear them."

"I'm sorry, Larry, if the truth hurts. But imagine how I feel. I'm his wife, after all, for better or worse. And while I know I'm not perfect, I don't believe I exaggerate Earl's imperfections one iota. I'm at my wit's end trying to understand what he wants of me!" Her eyes beseeched him. "I have to talk to someone, Larry. If you won't listen or help . . ." She bowed her head in distress.

"Laurette." He approached her awkwardly, shifting from one foot to the other, at a loss as to how to console her. "Why don't you get dressed, and we'll buy out every shop on Broadway? Some new bonnets should lift your spirits."

"I'm out of the mood now," she said, weeping openly now, removing the handkerchief from his breast pocket to blot her eyes.

"My dear," he murmured wretchedly. "We shouldn't be here like this."

"You're so kind, Larry, and I'm so glad you're here. I hope you stay forever."

Larry was never quite sure how she came to be in his arms, but suddenly he was holding her and whispering, "Don't cry, Laurie. Things will work out between you and Earl."

"No, I've lost him, Larry. He doesn't love me anymore, if he ever did. He cares more now for his horses and harlots."

"Nonsense! I'm sure this is just a temporary estrangement, Laurie, common in marriage. You haven't lost Earl. How could he not love you? You're sweet and lovely and gentle, everything a man could want in a wife."

"Am I, Larry?"

Her hand caressed his face, stroking the boyish cheeks, tracing the sensitive mouth. Her wrapper parted over her bosom, revealing bare flesh, soft and white and fragrant with narcissus, her favorite scent. Larry had an insane desire to fondle her breasts. His adolescent passion, never before so keenly aroused, threatened to overwhelm him. He released her abruptly and stepped back, heaving.

"You'd better leave, Laurie."

"Relax, dear."

"Relax? You're my brother's wife!"

"Have you ever had a woman, Larry?"

He glanced away, shaking his head.

"Never?"

"No."

"Nor seen one nude?"

"Not alive," he quavered. "Just art. Paintings, statues."

"Poor boy." Easing herself back into his embrace, she pressed her thighs against his genitals. "Aphrodite in marble is fine, Larry, but there's no substitute for a real woman."

"We're playing with fire, Laurette."

"Fun, isn't it? Kiss me, darling. You know you want to; don't be afraid. I won't bite you."

"Laurie, we can't do this! It's wrong. Please go, before it's too late."

Her lips curved in a sensuous smile. She kissed him tentatively, teasing until he responded, taking his tongue into her mouth and savoring it. Then she guided his nervous hands under her negligee and over her figure, from the proud breasts to the slender waist and smooth hips. Larry touched the erect rosy nipples, and everything except desire fled his mind. His feeble defenses trembled precariously and then collapsed.

"Lock the door," she cautioned, then moved toward the bed.

It was a humiliating fiasco in which he had barely removed his clothing before plunging eagerly into her body and ejaculating prematurely. He had intended to linger, to enjoy this fully, but he knew nothing about the delightful preliminaries of the act, or of the control necessary to prolong it. Should he apologize for his clumsiness? How could he ever face her again? Face Earl? Or himself?

Pulling on a robe and smoothing back his damp hair, Larry crossed the floor to stand by a window, gazing down at Fifth Avenue. Although it was not yet noon, heat steamed up from the pavement and seeped into the house. The brownstone mansions often became giant ovens in midsummer. The scorched trees now hung limp and withered, mimicking the way he felt.

Laurette lay languidly in bed, watching him with mingled pity and contempt. "What are you thinking, Larry? How wicked I am? Not at all. There's never been any other man in my life except my husband, until now. I don't know what possessed me. Loneliness, unhappiness, despair. Revenge, perhaps. To be untrue to Earl just once, for his myriad infidelities to me. You don't hate me, do you? Say something!"

His voice was hesitant, raspy. "What's there to say? It happened, that's all. We weren't strong enough, Laurie. We didn't fight it. Regret won't help now. Nothing will help."

"And you blame me?"

"No, myself. I'm weak, despicably weak, and I can't stay here any longer. I have to go away."

"Why?"

"Why? My God, after that—orgy!"

"Orgy!" She laughed. "Oh, Larry! You were an anxious little boy, too absorbed in your own pleasure to even realize you had a partner. And now you're behaving like a deflowered virgin, and making me feel like a depraved child-seducer! You can't even face me. Am I ugly to you now?"

"I've violated your hospitality and profaned my brother's house," he lamented. "Taken his wife in adultery!"

Laurette sighed, sat up, and shrugged into her robe again. "Stop moralizing, Larry, and look at me! I'm covered now. Try to be adult. This penitent-sinner attitude of yours will betray us both, and Earl will divorce me and quite possibly kill you in a rage. Is that what you want?"

"It's what I deserve."

"And do I deserve divorce, scandal, disgrace? The stigma of an adulteress? That's certain exile from society, comparable to death for any decent woman!"

"But we can't risk having this happen again!"

"Was it so terrible? You seemed to enjoy it."

"Laurette," he groaned, embarrassed.

"I only meant that it didn't ruin you, Larry. Nor was it incest, if that's troubling you. We're not blood relations, you know."

"Nevertheless we can't continue to live under the same roof, Laurette, defying temptation! If only I had gone to Charleston, or abroad."

"Good Lord, such dramatics, like a Greek tragedy! This house is as much yours as Earl's, and I don't intend to make a habit of seducing you. But run, if you must, like a fugitive fleeing a crime."

"Adultery *is* a crime"—he reminded her—"against the laws of God and man."

"Yes, of course. And guilty women were formerly stoned in the streets for it, put on the rack and in the stocks. Tortured, branded, beheaded, while their faithless spouses fornicated whenever they chose. Even now an adulteress can be jailed, charged, and tried like a criminal in domestic court, and deprived of every human right. But I trust you don't wish me such a drastic fate? Sackcloth and ashes will suffice?" She went to the bureau to groom her hair with one of his brushes.

"Laurette, I'm sorry."

"You must forget it, Larry."

"How can I forget it?"

"Try. I shall."

"You're certain no one saw you come in here?"

"The chambermaids know I sleep late," she said. "They're not allowed upstairs before luncheon."

In his doleful preoccupation, Larry missed the contempt in Laurette's manner. The miserable coward was afraid even of servants, whose livelihood depended upon absolute discretion. "What about Jacintha?" she asked, viewing him in the mirror.

"I hope she'll understand."

"Understand what, Larry? Jilting her without explanation, after pretending to court her? Will you throw the innocent little lamb to the big wolf?"

"Earl's not like that," he said in dogged defense.

"There are none so blind as those who will not see," she quoted. "But may I ask a favor of you? Please don't leave until next week, when Earl goes to Saratoga. It'll seem perfectly natural to him if you leave then." She waited anxiously. "Larry?"

He nodded. "All right, Laurie. Next week. Will you go with him?"

"No, I'd rather visit my parents, in Newport."

"Forgive me, Laurie?"

"We'll forgive each other, Larry."

And may God forgive us both, he prayed, certain that his brother never would.

Laurette opened the door a crack and peeked out cautiously, to insure a departure as furtive as her entry. Except for the lingering scent of her perfume, the incident might have seemed like an incredible dream. But even if it should eventually fade into merciful oblivion, he knew that the exotic scent of narcissus would always evoke this reality.

For the next few days Laurette held her breath, while Larry lived in a kind of sheepish agony. He avoided her as much as possible and refused to meet her eyes when confrontation was unavoidable. He passed his time in the library, reading and writing, or helping the valet do his packing. Laurette imagined that he visualized a scarlet letter on her forehead and locked his bedroom door at night, lest she sneak in and seduce him while he was asleep. At last, Larry revealed his intentions to his brother.

"So it wasn't love, after all?" Earl questioned, and Larry merely shook his head, glancing down at his plate.

Earl gazed at his wife. "Does this surprise you?"

"Not really. They were only friends."

"True, Larry?"

"True."

"You had me fooled," Earl said. "It appeared serious for both of you."

Laurette sipped her white wine. "Things are not always what they appear, darling. You should know that."

They exchanged wry smiles. "Yes, I should, darling. And, of course, Jacintha's going to regard me as the villain in this."

"Why should she do that?" asked Larry, concerned.

"And why should you care?" Laurette intervened, before her husband could reply.

Earl peered at her narrowly, and then at his brother, whose guilty expression irritated Laurette. Larry's cowering like a spineless puppy made her want to shake him. She was relieved when he excused himself and left the dining room suddenly.

Immediately Earl demanded, "What's going on here?"

"I don't know what you mean."

"Larry's miserable. Is he sick?"

"His asthma's been acting up," Laurette temporized. "Heat and humidity often aggravate respiratory conditions, along with dust and pollen. The voyage will improve his health and stimulate his appetite, put some flesh on his bones and color in his face."

"It's his spirit that's down, Laurette. Dragging."

"He's afraid of life, Earl. He's quaking at the idea of going abroad alone."

"Then why is he going?"

"Because he considers it necessary to his maturity," she

reasoned. "And it is, Earl. He's such a boy! You'd better bestow some Big Brotherly advice on him or hire a guardian angel to protect him. His emotions don't match his intellect. How could he graduate summa cum laude and remain so incredibly naive? The Continental women will frighten him out of his wits!"

"He could be running away from something," Earl mused. "Did Jacintha refuse him?"

"How should I know?"

"Don't be devious! You supervised his courtship, didn't you? He confided in you. Did she refuse him?"

"I don't think he proposed."

"Then what the devil is wrong with him? This tour is some kind of escape, and it shouldn't be. Travel is for knowledge, experience, and pleasure, not for running away."

Laurette laid her damask napkin aside. "You worry about him too much, Earl. No boy ever grew into a man, tied to his brother's shoelaces. Larry has been trying to fill your boots since childhood, and it's high time he walked out of your shadow."

"Maybe," Earl said grimly.

"I presume you're staying home this evening?"

"Yes."

"How nice! For a change."

"Save the sarcasm for later, Laurette."

"Oh? Shall I expect you later?"

"Am I welcome in milady's boudoir?"

"You always have been, milord."

"Horseshit," he muttered, pushing back his chair. "I think Larry's in the library. I'll have my coffee and brandy there. Some brotherly camaraderie might be in order."

Chapter 10

THE note and large bouquet of hothouse flowers were delivered to Riverview by messenger. Jacintha pondered the farewell tribute wistfully, thoroughly puzzled.

My Dear Jacintha,

Please accept these flowers as a token of my esteem and appreciation for your most enjoyable company these past two months.

I am sailing shortly on my Grand Tour and will think of you frequently during my travels. I know not if we shall ever meet again, as my long-range plans are indefinite.

I shall always treasure our friendship, however, and the pleasant times we had together. I sincerely regret that the exigencies of preparation prevent a personal goodbye, but I beg to remain

Your humble friend and servant, Lawrence Britton.

Jacintha brushed tears from her cheeks as Lollie arranged the long-stemmed white roses and lilies of the valley, reminiscent of a bridal bouquet, in a tall blue vase.

"I don't understand it, Lollie. I thought he liked me."

"He did, honey."

"Then why is he leaving New York so suddenly?"

"Who knows why rich folks do anything? And that boy's an odd one, anyway."

"I think he's being sent away, or driven off by his family —probably his brother."

"More likely his sister-in-law," Lollie suggested, picking up a fallen petal. "A witch, that creature. I bet she had ancestors in Salem."

"But Laurette Britton had nothing to fear from me. Why, she has everything a woman could want and more."

"That's not always enough, Missy."

"Well, I can't imagine what she lacks."

"Love, perhaps."

"Of others, possibly, not of herself. She's a narcissist, Lollie. And attar of narcissus is her favorite essence. She imports it from Paris."

"Vanity can be a burden," Lollie declared. "Vain women dread time."

"Men get old, too, don't they?"

"Not like us, unfortunately. But age ain't one of your concerns yet, child. And no point crying over spilt milk now, either."

"You mean clabber—it soured last night."

"I noticed this morning."

Lifting the damp curls off her back, Jacintha broke her winter vow never to complain about summer again. "This wretched weather! Food spoils so easily. The meat is tainted, too. I can smell it in here."

"I'll soak it in vinegar."

"No, throw it out, Lollie. We'll fix something else for supper. Soup, maybe."

"The vegetables are wilted."

"Good. They'll match the cooks."

Jacintha sighed. She envied Larry his journeys, and hoped he would enjoy his odyssey and find whatever he was seeking.

Her September allowance arrived early from Britton Bank, and it was one hundred dollars, double her regular stipend. Lollie considered this a generous gesture, but Jacintha took another view.

"Guilty conscience! Now I know *he* sent Larry away, and I'll never forgive him."

"Never is a long time."

"Not long enough to even my score with Earl Britton!"

"You could be wrong, honey."

"You always defend him, Lollie. But why else would he increase my money? I should send it back to him!"

The housekeeper shrugged. "Beggars can't be choosers, Miss Howard. But send it back, if you feel that way."

"I will," Jacintha decided vehemently. "No, I'll take it to him. Help me dress."

But halfway up the stairs she paused, remembering an item she had read in the *Tribune*.

Like so many other prominent New Yorkers, Mr. and Mrs. Earl Britton are departing for cooler climes on an extended holiday. They will sail on their luxurious steam yacht, the *Lorelei*, to Albany, where Mr. Britton will embark for Saratoga Springs and Mrs. Britton will board a train to visit friends on Cape Cod before joining her parents, the Robert Lancasters of Philadelphia, at their summer residence in Newport, Rhode Island.

Mr. Britton's younger brother, Lawrence, a June graduate of Harvard University, is currently on his Grand Tour, after which he will reside in the South, probably on the Evanston plantation, Rosewood, in the beautiful Carolina Low Country.

We wish them all Bon Voyage and Happy Landings!

"It's no use," Jacintha murmured. "He's not there, Lollie. And anyway, you're right. We do need the money."

PART II

Chapter 11

THE autumn afternoon was deceptively mild and golden, as if Indian summer had come to stay. Feathery white clouds were etched in the indigo sky. Except for the falling leaves and ripening apples, winter seemed far away—a mere illusion.

Jacintha sat in a wicker swing attached by chains to the stoutest limb of an old buttonwood tree. As she swung, the wide lavender sash of her pearl-gray poplin dress floated behind her, the full flaring skirt revealing glimpses of the lovely lingerie she had hopefully begun to assemble for a trousseau during Larry Britton's courtship.

He had been abroad over two months now, and several long letters assured Jacintha that he was enjoying his Grand Tour immensely. But an undercurrent of sadness ran through the pages containing poetic descriptions of museums, art galleries, castles, cathedrals, and opera houses. In the midst of so much beauty, why did he not sound happier? And why did he write that he planned to sail directly to Charleston upon his return to America?

Jacintha expected never to see him again. Nor had she heard from Earl or Laurette since Larry's departure, although the social columnists had exuberantly heralded their return to Manhattan prior to the fall season. Jacintha's own life had sunk back into its monotonous routine. Her former fears and anxieties, temporarily obscured by the happiness of Larry's companionship, reappeared and hovered now like ominous shadows.

Her financial plight grew ever more critical. Selling Riverview seemed the most sensible solution. Of course, she could not hope to receive the true worth of any of her possessions. Auctions were usually sacrifice sales. Tomorrow, then, she would begin listing the items, room by room, in a journal for the auctioneer. If only she could accomplish the fact without her guardian's knowledge, take the proceeds and go far away. Start a new life.

Hearing a noise, she glanced swiftly over her shoulder—and confronted her nemesis.

He smiled suavely, debonair in casual tweeds. "You should lock your house, Miss Howard."

Glad that she was not barefoot and in old clothes, Jacintha admonished tartly, "And you should be arrested for trespassing, Mr. Britton!"

"There was no response to my knock, so I came in and searched for you. Where's your duenna?"

"Marketing. What do you want, Earl?"

"To visit my ward," he replied blandly. "See how she's faring. Of course, I'm interested."

"And when did your interest begin?"

"I've always been concerned, Jacintha."

"Is that why you drove Larry away?"

There was a pause. Then Earl asked slowly, "Who told you that?"

"No one. I figured it out. And I hope you're satisfied."

"My God, Jacintha! You take me for a worse villain than I am. I didn't drive Larry from New York or try to influence him to live in South Carolina. He made both decisions himself, quite unexpectedly."

She shrugged nonchalantly. "It doesn't matter now. What can I do for you?"

"I came to invite you to a ball."

"Indeed? I thought that was done by formal invitation."

"You'll receive one," he said. "This is merely advance notice. That's a charming frock, but you'll need a ball gown."

"I shan't accept."

"Now, Jacintha, don't be difficult! You must meet some appropriate suitors."

"Your brother was eligible and proper."

"But only twenty, an immature boy. It wouldn't have worked, Jacintha. Believe me."

"Then you *did* deliberately stop our courtship?"

"No, I did not!" He glanced toward the Hudson, visible through the defoliating trees. "Something happened. I'm not sure what, but I have an idea."

"Is it a secret?"

He nodded gravely, his eyes remote.

"I don't believe you."

"That's your prerogative, my dear. But will you believe this? Your grandfather's estate is bankrupt. There's no more money, unless I sell this property."

Jacintha touched her feet to the ground, halting the swing. Despite her recent resignation to the sale of Riverview, facing the reality was not easy, nor was hearing the verdict from Earl. "Do you have a buyer?" she asked tremulously.

"I think so. A man I know is seeking a home in New York and could pay a good price."

"Where does he live now?"

"Various places. He travels a good deal, surveying his assets. He owns textile mills and shoe factories in Massachusetts, and real estate and other enterprises in New York, where he wants to settle."

"May I know his name—or is that a secret, too?"

"Cole Danvers."

"Has he seen Riverview?"

"Only in passing, but he likes it."

"And would I go with the property?"

"Certainly not, although I don't imagine he'd object to

such an arrangement. Legally, that is. You see, he's also in the market for a wife. But he's much too old for you, Jacintha, and unsuitable. Crude fellow, self-made."

"No silver spoon at birth? No nanny, governess, tutor, or college degree? Pulled himself up by his own bootstraps? My, he must be a terrible boor!"

"Spare me your sarcasm, please. I'm not belittling his success, Miss Howard, only his methods of achievement. He's ruthless, avaricious, and eternally ambitious."

She smiled bitterly. "Larry was too young and callow, and Mr. Danvers is too old and greedy. Just what age and kind of man does my cautious guardian recommend for me?"

Pretending to ponder the question, he drawled, "Oh, someone about thirty or so, with character and position in addition to fortune. A decent, God-fearing chap, who wouldn't barter his soul to Satan for profit."

"And where is this marvel of humanity to be found?"

An ingratiating grin. "You're looking at him."

She leaped from the swing, glaring at him furiously.

"You're insufferable, Earl Britton! The most arrogant person I've ever had the misfortune to know. And go ahead, sell Riverview. The sooner the better. I realize I can't keep it forever. Auction it all to the highest bidder, and Lollie and I will take the money and go West. I've been reading about the wonderful opportunities in the Territories. Wagon trains depart from Eastern stations every week, and it shouldn't be too difficult for you to hire a driver for us. If it is, we'll do it ourselves. I—I think it would be a great adventure!"

Instantly sobered, Earl said, "The proceeds will be put in trust for you in Britton Bank, as stipulated in the will. You'll continue to receive it by allotment, Jacintha, not in a lump sum. Nor will you leave New York without my consent until you reach your majority or marry."

"Also not without your permission?" she cried angrily. "Oh, how could Grandpa do this to me!"

"He didn't want his naive granddaughter hurt, and you should be grateful to him."

"Pooh! I'd rather be my own guardian, belong to myself, do as I wish with my life."

"You can, eventually. But not if you marry, for then you must defer to your husband."

"Does Laurette defer to you? I think not! She strikes me as most independent."

"Only because I don't demand subservience or exercise the control the law allows a man over his wife," he explained. "You may not acquire such a lenient spouse."

Jacintha was moving about the garden, trying to avoid the weeds and brambles. She snared her sash on a hawthorn and suffered his assistance in releasing her. Then she plucked a shaggy aster bloom from the rank perennial border and slowly pulled it apart. "I'm not sure I want to acquire any kind of spouse, ever."

"In that case, there's an alternative. And I don't mean the one Horace Greeley recommends to young men."

"You speak in riddles."

"Well, stand still and listen to me."

"Why? I'm not interested in any of your diabolical alternatives."

"Oh, Lord, Jacintha! Why do we always end up fighting? You know damned well something has to be done about your situation, and not this ridiculous idea of going West! You're not a pioneer—how long do you think you could survive alone in the wilderness? Why not simply let someone take care of you?"

"Someone?" She stared at him, then asked slowly, "You?"

"Yes."

"Take care of me how?"

"In every way. The necessities. And luxuries."

Jacintha could not believe she had understood him correctly. "Be your mistress?"

"I can offer you everything but marriage, my dear."

Her eyes widened; her jaw dropped. How dared he insult her so boldly, as if she were a harlot soliciting in the street! Decent, God-fearing chap? The sneaky snake had a high opinion of himself! She recoiled in shock.

"Why, I'd rather go to the wilds and be trampled by buffalo. . . . I'd rather die than be kept by you, Mr. Earl Britton!"

A nerve flickered about his tense mouth. "Is that so? Well, Miss Howard, since you're being so bluntly honest, why shouldn't I? I'm keeping you *now*. Yes, Jacintha, your allowance is coming from my bank account, not yours. Your funds have long since been exhausted. I've been playing Santa Claus!"

This was somehow even more degrading than his indecent proposal. Jacintha turned away, her face beet-red and her bosom heaving.

"Thank you for the information," she said in a quavering voice. "I'll find some way to repay you. And I refuse to accept another penny of your charity."

His anger melted in remorseful apology. "I'm sorry, Jacintha. I shouldn't have said that, but I was angry. You might have been a little kinder in refusing me." He rubbed his chin ruefully, as if she had struck him. "That was quite a blow to my pride."

"You deserved it."

"I know. Forgive me?"

Her mind was elsewhere, racing. "This Cole Danvers," she said tentatively. "Send him here as soon as possible, and I'll show him the place. If he buys it, I want the cash, Earl. If you won't give it to me, I'll go to an attorney, tell him the sort of proposition you made me, and have you declared an unfit guardian."

He almost laughed. "I have enough influence to keep such a petition out of court indefinitely, Jacintha. But it won't be necessary. I believe Danvers will purchase Riverview immediately. You may have the proceeds and do as you please."

Tears stung her eyes. "Good riddance?"

"I didn't say that."

"But I have been a nuisance, haven't I? A burden?"

Earl shook his head, smiling slightly. "A challenge, rather. But it'll soon be over . . . aren't you relieved?" He stood behind her, and she felt his hand touch her hair. "I'm going to miss you, Curly Locks, and worry about you on your westward journey."

"I—I haven't gone yet."

"May I kiss you goodbye?"

"Please go, Earl."

"Yes, I guess I'd better," he agreed. "I have an appointment with Danvers tomorrow. Are you certain you want to sell your home, Jacintha?"

Bewilderment, despair, defeat engulfed her. "I must."

"No, darling, I lied to you. You're not broke yet, and I haven't been supporting you."

But she was not beguiled. "Now you *are* lying, Earl, and I do intend to reimburse you. Tell Mr. Danvers he can take possession of Riverview very soon. Lollie and I can be packed and out in a few days, a week at the most."

"But where will you go, Jacintha? You can't be serious about this other business. It's lunacy!"

"Then we'll have plenty of mutual company on the trail," she replied. "A caravan of lunatic pilgrims. I'll expect Mr. Danvers in a day or two."

"Very well," Earl muttered. He turned and left abruptly.

Jacintha went into the kitchen and brewed a pot of tea to share with Lollie. The idea of two inexperienced women trekking West alone was indeed insanity. Even Lollie, who still believed in miracles, would consider it madness.

Expecting an elderly man, Jacintha was surprised by the robust, ruddy stranger who appeared at her door. Neither old nor young, Mr. Danvers was in his prime, and apparently in vigorous health. There was no silver in his thick auburn hair, groomed with a heavily scented pomade, or in the bushy russet mustache with which he tried to disguise a somewhat crooked nose, broken several times in his youth. His black frock coat and checked trousers, crimson cravat and flamboyant jewelry, patent-leather boots and fancy gloves reminded Jacintha of pictures she had seen of Tammany Hall politicians and Bowery dandies. He obviously enjoyed flaunting his wealth.

His awkward bow betrayed his lack of polish, but his broad smile conveyed his pleasure in introducing himself to such a lovely young lady. No wonder her guardian had tried to persuade him to let their lawyers handle the purchase, sight unseen! A clever rascal, Earl Britton! But Cole Danvers had insisted on a personal inspection of the property. Now his small shrewd eyes, pale brown with a reddish glint, carefully appraised Riverview's owner. If he played his cards right, there might be more than a business transaction involved here. . . .

"I'm mighty pleased to meet you, Miss Howard," he said in a guttural bass voice. "You were expecting me?"

"Yes, sir. Mr. Britton mentioned your interest in finding a residence in New York, preferably in Greenwich Village. Of course, this one is not in the best condition."

"Ah, but the foundation is there! Good design, excellent craftsmanship. I can tell it was once a very fine place and could be again, with proper attention. I want to see all of it, Miss Howard, from basement to attic."

"Certainly, sir."

As Jacintha escorted him through the mansion, he tested the beams, walls, floorboards, staircases, fireplaces for soundness. Pounding his fists, stamping his feet, shaking doors, rattling windows, scratching and probing exposed surfaces with his penknife, he explained, "Can't be too careful about dry rot and termite damage. Some old buildings are mere hollow shells verging on collapse. I got stung that way once, but never again. This structure is basically solid, though, built to last."

"I'm selling the furniture too," Jacintha said, disappointed by his cursory examination of the fine pieces. And her heart sank as he casually outlined the many gross changes he would make. Would he simply dispose of everything, start anew with the ornate and often hideous Victorian decor so popular now?

"I trust, Mr. Danvers, that you are aware of the valuable antiques? Why, you could never replace that Queen Anne settee in the parlor, or the pair of Chippendale sofas in the drawing room, which my great-grandparents purchased on one of their trips abroad. They and my grandparents made many voyages across the Atlantic in search of beautiful furnishings for their home and business. The dining suite is authentic Hepplewhite, and there are several genuine Adam mantelpieces—not reproductions. We have some Pembroke tables, Sheraton chairs, and a handsome Jacobean armoire."

"Yes, yes." He nodded, although the names meant little.

"I like this house," he decided. "I only wish there was more land with it. The grounds must have been large once."

"A veritable paradise, Mr. Danvers, and there's still enough for a lovely garden. A landscaper could work wonders with it. At least the residence doesn't sit right on the street. Notice the fine old oaks and graceful elms in front, and the Lombardy poplars lining the driveway. The iron fence and gates could be painted or replaced, and the pools and fountains restored."

He smiled, watching her animated gestures, fascinated by her unusual turquoise eyes. "You don't have to persuade me, Miss Howard, although you are indeed a persuasive saleslady. I've already made up my mind to buy Riverview, and I won't even change the name. But Mr. Britton has set a steep price. I'll have to haggle with him."

"Not too much, I hope? This is all I have in the world, Mr. Danvers. I would appreciate your generosity."

"Would you, now, Miss Howard? Enough, perhaps, to agree to supervise the decoration? Give the professionals the benefit of your knowledge and taste?"

Jacintha blushed delicately. "I think that might be arranged, sir."

"Good. Would tomorrow be too soon to start?"

"Well, my housekeeper and I shall be busy preparing to move, Mr. Danvers."

"You don't understand, Miss Howard. I'd like you to remain in residence during the restoration. Your servant, too. At no cost to you. In fact, I insist on compensating you for your time and trouble."

It was a generous offer, and Jacintha could hardly believe her good fortune. "That's very kind of you, Mr. Danvers. To tell the truth, we haven't located satisfactory lodgings yet, or made our future plans. And I assure you, helping restore Riverview will be a pleasure—a memorial to my forebears."

"Then we have reached an understanding?"

"Yes, we have," Jacintha agreed, shaking the bejeweled hand he extended. "And we'll try not to inconvenience you too long, sir."

"I'm in no great hurry, Miss Howard. I keep a suite at the Astor Hotel. I do considerable traveling, but will be coming here frequently to check the progress of the decorators. The finest decorating firm in New York will be put at your disposal—subject to your approval, of course."

Her pink mouth dimpled at the corners as she warned, "That's a temptation to stay on, Mr. Danvers. You may have to evict me before you can move in."

Was she flirting with him? "Things change, Miss Howard," he mused, admiring the portrait of the beautiful young woman in the bouffant white gown on the drawing room wall. "You may never have to leave at all. Life is sort of a kaleidoscope, I've found. Never constant, always changing. Yesterday we didn't even know each other. Today I'm buying your home. And tomorrow . . . who knows? A kaleidoscope, Miss Howard," he repeated, rocking on his heels. "Is that you up there?"

"My mother."

"Lovely," he said. "Every lovely lady should be painted. Does this one go with the house?"

"I'm afraid not, sir. I plan to take the family portraits with me. Sentiment, you know. Memories."

"I have no such keepsakes," he mused. "My ancestors were never immortalized on canvas, or even on tombstones, which they couldn't afford. Reckon I'll have to be the first in the Danvers gallery . . . or my wife will, when I find her." He paused tentatively, but Jacintha said nothing. "Now I'd best get to Britton Bank and negotiate the contract with that robber baron."

Jacintha accompanied him to the door, where he put on his black derby. A hired hack waited at the curb. Surely he would buy a fine carriage and horses when he became master of Riverview. Several vehicles, perhaps, and a stable of thoroughbreds, like the Brittons, Vanderbilts, and Astors.

Chapter 12

WITHIN a week Jacintha was conferring with the renowned firm of Bartell & Smith, pondering sketches, materials, colors, selecting and rejecting as carefully as if Riverview were going to be her permanent address. When in town, Danvers spent several hours a day there, badgering the contractors, carpenters, painters, and masons, who complained to Miss Howard in his absence and grumbled incessantly among themselves.

The decorators realized that their professional reputations would suffer if they followed their client's flamboyant wishes, and Smith, a nervous little man, was approaching hysteria. "Red, red, red! What a vile, delirious color! I fear that if we pleased Mr. Danvers in every respect, we couldn't get a job decorating Bedlam!"

Jacintha silently agreed and entered into a tacit conspiracy to prevent the transformation of Riverview into a monstrosity. Desecration of her ancestors' memories must be avoided by any means necessary. Messrs. Bartell and Smith gratefully commended her discrimination before Mr. Danvers and happily adopted many of her suggestions. "Miss Howard has excellent taste, sir, and we're incorporating many of her ideas. Our goal is enduring beauty and elegance, and we're convinced you'll find the end result esthetically gratifying."

Their client, not even certain of what they were saying, shrugged in acquiescence. Although partial to scarlet velvet and gold tassels, he would just have to trust their judgment. After all, he had hired them to do the job and was paying them a king's ransom. Moreover, Miss Howard was a lady of refinement. Her taste could be trusted.

"You must do me the honor of being hostess at my first party here."

"If you wish," Jacintha consented. "But it won't be ready for entertainment for a while, Mr. Danvers."

"Cole," he urged. "And your name is so pretty, may I please call you Jacintha?"

She nodded, lowering her lashes at the compliment. "Mr. Bartell thinks that Florentine tapestry would be an attractive wall-covering for the dining room, and flocked French paper in the parlor."

Danvers grinned. "If I don't agree, I fear that little fella would fly into a frenzy. I'm surprised he don't want ruffles and lace everywhere."

Dreading her approaching departure, Jacintha's thoughts were reflected in her face.

"Why so sad and quiet?" Cole asked. "Something wrong?"

"Just thinking," she answered. "And perhaps a bit fatigued."

"You've been working too hard, Jacintha, and all this stuff scattered about must be bothersome. Maybe I'm imposing on you too much?"

"Not at all!" she protested. "I'm enjoying it."

"Still, you should have some rest, my dear. And leisure. Let me take you to supper this evening. And the theater, if you like."

"Why, I think that would be very nice, Cole. There's a new play at the Park Lane. Do you enjoy drama?"

"Haven't seen enough to know," he replied.

"Not even Shakespeare?"

"*Hamlet,* once, in Boston. I prefer comedy. And pantomine. Puppets, too. I get a real boot out of Punch and Judy."

And burlesque? Jacintha wondered. Carnivals, boxing matches, cockfights?

"Well, I believe one of the Bowery theaters is featuring a company of Italian comedians on its bill. We'll go there instead. And for supper—well, Delmonico's is said to serve the finest cuisine in Manhattan."

"Delmonico's it shall be, then. Sunday we'll rent a carriage to drive in Central Park, and then watch the horse races on Harlem Lane. We'll have some fun together and get better acquainted—if you've no objections."

"What if I did?"

He laughed, enjoying the banter. "I'd just have to overcome them. And I warn you, I'm a determined fella. Don't give up easy. The wonder to me is that you're still free, an unclaimed treasure. Has your guardian kept you under lock and key?"

"The Brittons were supposed to sponsor me in society," she explained. "There was even talk of my living with them, but nothing came of it. I don't think Mrs. Britton approved."

"What wife would, under the circumstances? And I can tell you now Britton didn't want to sell me this place. He jacked up the price to discourage me. He was mighty displeased, hearing this news after the contract was signed. I'm surprised he hasn't moved you out of here."

Jacintha was carefully examining some swatches of fabric. "He couldn't, without force. I must confess to an undesirable feminine trait—obstinacy. We've done some guardian-ward battle over it, but he usually concedes. I'm sure he'll be greatly relieved when the relationship is finally ended."

"And you?" he questioned warily, studying her face through a cloud of cigar smoke.

She shrugged, her eyes wistful. "I don't know. I had a little-girl infatuation with him. Of course, that was long ago."

Danvers pressed her. "Maybe you still feel that way."

"Certainly not!" Her denial was vehement. "I was just a romantic child with silly ideas, and he was the only handsome young man who ever visited my elderly grandparents. I shouldn't even have mentioned it to you, and don't know why I did." Her hand smoothed a velvet sample, caressing the soft texture. "It's getting late, Cole. You may call for me at seven this evening."

He rose and reached for his hat, twirling it in his hands. "It's a proud gent I'll be, with such a charming young companion on my arm."

His punctuality was commendable, but his garish attire dampened Jacintha's enthusiasm. Nor had he brought her flowers, as a gentleman should, although he was sporting a scarlet carnation boutonniere in his lapel. His eyes boldly appraised her figure in the low-cut ivory moire gown, lingering lustfully on her smooth, fair shoulders and softly curving bosom. Jacintha blushed, feeling indecently exposed, and quickly donned her cloak and elbow-length gloves.

In elegant Delmonico's where the guests were all refined, Jacintha wanted to hide. Cole bellowed at the waiters, demanding extra attention, and scraped his plate noisily. Equally embarrassing later on were his boisterous laughter and obscene remarks at the Commedia del Arte. He seemed totally unaware of his gaucherie, and there seemed no discreet way to reform him at this stage in his life.

Jacintha tried not to think beyond the restoration of the estate or regard Cole Danvers as anything more than a benefactor who had arrived at an opportune time. The house and furniture she loved so dearly were not doomed after all, and for this she was grateful.

She breathed deeply of the pungent odors of paint and varnish. The din of hammers and saws was sweet music to her ears. The elements no longer posed threats to her beloved Riverview. Rain, wind, sleet, snow, hot sun—Riverview would stand in pride and dignity for another century, and more!

But when at last it was finished, the workmen and

equipment gone, Jacintha's spirits declined sharply. Now she was idle again, restless, despondent. Temporary illusions of ownership vanished in harsh reality, for now she had no further claim to Riverview.

In mid-December, as she was morosely preparing to leave, Cole suddenly proposed. Since she had not discouraged his attentions, he had evidently assumed that their courtship would culminate in marriage.

He did not speak of love. Possibly he feared to broach the subject. He said only that he had grown extremely fond of her and that she belonged at Riverview, which would not be the same without her.

"Please," he begged when she hesitated in surprise, "don't decide now. Think about it, Jacintha. But don't keep me on tenterhooks too long—I'm not a patient man." He added that he was taking a brief business trip to Boston and Lowell, and, after some persuasion, Jacintha promised to consider his proposal and give him an answer when he returned.

Lollie was indignant. "I knew all along that old cock was performing a mating dance to lure you into his nest!"

"I'm already in his nest," Jacintha said wryly.

"Better fly the coop, Missy, before he clips your wings!"

"Fly where, Lollie, and to whom? I was born here, this is my home, and I hate to leave it. Furthermore, I think Grandpa would want me to be mistress of Riverview."

"With Danvers as master? He's more than twice your age, child! And surely you don't love him?"

"What's love, Lollie? Do you know?"

"It's supposed to be a very special feeling you have for something in his touch, his kiss. What do you feel with Mr. Danvers at such times?"

Jacintha sighed. "Nothing much. I seldom allow him any liberties. And I don't have romantic dreams about him."

"Do you ever think of Mr. Larry?"

"Occasionally."

"And his brother?"

Jacintha's temper flared.

"Why do you ask that? Just because I had a childhood crush on Earl Britton doesn't mean——oh, it's too silly to discuss! Especially when I'm going to marry Cole Danvers. Why not? He's not so old or repulsive. And you and I can go on living here. What better prospects do I have?"

"Mr. Britton won't let you marry him," Lollie predicted.

"He can't stop me! If he tries, we'll elope. I'm of legal age, and the marriage couldn't be annulled without my consent. I'll tell Cole when he gets back to town." When Lollie did not speak for some time, she tapped her chin pensively and went on, "I wonder where we should go on our honeymoon? The travel editors say New Orleans is a most interesting city, with a mild winter climate, and I've wanted to ride on a Mississippi River steamboat since reading Mark Twain. I'm sorry you can't come along, but Mr. Danvers would expect you to mind Riverview while we're gone. Isn't it beautiful now, Lollie? And wait until it's landscaped! He has managed to buy the adjoining property on both sides! He plans to enlarge the carriage house and stables. Riverview will be an estate again!"

She rattled on breathlessly, lest she fall back into indecision. "We'll hire caretakers, a coachman and grooms, and more household help. You'll be in charge of the domestic staff, and have much less work to do. Won't that be nice? Oh, Lollie, don't look so glum! We're going to have a wedding, not a wake. Run downstairs now and fix some lunch in our wonderful kitchen with the new cook range, lead sink, and the shiny new copper kettles the scullery maid will have to polish. And what a fancy dining table we'll set with our Bavarian china, English sterling, Danish crystal——"

"Yes, ma'am."

"Ma'am? What happened to Missy?"

"It'll be 'madam' soon," Lollie said dolefully, "and I'll have a master."

"Every husband is master of his house, Lollie. But you won't be his slave—this isn't the South, you know. You didn't mind when Grandpa was your master, did you? Well, I don't think Mr. Danvers will be harder to serve.

And when he travels, we can do as we please, just as before, except that we'll have more time and money. No worrying about bills. No more patching our clothes and mending our shoes. No stews, chowders, and shepherd's pies on the menus, not unless we crave them. We can buy food out of season, keep the house warm, and burn gaslight. Go along now and brew some tea, too, since we no longer have to skimp on that either. Soon we'll have anything we want!"

"Not everything, Missy. Something will always be missing, and you'll know what it is when it's too late. But you can still change your mind."

"I'm resigned to my fate, and you should be to yours by now," Jacintha said softly.

"I am, child. It's easy for someone my age. But you may find it more difficult."

"I'm not so young Lollie."

"Still in your teens!"

"According to the calendar, yes. But I'm aging rapidly. Will you feed me, please—or shall I die of starvation before old age?" she joked, but without humor.

Lollie decided not to argue further. Jacintha would do what she wished.

Chapter 13

JACINTHA's news delighted Danvers. He had returned on Christmas Eve, muffled in a caped greatcoat, bright plaid scarf, and tall beaver hat. "I had no time for gift shopping," he said, to explain his empty hands. "But you couldn't have given *me* a better present, honey! We'll be wed before the new year."

"So soon?" Jacintha murmured, taken aback.

Lifting her in his strong arms as if she were a doll, Cole danced about the dainty parlor, his clumsiness threatening the bric-a-brac. "I don't believe in long engagements, Jacintha. Besides, at Britton Bank this morning, I learned that your guardian went to Charleston for the holiday season. We'd best marry while he's away, so he can't interfere. I don't think he regards me as a suitable mate for you."

Jacintha wondered if Laurette had accompanied Earl, and how she had missed that item in the social columns, if indeed it had been printed. Perhaps Larry had cut his Grand Tour short, and they were having a family reunion at Rosewood Plantation? Not that it really mattered now. She had accepted another man's proposal.

She could feel the tension in his body as he set her on her feet, enveloped her in a steellike grip, and kissed her lips. Her reluctant, closed-mouth response, suggesting virginal innocence, both pleased and disappointed him. He would have to teach her how to kiss, along with the more important pleasures. Could he arouse her dormant passions? Cole was weary of whores.

Snow was swirling outside, piling on the windowsills, and though a blazing fire crackled on the hearth, Jacintha shivered. "May we have a wedding trip?" she beseeched him, like a child begging a favor. "Preferably in the South, where it's sunny and warm. New York is so terribly cold and bleak now."

"Cold? With that new furnace, a ton of coal in the bin, ten fireplaces, and a full woodshed?"

"Oh, the heating facilities are adequate, Cole. But I'd like to travel to New Orleans on a riverboat."

"Way down yonder?"

She pursed her lips prettily, and her compelling eyes coaxed him. "Please, Cole?"

"All right, sugar. If that's your desire, I'll make the arrangements promptly. You know a parson, or will a judge do? I know a couple at the courthouse."

"It doesn't matter," Jacintha told him, convincing herself that it really didn't. Married was married. And love was . . . what? Would she ever actually *know?*

"Is there any liquor in the house?" Cole inquired. "Wine or beer, even, to toast our future together?"

Jacintha was watching the flickering reflections of firelight on the Christmas-tree decorations. Suddenly her whole world seemed made of false glitter and imitation. "Some cooking sherry in the pantry," she said.

"It'll do, until I can stock the cellar." He yanked the bell cord to summon the servant. "I don't want to seem forward, but I think I'll spend the night here, Puss, rather than risk that blizzard out there. We can talk cozily before the fire."

"It's your home, Cole." The stark truth of this statement appalled her. "We're having roast goose for dinner tomorrow, with chestnut stuffing, cranberry sauce, and apple pie."

"And cooking spirits?" He grinned. "Well, there was a time I couldn't afford much better, but that's past now. We're going to live in style, Jacintha. The best of everything! We'll crack that exclusive society shell in this town, too."

"Is that important to you, Cole?"

"Damned right! I know there's a big difference between new money and old, and family heritage counts for a lot. But with a wife like you, enough gold, and the right connections—"

Lollie appeared on the threshold, and Cole ordered her to bring wine and glasses. "Pantry stuff, or whatever. Miss Howard and I wish to celebrate our betrothal."

"Yes, Mr. Danvers." A gentleman would have provided vintage champagne, she thought contemptuously.

"And prepare a bedchamber for occupancy tonight."

Lollie glanced dubiously at Jacintha, who nodded.

The servant's dismay amused Cole. "Don't worry. I'll follow the rules and wait until the proper time. This is just an emergency, due to the weather. Well, don't stand there gawking like a ninny! Get the sherry."

"Yes, sir."

They went to Tiffany's for the rings, a less elaborate set than Cole would have selected alone. He was astonished when Jacintha protested that large gems were ostentatious.

"You prefer a one-carat diamond to a three- or four-carat?" He was incredulous.

"I really prefer that lovely star sapphire," she replied. "Or the turquoise circled with tiny diamonds. The pearl-and-opal ring is nice, too."

Cole appealed to the jeweler. "Convince her that big stones are not vulgar."

"Well, the lady has small, delicate hands, sir, and perhaps one of the other choices would be wiser for her."

"Poppycock! We'll take the diamond solitaire and band to match. Cut 'em down to her size as quickly as possible. We're in a hurry."

"You may pick them up this afternoon, sir."

Leaving Tiffany's, Cole said, "We got a few hours, sugar. Need anything for your trousseau?"

"I'd rather shop in New Orleans," Jacintha decided. "I've read about their fine French boutiques and modistes, and they import directly from Paris. Of course, fashion is inspired by the Second Empire now, and Monsieur Worth is the Court's favorite couturier."

"Those foreign words are beyond me," Cole said, pausing to admire a red leather Saratoga trunk in a luggage store window. "Got everything packed for the trip?"

"Yes. And you?"

"I've been living out of suitcases and in rented lodgings for years, sweetheart. Already gave up my suite at the Astor and ordered my stuff delivered to Riverview—it should be there by now. I made the appointment with Judge Hawkins, too. We're due in his chambers at five o'clock this afternoon. We'll leave early tomorrow on our honeymoon."

Jacintha clutched her hooded cloak tighter against the frigid winds and tucked her mittened hands deeper into her wool muff. Cole was saying, "I hope those oafs at the ticket agencies got the itinerary and connections straight. I won't tolerate any delays." The gutters overflowed with melting ice and sewage slop from broken mains. The air smelled of horse manure and urine, decaying fish and dirty pushcarts, slaughterhouses and tanneries, factory smoke and harbor stench—all the evidence of progress.

"You're very efficient, aren't you?"

"I can't abide bunglers."

"People do make mistakes, Cole. To err is human, you know. Don't your employees ever bungle?"

"Not often, if they want to hold their jobs. Even the youngsters soon learn that, although they get more chances."

"You employ children?"

"Every industry does," he said. "Many families couldn't exist without the money their kids earn."

"When do they go to school?"

"They don't. What a sheltered life you've lived!" he remarked, guiding her into an oyster bar for lunch.

Jacintha disliked these eateries, which were usually small and dingy and patronized mostly by men. They reminded her of saloons. She had no taste for the oysters, watching Cole swallow several dozen raw and gulp down six schooners of beer, the foam clinging to his mustache.

"My, my! such a delicate appetite," he teased as Jacintha nibbled crackers and sipped ginger ale. "Better eat something nourishing, young lady. You'll need your strength tonight." He winked.

The remark evoked anxiety, then suddenly dread. She had tried not to think about the physical side of marriage. Naturally the union had to be consummated, and a wife must forever after submit to her husband's desires. But she had no inkling of what to expect, or how to fulfill her marital obligations. She would be at his service . . . and at his mercy.

A court clerk witnessed the brief nuptials. Judge Hawkins congratulated the groom and kissed the lovely young bride's cheek. Afterwards they went immediately to Riverview, where Lollie served them a candlelight supper.

Cole was hungry again, but Jacintha ate no more heartily than she had at noon. The glittering new rings on her left hand felt strange and heavy; she would have to buy her gloves a size larger to accommodate the high-pronged solitaire.

Cole thought the moist gleam in her eyes was happiness, and imagined her quiet was timidity. His hand touched his groin furtively under the napkin. He was tumescent again, an almost constant condition since the vows had been spoken. How much longer could he restrain himself? He urged Jacintha to drink her wine, which she did to please him and to fortify herself. When Lollie came to clear the table, Jacintha rose to assist her.

"No!" Cole objected. "That's servant's work, not for a bride on her wedding night. And if we're going to keep our schedule tomorrow, we'd best retire early. Leave the dishes till later, woman. Go up and help your mistress now."

"Yes, sir."

The master chamber was in readiness; fresh linens on the bed, fire on the hearth. Jacintha's personal belongings, except for the clothes and toiletries in the luggage, had been placed in the closet, bureau drawers, and armoire. Now she sat on the satin-covered bench before the dressing table, nervously removing the pins from her hair, which rippled darkly on her shoulders. She picked up the brush, then put it down.

If only Lollie could give her some motherly advice! But Lollie was a spinster, with no real knowledge of such matters.

"Better get undressed," Lollie urged gently. "He'll be coming soon."

"I suppose so."

"Stand up, child, so I can unhook you."

"Oh, Lollie, can't you tell me *anything?*"

"Only what I've heard from other women. Matrons."

"Yes?"

Her fingers worked on the fastenings. "It'll hurt. They say it always hurts the first time. You'll bleed—that's natural for virgins, too. And you may get pregnant."

"Oh, God! What have I done to myself?" She began to shudder and weep, covering her face with her hands. "I don't love him, Lollie. I realize that now, and I don't want to be his wife and bear his children. I—I don't want him to touch me that way! What can I do?"

Lollie shook her head sadly. "Nothing, honey. It's too late. He can take you at will now. That's the law."

"If only I'd listened when you tried to warn me! But he acted differently during the courtship—generous, kind, trying to please me. Rather nice."

"I reckon even leopards behave tamely while wooing a female, but they don't change their spots after mating. And men show their true nature in marriage, too. Mr. Danvers is sly. He simply hoodwinked you."

Jacintha sighed wretchedly as the blue-green velvet dress was slipped down over her petticoats and hoops. "Those, too," Lollie said. "Everything must come off, Missy. I doubt he'll even let you keep the nightgown on. A husband wants to see his wife's body, and wants her to see his."

The frilly undergarments were removed, the stays unlaced, the white muslin bridal ensemble donned. She should have worn the traditional gown and veil, Lollie thought, and had a religious ceremony and proper reception—all the beauty and joy reserved for the virgin bride. And she should be eager to receive her groom now—not terrified of him.

"Try to relax," she advised. "Are you cold? I'll whisk the warming pan over the sheets before you get into bed."

"I'm not ready for that yet." Jacintha mulled over plausible excuses to delay the inevitable; headache, sore throat, unexpected menses. "Tell him I'm ill, Lollie. Indisposed."

"My poor baby." Lollie was comforting her when Cole entered without knocking and signaled dismissal.

"She's not feeling well, Mr. Danvers," Lollie said at the door. "Probably coming down with something. I hope it's not catching. Good night, sir."

Cole crossed the room to his wife, who winced and almost cringed before facing him. He felt her forehead. "You're all right, sugar. It's just first-night jitters. Did that old maid scare you? How the devil would she know?" He led Jacintha toward the bed and untied the bow of her wrapper. "Take these trappings off."

"Cole—"

"I've waited long enough, Jacintha." He stripped himself rapidly, flinging his clothes helter-skelter, while she stared at him in mute horror. Finally he stood naked before her, grinning proudly. "This is how a man looks raw, Mrs. Danvers. Not such a pretty sight as a nude woman, perhaps, but you'll get used to it."

His hairy body, with its barrel chest, heavy belly, and bowed legs, recalled the gorilla illustrations in her grandfather's anthropology books, and his erect penis with its dark-red tip appeared huge and grotesque. How could he possibly insert the terrible throbbing thing without tearing her apart?

Displeased by her frowning reaction, Cole grasped her timid hand and guided it over his torso, toward his turgid genitals, commanding gruffly, "Touch me; feel your spouse! I'm hard as any man half my age, and ready as any raring youth. You snared yourself quite a stud, madam!"

"No, please!" Jacintha shied away, as if burned on a hot stove, feeling truly ill now, afraid she might vomit. "Not yet, Cole."

"Stop this, Jacintha! You're not a child, and I won't coax you all night."

Delicate ribbons and lace were ruthlessly ripped, baring her shoulders, breasts, hips, legs, until she was helplessly exposed. He gloated, wetting his lips with spittle. "Not a blemish! Perfect! And you would deny me this pleasure? Ah, Jacintha, what a tease you are!" He tickled her under the chin, pinched her pert coral nipples. "Prettiest tits I ever saw, can't wait to taste 'em . . ."

There was no escaping his lust, and soon Jacintha was trapped beneath him on the bed, one loggish leg wedged between her thighs as his mouth devoured hers and his hands groped over her flesh. Wild with passion and desire for possession, her whimpering protests infuriated him. Spreading her legs like a wishbone to be broken, he forced penetration, ignoring her writhing. She felt torn in half, and each searing thrust was infinitely worse than she had imagined. Though it seemed to go on forever, the ordeal was over in less than fifteen minutes. The rooting ceased, and he lay inert, the cruel hardness softening. Finally releasing her, Cole reached for the huckaback towel Lollie had placed on the nightstand.

"Is it over?" Jacintha asked prayerfully.

"For now, sweetheart. Wasn't so bad, was it? Some ladies actually enjoy it. Maybe you will too, eventually."

Enjoy being raped and brutalized? she thought, outraged. Never, never, never!

"Go clean yourself up, Puss. You're a bloody mess. And then stoke the fire and douse the lights—I've got to get some rest. But don't be too disappointed. This cock will rise again with the roosters, and we'll be diddling regularly from now on. I promise you that."

When she returned from the bathroom, sore and aching, Cole was sprawled over most of the mattress, snoring. Jacintha crawled into bed carefully, lest she disturb him, and muffled her sobs in the eiderdown pillow.

So that was the marital act? That gory, excruciating ordeal was the ritual sacrifice of the subservient female to the dominant male? That brutal, disgusting activity was the "love" praised in romantic fiction, poetry, and song? What a dreadful initiation into the state of what was called holy matrimony! How could any woman survive repeated assaults for long?

Hours passed before she slept. All too soon she was rudely awakened and forced to endure the same terrible ordeal again. And yet again.

Chapter 14

DURING the long, tedious journey to Pittsburgh, Jacintha realized why trains were called "iron horses," and why most people preferred to travel by water whenever possible. The engines puffed and snorted and the clicking wheels kicked up as much dust as a horde of pounding hoofs. What little scenery was visible through the sooty windows was obscured by rain and sleet. Thank heaven Lollie had prepared a box lunch for them, for there was no dining car, and the food peddled by the newsbutchers was hardly palatable. Coffee, hot soups, and stews were available at the stations, but the weather kept most of the passengers aboard during the stops.

For Jacintha Danvers, however, the lack of sleeping accommodations more than compensated for all the other discomforts. Cole could not molest her, although he tried when the lights were out and the others were presumably dozing in their seats. His hands roamed familiarly under the lap robe, and he urged her to reciprocate. Appalled, she reproached him in whispers. What if someone woke, or the cover slipped, or the conductor happened to walk through the coach with his lantern?

Chagrined, Cole muttered that the couple across the

aisle, also newlyweds, were not hampered by prudery, and Jacintha knew their behavior aroused him. They bundled intimately, murmuring and sighing in the darkness, occasionally giggling gleefully. They were young, obviously in love and happy, and Jacintha envied the girl. Maybe lovemaking could be fun if you cared enough for your mate, be he husband or lover.

"Hush, Cole, and go to sleep."

"Not much chance of that, in this freezing boxcar! I wish to hell we had stayed at Riverview."

Jacintha assured him that the riverboat would be much better.

And indeed it was. The *Memphis Belle*, a large new sidewheeler, ornately tiered and appointed, was as luxurious as a floating hotel. They had a fine stateroom on the choice saloon deck, twenty feet above the water line. The balcony railing was ornamented with wood filigree, and gilded flowers, vines, and cupids encrusted the white-painted furniture. Murals decorated the walls, a thick Wilton carpet covered the floor, and the exquisite chandelier resembled a shower of crystal raindrops.

Negro attendants assisted the stewards. Excellent meals, impeccable service, delightful entertainments—Jacintha would have enjoyed it all immensely, were it not for the episodes in the double berth. There was less pain now, but certainly no pleasure. Cole's brutal selfishness stifled her own desire, which a perceptive partner might have manipulated into passion and mutually rewarding joy. Tenderness, finesse, and preliminary wooing could have made the difference between cooperation and conquest, rapture and revulsion.

As the gentlemen drank and gambled in the saloon, the ladies gathered in the pink-and-silver lounge to chat over tea and punch. But Jacintha never lingered long in their company, aware that she and Cole were often the subject of their idle gossip. The obvious discrepancy in their ages and breeding piqued feminine curiosity and evoked masculine speculation.

Cole strutted and postured in his wife's presence, vain as

a peacock in his gaudy finery, and pleased that her youth and beauty created such a sensation. He flaunted his bride in the dining room and made irritating references to her as "the missus" and "the little woman." Fortunately he could not parade her on the promenade deck. A fierce winter was on the Ohio Valley, isolating the farms and villages in snow and ice and keeping indoors the inhabitants of even the large port towns of Cincinnati and Louisville.

Only hardy young folk greeted the *Memphis Belle* when her whistles and steam calliope signaled her arrival at the public landings. Most of the first-class passengers were Southerners returning from Northern holiday or business trips, some with personal slaves. The humble occupants of the cheap accommodations below the boiler area were seen only on boarding and debarkation. Many were immigrants en route West, and Jacintha pitied them. Poor souls, quartered in steerage, toting their belongings in bundles and sacks.

"Save your pity," Cole told her. "Some of them crossed the Atlantic under worse conditions than these. My own family did, in fact."

Except for the semesters she spent in boarding school, Jacintha had never been separated so long from Lollie, and she missed her in many ways—none of which Cole could possibly understand. She had either to summon a maid or request his clumsy assistance in dressing, usually with regrettable consequences, for his animal instincts were strong.

Since he was still vigorously potent at forty-one, Jacintha feared he would impregnate her on the honeymoon—in which event, according to Lollie, her menses would cease. The date of her last period was indelibly etched on her mind, and she had never imagined that she would be elated to welcome another one. In the months ahead she would eagerly anticipate the once dreaded menstrual cycle, mark it faithfully on her personal calendar, and regard it as a blessing rather than a curse. Now she was just relieved to remain in seclusion, pretending greater discomfort than she felt, while Cole amused himself drinking and playing cards.

"Not bad for a day's take, eh?" he bragged, counting his winnings before locking them in a valise. "This boat is teeming with gamblers, and my luck is running high."

"Do you keep that little pistol up your sleeve in case your luck runs out?" Jacintha asked mockingly.

He grinned. "Observant, ain't you? Well, it's a sorry gambler that has but one trick up his sleeve. Does the gun bother you?"

"Yes. We're in the South now, Cole, and men challenge one another on the slightest excuse."

"Don't worry, I can handle a weapon."

"Have you ever fought a duel?"

"Not with a derringer. Afraid for my life, sugar?"

"I wouldn't want you to be killed, or kill someone else. Have you ever?"

His look warned her not to pry further. "A man should have some secrets, my dear, even from his wife."

"Especially from his wife," Jacintha quipped.

"Now you're being impertinent, madam. Better learn to curb your feminine curiosity, or you'll be in a constant ferment, suspecting the worst of your husband."

Jacintha turned toward the window. They were in Delta country, heartland of the great cotton plantations. The fields lay plowed and fallow now, awaiting seasonal planting. Slaves labored along the banks, shoring the levees against the floods that rampaged down the Mississippi during spring thaws, flushing acres of alluvial soil into adjacent swamps, wasteland, and eventually the Gulf of Mexico. Occasionally she glimpsed a magnificent white-pillared manor high on a hill, above and beyond the river's destructive path, smoke pluming from the multiple chimneys, surrounded by gardens, outbuildings, slave cabins—a miniature community sufficient unto itself.

Cole interrupted her thoughts. "We'll be in Natchez in an hour. Want to go ashore and gander a bit?"

"I don't feel up to it," Jacintha declined. "But you go ahead, if you like."

"You have this much trouble every month, honey?"

She nodded, courting sympathy and buying time for herself. "Sometimes more."

"Well, pregnancy is supposed to cure such things," he said. "I hope you're not too delicate for childbearing. I'd like some kids. Preferably boys, to follow me in the mills and factories. Girls are a nuisance, mostly."

"Indeed? And how would men beget sons without them? I presume your mother was a female?"

He smiled, tapping the bowl on her tray. "What a sharp little tongue! Did you have razor soup for lunch? You warned me beforehand that you were stubborn, but you forgot to mention you also have a temper."

"And a spine!" Jacintha added defiantly. "I'm no rag doll."

"Certainly not," he agreed. "And I like your spirit. Our union shouldn't ever be dull. Will you be dining with me in the salon this evening?"

"I'm sorry, no. I'll just order another light meal sent here. You can drink and gamble all night."

"I gather you don't approve of my vices, Mrs. Danvers? But most men indulge in them, one way or another. Members of the Stock Exchange, including your Prince Charming, are gamblers at heart, speculating in the market. Life itself is a risk. Any bookmaker will give odds that a newborn babe won't reach its first birthday, and most insurance companies refuse policies on them before age two.

"There are respectable gentlemen aboard now, who are gambling on the future of this country. I was listening this morning to a big Philadelphia banker advising his audience to invest their ready cash in war materials. Said he himself was bound for New Orleans, to buy as much cotton as possible, have it shipped to Northern warehouses, and held on speculation. It's sound advice, which I plan to follow."

"Naturally," Jacintha murmured, gazing uneasily at the changing landscape. They were nearing an area of deep, dark, dismal swamps. The growth on the riverbanks was dense, impenetrable, vines and trees tangled in moss, a pristine jungle in which she visualized runaway slaves hunted by the merciless law and their masters' bloodhounds. The steamer moved cautiously through the treacherous, shallow waters.

"Do be careful in your games, Cole. Don't provoke any quarrels with the natives. The way things are now, Yankees aren't too welcome in these parts. Above all, avoid any political discussions."

"That's not easy in this territory," he declared. "John Brown's raid on Harper's Ferry last October still rankles, while we sing about his hung body moldering in his grave and his soul marching on. Now they're worried that the Republicans will nominate Abraham Lincoln at their convention in Chicago next May. Not that he has much chance of winning against New York's favorite son, William Seward, even if he makes the ticket. He's not a popular fella, North or South. Or a smart politician, either, in my opinion. Hell, Douglas made a damn fool of him in their silly series of debates. Mr. Lincoln contradicted himself on nearly every vital statement he made. The people wouldn't send such a changeable windbag to Washington. Besides, there's never been a Republican president."

"Perhaps," Jacintha mused, "that's why there'll be one this time. Grandpa used to say that America couldn't survive another do-nothing Democrat like President Buchanan."

"Could be he was right, too. But I don't think a war will depend on who sits in the White House, come November. The South is ripe for rebellion."

"The slave states we've passed through seem peaceful," Jacintha observed. "I've seen some great plantations, grand mansions, fine horses . . . the planters live like royalty. Why should they risk losing their wealth in a war?"

"They wouldn't expect to lose the war, Puss. If they fight, it'll be to keep their lands and slaves and castles and go on living like kings. Not that I blame 'em. Some day I'm going to build a palace on Fifth Avenue, among the Manhattan aristocracy."

"I don't want a palace on Fifth Avenue, Cole. I want to stay at Riverview, no matter how rich you become."

"Well, we won't debate it now, Mrs. Danvers. But I trust

you have more social ambition than you pretend? And you know some members of the Charmed Circle—"

"If you mean the Brittons—" Jacintha said, interrupting him.

"Who else? A few invitations from them would get our feet in the right doors."

Jacintha briefly considered Laurette . . . haughty, condescending. "Have you ever met Mrs. Earl Britton?"

"Once, at the bank. Gorgeous creature, with red-gold hair and emerald eyes. I know she's a Philadelphia blueblood and has a lot of clout in high society. Nobody would dare snub a guest in their home."

Jacintha set her chin firmly. "I won't grovel to snobs, Cole, and particularly not to that one!"

He grinned, tweaking one of her bouncy curls. "Jealous of her, Puss, because she married your Prince Charming?"

Her brilliant eyes glittered in tempestuous defiance as she pushed his hand away from her head. "Stop calling him that! Earl Britton is nothing to me, his wife is even less, and I won't be goaded into cultivating them for your benefit!"

"Yours too, Mrs. Danvers. Think of the future. You want our children to have all the advantages, don't you? Wise parents plan these things in advance."

"We're not parents yet, Cole."

"But we will be, Jacintha. You don't look barren to me, and I'm in fine fettle for fatherhood. Never had a bad sickness in my life, except for that siege of mumps when I was twenty. The doc said the disease went down on me, and my balls swoll up something awful. Damned near died then, but been healthy as an ox since. No, there's nothing wrong with Cole Danvers."

The whistles blew, the calliope began to play a sweet Stephen Foster tune, and the bluffs of Natchez came into view. As in other busy port towns along the Ohio and the Mississippi, the wharves were stacked with cargo—mostly bales of cotton awaiting shipment.

"I think I'll go ashore with that Philly banker and try to buy some cotton on consignment," Cole said.

"Didn't you buy enough in Louisville and Memphis?"

"Only a thousand bales or so," he complained. "No more was available. I want to stock my textile warehouses, as well as speculate in the market. Wheat and grain will be valuable future commodities, too."

He donned his beaver-collared greatcoat and tall beaver hat, picked up his gray suede gloves and the gold-headed cane he affected, and stood admiring himself in the mirror. Then, planting a perfunctory kiss on her cheek, he made a swaggering exit.

A would-be king, Jacintha thought grimly, hoping to conquer the world by cornering the essential markets.

Chapter 15

A FEW months ago Jacintha would not have believed that she could sit in a French dress shop in glamorous New Orleans—surrounded by gorgeous gowns, bonnets, and accessories from which she might choose any number—and feel so little enthusiasm. How she had envied Laurette Britton's shopping sprees in Manhattan! Prodigal creature, acquisitive as a squirrel, hoarding more apparel than she could possibly use in any one season.

Jacintha had no ardent desire to shop, but Cole insisted that she enlarge her wardrobe. Their tastes clashed on nearly every selection. He preferred bold colors, elaborate styles and fabrics. High-heeled satin slippers studded with imitation jewels and garish paste buckles; bonnets loaded with artificial fruit, flowers, dancing plumes; the scantiest lingerie, transparent if possible; and the sheerest silk hosiery, like lacy cobwebs, with gaudy embroidery on the ankles. Jacintha's rejection of most of his choices bewildered and exasperated him. He could not appreciate subdued hues in clothing any more than he could pastel paintings. Cole would never discover elegance in simplicity. Moderation in any form bored him. This was partly because he had been raised on a diet of strictest moderation.

"I'll dress you like a queen," he told Jacintha.

A gypsy queen, she thought, fit for Mardi Gras!

The pink stucco shop in the Vieux Carré was strewn with boxes and tissue paper, while the confused proprietess sought to placate madame and please monsieur, concentrating her efforts on the purse-holder. Surmising that this was a *mariage de convenance*, with which she was professionally familiar, Madame Dauphine cleverly catered to the boorish Yankee who appeared so flush with American gold and so reckless with it, too. Fortunately her stock had just been replenished with new shipments from France. There were racks and glass cases filled with vivid garments, rows of papier-mâché heads displaying chapeaux with rue de la Paix labels, drawers full of delicate, convent-made underwear.

When they progressed to the ball-gown stage, the proprietress produced a flamboyant creation of vermillion satin with a precariously low décolletage bound in flaming marabou, and Cole insisted that Jacintha buy it. She refused, emphatically, and neither flattery nor cajoling could persuade her.

"Why not?" he cried angrily.

"It's indecent! Conspicious and vulgar."

The Frenchwoman, a fashion plate in gray-and-maroon striped taffeta with flaring bishop sleeves, was horrified by the heresy. Her thinly plucked brows arched, her frisette of false hair fluttered, her trussed bosom quivered. "It's à la mode in Paris, Madame Danvers! An exact copy of one of the Empress Eugenie's most successful costumes, and created quite a sensation at the French Court. Napoleon adored it!"

"Indeed?" Jacintha murmured, unimpressed. "Then I fear for the morals of the French Court and its rulers. I much prefer the turquoise tulle and Chantilly lace. I'll also take the pale gold brocade, the ivory moire, the rose velvet embroidered in seed pearls, and the iridescent silk."

"*Mais oui,* madame! Excellent, every one. And for your winter evening wraps, may I suggest this exquisite black velvet cloak trimmed in ermine, a cashmere shawl, and a fur cape? My furrier is an absolute marvel, divinely inspired!" she declared, raising her eyes heavenward and clasping her hands in homage. "And remember, your husband wants only the best for you." She murmured in French to her chic assistant, who brought out several of the most expensive selections. *"Voilà, chérie! Magnifique, n'est-ce pas?"*

Jacintha nodded, admiring the regal furs, unable to decide between the mink and sable capes, until Cole, growing increasingly irritable, decided the issue by purchasing both.

"Oui, monsieur," the proprietess purred. "Would you care for *café au lait* or wine while madame ponders the *robes de chambre?"*

"You needn't bother," Jacintha said quickly, feeling that she had more than enough seductive boudoir ensembles already. "I have finished shopping for the day. Send my purchases to the Chartres Hotel, *s'il vous plaît."* She glanced at Cole, who sat with his stocky legs crossed, puffing a long, thick cigar. "Shall we go? I have a wretched headache."

"Not again," he muttered, disgusted. "Madame, perhaps you know a cure for female complaint?"

Madame Dauphine nodded, smiling knowingly. "Jewelry is often a sovereign remedy, monsieur. Most efficacious when administered in large carats, and I can recommend a fine shop on Royal Street."

"You don't know my wife, madame. Unlike other women, she's immune to such treatment. Much obliged, anyway."

They rode back to the hotel in a hansom cab driven by a liveried Negro, Jacintha quietly observing the quaint architecture and atmosphere of the French Quarter. The small frame and stucco houses boasted brightly painted shutters and wood stoops called *perrons.* Two- and three-story buildings with connecting walls and galleries decorated with ornamental ironwork showed a French-Spanish influence. Through grilled gateways and porte-cocheres could be glimpsed tiled patios, fountains, and courtyard gardens planted with semitropical shrubs and flowers—oleanders, camellias, jasmine, gardenias, bananas, yucca.

Trees flourished in the temperate climate, where frost was rare and snow a novelty, and Jacintha admired the magnificent magnolias, the delicate mimosas, palms clacking in the Gulf breezes, venerable live oaks draped in silvery moss. On the sidewalks she saw female slaves toting huge bundles on their turbaned heads and baskets of laundry on their hips, youngsters both white and black clinging to their skirts and apron strings. Vendors hawked wares, which included produce, fish, delicacies, voodoo charms, and magic potions, in a babble of Gumbo-French.

Jacintha had already sampled some tempting and exotic confections, consoling herself with pralines, glazed fruits and nuts, candied orange blossoms, rose and violet petals. In the many fine restaurants, she enjoyed gourmet Creole dishes, including bouillabaisse and various seafoods, none surpassing the pompano and creamed oysters in patty shells. Dining was a cultivated art in this leisurely city, where the natives ate seven-course breakfasts and spent hours at the dinner table. Jacintha would have loved all of New Orleans, had she only been in love with the man who had brought her there.

"I didn't care much for some of the things you bought," Cole complained. "About as exciting as warm mutton soup. Now, that red gown—"

"I'm sorry, Cole. But if you want your wife to be a lady, don't expect her to dress like a tramp!"

"Tramp? That dress had a thousand-dollar price tag!"

"Cost does not determine true value, Cole. No decent woman would be seen in that cocotte's costume! And while we're on the subject of appropriate attire, I wish you'd visit a good tailor and dress more soberly."

"Like a pallbearer?"

"A gentleman. Isn't that what you want to be? Not in loud plaids and checks, but in conservative suits. And with less ostentatious jewelry."

He was aghast. "Roxy thinks I'm the Beau Brummell of the Bowery!"

"Who's Roxy?"

"Just—someone I know there," he said curtly, regretting the slip.

"An actress?"

"Yeah, at the National Theater. Her stage name is Roxy LaFlame. She sings and dances, too. Very talented."

"I'm sure," Jacintha murmured.

"She's only a friend," he insisted.

They were passing Jackson Square and the solemn gray towers of St. Louis Cathedral. "You needn't explain, Cole. You were a bachelor, after all, and no monk. Does Miss LaFlame know you're married now?"

"Not yet."

"Would you like to keep it secret?"

"Enough of this, Jacintha! You got any ideas about this evening?"

"Dinner at Antoine's," she suggested. "I'm hungry for some lobster bisque."

"And afterwards?"

"I thought you might like to go to a casino," she said, offering him a night on the town.

Pleased by the offer, he nodded. "But you'd have to stay in the Ladies' Salon. No petticoats allowed in the gaming rooms, except the house shills."

"I'll return to the hotel and retire early."

Cole thought her deference was pique over the woman he had inadvertently mentioned, and he humored her, although he was not inclined to pamper females. Some husbands would tame such a recalcitrant spouse with a whip, and eventually he might have to resort to some kind of force to establish his mastership. She must realize that he would not be henpecked! "All right, honey. I reckon you're tired, after all that shopping and spending my money."

"It was your idea!" she snapped, like a puppy with its sensitive tail tweaked. "How long will we be in New Orleans?"

"Another week or so. I'm dickering with some cotton, rice, and sugar brokers. And planters' agents."

"My word! You'll be as rich as Croesus."

"Who's he?"

"He *was* a wealthy king of Lydia before the time of Christ. You really must do some reading, Cole."

"I'm a self-made man, Jacintha. Not much education. I read the daily journals to learn what's happening today. I have no interest in ancient history, mythology, or literature. What good does all that do a person?"

"It's knowledge, Cole, and often wisdom."

"Will it make money? How much book learning do you think John Jacob Astor had, living over his father's butcher shop when he was a boy? Yet he was shrewd and ambitious enough to make a tremendous fortune! And the richest fella in America now speaks the worst English I ever heard, far worse than mine! But he's a clever bastard, that Cornelius Vanderbilt."

"Astor endowed a library," Jacintha pointed out.

"Sure, to perpetuate the family name. But his money alone would've done that. Gold has magic. Don't it prove something that a king who lived two thousand years ago and must've had *some* personal qualities is now remembered for his wealth? Success is all that matters in this world, Jacintha."

Exercising his masculine license to freedom even on the honeymoon, Cole idled considerable time at the Absinthe House, Maspero's Exchange, and squandered much money at the casinos, cock- and dogfights.

Jacintha browsed in the boutiques, art studios, antique shops, and bookstalls. Dining in the hotel tearoom, she met an elderly dowager who was also a guest at the Chartres and who said she spent her winters in New Orleans and her summers at Saratoga Springs. Still superficially mourning her late spouse, she wore the traditional weeds and veils. Her small speckled eyes, constantly darting here and there, had a birdlike brightness. There were white winglike streaks in her crest of dark hair, and her long withered neck seemed to crane from her slight body. Hungry for companionship Maude Franklin latched onto Jacintha, invited her to her suite, and offered to accompany her about town.

"I've been noticing that your husband ventures off alone sometimes, Mrs. Danvers," she said, "and you strike out on your own too. That's dangerous, you know, for a lovely young lady in this wicked city. You need a chaperone, and I'm available. I know this place thoroughly—the right people, the sights worth seeing, and the things worth doing."

"I'm afraid we're not here for the season, Mrs. Franklin," Jacintha apprised her, adding as the old lady's face fell, "but I'd enjoy going to the theater or opera with you. My husband doesn't care much for those things."

"How fortunate that we met! I have boxes at the St. Charles Theater and the new French Opera House, which is still celebrating its premiere performance with *Guillaume Tell*. Please be my guest this evening."

"That's very kind of you, madam."

"Not a'tall, dear girl. Why should you be alone while your thoughtless mate pursues his male pleasures? Men are selfish creatures. Why, I've known bridegrooms to visit bordellos on their honeymoon! And married or single, a mistress is the rule, not the exception. In New Orleans, they fancy *femmes de couleur*."

While Jacintha struggled with her French, her officious mentor explained, "Negroes, my dear. But not black or chocolate brown! They prefer the *café au lait* quadroons and choose them at balls held expressly for this purpose. They are very beautiful, these persons of mixed blood, and cherished by their lovers, who give them fine homes, servants, carriages, all the necessities and luxuries. The issue of these unions are born free, and educated in the North or abroad. The arrangements are generally completed beforehand by the girls' mothers. It is common to list conditions and demands in writing and to require signed legal documents. These provide for legacies and settlements, and often the prospective keeper must also agree to support the mother of his mistress."

Jacintha's eyes widened, and she could not suppress her curiosity. "Don't the married men's wives and families object?"

"Oh, yes! Strenuously, in some cases, often giving society some violent confrontations. The same relationships exist in the East, particularly in New York and Washington, though somewhat more discreetly, perhaps."

At that moment an exquisitely gowned and groomed young woman entered the tearoom on the arm of a debonair gentleman, and Mrs. Franklin nudged her luncheon companion under the table. "There's a couple now."

Fascinated, Jacintha tried not to stare at the absolutely stunning quadroon with satin-smooth golden skin, light brown hair stylishly coiffed, delicate features, and perfect teeth. Her entire costume, from the tiny floral chapeau to the dainty French-kid slippers, was Parisian haute couture, and she wore it with grace and flair. Removal of her elegant fox-trimmed cloak revealed a plum-colored silk gown intricately designed to enhance her slender, supple, seductive body. Jacintha had expected a more voluptuous figure and flamboyant garb. A gold locket nestled in the cleavage of her golden breasts, and tiny loops of gold adorned her small pierced ears. She was exotic, poised, cultivated, proud of her blood and position. Once or twice her escort's eyes roved in Jacintha's direction, as a curious stranger's might, but for the most part his attentions were devoted to his mistress, and she appeared to idolize him.

They're in love, Jacintha thought with amazement. She's not just a convenience to him, or him to her. They're actually in love! So true love was possible in such a relationship, after all. Why had she imagined that it was not?

"Gorgeous, isn't she?" Mrs. Franklin remarked. "And he's so handsome, polished, and obviously wealthy. A most attractive and compatible pair!"

"More important," Jacintha wistfully observed, "they care deeply for each other. He worships her, and she adores him. They're happy and content."

"But of course, my dear! Why else would they stay

together? It's not a compulsory union, as in marriage. He does not own her in any sense and cannot regard her as a slave. Their commitment is mutually rewarding. A man often loves his mistress more than his wife, you know, and often with good reason."

"I suppose so," Jacintha agreed, suddenly remembering the puzzling occasion on which she had seen Earl and Laurette Britton together in their magnificent home, their cool politeness verging on hostility. She found herself wishing for a romantic tragedy at the opera this evening: *Tristan and Isolde* rather than *William Tell*.

Chapter 16

DURING their first week back in New York, Jacintha had little time to think much about either her husband or herself. She and Lollie were busy interviewing applicants from a domestic agency. A middle-aged widow was employed as cook and a buxom Irish lass as maid, both requesting permission to reside off the premises because of family commitments. They also hired a black laundress named April Martin, who promised to come five days a week, rain or shine. April's solemn face and manner suggested some tragedy or secret in her life, and Jacintha wondered if it had anything to do with her race. April said she had no family except her twin sister, May, who was married and had five children. Were they escaped slaves, perhaps, concerned about the fate of relatives still in the South?

A coachman, footman, stablegroom, and gardener were added to the domestic staff. All the servants were under the immediate supervision of the housekeeper, whom they addressed as Miss Lollie. "I'll get fat and lazy," she complained, "with so little to do."

"I doubt that, Lollie. Mrs. Paxton and Peggy Ryan must have an afternoon off each week, and time for Sunday worship. There'll be plenty to occupy you. Mr. Danvers likes to be waited on, you know."

Lollie nodded. Unlike some not-to-the-manor-born, the master of Riverview had no difficulty adjusting to luxury. He was never far from a bell cord. The time would come when Riverview's servants would look forward to his absences almost as much as his wife did. "That's what they're paid for!" was his blunt rationale when Jacintha suggested that perhaps he demanded too much attention.

She pitied his factory and mill workers, especially the poor little children, and had no desire to visit any of his sweatshops. His generosity in other ways, particularly toward her and the estate, was a puzzling paradox. There were many facets to his nature, some dark, the understanding of which, Jacintha feared, would make life with him totally intolerable.

Acceding to his wife's good taste in the matter of family transportation, Cole bought an elegant clarence, royal blue with gilt trim and velour upholstery, finely detailed by a famous London coachmaker. A pair of shining, perfectly matched bays acquired at the Horse Mart moved into the stables, joining frisky roans purchased for Cole's personal vehicle, a bright red phaeton with a convertible top. He was also in the market for an English curricle and some fast trotters to race against the Wall Street competitors. "Come spring," he told Jacintha, "I'll buy a fancy victoria or landau for summer driving."

But the city was still in the throes of winter when Jacintha took her first ride alone in the imported clarence. With a small brazier of live coals at her feet and a fur lap robe tucked about her knees, she ordered the coach attendants, Clancy and Job, to drive her to Central Park so that she could watch the skaters.

It was Saturday afternoon, and the frozen lakes and ponds were thronged with frolickers on steel blades. Laughter, singing, music, games, hawkers—it was a carnival on ice, with expert, novice, and clown vying to amuse the spectators. The coachman and footman had brought their blades along and, with their mistress's permission, were in the midst of the merrymakers. Jacintha was astonished by their agility, for they were both rather clumsy on dry land.

She opened the carriage door to hear the calliope better, and sat, vicariously enjoying the happy scene, too absorbed to notice the prancing black stallion approach from the rear and the rider dismount.

"Mrs. Danvers, I presume?" said a smooth baritone voice, and her heart leaped.

With the memory of their last meeting still vivid in her mind, Jacintha could not meet his eyes comfortably. "Good afternoon, Mr. Britton," she greeted primly. "This is a surprise!"

He smiled, looking young and boyish in a Scotch-plaid mackinaw and muffler, a knitted cap cocked jauntily on the side of his head. Although the other men's faces were chapped with the cold, Earl had a summer tan. Had he gotten handsomer? Or was it just that Cole suffered so badly by comparison?

"A pleasant one, I hope?"

"Of course! But what are you doing here?"

"Exercising my horse. Haven't ridden the devil much lately, and he's getting out of shape."

Stripping off his gloves, he warmed his hands over the hot brazier. Jacintha was conscious of his long, slender fingers and manicured nails—the hands of a gentleman. Would they be tender in caress, knowing in exploration, thrilling on bare flesh?

"Why haven't you called on us?" she asked petulantly.

"Not having received an 'At Home' announcement, I thought the newlyweds still treasured their privacy," he replied wryly. "But I see you haven't lost your pouting technique, nor have your eyes lost any of their fascination. Marriage hasn't changed you as much as I feared. You're still the most charming, vivacious little minx in Manhattan."

"You mustn't say such things," she admonished.

"Why not? We're old friends, aren't we, even though no longer guardian and ward? Where's your bridegroom?"

"He had some business on the Bowery."

Earl wondered if she knew the extent of her husband's enterprises there, the saloons and brothels he owned, in addition to the rabbit-warren tenements. Other questions came to mind: Why did you marry him? Do you love him? Is he good to you? But Earl did not voice them, perhaps because he was afraid of the answers.

A curtain of silence separated them briefly. Then he gestured toward the activity. "Why aren't you out there, giving the men a treat?"

"I forgot my skates," she said. "Did you have a nice visit in Charleston?"

"How did you know I was in Charleston?"

"Cole heard it at the bank."

"I see. Yes, we had a nice holiday. Lots of gifts and entertainment. Christmas is celebrated grandly in the Low Country." He paused. "How was New Orleans?"

"Oh, it's quite a place! I bought trunks of clothes, and Cole bought tons of cotton, sugar, and rice to hold on speculation. He's very rich, you know. We've restored Riverview, and the grounds are being landscaped now. You must come and visit us soon, Earl."

He nodded, but said only, "The proceeds from the sale of Riverview are in your account, Jacintha. Fifteen thousand dollars. That's a small fortune. What should I do with it?"

"I thought it belonged to Cole."

"No, he owns the house now, Jacintha. But the money is your inheritance, and I won't allow anyone to touch it without your permission. Understand?"

Jacintha sighed. "How strange! Now that I don't need money, I have it. Take what I owe you, Earl, and keep the rest to gain interest. If Cole wants to borrow some, let him. He has given me a great deal."

"A great deal of what, Jacintha? Happiness?"

"Security," she murmured. "He saved my home."

"And you're grateful? Gratitude is a sorry basis for marriage, my dear, and someday you may regret it."

Someday? she thought ruefully. Oh, God, if only he knew how much she already regretted it!

Their attention was arrested by a small, straggly band of demonstrators, white and black, carrying flags and placards, their boots crunching in the snow as they marched toward the park. A man, leading another on a rope, walked ahead of the rest, and all were singing.

> John Brown's body lies a-mouldering in the grave,
> John Brown's body lies a-mouldering in the grave,
> John Brown's body lies a-mouldering in the grave,
> But his soul goes marching on!
> Glory, glory hallelujah!
> Glory, glory hallelujah!
> Glory, glory hallelujah!
> His soul is marching on!

"Why do they keep up this John Brown cult?" Jacintha cried impatiently. "He wasn't any great hero, stirring up that hornet's nest in Virginia!"

"Don't let an abolitionist hear you say that. He's a martyr in their eyes, revered as much by his admirers as despised by his detractors."

"War is getting closer, isn't it?"

"I'm afraid so."

"If it comes, will you go?"

"Probably."

"Why?" she demanded anxiously, her lips slightly parted.

"Why not?" he asked quietly.

"Well, what about the bank? Who would run it?"

"Uncle Peter and a highly competent staff. No man is indispensible, Jacintha, however much he might like to think so. And though the Britton clan were primarily bankers, there were a few soldiers and sailors, too. One at Bunker Hill. Another at Lake Champlain, in 1812. One was scalped in the Seminole Indian Wars, and another died fighting the Mexicans in Texas. That's why there are so few of us left. If Larry and I don't have sons, the Brittons will vanish completely."

"Then you owe it to your ancestors to remain alive as long as possible," Jacintha insisted. "Why do you want to get yourself killed?"

"I don't intend to be killed."

"No man expects to die in war, Earl. He always assumes it'll be another who's killed. He thinks he can be on a battlefield, with bullets and cannon balls flying thick as locusts in the wheat country, and be miraculously missed."

"Most are miraculously missed."

"But you wouldn't have to go, Earl! Rich men never have to fight wars."

He laughed. "Where did you get that idea?"

From her husband, but Jacintha did not tell him so. "Isn't it true?"

"Not necessarily."

"Well, I still don't see why you want to go to war."

"I don't *want* to go, Jacintha. Only a fool or ignoramus would want to go to war. But once it comes, somebody has to go, and I'm no better than the next man."

"You are too!" she cried impulsively. And then, appalled by her own audacity, she lowered her eyes, a queer tightness in her throat.

"Would you care, Jacintha, if I did go?"

"Yes," she murmured.

He caught her mittened hands in his. "That's very flattering. I hope it's true."

Jacintha trembled, disturbed by the intimacy of his clasp, the smooth, rich timbre of his voice. Abruptly she broke his grip and gazed toward the skaters. "Look at them! What fun they're having!"

"And why aren't we having fun with them? Come with me! We'll rent some skates and be the fanciest couple in the show."

"Oh, no," she demurred, sorely tempted. "I'm really not very good on ice."

"Nonsense! I'll bet you're a ballerina. Are you afraid I'll trip over my feet and embarrass you?"

"I know better than that, Earl Britton! You were a skating champion at Harvard."

"Good Lord, that was a decade ago! How could you possibly know what I did in college?"

Her answer was ready. "Grandpa told me."

"Oh? What else did Grandpa tell you about me?"

"Enough." She grinned. "You asked me to skate, remember? Well, I accept your invitation, sir."

They had difficulty finding a pair of skates small enough for her feet, but finally succeeded, and Jacintha chuckled as Earl put them on for her. "I feel like Cinderella."

"Cinderella's feet were cloven hoofs beside yours," he said, fastening the buckles. "Ready?"

"Uh-huh, but do go slowly, Earl. I haven't skated since my school days in Brooklyn."

"Nor I since mine in Boston."

"Doesn't Laurette like to skate?"

"No, she doesn't care much for sports, especially outdoor winter sports."

They were somewhat stiff and overly cautious at first, but Earl soon limbered up, and Jacintha saw that he was as skillful as anyone on the ice. "Relax," he urged. "I won't let you fall. There, now, you're doing fine. We'll try some figures, simple ones to begin with."

His arm about her waist was steady and reassuring. With his encouragement and guidance, Jacintha forgot herself and entered into the jubilant spirit around her, laughing and singing with the crowd. Her dark curls bounced vivaciously under her white fur bonnet, her turquoise eyes sparkled, her pink cheeks glowed. Occasionally she changed partners, but was happiest when gliding back to Earl.

"Having fun, little girl?"

"Oh, yes! Are you?"

He grinned. "I feel twenty again."

"You look twenty."

"Bless you, my dear. I had begun to feel ready for the bone yard."

"You can't mean that?"

"Not exactly," he said, "although at times I think life has passed me by, and what's left isn't worth living."

Jacintha nodded. "I suppose everyone feels that way sometimes. But I've never felt better or more alive than now."

"Nor have I."

"I'm hungry," she said suddenly. "Will you find us something to eat? I'll stake that empty bench by that twisted tree. Hurry, before someone else grabs it!"

Earl whistled at a vendor, sprinted across the pond, and joined her in minutes. "By God," he said as they sat munching, "this tastes good! The chestnuts are roasted to perfection, and the popcorn and peanuts are still hot. I used to think only children and monkeys enjoyed these things."

"We'll get some taffy later. And hot chocolate."

"You'll be sick, Curly Locks." He smiled. "That was my pet name for you, wasn't it?"

"Mmm, and you used to bring me candy."

"Gumdrops and jelly beans were your favorites," he recalled. "Pretty sharp memory, eh?"

"Well, you're hardly senile, for heaven's sake! But you forgot licorice whips and jawbreakers. Oh, Earl, why do you always tease me? You never take me seriously."

"Perhaps because teasing you gives me pleasure, and I'm mean enough to enjoy it." And perhaps, he thought ruefully, because I don't *dare* take you seriously. "So you see, I'm really a brute."

Jacintha wrinkled her pert nose at him. "You're not going to have much appetite for supper."

"Supper? Holy smoke! I was just bragging about my keen memory, and I've forgotten that we have an early dinner engagement." His expression changed immediately. A somber mask fell over his face, obliterating all the joy of a moment ago. "I'm sorry, Jacintha. I'll have to leave now, or I'll be late. Let me remove your blades for you."

"No, don't bother. I think I'll stay awhile longer."

"Well . . ." He rose, hesitating, his eyes on her lovely face, tilted to his like a flower to the sun. "Thank you for the pleasure, Jacintha. Goodbye."

"Goodbye, Earl. And thank you, too."

She watched him cross the frozen water, weaving between the skaters. He returned his skates and paid the rental for both of them. Untethering his horse, he mounted and gave her a farewell salute as he galloped off, flying hoofs kicking up a miniature snowstorm.

A small boy wandered over to Jacintha. "Wanna skate?"

She smiled at him and rubbed her mittens across her moist eyes. "No, thank you, sonny. I'm just leaving. Here, have some popcorn and peanuts. . . ."

Chapter 17

A CHARMING octagonal gazebo and large hothouse were under construction at Riverview, and there were plans for an intricate boxwood maze and a circular rose-bed. A graceful white marble nymph replaced the broken statue in the reclaimed pool, where fragrant water lilies and hyacinths would soon float. A new fountain, birdbath and sundial were also added, along with the fashionable iron lawn animals and ornamental iron furniture.

By the time the landscapers finished, in late March, the transplanted lilacs, forsythia, and dogwood were budding, and with the acquisition of the new property, Jacintha could stroll to the rocky escarpment of the Hudson and meditate in a renovated lighthouse or a replica of a Dutch windmill while watching the river traffic, or gazing at the New Jersey Palisades.

Cole spoke of building a private wharf and acquiring a steam yacht as large and luxurious as Earl Britton's or Commodore Vanderbilt's. Jacintha had no such aspirations, nor did she share her husband's ambition to be launched into the mainstream of Manhattan society. This could not be accomplished, she insisted, without the sponsorship of a member of the elite coterie, and she refused to kowtow to Laurette Britton in the hope of achieving it.

"You'll just have to be content with the company of other *nouveaux riches,* Cole. And *parvenus.*"

"What the devil does that mean?" he demanded, always angry when he could not understand something.

"Newly rich," Jacintha explained. "And upstarts."

"Then why don't you just say that? Why do you confound me with those goddamn foreign words!"

"Believe me, those are familiar terms in high society, Cole, for people like you."

"Yeah? Well, I still think money can change that!"

Toward this end, he was too busy to take a vacation. They were among the few affluent New Yorkers who did not leave the city to escape the abominable summer heat. Once again the social pages listed the names of prominent families fleeing to popular seaside and mountain resorts, or abroad. Apparently the Brittons were going in different directions again this season, Laurette to Newport and Earl to Saratoga Springs. Perhaps separate holidays, like individual bedrooms, were the marital vogue in their class? Jacintha hinted hopefully at the subject, but Cole was not swayed.

"I reckon we'll just be out of style in that respect, Mrs. Danvers." He grinned, pinching her buttocks and adding one of his disgusting vulgarities.

When not away on business, Cole was occupied with his Manhattan enterprises, including a recently purchased tannery and clothing factory. Still unaware of his Bowery establishments, Jacintha did not know how much time he spent there. She suspected, but did not really care, that the Roxy he had inadvertently mentioned was more than a platonic acquaintance. Even so, he still bothered her too often in bed, and his violent mating invariably left her tense and restless, yearning for something she could not quite identify.

His foul breath and the strong residual odor of his sweat and semen on her flesh repulsed her. She could not wait to scrub it off. There must be something more to sex, she thought, bewildered. The Creator couldn't have designed it solely for the pleasure of man and the misery of woman!

She had not seen Earl Britton since their chance meeting in Central Park. Although aware that Cole saw him occasionally at the bank, Jacintha dared not ask if Earl ever inquired about her. She had hoped he would call at Riverview, but he was either too busy or simply not interested. Had his compliments and apparent enjoyment while ice skating been mere pretense? And would he always remain an enigma, defying comprehension?

"I didn't expect Mr. Britton to congratulate Mr. Danvers on our marriage," she told Lollie. "But I thought he'd at least be curious about the house."

"He saw it," Lollie said.

"He did? When?"

"While you were traveling."

"Mr. Earl was here then? Why didn't you tell me?"

Lollie shrugged. "He'd just returned from Charleston and didn't stay long after learning about the wedding."

"What did he say?"

"Nothing much, but I never saw anyone look more miserable. I offered him some coffee or wine, but he shook his head sadly and left. He was deeply hurt, Missy."

Jacintha sighed remorsefully. "I made some unfortunate mistakes, Lollie, but it's all too late now."

Remembering wryly the lean days of early rising and hard work, when she had longed to luxuriate in bed until noon and dine from a tray, Jacintha found it difficult to enjoy her leisure now. Lollie managed the household so efficiently that there was little for Jacintha to do beyond menu planning, cutting and arranging fresh flowers, strolling, and shopping. Afternoons she read, embroidered, or played the now well-tuned spinet in the parlor.

Occasionally, at Cole's insistence, she entertained the wives of his business associates at tea and accepted their invitations, but the only thing the women had in common was their husbands' ambition. Overdressed and over-jeweled, they lived in overdecorated mansions, attended by overliveried servants. Some enrolled in dancing and riding academies, anticipating grand balls and fox hunts, and were convinced that Mrs. Danvers possessed an open sesame to the closed portals. All were older than Jacintha, some by many years, and she was bored by their petty gossip, fretful anxieties, frustrations, and futile struggles. Poor souls, doomed to disappointment!

One evening a brigade of Lincoln supporters passed Riverview, ringing bells and rolling drums to announce a rally in Washington Square, which Jacintha thought might relieve the monotony of her life. With the presidential campaign reaching a feverish pitch, political gatherings were numerous all over the city.

"Let's go, Lollie!"

"What for? We can't vote."

"But it's something to do! Brass bands always play between the speeches, and often minstrels perform. Come!"

People flocked to these public gatherings, cheering loudest for the party providing the best show and serving the most refreshments. Few actually knew much about the candidates or cared who was elected, since the results seldom affected their personal lives one way or another. This audience was disgruntled, however, because the conservative Republican Wide-Awake Club could not compete with the liberal Tammany Hall Democrats in either the quality or quantity of entertainment.

Jacintha and Lollie were jostled in the stampede, their bonnets knocked away, shoes scuffed. They had been on the scene less than half an hour when a drunken lout spilled a tin cup of beer over Jacintha's new flocked voile dress. This infuriated Lollie, who had just pressed the rows of ruffles on the billowy skirt and the long taffeta-ribbon sash. "Swine," she muttered, pushing the sot away. "Mind your manners!"

Instantly his tipsy wife dashed her suds into Lollie's face. A black man rushed to Lollie's defense and tangled with the woman's burly husband. Others joined in the fray, indiscriminately fighting and cursing one another. Jacintha watched in dismay until a policeman's shrill whistle sounded nearby. She grabbed the housekeeper's hand. "Let's get away!"

They ran wildly, hoops swaying and crinolines rustling, through the milling horde until they were safe. Lollie clutched her chest, her heart pounding, and panted. "Whew! We left just in time. The paddy wagons are coming now!"

"We nearly landed in jail," Jacintha breathed in awe. "Our clothes are torn, I lost a slipper, and we smell like a brewery! I swear, trouble stalks me. I must have been born under an evil influence."

"Matter of fact, the caul was over your head, which means good luck."

"Good luck? Then a wicked witch cast a permanent spell over me afterwards!" She shivered, suddenly cold despite the intense August heat. "I'll never attend another political shindig!"

But less than a week later, again prompted by ennui, she went to a Temperance lecture at Cooper Union and ended up marching on the Bowery, only to encounter her husband in the first concert saloon they attempted to enter.

Jacintha quickly broke ranks and retreated, but not quite soon enough. Cole chased her down the street, finally catching her as she attempted to escape across Chatham Square, and demanded while maintaining a bone-crushing grip on her arm, "What in hell is the meaning of this?"

She glared at him sullenly. "How could I know you'd be patronizing that place?"

"Patronizing? I own it, Jacintha! And several more."

"Concert saloons? The ministers and news editors say those are nothing more than brothels!"

"The hostesses dance with the customers," he explained. "If some do business on the side, that's their affair."

"They're prostitutes, Cole—and perhaps you also provide convenient rooms for their transactions?"

His silence betrayed him. Jacintha turned away, gazing at several garishly garbed streetwalkers in the square.

"You have prosperous legitimate enterprises, Cole. Why do you deal in this illegal filth?"

"Concert saloons are perfectly legal, my dear, and favored by some of the finest gentlemen and studs in this city. Likewise, the parlor houses. You're a child, Jacintha, and your notions of life come from fiction—those silly romantic novels you dote on! The facts are somewhat different. It's time you grew up. I won't have you butting into my business. Go home now! Mind your knitting, and stay away from those crazy temperance and suffragist fanatics! You hear?"

"You're hurting my arm, Cole."

"I'll paddle your ass if you continue to provoke and disobey me," he warned, signaling a hackney. "You need some brats to keep you busy. You should be six months pregnant by now! Not doing anything to hinder nature, are you?"

Since the middle-aged matrons of her acquaintance discussed menopause more than pregnancy and contraceptives, Jacintha learned little about these matters from them. "I don't know what you mean," she said, and Cole believed in her innocence.

He handed her into the cab, giving the driver the address and fare. "I'll probably be late getting home."

Jacintha nodded, avoiding the perfunctory kiss he would have planted on her cheek. "We're creating a public spectacle," she admonished him, embarrassed by the gawkers. "Go on, driver!"

She pretended to be asleep when Cole got in that night, and mercifully he did not disturb her. She rose at dawn, strolled in the dewy garden, then breakfasted alone on the terrace. When Cole finally came down, she was working petit point in the parlor, a pretty picture of domesticity. She ignored his greeting, concentrating on the fabric stretched tautly across the hoops.

Her petulance amused him. "Now, Puss, you can't stay mad at me forever."

"I'm not angry, Cole. Just disgusted. Tell me, is Mr. Britton aware of your Bowery dens?"

He shrugged negligently. "Why?"

"Because I think that's one reason why you rushed our

marriage in his absence," she accused him. "And you'll never make it into decent society, Mr. Danvers, while you own disreputable places!"

"Oh, I don't know about that," he drawled confidently. "His Honor, Mayor Fernando Wood, is one of my customers, along with Boss Tweed and other Tammany toffs. Also some prominent Wall Street gents."

The needle slipped, and Jacintha accidentally pricked her finger. "Are you implying that Earl Britton . . . ?"

Cole grinned slyly. "I'm not implying anything, Pussycat. But he's a man, isn't he? You think he's never known any woman but his wife? Such a handsome bastard probably has petticoats chasing *him!*"

Jacintha pursed her lips primly. "I don't care to discuss it further, sir."

"Good. Just behave yourself, madam, and we'll get along fine. No more surprise raids on my territory, understand?"

She mustered the courage to speak her mind, and said in a rush, "Our marriage was a mistake, Cole, and should be dissolved."

"Indeed? Well, I don't happen to agree, Mrs. Danvers. We're husband and wife—and will remain so till death do us part. Now, stop this prattle and look at the pretty trinket I bought for you." Producing a velvet case from his robe pocket, he opened it to reveal a fabulous diamond necklace, bracelet, and pendant earrings. "Ten thousand bucks," he bragged, dropping the gift into her lap.

"One night's take from your fleshpots?"

"Ah, my little spitfire! You're hotter than usual today. Can it be you're jealous of the pretty young ladies in my employ and curious if Roxy LaFlame is one of them?"

"Is she?"

"Miss LaFlame is an actress," he said, stroking his mustache, "like I told you in New Orleans. Tony Pastor signed her for a role in a new play opening in his theater this fall. She's rehearsing now."

"Were you with her last night?"

"For a while," he admitted. "Just watching her practice on stage. It's a dancing part, and Roxy's a good dancer."

"Naturally, after her experience in your concert saloons! It's strange that you advocate independence for her kind, but not for other women! All the feminists want is equal rights with men and fair treatment."

"Plus the vote."

"Is that so terrible, considering that the government concerns them too?"

"God help the country if females ever gain control. That Buchanan is muddleheaded. What improvements do you suppose a she-president would make, besides rearranging the furniture in the White House?"

"Queen Victoria isn't doing so badly ruling the British Empire!" Jacintha retorted indignantly.

Cole scoffed. "Poppycock! She sits on the throne, but Prince Albert and the Prime Minister tell her what to do. And I'm telling you again to stay clear of those loony Amazons!"

Jacintha refused the gauntlet. "Some mail came from Boston and Lowell this morning," she said. "It's on the desk in the library. You'd better take care of it, Cole. I want to go over the dinner menu with Cook now. Will you be dining here this evening?"

"Yeah, and I'm hungry for roast beef—rare. The last rack of ribs was overdone."

"I'll tell Mrs. Paxton."

"And now I'd like some breakfast." He yanked the bell cord impatiently. "Goddamn servants, never around when you need one! What am I paying 'em for?"

To suffer a monstrous master, Jacintha thought, but held her tongue. She had crossed him enough for one day.

"Lollie is coming now," she murmured, returning to her needlepoint.

Chapter 18

EARL Britton had just returned from the polls, where he had cast his ballot in the presidential election. The sky was heavily overcast, and a strong, bitter wind was blowing from the South, across the Battery and Bowling Green, into Wall Street. He warmed himself at his office fireplace before removing his topcoat and sitting down at his desk. His secretary had placed his personal mail there, and on top of the stack lay a letter addressed in a familiar hand. Instantly Earl reached for the silver letter-opener.

Charleston, S.C.
October 22, 1860

My Dear Brother:

This will be a big surprise to you—and, I hope, a pleasant one. I am married! I still find it a little incredible, but it is happily true. I am an old married man of one week!

The lovely lady I am so fortunate to have as my wife is the daughter of one of this state's oldest and finest families. She is the former Geraldine Kenyon, whose father, you will recall, served four terms in the

United States Senate before ill health forced his retirement from public life.

My bride is a few years older than I—five, to be exact—but I couldn't let a little thing like that stand in my way. She is beautiful, charming, gracious—all that a man could desire in a lifelong mate, and my supreme desire is to make her happy.

The Kenyons have just returned from a three-year sojourn in Europe, where the Senator took the waters of St. Moritz and Baden-Baden, while Geraldine continued her music studies at the Conservatory of Vienna. She is a magnificent pianist, the one person who could, I believe, give you some competition on the "ivories." She also paints quite well and writes lovely poetry. If I sound boastful, it is because my pride in her drives me to superlatives. She is truly a wonderful person, brilliant and talented as few females are, and I am certain that you will be as proud and pleased as I to have her in the family.

By now you are undoubtedly wondering, and rightly so, why you and Laurette were not invited to the wedding. But do not feel slighted, dear brother. It so happens that, as weddings go, we didn't have one. The Kenyons were visiting friends in Charleston when I arrived on the last day of September. We met at a reception, it was love at first sight, and we eloped a week later. Didn't I outdo you a bit there, old man? If memory serves, it took you somewhat longer to woo and win your fair lady!

Of course we were properly admonished by Mother and Aunt Evelyn for our impetuosity—remember that Mother thought you had rushed matters too much? You can imagine what she thought of me! And poor Mrs. Kenyon, who had always dreamed of seeing her only daughter wed in a brilliant ceremony at Foxhall, their ancestral plantation near Columbia, was astonished by our secrecy and undue haste. Things are not done so swiftly in the leisurely South, you know.

We are both back in the good graces of our respective families, however, and being most cordially received and entertained. Southerners are too romantic to remain peeved at happy newlyweds! After a brief honeymoon in the Georgia sea isles, we shall make our home at Rosewood, thereby fulfilling Mother's ambitions for me as a planter.

I have told Geraldine much about you, Earl, and she is most anxious to meet her suave and handsome brother-in-law. I trust that meeting is not too far in the distance. Write to us, and give my regards to Laurette and Uncle Peter. Hoping to hear from you soon, I remain

your loving brother,
Larry.

"Well, I'll be damned," Earl muttered to himself, smiling and shaking his head. "I'll be goddamned!"

That evening he told his wife the news.

"Larry is married?" Laurette stared at him incredulously. "Why, I can't believe it!"

"It's true, Laurette, and he seems very happy."

"Happy?" she scoffed. "You're a fool, Earl Britton! Larry was in love with Jacintha Howard. He just married some simpering little belle on the rebound."

"No, I don't think so," Earl mused. "His letter sounds sincere, and Larry was never good at lying, Laurette. He couldn't pretend a happiness he didn't feel."

"Perhaps not." She shrugged. "Well . . . if his heart was broken, it certainly mended rapidly. He worked much faster with Miss Dixie than with Miss Howard. I swear I don't believe Larry so much as kissed Jacintha once in the two months he courted her."

"How could he, under your constant surveillance?"

"Oh, I didn't watch them that closely! Larry was just too bashful, but apparently Miss Dixie Belle overcame his shyness."

"Her name is Geraldine," Earl said angrily. "She was Miss Geraldine Kenyon."

"Senator Kenyon's daughter?"

"Yes. The Senator is retired now. Ill health."

"Well, at least she comes from a proper family. I wonder what she's like."

"Quite a lady, from his description."

"I'll decide that when I meet her!" She laughed suddenly. "What a jolt this will be to Jacintha!"

"Why should it be? She's no longer interested in Larry. Jacintha has been married for almost a year."

"Even so, no girl likes to feel that a former beau could forget her so easily. Besides, she can't possibly be in love with her husband. Cole Danvers is more than twice her age, and rough-cut. Remember his boorish behavior the first time I met him at your office, his unsubtle hints for an invitation to our home? Jacintha undoubtedly married him out of desperation, and Larry's marriage will be quite a shock to her pride."

"It's a bit of a shock to yours too, isn't it?"

Laurette cast him an oblique, wary glance. What was he insinuating?

"I don't understand."

"Oh, come, now, Laurette! You didn't expect Larry to forget *you* so swiftly, either, did you?"

He knew! That weak little coward had told him—betrayed her and himself!

For a few moments, remembering Earl's great affection for his brother and his greatly superior strength, Laurette was truly afraid. But fear soon gave way to arrogance and a malicious desire to flaunt her adultery. She challenged him recklessly. "So he told you?"

Earl scowled, disgusted. "No, he didn't tell me—he didn't have to! His face and manner betrayed him. I told you he was never good at deception. You planned to seduce him, Laurette, from the day he arrived here. I could see you working on him, and see him weakening. I knew it was going to happen, but I didn't know how to prevent it. Why did you do this, Laurette? Why did you want to ruin his life too?"

"Ruin his life? How dramatic! And how absurd, coming from a roué like yourself!"

"Dispense with the satire, Laurette. I'm in no mood to bandy witicisms. You know damned well what I mean! Before he left, Larry couldn't face me once without flinching. He was miserable, in an agony of self-hatred. It may seem trivial to a dissolute slut, but to an honorable man, cuckolding his own brother is no mere peccadillo, I assure you! Larry will probably feel guilty the rest of his life, believing he did me a terrible injury. My God, if he only knew the truth! But perhaps he has guessed it by now. There's a name for women like you, Laurette, and it's not a pretty one."

Her contempt matched his as her lips curled in an insolent smile. "What do you intend to do about it?"

"I could divorce you," he said.

"And name your brother as corespondent?"

Earl frowned, aware of her advantage. "No, I'll let you accuse me of infidelity."

"Not a false accusation, I'm sure! But I don't choose to make it *yet*, Earl. And whatever else you may think of me now, I regret what happened with Larry." She paused. "It was a wretched experience for both of us, but I don't think it destroyed him. He seems to have recovered from his one terrible sin."

"He was a virgin, wasn't he? Jesus, Laurette! What a memory of sexual initiation, seduced by his sister-in-law! And in his brother's house. My bed too?"

"No. His."

"You went to his room?"

"Yes."

"Dressed?"

"In dishabille, darling."

Earl winced and turned to leave.

"Where're you going?" she asked.

"To get some fresh air!"

Laurette ran after him, catching his arm. "I'm sorry, Earl. It's wicked of me to taunt you this way. Please forgive me. You've cheated on me, many times, haven't you?"

"Not with a sister."

"I no longer have a sister."

"You understand the point, Laurette."

"Well, I've been unhappy, Earl. Lonely and bored, and maybe I did it just to hurt you, because I realize that you don't love me anymore."

"That's right!" he snapped. "And I don't believe you ever loved me, Laurette. Why in hell did you marry me? You never wanted children. You were angry the first time you got pregnant and relieved when you miscarried. You were furious the second time, and I think you had an abortion. You freeze up whenever I approach you, still fearing pregnancy—although it's hardly likely anymore. Whatever butcher aborted you—probably Madame Restell —apparently made you sterile. And thank God for that, lest my brother's child were also slaughtered! Or would you have borne it, to humiliate me further?"

"You're weaving fantasies, Earl."

"I could forgive you anything but this, Laurette. This treachery I can neither forgive nor forget."

"Why did you wait so long to confront me?"

"Because I had only suspicions, and I hoped they were wrong. I even made love to you, trying to convince myself that you couldn't seduce Larry and continue to lie with me. Only a heartless bitch could do that! But you could, because that's precisely what you are, Laurette! A despicable bitch! Now I know the truth, and I can't delude myself any longer. Your name should be spelled 'Lorette,' the French word for harlot."

She blanched. "I know my French, you bastard." She wanted to wound him but did not quite dare, except with her tongue. "Maybe I did you a favor, darling. If Larry had stayed, he might have married your innocent little ward. Would that have pleased you? I think not. You coveted Jacintha Howard's virginity yourself, didn't you? But that greedy old money-grubber got her instead. How that must rankle!"

Earl brushed her aside, glowering with suppressed rage. "I'd better leave, before I give you the beating you deserve," he growled, and Laurette knew it was dangerous to provoke him further.

Chapter 19

ANNOUNCEMENT of Abraham Lincoln's election to the presidency by a slim majority of electoral votes was carried to the people via telegraph, newspapers, pony express, town criers. It had not yet reached some remote regions in the backwoods and mountains, inaccessible to the courier and grapevine, when the first serious repercussions were felt in the South. Barely a month later, on the twentieth of December, South Carolina seceded from the Union, and the thin thread holding the peace began to snap ominously.

At Britton Bank, while seeking another industry expansion loan, Cole Danvers heard that Earl had gone to Charleston to try to bring his family back to New York. He also learned from Peter Britton that Earl's younger brother had married, soon after his Grand Tour, news which Cole imparted to his wife, unaware that Lawrence Britton had once courted her.

Jacintha scarcely glanced up from the new Charles Dickens novel, *A Tale of Two Cities,* in which she was currently engrossed. She had become an avid reader, but contrary to what her husband thought, not everything she read was romantic fiction or poetry. History, biography, philosophy were also included, along with the tracts of some controversial feminists, past and present, such as Mary Wollstonecraft, Abigail Adams, Madame de Stael, and George Sand.

Cole's information came from the daily journals, and he favored *The New York Herald*, whose publisher, James Gordon Bennett, was one of his friends. The cogent editorials of Horace Greeley, the strange little man who owned and edited the *Tribune*, bored and often irritated him. Cole used the library as an office, and Jacintha thought it desecrated the memory of her grandfather, whose sanctuary it had been. Seeing Cole at the Jeffersonian desk, or lounging in the leather easy chair with his feet propped on the hassock, made her want to beg her grandparents' forgiveness for making him master of Riverview.

As the national situation worsened, Cole's business trips became more frequent, and Jacintha eagerly helped him pack his carpetbags. His factories were preparing for around-the-clock production. His warehouses now bulged with raw materials, and his tannery was processing leather as rapidly as the hides could be purchased. He increased his stocks in railroads, shipyards, ironworks, munitions companies, granaries, and he was also investing heavily in coffee, tea, sugar, flour, and other vital staples. It appeared inevitable that the vast fortune he had long ago envisioned, was about to be his.

But Jacintha's wistful expectations were fading into a nebulous haze. She sat on the padded windowseat in the library oriel, gazing glumly at the somber January sky, from which the sun seemed to have disappeared forever, lonely as a shut-in, and convinced that nobody anywhere on earth could be more miserable than she. The silence was broken when Lollie announced a visitor. "Looks like one of Mr. Britton's magnificent mounts."

"Let me see. Good heavens, it is!"

"Will you receive him?"

"Yes. It may be important." Jacintha patted a stray curl into place and smoothed her lace collar and cuffs, nervous and excited. "Do I look all right? Stop grinning like a sly cat, Lollie, and answer the door."

She was posed on a small tapestry sofa, the silken folds of her gown neatly arranged over her crinolines, when Earl entered the room. He approached, smiling, holding his crop under his left arm, as he removed his gloves. A raw-silk ascot was tucked into his tweed jacket. His tight fawn twill breeches emphasized his muscular thighs and even his sex, which never seemed to embarrass men who fancied English riding clothes. The habit was incomplete, however, for he rode too swiftly to bother with a tall, clumsy hat, and his dark head was bare.

"Good afternoon, my dear. I trust I'm not disturbing you?"

"Not at all," Jacintha assured him, closing the heavy tome she had indiscriminately grabbed from the history section. "I'm grateful to you, actually, for rescuing me from a rather dull account of Pompeii."

"Then it's fortunate I came. I have a rather interesting book on Pompeii, however—privately published and long-banned in many countries, including America."

"Really? I'd like to read it."

He grinned devilishly. "Remind me to lend it to you, when you're a little older."

Jacintha blushed. Still teasing her, the rascal!

"Sit down, Earl. I'm sorry Cole isn't here." She flushed at the lie, for she wasn't the least bit sorry.

"Do you expect him soon?" he asked, taking an armchair opposite her.

"Not soon, no. He's somewhere in Massachusetts—Boston or Lowell. So if you came on business—"

"No, I just happened to stop by."

She smiled prettily. "I'm glad you did. Would you like some coffee? Tea? A drink?"

"A glass of port, if you have any."

"There's a cellaret in almost every room," Jacintha said, rising to serve him, "and the basement has been converted into a liquor storehouse. Cole expects a shortage of alcoholic beverages, and he's an instinctive hoarder."

Earl wondered about Danvers's other instincts, especially with regard to his wife. "Thank you," he said as she handed him a crystal goblet of vintage port along with a tiny linen napkin. "Won't you join me?"

"If you like," she agreed, pouring herself a small portion and returning to her seat. "What do you think of Riverview now?" She was anxious for his opinion.

"It's beautiful, Jacintha, and just about its original size. The grounds extend to the Hudson again, and they're well landscaped. The restoration must have been quite expensive."

Jacintha nodded reflectively, thinking that the personal costs to her far exceeded her husband's monetary outlay. "There were some temperamental clashes between Cole and the decorators. His taste is somewhat flamboyant, as you know. But it was three against one, and we finally triumphed."

"Your grandparents would be very proud of Riverview now, Jacintha."

"I wonder," she murmured, sipping her wine pensively.

"You sound skeptical."

Her eyes avoided contact with his. "Just one of my moods."

"I·didn't know you had moods," he said, crossing his long booted legs. "I thought that was my province." He paused, weighing his next words. "I suppose you know that my brother is married."

"Yes, your uncle told Cole."

"Gossipy as an old woman, Uncle Peter! I meant to tell you myself, Jacintha, but there wasn't time before I left for Charleston."

"I trust your family is well?"

"Yes, but still determined to remain in Charleston, whatever the consequences," he replied gravely. "South Carolina considers itself an independent state since its secession, and the Home Guard was already drilling in the streets when I was there. The Union is dissolving, Jacintha. Florida, Alabama, and Georgia are considering secession now. It's just a matter of time before the other slave states follow. I believe the South intends to form a confederacy and inaugurate its own president before Abraham Lincoln takes office, if he's not assassinated before then. Threats have been made, and he'll need heavy security throughout his term."

"Maybe not, Earl. Mr. Lincoln's presidency doesn't necessarily mean war, does it? The Southerners claim they want only to be left alone, to live as they please without Northern interference. Perhaps we should give them a chance to prove it."

"That would mean two nations, Jacintha."

"Well, this is a big country! There should be room enough for people with different ways of life to exist in peace."

Earl was gazing into the fire; a blazing log had fallen from the grate and was consuming itself in molten ashes. "No doubt some political overtures will be made in that direction," he responded, finishing his port.

"We might even reunite!"

"My dear, America has never been truly united. But there's no harm in hoping."

And praying, Jacintha thought, remembering what he had told her in Central Park. But surely he would change his mind about volunteering, rather than risk alienating his family, and possibly even fighting against his own brother!

"How is Laurette?" she asked reluctantly.

"The same." His voice held no emotion.

"Did she go with you to Charleston?"

"Yes. She was anxious to meet our new sister-in-law. Laurette spent most of her time in the city, however, with Mother and Aunt Evelyn. I stayed at the plantation with Larry. I think he'll make a good planter, and his wife will be an excellent mistress for Rosewood. She was raised on a plantation and trained by her mother in manor management."

"I know, Earl. I've read about the Kenyons of South Carolina, and the marriage of their daughter, Geraldine, to your brother. Someone sent me lengthy clippings from the Charleston and Columbia papers."

Earl did not need to guess the name of the anonymous sender. Laurette, of course. "I see."

"Don't misunderstand me, please. I'm delighted for Larry and his bride, Earl, and wish them eternal bliss. I'm sure they belong together."

"Yes," he said, standing.

"You're leaving?"

"I want to visit the Britton estate," he explained. "If I ride swiftly, I can reach it before dark."

"The house on Kip's Bay?"

"You remember it?"

"Oh, yes! I went there several times with Grandpa, at your father's invitation. It's a grand country place, but I thought it had been sold."

"No, although I seldom go there anymore. Too many boyhood memories of our summer and winter holidays." Nostalgia mellowed his recollections. "That's where Larry and I learned to ride, hunt, fish, sail, and scull. The dust-covered furniture seems ghostly now. But I suddenly have an acute yen to see Greystone again, spend a night in the lodge we boys used to share with our friends and dogs. I'm sure the caretaker will have some extra food and firewood."

"But what will you do there, alone?",

"Think," he replied, reaching down a gentle hand to urge her to her feet. "Ponder the past and present, and try to foresee the future. What do lonely people do, Jacintha?"

The admission was a surprising revelation. "I've never thought of you as lonely," she said softly.

"No? Well, I often am, my dear." His expression was sad, brooding. "Now I'm being maudlin. Forgive me, Jacintha. I shouldn't have come."

"Don't say that!" she cried, astonished by her own emotionalism. "You certainly took long enough, Mr. Britton! And you must come again, soon."

Their eyes fused momentarily, then he shook his head vigorously, as if to clear it. He had dreaded to find her pregnant by now, but there were no changes in her appearance. Her body was still slender and supple, the elevation of her pert breasts in the tight bodice suggesting unnecessary lacing. All woman, Earl thought. Too damn much woman!

Larry had gotten an affluent and talented wife in Geraldine Kenyon, but also an exceptionally plain one, with straight, drab hair and dull eyes, pale-lashed and slightly protuberant, and a flat-chested, almost boyish figure. Compared to this vivacious, brilliant-eyed beauty, Geraldine was a wren beside a bird of paradise. God, how he longed to take her in his arms, kiss her tempting coral mouth, caress her tantalizing curves. How he longed to make urgent love to her!

"Jacintha—"

She swayed toward him involuntarily, as if magnetized, and whispered, "Yes?"

He clasped her hand briefly, released it, and touched her cheek tenderly. "Goodbye, Curly Locks. Be a good girl, and I'll bring you some candy next time."

Jacintha stood like a statue ready to crumble. She had sensed his emotions and imagined that he sensed hers. She had even closed her eyes and parted her lips expectantly. She was deeply hurt by his hasty retreat, and was wistfully rubbing the part of her face he had touched, when Lollie wheeled in the teacart.

"I thought you might like some refreshments. Did Mr. Britton leave already?"

Jacintha nodded, her eyes misty. "Oh, Lollie, I think I'm in love with him!"

"And you're just now realizing it? I knew it when you were nine years old."

"Well, then, since you're so astute, tell me what to do about it!"

The older woman sighed sympathetically. "Nothing much you can do, when you've got a dragon by the tail. And we both know that's what the master of Riverview is!"

And eventually he'll destroy me, Jacintha mused morosely. I'll die a little each wretched day . . .

Snow fell that evening and, intermittently, for a week.

Jacintha wandered aimlessly through the house, upstairs and down, pausing at the windows, hoping to see Earl galloping up on his swift black stallion. She was too restless to read for any length of time, too nervous to concentrate on fancy work.

Finally she ordered the stablegroom to prepare the pretty little green-and-gold sleigh Cole had given her for Christmas and drove herself to Central Park. Perhaps they would have another chance encounter and waltz together on the ice. But Earl was nowhere in sight, and after an hour of waiting on the perimeter of the frozen lake in her beaver parka and fur-lined mittens, she left. Was he snowbound at Greystone, and still meditating? Two more Southern states had seceded, another was in the process, and Earl's pronouncement seemed correct. The Union was indeed dissolving.

Dear Lord, if only Cole would get marooned in Massachusetts and remain until the spring thaw!

❧ PART III ❧

Chapter 20

JACINTHA was on her way to do some shopping, heartened somewhat by the new season. She smiled at the motley group of youngsters accompanying a hurdy-gurdy entertainer and laughed aloud at the amusing antics of the chattering monkey. She ordered the coachman to stop so she could purchase a nosegay of fresh violets from an old flower-woman, and regretfully passed up the bird-men peddling singing canaries, colorful parakeets, and squawking parrots in wicker and gilded metal cages. Cole would allow no pets in the house.

Always rapid, the pulse of the city was beating furiously on this bright April day as shoppers rushed to spring sales. Jammed horsecars and omnibuses rattled along Broadway, their bells clanging. Vendors hawked fresh produce, beef, bakery and dairy products. Vehicles jockeyed for position on the busiest thoroughfare in town, the drivers yelling and swearing at one another.

The largest shops and department stores were located in this area, and their show windows displayed every conceivable luxury and necessity—from elegant clothes and jewelry to cuspidors and chamber pots. Every corner had its prostitute, beggar, and pickpocket. Jacintha agreed with P.

T. Barnum that New York was the most vibrant, exciting city in the world; and though she longed to see London, Paris, and Rome, she knew she never wanted to live anywhere else.

As she approached City Hall, the traffic slowed considerably. People were hurrying out of buildings, into the streets, running toward City Hall Park and Newspaper Row. A fire or accident? She heard no alarms. The attraction was Printing House Square, where most of the daily journals were published—and the news had been ominous the past few months.

MISSISSIPPI FOLLOWS SOUTH CAROLINA IN SECESSION. FLORIDA FLEES UNION. ALABAMA SECEDES. GEORGIA JOINS MARCH OF SECESSION. LOUISIANA LOST. TEXAS OUT. UNION DISSOLVED. JEFFERSON DAVIS PRESIDENT OF CONFEDERACY. MONTGOMERY, ALABAMA TEMPORARY REBEL CAPITAL.

And all, people said, because Abraham Lincoln occupied the White House!

"Stop!" Jacintha called to the coachman, rapping her parasol against the perch. "What is it, Clancy? Some emergency?"

"I don't rightly know, ma'am. Hey!" he shouted at some boys passing the landau, which Cole had bought primarily for the Central Park carriage parade. "What's going on here?"

One of the youths paused, speaking rapidly, his pimpled face flushed with excitement. "It's war, mister! They done it! Ain't you heard? Them dirty dogs fired on Fort Sumter —that's somewhere down South! Fired on their own country's flag, the goddamn rebel traitors!"

"War has been declared?" Jacintha asked tremulously.

"It will be, lady!" he jubilantly assured her. "We gotta fight now; we been attacked! And we'll whip hell outta them lousy slave-holdin' bastids, too—quicker'n you can say Uncle Tom's Cabin!" He sprinted back to his Five Points gang, giving a high-pitched whoop that chilled Jacintha's blood.

But before she could assimilate the news, she heard a familiar feminine voice say, "Why, it's Jacintha Howard, isn't it? I mean, Danvers. I thought I recognized you. My carriage is stalled a few feet away, and we may as well chat a bit."

Laurette Britton stood beside the landau, poised and smiling, in a suit of beige Saxony wool and a plumed Empress Eugenie hat dipped coyly over her forehead—the one perfectly calm and collected person in the crowd of thousands.

Jacintha affected a cordial greeting. "Hello, Laurette. How are you?"

"Exhausted!" she declared brightly. "I spent the entire morning at Stewart's, selecting new materials and trimmings, bonnets and slippers. My modiste is going to be very busy in the next few months. May I sit with you, dear? I fear I'll be trampled if I stand in the street."

"Please do," Jacintha invited, opening the door. Clancy would have left the box to assist her but Laurette waved him back. Lifting her skirts well above her slender silken ankles, she climbed in and sat vis-à-vis.

"What a handsome carriage this is, and brand new! You're riding in style these days, Mrs. Danvers. We must have ours refurbished or buy another, although Mr. Britton seldom uses any of the family vehicles. He prefers to drive himself in his phaeton or chaise, race his curricle, or ride that wild black beast so aptly named Rocket."

How could she rattle on about trivia? Jacintha wondered.

"You've heard the news, Laurette?"

"Oh, yes." She glanced contemptuously at the milling multitude. "Look at the fools! They'll stampede like crazed cattle before long."

"I guess you can't blame them for being disturbed," Jacintha said. "It means war."

"Well, it's been coming for years. The ironies of fate, I suppose. Death for some men, opportunity for others."

"Opportunity?"

"Of course! It's common knowledge that wars generate prosperity. Some individuals profit from them. History indicates that some rulers have actually precipitated wars in order to save their countries from depressions. Every domestic crisis is basically economic, you know, and America hasn't yet fully recovered from the Panic of Fifty-seven. Slavery is not the fundamental issue here, it's merely a convenient scapegoat. But it'll satisfy the crusaders' cause while serving the interests of commercialism. Fortunes will be made by men shrewd enough to take advantage of it."

"I'm thinking," Jacintha said quietly, "of the men who will die, or be maimed."

"A noble thought, but surely you realize that Mr. Danvers will never see a battlefield!"

Jacintha blushed, and Laurette gave a short, throaty laugh. "You should see your face, darling! You look as guilty as a schoolgirl caught kissing her sweetheart in the cloakroom. Can it be that the naive little Village maid has adopted that old Continental custom?"

"What old custom?"

"Why, a *mariage de convenance,* as the French call it. Take a wealthy husband, usually old and unattractive, for security—and compensate for his physical shortcomings with a handsome young lover. The practice is fairly popular in America, too—though our conventional wives are more cautious. Or perhaps just more hypocritical. What do you think, dear?"

"I wouldn't know," Jacintha murmured, disturbed by the barbed insinuations.

"Never given it any thought?" Laurette persisted.

"No—why should I?"

"Because I've seen your husband, Jacintha, and am aware of your former financial straits. I find it hard to believe that love motivated your marriage. Nevertheless, I think you made a wise bargain. Cole Danvers is a clever and ambitious man, determined to get what he wants from life. He will prosper greatly from this war, believe me. So could my husband, but Earl lacks Cole's ambition, and is rather exasperatingly patriotic—gallant enough even to enlist. You're a lucky lady, Jacintha. Count your blessings."

Jacintha had difficulty controlling her temper. This was Earl's wife making these incredible statements, lamenting his patriotism and integrity while admiring the lack of those attributes in other men. Suddenly she felt very sorry for Earl, married to someone who apparently neither loved nor respected him. Indeed, Laurette seemed to consider Earl a fool. Once Jacintha had envied Laurette Britton for her beauty and sophistication. Now she despised the woman.

"Mr. Danvers would be flattered to hear you speak so favorably of him," she said. "I must convey your sentiments, although I don't share them."

Laurette's oval eyes narrowed to jade slits. "I don't know whether you're being naive or sanctimonious, Jacintha. But the sweet-innocence bait that failed in your trap for Larry Britton obviously worked on old King Cole! I assume you know that a cunning Carolina spinster snared the poor boy?" she inquired without waiting for an answer. "Charity prevents an accurate description of his thirty-year-old bride," Laurette declared, adding five years to her sister-in-law's age. "Suffice it to say that homeliness is one of her virtues."

Jacintha missed the last snide remark, distracted by a familiar mounted figure slowly clearing a path toward them. Her heart raced wildly, and she tucked her nervous hands under her reticule.

"Why, there's Earl! And *à cheval,* as usual." Laurette hailed him casually, lifting a gloved hand. "Hi, Cavalier!"

Earl dismounted and tossed his reins to the coachman. "Hello, ladies." His bland smile was directed at Jacintha. "Fancy meeting you two together!"

"Oh, we didn't start out that way," his wife assured him. "It just developed."

"Caught in the traffic," Jacintha explained.

"Well, we don't need a crystal ball to predict the future now," Earl said musingly as the crowd scrambled for the bulletins dropped from the publishers' windows and passed them from hand to hand along Park Row and through Printing House Square.

"Jacintha is quite distressed about it," Laurette said mockingly, her claws unsheathed.

"Judging from the frenzy here, she's not alone."

"Is Wall Street excited?"

"The banks, brokers, and the Stock Exchange are all closed," he said.

"But they'll be open for business as usual tomorrow, and concentrating heavily on war materials. Will you invest in war materials, darling? No doubt Jacintha's husband will! I was just telling her what a fortunate match she made."

Earl ignored that, Jacintha averted her eyes, and Laurette assumed the role of protagonist in the tragic street drama. "Were you on your way to a recruiting station, dear? They're probably mushrooming all over town."

Hanging on his response, Jacintha could not mask her emotions, which spoke more eloquently to Laurette than words. Laurette glanced at Earl warily, seeking similar clues in his face. But he seemed impassive, his gaze remote. He appeared intensely preoccupied, isolated in one of the somber moods that so often possessed him. Laurette wondered if it was unrequited love on Jacintha's part. A ward's affection for her older guardian? A romantic girlhood crush? The poor little ninny!

Laurette laughed, snapping her fingers in the air. "Come out of your trance, Earl! And you too, Jacintha. It's not the end of the world, you know."

"It will be for some people," Jacintha said softly.

The horses were restive, snorting and neighing, frightened by the uproar. Police, mounted and on foot, were trying to move the traffic.

Earl opened the door, grasping his wife's arm insistently. "I'll help you to your carriage, Laurette."

"Don't bother," she snapped, stepping out. "I can take care of myself." And to Jacintha, smiling cynically: "It was nice seeing you again, my dear. You and Mr. Danvers must visit us sometime."

"Thank you," Jacintha replied, aware that Earl was watching her reaction.

"Are you all right?" he asked as Laurette departed, using her parasol like a sword against any obstacle in her path.

"I think so, Earl. What will happen now?"

He shrugged. "God knows, Jacintha—but it can't be anything good. Do you want an escort home?"

"No, I'm sure Clancy can manage."

"You'd better leave, then, while you can."

Reclaiming his reins, Earl mounted Rocket and started off at a slow trot, turning once in the saddle to wave at Jacintha.

"He's right," the coachman agreed, trying to calm the pawing team. "Can't tell what a mob like this might do."

"Drive on," Jacintha told him. "Take me home."

"Fast as I can, ma'am."

Jacintha alighted from the carriage, dabbing at her eyes. War had come. She was resigned to Earl's enlisting; but she could not think beyond that point, lest she go to pieces. She let herself into the house, wanting to be alone.

"Come here, sugar!" Cole called drunkenly from the library. "You've heard about Fort Sumter?"

She nodded, moving hesitantly into the room. "I've just come from Printing House Square. The town's going mad."

"But why have you been crying? Ah, my poor little poppet! Save your tears—I won't be toting a gun. And this isn't a sad occasion for us, Mrs. Danvers. *We've* nothing to lose and everything to gain."

"You're drunk, Cole."

"If so, I'm not the only one today. Men react to war in many different ways, but three are most common. I'll wager the saloons, casinos, and whorehouses are packed with customers."

"Which means more business in your Bowery establishments, doesn't it? More tainted money in your tills! You have the Midas touch, Cole."

He grinned. "I've also got foresight. Have some wine, and we'll celebrate together. Madeira or sherry?"

"Neither," Jacintha declined. "I won't drink to war, Cole, or to your prospering from it."

"What's chewing at you, woman? Don't you realize what this means to us? We'll be richer than I ever dreamed!

Soldiers must have uniforms, boots, blankets, and tents. And these things don't grow in gardens! I'll build an empire that will make me a powerful man in this country as long as I live, and my sons and grandsons after me—if we ever have any!"

"That's up to God," Jacintha said, tired of being blamed for their childlessness, "and maybe He has His reasons—"

"Well, never mind that now. There's time. Just don't act as if being a millionaire's wife offends you. You would never have married me if I were poor, and you damned well know it!" He sloshed rye whiskey into a hobnail tumbler, spilling it over the cellaret and staining the Persian carpet. "Don't sit in judgment, madam! Where would you and your precious Riverview be without my gold?" He was shouting now.

"It's the war I object to, Cole, not wealth."

How right Laurette was about Cole! Was it a case of bitch understanding bastard?

"I met Mrs. Britton in town today, and she invited us to call sometime."

Cole smiled, humor restored. "Smart lady, knows a smart fellow when she meets one."

Never had she felt greater repugnance toward him. She turned away, untying her bonnet as she crossed the foyer. In the master suite she put the wilted violets on her dressing table and was pondering them sadly when Cole flung open the door. One glance in the mirror at his face revealed his intentions. Oh, Lord, why had she come home!

"I'm not feeling well," she said, dissembling.

"Excuses, excuses! What is it this time? Another headache? The vapors? Female complaint? Don't tell me you're wearing the rag again, because that was last week, and I'll accept only one period per month. Goddamn it, Jacintha, we'll never have a kid at this rate!"

Swinging her off her feet in arms of steel, he dropped her on the bed and began disrobing. "Get undressed!"

Jacintha leaped up and ran toward the portal, impeded by her wide hoops. Cole caught her before she reached it. His mouth smashed down on hers, and his rough hands

abused her body. In her panic, she became irrational, crying and screaming, hammering her fists furiously on his
chest. But it was like attacking a stone wall, and only
bruised her own flesh.

"Let me go, Cole!" She struggled fiercely against his
embrace, determined not to submit again. "Let me go or
I'll kill you!"

The threat made him laugh, and her violent protests
served only to stimulate him. He kissed her again, harder
and deeper, deliberately hurting her. Jacintha retched at
the salty-acid taste of him, but the desire to bite him was
curbed by fear. Wild with rage and frustration, she cursed
and clawed at him, trying to thrust her knee into his groin,
but it was hopeless.

"So I've got a red-hot little rebel in my own house, eh?
Well, then—we'll have our own private war, Mrs. Danvers.
And we shall see who wins, Puss. We shall see who wins!"

Chapter 21

LAURETTE was pacing her bedroom carpet, indignant over her husband's news. Although she had complained about his patriotism, she had not really expected him to volunteer.

"Have you taken leave of your senses?" she demanded furiously. "Why did you do it, Earl, and without even consulting me?"

In her self-absorption, she had not heard a word of his explanations, all of which he now repeated. "There are fewer than thirteen thousand troops in the Regular Army, Laurette. Most of them are scattered over the Far West, dealing with the Indians. The frontier posts have priority on the infantry and cavalry, and the coastal fortifications have priority on the artillery. The attack on Fort Sumter could not have succeeded if the fort had been sufficiently manned. The National Guard units are neither up to regimental strength nor properly trained. There has been no serious recruitment since the Mexican War! The situation is critical."

"But that's the government's fault, not the people's! And it needn't affect us."

"Listen to me, goddamn it! The Union is desperate for officers. Every cadet graduated from West Point could not begin to fill the need. A great many men will have to be commissioned from the ranks and volunteers, to command the seventy-five thousand militia Lincoln has requested. Evidently the bald heads in Congress were caught napping, concentrating on civilizing the savage West, when all along the real threat was from the genteel South. Beauregard fires a shot, takes over a fort, and we are unable to defend ourselves, much less force him out! The President is calling for help, and—"

"You're a banker, Earl, not a soldier. You've had no military experience. How can you fit in?"

"Every able-bodied man is necessary. He need only learn the contents of a manual of arms and indicate a preference for a branch of the service. If he can handle a horse, a pistol, and sword, he's prime officer material for the cavalry. Colonel Forbes offered me a captaincy, and I accepted it."

"In the cavalry? Good grief! The Navy would have been more appropriate for a yachtsman. And with your knowledge of economics and your political connections, you could ride out this mess at a desk in the Treasury Department."

"If I wanted to do that, Laurette, I would remain in my office on Wall Street."

"As you should! And you should have discussed it with me. I'm your wife, Earl, for better or worse, and not anxious to be a widow. You're not free to dash off to high adventure like some swashbuckling figure. You have responsibilities."

"You'll manage, Laurette. There'll be many other women in the same circumstances, you know."

"Not among our acquaintances! Few men in your position behave so rashly. I don't understand you, Earl, but I think there's more to this than patriotism. Is it that unfortunate episode of mine with Larry?"

His hand made an angry silencing gesture. "Let's not discuss that, Laurette!"

"But it is the reason for your foul moods and this foolish decision, isn't it? I've admitted my wrong and asked forgiveness. Should I recite my mea culpa on my knees? Or perhaps you'd prefer to have me branded and stoned in the streets?"

Earl scowled darkly, flexing his hands. "Just stop talking about you and Larry."

"Why, when you're going out to fight him? You know his allegiance is to the South. Is this how you plan to avenge your honor, in a mass duel?"

"I bear my brother no ill will, Laurette. He was simply your pawn. I blame you entirely. And that has nothing to do with my decision to fight."

Laurette tried harder persuasion. "What about your mother? Does she deserve the agony of having her sons become mortal enemies on the battlefield? It may very well kill her."

"She won't know," he said gravely. "The mails will be cut off, eventually."

"I'll tell her."

"You do, and I'll break your neck," he growled ominously.

But he had already taken precautions to prevent his family from knowing the truth. A correspondence plan had been arranged through Uncle Peter, whereby Earl would send letters to New York from his location, to be forwarded to Charleston in envelopes previously addressed in his own hand, for however long the postal service between the Union and Confederacy continued.

"I believe you wish to die," Laurette surmised. "You want to see action, and you intend to challenge fate."

"I intend to serve my country to the best of my ability."

"Meanwhile deserting your wife. You must still love me, Earl, to be so vengeful."

"You flatter yourself, Laurette. I care nothing whatever for you now, and in my absence, you may do as you wish. Take a lover, if you like. You'll need an escort, and no doubt some of my best friends would be happy to oblige you. Do as you please, madam, for I shall do the same."

"Haven't you always?"

"Not always, no."

There was a pause, and then she blurted, "Am I wrong in suspecting something between you and Jacintha Howard?"

"Why is it a wife always seeks to blame another woman for her own failures?"

"You expect me to believe your interest in her is purely platonic?"

He frowned, angry and embarrassed. "Believe what you like, madam. You will anyway."

"I see the look in your eyes. And I watched her closely, that day in Park Row, when I mentioned the military. Surely you realize she's in love with you. Is that the real reason for your going to war? Because she belongs to someone else?"

"I refuse to discuss this, Laurette." Pacing, he changed the subject abruptly. "Uncle Peter will be in charge of the bank and my monetary affairs while I'm away. Your household and personal allowances will come through him."

"Oh, Earl, won't you reconsider, please? Now that we've reached this stage, I'm afraid our separation will be permanent. And despite what you may think, I don't want it that way."

"That's too bad, my dear, because that's how it is. I'm sorry."

An angry gesture halted her approach. "It's over for us, Laurette. Why not accept the fact with as much dignity as possible?"

"Very well, Earl," she sighed. But it was only a temporary resignation.

In less than a month Captain Earl Britton would leave for Washington to join forces being hastily organized under General Irvin McDowell into the Army of the Potomac, to aid in the defense of the Capital. Bank business occupied Earl's days, and social obligations took all his evenings. It seemed that he would not have an hour to

182 • *Patricia Gallagher*

spare for the one farewell that mattered, and that had begun to obsess him. Finally he contrived to arrive when the master of Riverview was least likely to be at home.

In the afternoon sun, the garnet bricks reflected an odd crimson glow, like fire, and the tall smoke-blackened chimneys were etched darkly against the sky. Earl contemplated the strangely illuminated house for several minutes, wondering if he would ever see it again.

A gardener told him that Mrs. Danvers had strolled toward the river. Earl followed the garden path, pausing some distance from the spot where Jacintha sat gazing into the distance.

A ferry tooted on its way to Hoboken. Passenger steamers, crowded to capacity, plied upstream and down. Freight boats and barges arrived continuously via the Erie Canal. New York was the busiest port on the Atlantic Coast, its rivers and harbor jammed with foreign and domestic trading ships, and now with war vessels too. Like Commodore Vanderbilt, Earl Britton had offered his large steam yacht to the government, and the *Lorelei* was currently being converted into a gunboat at the Brooklyn Navy Yard.

The donation had infuriated his wife, who raged, "More insanity! The *Lorelei* will be ruined or sunk. We'll never see that beautiful yacht again!"

"Your family can easily replace it, Laurette. They are shipbuilders, after all."

"For the Lancasters, not the Brittons! You constantly amaze me, Earl. I think you must be utterly mad, to do the things you do!"

Earl sighed and brought himself back to the present.

"Jacintha," he called softly.

Was her imagination playing tricks on her? She glanced cautiously around and saw him beside a shirred boxwood tree. He was in blue cavalry uniform, and Jacintha thought he must surely be the handsomest officer in the Union Army.

As she approached him, restraining the urge to run, he swept off his black felt hat, with the cavalry insignia of crossed sabers on the crown, and placed it on the hedge. "I have a bad habit of sneaking up on you," he said apologetically. "Did I frighten you?"

"Oh, no," she assured him, smiling. "Well, maybe a little. How fine you look, Captain Britton!"

"I couldn't leave without saying goodbye, Jacintha."

"I—I didn't think it would be so soon . . ."

"I didn't either, actually. I've had only a few briefings at the Armory, along with scores of other commissioned civilians. But the emergency demands extreme measures. Troops are being shipped South as rapidly as possible, many without any training whatever. We hope they'll get some training in camp, with seasoned units, before they have to fight."

"Is your destination a secret?"

"Not at all. Every platoon, no matter how small or poorly equipped, is dispatched with some fanfare. Did you see the grand parade of the Seventh Regiment down Broadway as they embarked for Washington?"

"I read about it," she said. "The editors compared it to a Roman holiday."

"Well, our departure won't be so spectacular, but we're headed in the same direction."

"It's what you want to do, isn't it? What every man wants to do?" No, not *every* man, she thought.

"Somebody has to fight, Jacintha. You can't wage war without warriors."

"How does your wife feel about it?"

"Like most wives, I suppose."

"I'm sure you'll be a good soldier, Earl."

"I hope so, Jacintha." He put his hands lightly on her shoulders and gazed into her eyes. "Do you know, my dear, that it's customary to kiss a soldier who's going off to battle?"

"It is?" she whispered hoarsely. Was the ardor in his eyes only the reflection of her own passionate desire?

"It's supposed to bring the departing warrior good luck."

"Oh," she murmured, suspecting that he was teasing her again. "Well . . . I wish you luck, Captain. And Godspeed."

They stood, almost touching; so close, their breaths mingled. The scent of her cologne surrounded him, and she could smell his spicy shaving lotion, the tobacco smoke on his clothes, the leather of his boots and scabbard. Then, in a motion so sudden it took both by surprise, Jacintha was in his arms. He held her tightly for a few silent moments. It was all too brief, and unbearably sweet. He did not kiss her. She felt his body tense, his muscles harden and quiver, before he abruptly released her.

"Maybe we'd better dispense with the good luck token."

"Why?" she asked, feeling cheated.

"I think you know why. I can't fool with you, Jacintha. Oh, hell! Why did I come here and subject myself to this torture?" He abruptly donned his hat, giving the brim a sharp snap. "Goodbye, Jacintha."

Don't cry, she commanded herself, or tell him what you feel. The last thing he needs now are tears and a confession of love.

She even managed a cheerful smile. "Be careful, Earl. Don't take too many risks, and try not to whip the Rebels all by yourself." She wanted to ask him to write but did not dare.

Still he hesitated, reluctant to leave, his towering stature dwarfing her. A shadow fell across them, an omen that would later haunt Jacintha. "Little Curly Locks," he murmured gently. "God bless and keep you."

Very quickly then, he bent and kissed her cheek, so lightly and tenderly that she barely felt his lips. Then he was walking out of her garden, the spurs on his varnished boots jingling faintly, his silver-sheathed sword glinting in the rays of the setting sun. Moments later Jacintha heard the metallic clatter of his mount's hoofs on the cobblestones, the sound echoing, fading, then dying.

Goodbye, darling. *My heart, my love, my life.*

Chapter 22

LAURETTE BRITTON went into war work with the same élan with which she always took up any new fashion. She soon had positions of authority in both the Ladies Relief Union and the Ladies Army Aid Association.

Mayor Fernando Wood invited her to share the rostrum with him and some other city fathers at a Citizens' League meeting in Union Square, where her excellent speech in behalf of the cause received as much applause as any male speaker's.

"Congratulations, Mrs. Britton," he said as Laurette returned to her seat beside him on the bunting-draped platform. "You seem to have captured the audience faster than some of our blustery patriots. And why not? Such beauty, grace, and fervor would inspire the hardest-hearted! With you on his side, a politician could hardly lose an election. What an effective campaigner you would make!"

Laurette smiled. "I didn't think squaws were permitted in the Tammany wigwam, sir."

"They're not, madam. But some do work quite effectively behind the scenes. All the sachems like to point to their wives with pride. There's something suspicious about a bachelor politician."

"Indeed? William Buchanan managed to be elected president without a wife. His lovely young niece, Harriet Lane, was his official hostess throughout his term in the White House, and in London when he was minister to Great Britain."

"Ah, but he was not renominated for the office, was he? Now, if he'd had a beautiful and brilliant wife like you—"

"I'm flattered, your Honor. But my husband has never had political ambitions. He is also a Republican, you know. And so is my father, Robert Lancaster of Philadelphia."

"I know, dear lady. And I think our next mayor is going to be a Republican espoused by Mr. Tweed. Mrs. Wood and I are entertaining the Tweeds and some other friends at dinner next week, and we would be honored if you would come. You will, of course, receive a formal invitation."

"Thank you, sir. I hope I can accept." Did this turncoat chameleon, who changed his party colors to suit the political climate, expect her to charm him back into Tammany's favor, or to employ her family's Washington connections in his interests? Fool! She had more fascinating personal uses for her powers of persuasion....

Laurette enjoyed the new attention focused on her in the press, where her name now appeared in other than the social pages. Articles extolling her patriotism were excitingly captioned: LINCOLN'S LADY GENERAL; SOLDIER WITHOUT A RIFLE: CAPTAIN OF THE HOME FRONT. Thomas Nast, the brilliant young cartoonist, caricatured her without employing his usual caustic satire. Harriet Beecher Stowe was said to be writing a novel, with Mrs. Britton as the heroine. Susan B. Anthony, Elizabeth Cady Stanton, Lucretia Mott, and the Grimke sisters implored her to join the women's suffrage movement. *Godey's Lady's Book* asked her to write a column for the magazine.

Rumors circulated that Longfellow and Whittier were composing odes to her, that Bronson Howard was writing a play about her, that Thomas Sully and John Neagle were clamoring to paint her portrait, and that President Lincoln himself had invited her to the White House to receive a personal commendation.

Laurette neither confirmed nor denied the rumors, having instigated most of them herself, in the hope that they would materialize.

She wrote to Earl, enclosing clippings about herself, although the Northern journals were available in Washington and he must surely by now be aware of her fame and glory. Earl did not seem much impressed, however. Indeed, he insinuated that vanity and self-interest inspired her zeal. Furious with him, Laurette did not write again for over a month, long after the Battle of Bull Run—and then she pettishly informed him that she was homesick for her family and would be visiting them frequently.

"A fine idea," Earl wrote back. "I'm sure some of your old beaux will be delighted to entertain you, particularly Cousin Norman."

It's Jacintha's fault! she thought furiously, crumpling the letter and tossing it away. Though Earl denied any serious interest in his former ward Laurette believed otherwise, and she sought ways to taunt and humiliate the younger woman whenever possible.

Jacintha was working five days a week at the Army Aid Association, whose members gathered in the great Quaker Meeting House, where the Quakeress Lucretia Mott often spoke on the evils of slavery. The immense hall was filled with long tables, stacked with bolts of muslin, flannel, and cheesecloth, spools of thread, boxes of needles and thimbles. Tearing and rolling bandages, scraping lint from the bins of cotton, and making hospital linens and garments occupied the volunteers for long, tedious hours. But Jacintha was glad to have a useful purpose, to feel that she was contributing at least in some small measure to the needs of the servicemen. She lived in constant fear for Earl's safety, having nothing to reassure her but the absence of his name on the newspaper casualty lists. And everyone knew the lists were not always accurate.

Busy keeping her place in the limelight, Laurette Britton seldom participated in the various organizations which she ostensibly supported—and never participated in the dull routine tasks. When she did appear, she was usually accompanied by a high-ranking political or military personage, including visiting senators and congressmen, a general or admiral, the Mayor, and occasionally even the Governor. Like an inspector-general, Laurette took note of work accomplished and delivered laudatory speeches, then hurried off.

Thus, to Jacintha's immense relief, her presence in the Quaker Meeting House escaped Laurette's attention for many months. Conservatively dressed, she sat inconspicuously in a corner, behind huge piles of cloth and cotton-batts. Once she remained in the cloakroom during Laurette's tour of the hall; another time she fled to the lounge. But an encounter was inevitable, and when it occurred at last, Laurette had the advantage.

"Why, Mrs. Danvers!" she cried, pausing beside the table where Jacintha was making cotton pledgets. "I didn't know you were among my home-front troops."

The possessive pronoun irritated Jacintha. "I've been working here since the Army Aid Association was organized," she said lightly, aware of her appearance, with lint flecking her dark hair and clothes.

"Really? How commendable!" A gloved hand patted Jacintha's shoulder. "But you look as if you've been in a snowstorm, dear!"

"We cotton pickers all look that way," Jacintha replied testily. "Most of the ladies prefer to roll bandages, sew, or pack emergency kits. Lint scrapers are in the minority."

"Well, we need every volunteer we can muster, to aid in any capacity whatever."

Except the queen bee, Jacintha thought resentfully, who never lifts a finger!

A young woman from a nearby table, whose husband was also in the Army of the Potomac, inquired if Mrs. Britton had heard from Captain Britton recently, and Jacintha listened anxiously for her response.

Removing a lacy kerchief from her chinchilla muff, Laurette touched her elongated green eyes delicately. "Not recently, but I trust he's all right." She shook her head and sighed. "Beyond our feminine contributions to the cause, what more can any woman do except hope and pray for the men's safety? They also serve who wait, you know."

The other woman nodded, thanked Laurette, and resumed her chores, fingering the rosary in her pocket.

Laurette peered down at Jacintha. "Perhaps you've had word from Earl lately?"

"No, he doesn't correspond with us, Laurette."

"Not even with Cole?"

"Why should he?"

"Well, you are friends, aren't you? And friends do communicate occasionally, don't they?"

"I imagine his military duties keep him occupied."

"Oh, I doubt he's that busy! The Army of the Potomac has been rather idle since the Manassas Creek disaster. The correspondents on the scene say the President was especially disappointed in the cavalry's performance," she added in a low tone intended only for Jacintha's ears. "Imagine their red faces when they were forced to retreat back across the river to the ramparts of Washington!"

"One battle won't decide the war," Jacintha said in quiet defense.

"It might, with the right commander," Laurette quipped, "and if some of our officers weren't so absorbed in other matters. According to the gossip columnists, they are the social lions of the Capital—much in demand at government functions and private parties. The hostesses supposedly vie over the handsome ones and use lovely young girls to lure them to their parties. In her newsletter to the *New York World*, Jenny June, who's not usually given to silly romanticizing, described Captain Earl Britton as 'a princely officer on a splendid white charger, lacking only a suit of armor to epitomize every maiden's dream of a perfect knight.' Pure treacle. I almost retched to read it."

"I thought his horse was black."

"Didn't you know? That satanic beast was shot out from

under him at Bull Run. Now Earl has a noble white Arabian steed named the Sheik of Araby. The Sheik was a gift from Philadelphia banker, Jay Cooke, whom we both know well."

"I trust Captain Britton wasn't injured in the battle?" Jacintha inquired, quivering inside.

"Bruised slightly when Rocket fell, but he was dancing at one of Kate Chase's famous candlelight balls the next week. Her honored guest, in fact, and appropriately so, since her father is secretary of the Treasury, and a friend of both our families. Miss Chase is very young and beautiful, admired by many gentlemen, including the President, and she especially admires men in uniform."

Jacintha blanched. "Entertainment is good for the soldiers' morale," she rationalized.

"Yes, indeed—and all male privileges apply during wartime. No doubt my cavalier is having his share of romantic adventures. Why not? He's male and mortal."

Confident that she had wounded, Laurette moved on, clasping outstretched hands along the aisles, pausing briefly to encourage, bestowing her gracious personality like a benediction.

The experience sent Jacintha to bed with a melancholia so debilitating that Cole thought she was finally with child, and summoned a physician.

"Just exhaustion"—was the doctor's diagnosis, dashing Cole's hopes—"complicated by a touch of grippe. Two to three weeks of rest, a nourishing diet, and herbal tonic will put her on her feet again, Mr. Danvers."

Jacintha was relieved but not surprised. She had begun to believe and hope that she was barren. She liked children, but she had no wish to bear them for a man whom she did not love and could not respect. Moreover, she feared that only a monster could be conceived during their monstrous matings.

While she was confined, pale and listless despite Dr. Selby's potent elixir and Lollie's expert nursing, the North celebrated its first major victory since the beginning of the war. Jacintha sat pensively in bed, a coral satin sacque over her nightgown, chilly despite the crackling logs on the hearth. She was surrounded by newspapers detailing General Ulysses S. Grant's spectacular capture of Fort Donnelson on the Cumberland River, which had followed by only nine days the fall of Fort Henry on the Tennessee. These were strong sister forts of the Confederacy, just nine miles apart.

New York went wild with joy. Plagued and sorrowed by failures and inactivity in the East, the Union would have celebrated any victory enthusiastically. A new star of hope had risen in the West, and General Grant was now a national hero.

Lollie, who had just returned from the apothecary with yet another prescription for her ailing mistress, excitedly described the jubilance. "Whee, it's bedlam out there! Like the Fourth of July and New Year's combined! Church bells ringing, factory and boat whistles blowing, rockets hissing!" Removing her snow-powdered hooded cloak, she spread it across a chair before the fireplace. "There's going to be a torchlight parade tonight. Oh, Missy, I think the war will soon be over!"

Cole, knotting a flamboyant cravat of East Indian silk before the bureau mirror, snorted scornfully. "Over? Because we've had a couple of piddling wins in the West, after all this time? It's in the East, by God, where we need some decisive action! I agree with Horace Greeley. The war will be won or lost in Virginia. Look there on the front page of the *Tribune*: ON TO RICHMOND! Grant's going in the wrong direction. But at least he's moving, which is more than can be said for General George McClellan. Lincoln might as well have left McDowell in command of the Army of the Potomac; they ain't lifted a boot to march, or straddled a horse to ride, since they turned tail at Bull Run and ran away in miserable defeat. Seven months now, they've been sitting around Washington, polishing the seats of their breeches!"

Jacintha cast him a contemptuous glance. The biggest cowards were invariably the bravest critics! "That Army may be keeping its operations secret."

Cole shrugged. "My business is terrific. The government obviously expects the war to last. The War Department is tossing out contracts like confetti. Their buyers purchase everything and inspect nothing. Worthless steamers, shoddy clothing, rotten blankets and tents, shoes with cardboard soles, guns that jam and powder that won't fire, food no better than swill. Small wonder that Congress is fixing to increase excise taxes and tax individual incomes. At the rate they're spending, the Treasury will soon be empty. Everybody else is getting a share; why shouldn't I?"

"Congress should first pass some stringent laws against war profiteering and speculation," Jacintha said musingly. "That would halt some of the graft and other corruption."

"Mind your mouth, Mrs. Danvers. Your loving spouse's speculations run the gamut, from food to gold, and I'm profiting handsomely. I'm now among the largest depositors at Britton Bank and The Bank of Boston."

"Do you ever think of anything but money, Cole?"

"On occasion, honey. Do you wish me to think of something else now?" He grinned at her petulant frown. "I thought not, so keep your pantalettes on, Puss. What're you pouting about today, anyway? Haven't I been a good husband lately? Gone a lot, maybe, but so were you before this illness, working so much at your charities, I could hardly keep track of my Good Samaritan. At least you know my whereabouts when I'm in town."

"Your Bowery establishments, I assume."

"Yeah, they're regular mints now," he boasted. "Especially the concert saloon, since I've added a star attraction."

"Mademoiselle LaFlame?"

"Who else? Roxy draws business like a magnet. The fellas flock around her like flies to honey. She's got a new act, and the boys in blue love it. Wears a costume made of flags and apologizes for the scantiness of the Stars and Stripes since secession. They cheer and beg for more of her dancing. Then she sings songs with 'em and takes a hundred bows every performance."

"That's disgusting, Cole! It's a desecration of the flag."

"It's all in fun, and we've had no complaints. Let the poor bastards enjoy themselves. Some won't be here long. I feel sorry for them. Youngsters, mostly, barely weaned. Some ain't even shaved yet, or had a woman, and might die before they're man enough for either one."

"So you show your compassion by watering their drinks, rooking them at the gaming tables, and debauching them with half-naked dancers?"

Cole scowled. He poured some heavily scented Macassar oil on his auburn hair, parted it in the middle, and combed two low loops on his broad forehead. Then he waxed his rust-colored mustache, which now drooped in the cavalier fashion sported by many cavalrymen. He began to croon in his faulty bass.

"Dearest one, do you remember when last we did
  meet?
You told me how you loved me, kneeling at my feet,
Oh, how proud you stood before me in your suit of
  blue,
When you vowed from me and country ne'er to go
  astray,
Weeping sad and lonely, sighs and tears how vain,
When this cruel war is over, pray that we meet
  again."

The song was terribly sad.

"Please," Jacintha pleaded, her eyes blurring, "don't sing that, Cole."

He donned a caped greatcoat and set a new black derby on his head at the rakish angle worn by the Bowery dandies and Tammany politicians. Picking up his fancy ebony cane and gray suede gloves, he stood, posturing fatuously, admiring his image in the cheval glass. Finally he crossed to the bed and bent to kiss his wife, but his mind was obviously elsewhere.

"I may not come home tonight," he said, his lips casually brushing her cheek. "You being sick and all, I don't want to disturb you. So take your medicine like a good little girl and have a nice rest."

It infuriated Jacintha to think that he considered her so naive. As if he cared about disturbing her! Jacintha longed to laugh in his face. She had never believed that their marriage had interrupted for very long his affair with Roxy LaFlame, if it had at all. Cole would spend this and any other night he wished in his lair above his concert saloon, with a companion who, Jacintha imagined, was well versed in the tricks of her trade.

But she felt only relief, even gratitude. She might have sent Roxy LaFlame a note of appreciation—for the more he copulated with his concubine, the fewer demands he made on his wife.

Moreover, submitting to Cole, however reluctantly, had begun to seem like infidelity to her true love.

Chapter 23

DREADING future encounters with Laurette Britton, in which she might not be able to control herself, Jacintha did not return to the Army Aid. But once she had recuperated enough to do more than trail forlornly about the house, getting in the way of the servants, she knew she must find some useful occupation.

She and Lollie set up a temporary workshop at Riverview, preparing supplies for the Medical Depot of Cooper Union. But the difficulty that individuals had in obtaining these vital materials, on which the large organizations had priority, soon forced them to discontinue their small operation. Next they tried collecting clothing, bedding, shoes, and cash donations for Clinton Hall to distribute to the needy families of servicemen. But this too was unsuccessful, for most citizens preferred to contribute directly to established agencies.

The need for nurses and assistants was urgent, however, and Jacintha decided to offer her services to a hospital. Trainloads of wounded men arrived from the battlefronts after each new engagement, and the majority landed in the large Northern cities, which were best equipped to handle them. In New York, vacant warehouses, large old homes, and other buildings were converted into hospitals and receiving stations, and the cry for medical staffs echoed across the island.

Many women responded, but not all could qualify for service. Pregnancy and motherhood kept many young wives at home. Elderly matrons were often infirm. The intimate nature of a profession involving naked males discouraged many women. Jacintha was accepted readily, but the matron to whom she reported for preliminary instructions gazed at her skeptically. "I hope you'll be strong enough to bear up, Mrs. Danvers. You look rather frail. Have you been ill?"

"I had a lingering case of influenza, Mrs. Timmons. But I'm completely recovered now—and anxious to serve."

"Bless you, my dear, and welcome. You may either furnish your own uniform or wear a simple cotton dress and an apron, a cap on your head, if you wish, and comfortable walking shoes. I recommend canvas slippers or Scotch brogans. We'll train you as best we can, but time doesn't allow for a probation period. You'll be given immediate duty. Report to me tomorrow morning at seven o'clock. That's all for now, Mrs. Danvers. Thank you. And good luck."

After her first month on the wards, Jacintha knew that this was back-breaking work. These workers received no glory, and unlike bandage-rolling, the labor provided no chance for camaraderie. But Jacintha welcomed the anonymity of nursing. Her emotions were too sensitive to share with anyone but Lollie.

Decisive victories at Nashville, Shiloh, New Orleans, and Memphis were enthusiastically celebrated in New York. But the roaring noises and the cannon salvos fired from the harbor forts and the Brooklyn Navy Yard often drove the shell-shocked patients into hysteria. Frequently Jacintha had to have assistance in restraining some raving soldier whose mind had been left on the battlefield.

"Jesus!" yelled one artillery sergeant, leaping off his cot and diving under it. "That was close! The sons of bitches got our position spotted. They're homing in. Git in them trenches, men! Don't just stand there gaping, you stupid fools! Hit the pits before you git your goddamn heads blowed off!"

While Jacintha was trying to coax him from his shelter with soothing assurances, a cavalryman went berserk, straddled a broom, and galloped wildly through the aisles, wielding an imaginary saber and commanding, "Charge, charge! Run the bastards through the belly! Trample their guts out! Charge, charge! Oh, shit, they done shot my mount in the ass—and we're goin' down!"

Later that same day, Jacintha was summoned to assist a surgeon in the amputation of a gangrenous leg. It was her first such experience, and though she managed to function during the crucial procedure, she fainted immediately afterwards. Impatient with the delay, the doctor revived her with spirits of ammonia and bluntly inquired if she were menstruating. Jacintha nodded, embarrassed.

"Why didn't you say so? I'd have gotten someone else. Although it's a mystery to me why the sight of blood should affect a woman accustomed to the menses since puberty! Go back to the wards, Mrs. Danvers, and tell the head nurse to send me an experienced assistant for the next surgery, which is due in ten minutes."

That evening Jacintha collapsed on the bed in exhaustion and slumbered deeply. But even in sleep, she could hear the horrible grating of the saw severing the bone, smell the rotting flesh, hear the victim's desperate pleas to spare his leg and let him die in one piece, and see his agony, which could not be totally alleviated by anodynes. Then the ghastly dream became a nightmare, for the man strapped helplessly to the table was Earl Britton. It was his terrible suffering she witnessed, his pitiful supplications she heard, his mortified leg that dropped into the bloody tub.

She woke in a cold sweat, her pillow sodden, her body shaking so violently that her teeth rattled. A glimpse of her bloodstained uniform in the morning sickened her again, but she ignored Lollie's suggestion to stay at home.

"I'll get used to it," she said doggedly.

"But you know Mr. Danvers has forbidden you to do any more war work, much less nursing!"

"I don't care about his orders! Besides, he won't know. He's gone most of the time."

In July, Confederate actions in the East dimmed the bright hopes recently created in the West. The Army of the Potomac was bogged down in the marshlands of the James peninsula! As returning soldiers apprised relatives of what had happened, the demoralizing facts had to be published. Numerous futile skirmishes and stupid strategic blunders by leaders had resulted in the disastrous Seven Days Battle, in which the formidable combination of Robert E. Lee and Stonewall Jackson had solidly checked the Union offensive within sight of Richmond.

Public opinion was like a weathervane, and now the wind from the East blew ill. General George McClellan's monumental defeats in Virginia eclipsed Grant's victories in the West. Gloom pervaded the North again.

When not on duty at the hospital, Jacintha was waiting with the curious, anxious crowds in Printing House Square for the latest bulletins and casualty lists. She lived in constant suspense, alternating between hope and despair. There was no certainty of any fighting man's fate—especially not when the losses were as staggering as those of the Army of the Potomac. Captain Britton might be wounded, dead, missing, or captured. The propaganda printed about Richmond's Libby Prison, which was used primarily to incarcerate Union officers, sent cold shivers up her spine, for the men were said to be systematically tortured to reveal military information. And God help any prisoner in Georgia's infamous Andersonville!

Had he been less involved in his own affairs, Cole might have noticed his wife's failing health. Her eyes were often darkly shadowed from lack of sleep and puffed from secret tears. She had dreadful premonitions, and the horrible nightmare kept recurring. Her once radiant complexion was so pallid now that subtle applications of rouge were necessary to keep her husband from suspecting anything was wrong. She camouflaged her weight loss with broader hoops and more stiffly starched petticoats.

Lollie prepared herb tonics and tisanes from the formulas in the old family pharmacopoeia. But she knew there was only one real cure for what ailed her mistress—and that cure was impossible to obtain.

After the Second Battle of Bull Run, at the end of August, the superintendent of the hospital assembled the nursing staff for a highly important announcement.

"Ladies, I have just received a very disturbing communiqué from the Surgeon General! As you know, Washington has been the principal receiving station for the casualties of the Army of the Potomac. But this new and calamitous defeat at Manassas Junction has changed that, at least temporarily.

"The capital's hospitals are packed, and the excess is overflowing into government buildings. The Patent Office, Capitol chambers, Georgetown College, and even some private residences are now in use. Convalescents must surrender their cots to the litter cases. The absolute limit has been reached, and they must now turn away all but the most critically wounded. We can expect our quota to be greatly increased, even if our facilities are not. Naturally, this means more work and longer hours for everyone. Be advised and prepared," he concluded.

The ladies looked at one another in wordless wonder. More work? Longer hours? How was it possible for them to do more without collapsing?

Summer passed in a blaze of white heat and red fury on the battlefronts, and the ambulances meeting the trains and ships brought in the grisly evidence of Confederate might and determination.

Jacintha dreaded going into town these days. She heard so many dire predictions and saw such pathetic sights everywhere. Young veterans thumped along the streets on wooden pegs and navigated precariously on new crutches.

Empty coat-sleeves, arms in slings or stumped at the wrists, black-patched eyes, disfigured faces—the legions were returning, and still peace was a remote mirage on the horizon. Already some indigent heroes, wearing ragged blue uniforms and caps, had turned to peddling notions or begging for handouts on Broadway.

To brighten the depressing wards of the dismal brown brick building near Tompkins Square, Jacintha often arrived with bouquets from Riverview's gardens. This morning she carried a variety of brilliant blooms. It was truly touching how sentimental a lonely man could become over a simple flower. A rose or lily or daisy might remind him of his mother, wife, sister, sweetheart—and then he would want to write a letter home, or speak with a chaplain, if the loved one were dead.

"Thank heaven you're here, Mrs. Danvers!" an aide greeted her in the lobby. "We've just been notified by the New Jersey depot that the Antietam casualties are arriving. They are being ferried across the Hudson now, and the ambulances will be delivering some of them here soon. I don't know where we're going to put them, or how we'll care for them! But Philadelphia and Trenton couldn't accept any more, and sent the trains from Maryland on to New York and Boston. Some of those poor fellows have been traveling for days, which means a lot of gangrene and amputations. . . ."

Jacintha gazed at her in dismay. She should be accustomed to such news by now, but she knew she would never get used to the abominations of war—the slaughter and maiming, or the realization that Earl Britton might be one of them.

"I'll do what I can," she promised. "If only it weren't so warm! Wounds fester so easily in hot weather. And if only we had some screens on the windows and doors! The insects annoy the patients cruelly."

Within an hour, official ambulances and donated conveyances were hauling in some of the victims of the carnage at South Mountain and Antietam Creek. The call for more cots had not been answered, and many men were placed on the bare floor, without even a blanket under them. All space was exhausted and the authorities bolted the doors and refused to admit any more.

Jacintha and the other attendants moved among the fallen men, trying to locate the most critical cases. Those with severe wounds in vital organs were considered hopeless, given large doses of morphia to ease their suffering, and left to the ministers of the gospel.

The battle had been fought on the seventeenth of September, almost a week before, and many of the wounds had not been re-dressed since the field medics had tended them. Infection was rampant. The greenish-black tinge of gangrene meant immediate amputation of any injured limb or certain death. The surgery soon resembled a butcher shop, strewn with parts of the human anatomy.

Jacintha was dashing back and forth with pitchers of cool water to quench dry throats, with basins of warm water for cleansing, when a feeble hand tugged at her skirts and she heard a hoarse whisper.

"Help me, please . . ."

She paused and gazed down at the figure at her feet. His head was swathed in blood-caked bandages concealing all but his eyes, swollen shut, and his grimly clenched mouth. His right arm was in a crude splint and she saw evidence of infection. His immobility suggested an injured spine or some other form of paralysis. But something in his voice, although distorted with pain, penetrated to Jacintha through all the noise and confusion, and her heart skipped a beat. Could it be? Oh, no! Please, God, no!

She set the vessel down and knelt beside him. Even lying down, his tall, broad-shouldered physique was impressive. He was built like Earl, and wore a cavalry uniform with a major's insignia. Very carefully her fingers pried open his eyes. They were glazed with fever and not focusing properly, but were the color of Earl's eyes. The mouth was also similar. Jacintha searched for his identification papers but could not find any. Lost credentials accounted for a great many men being placed in the "missing" category.

His heartbeat and pulse were strong, but he was burning

with fever. Bending close to his ear, Jacintha inquired, "Can you hear me, Major? What is your name? Tell me your name, sir. State your name and rank, please!"

"Britton," he murmured. "Major Earl Brit—" His voice faded away.

Jacintha gasped, and stifled a scream. Her nightmare was coming true!

Just then a surgeon in a blood-spattered white smock appeared in the doorway.

"Attention, staff and aides! The mortality rate in cases of severe infection is too high to warrant delay by standard methods of treatment. Therefore we will proceed to amputate all infected limbs, whether gangrenous or not. We shall begin with wards One and Two. Barring additional complications, we should reach this one tomorrow. That's all for now. Resume your duties, please, and properly identify all patients scheduled for surgery."

Horror filled Jacintha. Earl's right arm to come off? Earl to lie on that terrible slab, writhing and pleading? His arm to be dumped in a basket with other bloody stubs and stumps, and carted off somewhere for anonymous disposal? No, they couldn't do that to him! There was no evidence yet of gangrene in his flesh. It was swollen and bruised—infected but not putrefying. She would not allow him to be permanently maimed as a mere precautionary measure!

She had to think quickly. Fortunately the surgeons were not starting in this section, and could not possibly reach it before dawn, at the earliest. Thank God for his lost papers! His name was not listed on the receiving records. He would be tagged "unknown," and, if she moved him, he would not be missed.

Jacintha covered him to the neck with a sheet and hovered nearby to prevent transfer. She was off duty at seven o'clock this evening. She had until then to make her plans.

Chapter 24

THE owner of the livery stable scratched his head and picked his teeth with a straw. "Let me see if I understand. You want to rent a horse and small wagon, and you need a couple of men to get a soldier out of a hospital?"

"That's right. I can borrow a stretcher from the supply room. I work there."

"Where?"

"In the hospital on Tompkins Square. It's that old brown brick building that used to be a warehouse."

"Yeah, I know the one. The fella ain't dead, is he? We don't snatch bodies or rob graves. Stealing cadavers is too goddamn risky."

"I merely want to transfer this patient to another location," Jacintha explained, "so he can receive better care. I'll pay forty dollars for your services, plus the rental fee and deposit. But we have to wait until four o'clock tomorrow morning."

"How come?" he inquired suspiciously.

"Rules and regulations, sir. The nursing shifts change at seven A.M., and I want to be in and out before then. Naturally we have to be quiet and cautious, so as not to disturb the other patients in his ward. This lady"—she indicated Lollie—"will be waiting for us outside in the wagon. That's all you have to do. The horse and wagon will be returned to you later. Do you agree?"

He consulted his stablehand. "How about it, Joe?"

"For that much cash, I'd carry Abe Lincoln out of the White House and set him on General Lee's horse."

"This won't be nearly that dangerous," Jacintha told him. "It's not a crime. I'm merely trying to save a soldier's arm—and possibly his life."

"Must be somebody mighty important to you. Your husband, brother, sweetheart?"

Jacintha did not satisfy his curiosity. "Be expecting us at three A.M. sharp. Good evening, sir."

The plan worked smoothly enough, except for a few precarious moments when Earl, delirious with fever, began to mumble in the dimly lit corridor leading to the rear exit. Hastily clamping a hand over his mouth, Jacintha urged the litter bearers to hurry, offering an extra ten dollars if they got him out safely. The bonus provided an effective incentive, and they moved as swiftly and steathily as thieves in the night.

Using the comforters and pillows they had brought along, Lollie had already prepared a bed in the wagon. Earl was placed on it and covered with a dark blanket.

Jacintha paid the men in crisp new greenbacks, now legal tender. Then she climbed onto the narrow plank seat and picked up the reins. The iron-rimmed wheels rumbled noisily through the quiet moonlit streets.

"I tell you," Lollie said worriedly, "if Mr. Danvers finds out, he'll take a whip to both of us."

"He won't find out, if we're careful. How much time has he spent at Riverview lately? He was in Massachusetts for two weeks last month, and when he's in New York he's either at the tannery, the clothing factory, or one of his Bowery establishments. He doesn't even know that I still work at the hospital, Lollie. Mr. Danvers has other matters on his mind. Between us, we can nurse Earl without anyone knowing."

The housekeeper was dubious. "Won't the staff wonder about our long absences from home?"

"Not if we take turns staying with the major, and alternate our days and nights. Oh, Lollie, you've simply got to help me!"

"But it's so risky, and he seems so badly hurt! His head is bound up like a mummy's. Was he shot there too?"

"Not seriously, or he'd be dead by now. Bad cranial injuries are almost always fatal. A bullet may only have grazed his skull. Maybe someone applied too much bandage."

"We're taking him to his own place?"

"Yes. The Britton country estate is in the Kip's Bay area, not far from Turtle Bay. I remember Greystone from my visits there with Grandpa, and I also have a map. We follow the thoroughfare north of Union Square toward Murray Hill, and then turn eastward. There'll be markers. We'll use the hunting lodge, which is more private. I think I can find it without too much trouble. It's almost dawn. We should be there in a few hours."

"A few hours! Child, he may be gone by then. His temperature is raging, and this jouncing crate won't help."

"The padding should provide some protection, and I'll drive slowly. You have the medical kit?"

"Yes, and some groceries I borrowed from the pantry, too. But I don't like it, Missy. He needs a doctor!"

"I told you how the Army surgeons treat these cases now, Lollie. Wholesale amputations! That's a last resort, and I refuse to consider it unless it's absolutely essential for saving his life. Dysentery or some other stomach ailment is more likely causing his fever than an infection in his arm. Most combat soldiers suffer from bowel troubles."

Once they left the city proper, the streets became narrow, rough, winding lanes. The wheels grated and lurched in the deep ruts. The spavined old mare plodded along. They passed a miserable colony of ragged tents and tarpaper shacks and pit toilets. Dogs barked, chickens cackled. Lollie kept one hand on the loaded pistol, expecting some desperate character to rush at them. She shook her head. "Two foolish women carting a sick man into the wilderness. It don't make sense."

"Would you suggest Riverview? It had to be some place private, and Greystone was all I could think of. I just hope it hasn't been leased for the duration. If so, we'll find a nice inn somewhere—and pretend he's my husband."

"What about his wife? If he's missing in action, won't the authorities notify her?"

Jacintha winced. "Eventually, yes. But notification will be delayed while the official medical and burial records are checked. It's a long, tedious process, even with proper identification, much less without it." After a silence, she spoke again. "Do you understand, Lollie? I've got to help him, no matter what the consequences. I—I care for him deeply."

"I know, honey. But you've kept it from him all these years. If he lives, it won't be a secret any longer. You realize that, don't you?"

"Yes, I realize it."

Lollie sighed. "Well, I reckon he has to find out sometime. Maybe God willed it."

"God could have chosen a better time and way," Jacintha said ruefully, slapping the reins across the animal's bony rump. "Is the major's face uncovered? Put a pillow under his head. It sounds like he's gasping for air."

"That ancient nag is what you hear heaving! Mr. Earl is breathing all right. Just watch where you're going."

They were approaching a moon-dappled thicket. A covey of grouse, disturbed in the brush, flew out with a terrifying flutter of wings, startling the horse and the women.

"Jesus mercy!" Lollie cried. "What was that?"

"Partridges, I think. We scared them."

"*We* scared *them?*"

Jacintha glanced up at the starry sky. "It should be getting light soon."

"It's fall. The nights are longer."

"I'm glad we brought a lantern along."

"And a gun," Lollie added, pulling her shawl closer about her shoulders as she hoisted the light higher.

Finally they came upon a farming area, with fields and meadows and several cottages. They heard the predawn sounds of domestic animals and saw scarecrows guarding the vegetable patches.

"We're coming to a crossroads, Lollie. We'll have to stop and read the signs. I think we're headed in the right direction. If not, we can ask a farmer. They are awake early."

"They're also suspicious of strangers, and we're two women toting a half-dead soldier."

Jacintha drew rein before a group of markers, reading them aloud. "There's the right way!" she cried jubilantly. "My memory didn't fail me."

Soon they entered a pleasant rural region of large country estates. Steep gabled roofs and towering chimneys were visible above the treetops. A glorious sunrise was breaking on the eastern horizon, beyond Long Island Sound, as they reached their destination.

Jacintha had no difficulty locating Greystone. The stone pillars flanking the arched gateway bore the family name. The hunting lodge seemed an ideal sanctuary, isolated in the woods.

"What is there to hunt here?" Lollie inquired.

"Nothing much now, except rabbits and birds. But Grandpa said there were deer, wild hogs, and other game on the island when Greystone was built."

"Do you have a key?"

"No, I'll have to break in through a window and unlock the door." On the ground now, Jacintha picked up a rock and smashed a window. "I hope there's water in the cistern. And wood, and cooking pots."

"This is trespassing, you know."

"I don't think the owner will press charges, Lollie."

Except for accumulated dust and the shattered window glass on the floor, the lodge was neat and comfortable. It consisted of two large rustically-paneled rooms with open-beamed ceilings and unique bronze lighting fixtures. The sturdy furniture included a double bed, stacked bunks, a captain's table and chairs, rugged sea-chests, and shelves of books. Bearskin rugs lay on the varnished board floors. A box of wood and tinder stood by the native-stone fireplace, and another in the handily-equipped kitchen, which featured a Franklin stove, water pump, and galvanized sink.

Somehow, with the strength born of necessity, they managed to lift Earl out of the wagon and carry him inside to the bed. While Lollie kindled a fire and put a kettle of water on the hearth crane to heat, Jacintha partially stripped the patient, working with the speed and facility she had learned at the hospital. She would have to invent some excuse for her absence from Tompkins Square, but right now Earl needed her as desperately as the other patients did. She would compensate later for the time she gave him.

Carefully, using surgical scissors, she cut away the arm bandage and observed the familiar round raw hole caused by a Minié ball. There was a slight infection, some pus and proud flesh, which were considered normal in such cases. The wound had been inexpertly cauterized with acid or a hot iron or both, and a permanent scar would result—but Jacintha was confident it would heal.

Hesitation accompanied her tender removal of the dirty, bloodstained head wrapping. She was afraid of finding a disfigured face or damaged eyesight. But, mercifully, Earl had been spared. There were some superficial lacerations on one cheek and a short gash in his neck, below his left ear. Either a Rebel sword had nicked him or he had fallen from his horse when the bullet struck. Jacintha cleansed the wound with warm water, hampered somewhat by a week's growth of beard, and then applied the standard medical remedies of diluted carbolic-acid solution and iodine.

Lollie asked, "Shall we bind up his head again?"

"No, some inexperienced field medic nearly smothered him in yards of unnecessary gauze. Patches on the throat and arm wounds will be fine."

It required several days and numerous concoctions of camomile, boneset, and mullein leaves to bring Earl's fever and intestinal ailments under control. When he was able to take light nourishment, they spoon-fed him broth, tea, custard, and soft-boiled eggs. But even before this stage, he had recognized his nurses and surroundings and asked questions, most of which were cleverly evaded.

"You're not well enough to talk yet, Major."

"Go back to sleep, sir."

"We'll tell you about it tomorrow."

Earl obeyed, dominated by his keepers and privately enjoying his confinement—the first decent rest he'd had in over a year. The admiration and gratitude with which his eyes followed Jacintha's every movement wrung her heart.

Finally the day came when he would no longer be eluded. Lollie had gone to the community market for supplies, and Earl seized the opportunity of being alone with Jacintha.

"I must look like a hermit," he began, tentatively rubbing his whiskers.

Jacintha was trying to repair his damaged uniform. She glanced at him, smiling. "You must be feeling much better, Major, if you're worrying about your appearance."

"Well enough"—he agreed—"to do some thinking. My memory is clear now. I remember just about everything, from the time the Minié ball hit me at Antietam and Johnny Reb's saber narrowly missed decapitating me while I lay on the ground with hundreds of other casualties. Quite a long time later, I was lying on a hard floor, among a lot of other soldiers and rushing women. I clutched at a passing skirt—and heard the voice of an angel. It was you, wasn't it?"

Jacintha nodded.

"And you and Lollie brought me here?"

"Yes—and I trust you still own Greystone. If not, we're poaching."

"It's still Britton property," he assured her. "I used to ride out here fairly often. But I never stayed at the manor. It's too large and formal for one person. I prefer these quarters."

"Well, you'll have to replace a broken window, Major. I had to break it to let us in."

"A small item," he said, gazing at her curiously. "Why did you go to so much trouble, Jacintha? Couldn't I have been treated at the hospital?"

"Probably, but—" She hesitated, lowering her eyes.

"Yes?" he prompted.

"You would have lost your arm, Earl. The surgeons were sawing off arms and legs even if they were only infected. There was no indication of gangrene in your arm, and I thought it could be saved. And it has been, too! It'll be good as ever before long."

"Thanks to you," he said, and the awed realization in his voice made Jacintha nervous.

"Were you in the James Peninsula Campaign?"

A grim, reflective nod. "God, what a debacle! Thousands of men killed and left rotting in the swamps for nothing: The cavalry did more walking than riding. We were humorously known as the Dismounted Horsemen. Rain, rain, rain. March and retreat. Stand and fight and die. Bury the dead in the mud, dig the animals and equipment out of the slop, carry the wounded on your back—struggle on! Sickness, lice, filth, short rations. We lived like jungle beasts, and soon we began to look and smell like them. Disease and exposure claimed almost as many lives as Rebel fire. Some men turned yellow with jaundice. Swamp fever caused others to lose their hair and teeth. I was one of the luckier ones."

Jacintha did not raise her face, lest it betray her. She was thinking of the time when he must return to duty. She kept at her sewing, fumbled a stitch, and pricked her finger, drawing blood. "Oh," she cried, vexed. "A fine seamstress I am! I should have let Lollie mend your uniform."

"Don't concern yourself, Jacintha. I'll have to buy another one. Some new boots, too. I wonder what happened to my pistol and sword? They weren't on me, were they?"

"No. Probably lost in battle."

"Or stolen by the enemy."

Taking a deep breath, he allowed himself to ask about what was on his mind. "I notice you're still wearing your wedding ring."

She grimaced, concentrating on the tunic.

"Any children yet?"

"No, nor prospects."

This seemed to please him. "How can you spend so much time here? Won't you be missed at Riverview?"

"Not much. The servants think I'm at the hospital, and Cole is seldom at home. He's busy amassing a great fortune, Earl. He has many . . . interests, in and out of Manhattan."

"Business interests?"

"And personal."

"Another woman?"

Jacintha shrugged negligently.

"Don't you care?"

"Not really."

"Why did you marry him, Jacintha?"

A sigh, then a frown. "Desperation, I guess. And I didn't actually know him, either. He was on his best behavior during the courtship, rather kind and gentle, and not exactly repulsive then. Besides, I was totally ignorant of— some aspects of marriage." Embarrassed, she rushed on. "Cole is generous with gifts, buying me jewelry, furs, and other luxuries I don't want."

"A selfish generosity," Earl surmised. "He wants his friends to envy him his lovely young wife. He flaunts you as one of his possessions. It's all wrong, Jacintha. You don't belong with Cole Danvers."

"It's too late for recriminations, Earl. What's done is done, and can't be undone."

Unable to think of a comforting reply, Earl asked wryly, "Is Lincoln's Lady General still commanding the relief battalions on the Home Front? I know she isn't nursing. That would not appeal to Laurette," Earl mused ironically. "She prefers her men whole and healthy."

Her *men?* Jacintha thought. Why had he used the plural?

"Well, you'll have to let her know you're all right, Earl. She may already have been told that you were wounded. Will you get a recuperation furlough?"

"A short one, probably."

"And since you're convalescing so nicely, Major, I think you may be permitted a few indulgences. A drink from that bottle of brandy in the pantry, if you like. Tomorrow I'll bring some cigars and smoking tobacco. The humidors are empty."

"You don't mind a pipe?"

"Not at all. Grandpa used one, you know. I think the smoke of his old meerschaum and the tapping of his Malacca cane were two of the things I missed most after he was gone. Maybe I should have buried them with him. I've read that Indians bury their loved ones with some of their favorite personal possessions to enjoy in the next world."

"Many cultures do that, Jacintha. Are you studying the American aborigines?"

"I'm curious about why some of the tribes are friendly to the white race and others are not. And why some tribes even fight among themselves."

"Like our own people?" Earl suggested laconically. "Are we more civilized than the red savages? Not much! I feel fine now, Nurse. May I get up?"

"Not just yet, Major. And you'd better cover your chest. It wouldn't do to get chilled now and have a relapse. Did Lollie bathe you this morning?"

"Half of me. I did the other half. But I'm clean all over, Nurse, and hungry."

"You'll have a hearty supper when Lollie returns. I'll have to leave then, in order to reach town before dark."

Earl objected. "It's dangerous for you to drive that distance alone, Jacintha. Take Lollie and the gun with you. I can manage now."

"With one arm in a sling? I'm not afraid to travel by myself in the daytime, Earl. I rather enjoy it. The countryside is pleasant this time of year. I saw some farmers shocking hay yesterday, and I followed a wagonload of ripe pumpkins to town." Hearing hoofs and wheels grating on the gravel lane, she glanced toward a window. "Here comes Lollie now, and I'm sure she has a big, thick, juicy steak for you. She'll broil it with mushrooms and fix a vegetable casserole with cheese sauce."

"Sounds delicious," he said. "Jacintha—"

She rose quickly. "I'd better give her a hand."

Chapter 25

DRIVING up to the lodge a few mornings later, Jacintha found Earl up and waiting for her outside. He was freshly shaven and casually debonair in riding breeches and tweed jacket from the wardrobe he maintained at the lodge, and had even managed to clean and polish his battered cavalry boots. His facial abrasions were nearly healed, and his normally healthy color was returning. The sling was off his arm. He was smiling eagerly.

Though Jacintha had been too concerned about him to pay much attention to her own appearance, her color had also improved, and she had regained a few of the pounds she had lost. She looked girlishly pretty in a bright blue wool suit and saucy poke bonnet tied in a bow under the chin. As always, at the prospect of a few hours with him, she was happy and excited, her turquoise eyes sparkling.

"Well, Major Britton," she greeted him pertly, "you're looking mighty spruce again!"

"Why not, with two excellent private nurses tending me? And where is Miss Fairgale today?"

"She woke with a touch of rheumatism, because of the changing weather. Lollie claims to have a barometer on each kneecap. I told her to stay in bed and let the staff wait on her."

"I'm sorry she's ailing. You needn't have left her, Jacintha. The larder is well stocked, and I'm no longer helpless."

"I know, Earl. But I thought you'd worry if one of us didn't appear—that you would assume we were waylaid along the road."

"I would have, yes, and probably walked to town to find out what happened." He assisted her out of the cabriolet. "Let me take those bundles."

"Watch your arm."

"Stop pampering me. I'm strong as an ox."

Inside, they set the packages on the kitchen table.

"Have you had breakfast, Major?"

"At six this morning, Nurse. I'm a habitually early riser now; reveille blows at five, you know. Anyway, though I'm a bit out of practice on the griddle, my buckwheats and maple syrup tasted fine. After a year of Army chow in the field, almost anything would be delicious. Soldiers have a saying: If Rebel bullets don't get you, the mess sergeant's beans will."

Jacintha was putting some staples in the cupboard. "I've heard boys in the hospital complain about the camp food, and their complaints don't bear repetition."

Earl laughed. "Soldiers exaggerate notoriously about army life—but I can vouch for the awful food."

"I brought the papers, Earl. There's some good news. Czar Alexander may enter the war on our side! Two Russian fleets have been sighted in American waters, one off San Francisco, the other near New York."

"That's propaganda, Jacintha. It sells newspapers and boosts morale, but has little substance. Russia has had ships off our shores since the war began, but more in her own interest than the United States'. They are merely protecting their commerce. Russia won't cast in with the Union, any more than England will with the Confederacy."

"But the Czar freed the serfs, which means he's against slavery! And England will help the South, because her textile industry depends on Southern cotton."

"True, but their mills prepared themselves with heavy purchasing before the war began. Moreover, blockade runners are still delivering plenty of cotton from Southern ports to Liverpool." Earl shrugged, a gesture denoting helplessness. "It's very difficult to maintain your sanity in these crazy times, Jacintha. Rebellion is the worst kind of mania that can afflict a nation. I realize that all over again, every time I go into battle. We're destroying our brethren and our land. It has to be mass madness! You've seen the consequences in one hospital, Jacintha. Multiply them by hundreds and thousands."

"Insanity," Jacintha agreed, her voice somber with reflection.

"I wish I knew what's happening in South Carolina now. I've tried to pull some political strings to learn something about my family."

"Any success?"

He shook his head, pondering the front page of the *New York Tribune*. "War news should be printed in blood."

"Those letters I mailed to the War Department for you," Jacintha said. "How soon do you expect an answer?"

"Too soon. I'd better go into town with you today, Jacintha. I have some business to take care of, both at the bank and at home. Laurette may have heard something by now."

Any reference to his wife was a sharp dart in Jacintha's heart.

Earl was saying, "She may not be in New York at all, but in Philadelphia, visiting her family."

Jacintha ventured shyly, "Laurette has been sponsoring some 'morale parties' and other entertainments for the servicemen. General Ralph Cutter usually acts as host, and many prominent people attend."

Earl grinned cynically. "Christ, what an inventive mind that woman has! Those functions are simply a means to make merry with the sanction of the community. Not many men from the ranks will be invited—a few token soldiers and sailors, perhaps, who'll feel as out of place as commoners at court. Well, I knew she wouldn't be lonely in my absence, or lack for escorts. Not that I care, Jacintha. Believe me, I don't."

"But you won't be staying here much longer?" Her voice cracked as she asked.

"No. I want to reimburse you and Lollie for your time and expense. Of course, I can never repay you for your kindness. Or for saving my arm."

His humble appreciation was deeply touching. "That's not necessary, Earl. We were glad to help."

"You're so wonderful, Jacintha. Naturally, I won't mention any of this to Laurette. She'd never understand." Or maybe she would, he thought . . . only too well.

"Do you want to leave now?"

"Do you?"

"I suppose we may as well."

"That wasn't my question," he said.

"I—I'll get your gear ready, Major. What shall I do with the extra food?"

"Put it outside for the scavengers. But first, my wounds need re-dressing, Nurse. Will you oblige me once more?"

"Of course, Major." Jacintha moved industriously about the room, poking up the embers on the hearth, then filling the kettle hanging on the crane. "It's chilly in here."

"Normal for the season," Earl said, "and much cooler upstate, no doubt. I built a cozy fire last night and sat before it, smoking my pipe."

"All you lacked was your faithful retriever?"

"No," he said harshly, "that wasn't all I lacked." His eyes sought hers, refusing to retreat. "Look at me, Jacintha! How much longer can we avoid the truth? All this hedging and pretense—are we fooling each other? I've stood all I can. I can't take any more!"

"You too?" she whispered, searching his face, finding it tense and grave.

"Me too." He nodded. "I love you, Jacintha."

"Oh, Earl—you're not just saying that because I've been taking care of you?"

He stepped swiftly to her. "There are ways to convince you, my dear, if you need convincing."

She forgot what she wanted to say but it did not matter, for his mouth silenced hers and his arms captured her. Passion smoldered in his ash-gray eyes. His hands were infinitely tender and sensitive—and exquisitely stimulating. Jacintha ached with eager anticipation. It was as if she had waited all her life for this. Nothing must delay it.

His lips progressed down her throat to the tempting mounds beneath her blouse, burning through the thin silk, one hand working expertly to free the hampering bow and buttons, the delicate camisole. "Lovely," he whispered after the revelation. "Your breasts are even lovelier than my fantasies of them." His hungry tongue licked the soft, luscious flesh as if it were succulent fruit, lingering over the deliciously ripe nipples, teasing her and himself, relishing her passionate response.

Jacintha caught her breath sharply, thrilling to each new sensation, to every emotion, after her long-suppressed sexuality. "I—I hope you like the rest of me too," she murmured, close to pleading.

"I'll adore every precious inch," he promised, proceeding to disrobe her. "Just don't turn away from me, Jacintha. Let me enjoy your beauty."

During his slow, probing kisses and intimate explorations, her head reeled dizzily and her eyes blazed as though fevered. She pressed her pelvis against his lower torso, longing to feel his throbbing manhood.

"Say it," he demanded. "Say you love me too!"

"Yes, yes," she cried, nearly frantic now, her body trying to absorb his through his clothing. "I do love you, Earl! So much, so long!"

"How long?"

"All my life, it seems."

"Is that why you pushed me away so often—and would never let me touch you?"

"I was afraid you'd discover my real feelings, and think badly of me."

"And now?"

"Now I want you to know everything! I want to lie naked in your arms however long we have."

His arms enveloped her again, drawing her between his spread legs, where her squirming presence tantalized him. He caught the fragrance of damask rose in her hair, the honeyed sweetness of her young breath on her parted lips. He felt all of her yearning. "That's what I wanted to hear, my beloved. I had to know you feel the same need and longing I feel."

She burrowed her face in his shoulder, whimpering. "I've felt it for years, but never deeper or stronger than now. Oh, darling, don't wait any longer!"

The fire had died down to embers. Outside, fresh north winds swept down from Canada, chilling the great Hudson Valley and Manhattan Island. But it was warm and still in the cabin, which seemed luminescent with the afterglow of their love. Jacintha reclined against the propped pillows, Earl's head in her lap, her fingers playing idly with his thick black hair. A roseate translucence still suffused her skin, reflecting the total stimulation of every fiber of her being. Pleasure still gleamed in her eyes.

Earl reached for her caressing hand, humbly kissing each fingertip. "You're not sorry?"

Jacintha wanted to tell him that it was the most wonderful thing that had ever happened to her, but she was still somewhat dazed and unable to express herself. She knew now, without a doubt, the identity of the phantom lover who had visited her in erotic dreams.

"No, dearest, I'm not sorry. I'll never be sorry." And she meant what she said. Whatever the consequences, she would never regret this.

"Were you pleased?"

"In every way—and some I didn't realize were possible for a woman."

"You thought ecstasy was only for men?"

"Thank you for showing me, Earl."

"Oh, darling, it was my pleasure." He was deeply moved.

Several minutes lapsed while they relaxed in silent enchantment. Then reality ruptured reverie.

"What shall we do, Jacintha?"

"What *can* we do?"

"I wish I knew," he sighed.

Slowly he raised himself beside her, his shoulders slumped. The sheet slipped from their nude bodies, and Jacintha impulsively kissed the healing saber wound on his neck. His eyes darkened as her breasts brushed his chest and she hoped he would take her again. Then a somber frown spread over his features, replacing the former tranquility with dark despair.

"The die seems fairly well cast for both of us," he remarked grimly. "Hell of a time to realize it, isn't it? In addition to the legal problems, there's a war, and I'll soon be back in it. I didn't request a recuperation leave, Jacintha, because I had no idea that anything like this would occur between us. I asked for immediate orders, and no doubt the War Department will oblige me."

"You were running away, weren't you?"

"I suppose so." He shrugged. "From some gremlins that have tormented me for years."

"And I was one of them? Poor darling! All along I thought I was suffering alone. How ironic!"

"What?"

"Lollie's rheumatism tripped us both. But please believe I have no regrets, Earl. And I don't want you to feel any remorse—or any obligation to me because of this, either. Understand?"

"My dear, that's utter nonsense! Good Lord! Do you think I make a habit of telling a lady I love her, seducing her, and then just conveniently forgetting it?"

She smiled poignantly, restraining tears. "I hope not, sir, although we both know the seduction was mutual."

"Then don't try to be so damned noble! It wasn't just momentary lust, you know. A furlough fling for me and fleeting infidelity for you. We love each other!"

"Of course, darling—eternally, I hope. But we can't change our circumstances, and we may never have another opportunity even to speak of it together. All we can count on now is this moment in time."

"And when this moment is over?"

"We won't think about that."

"How can we *not* think about it, Jacintha?"

"I don't know!" she cried, crushing him to her breast. "Make love to me again, Earl. Now and as often as possible before we must part. Please?"

"Oh, God, I may desert!"

"No, you won't, Major—that's not like you. And we're wasting precious time. If only we could make time stand still!"

"We can try," he said desperately, embracing her again —and for a brief, blissful interlude they seemed to succeed.

Chapter 26

FOR several weeks after the first symptoms appeared, Jacintha tried to rationalize them away. She was merely tired, overworked at the hospital, miserable in her marriage, and worried about Earl. Or maybe she had the "green sickness"—an anemia peculiar to young women, which caused irregular menses. Surely, if she were capable of pregnancy, it would have long since occurred, for Cole took no precautions, and Jacintha dared not use any.

The persistent nausea, vertigo, and exhaustion forced her to consult a physician. Some questions and a preliminary examination confirmed her suspicions.

"No doubt about it this time," Dr. Selby concluded. "You have an heir on the way, Mrs. Danvers."

Jacintha sat before his desk, nervously twisting her kerchief. "You're positive, Doctor?"

He smiled indulgently, stroking his gray beard. "Well, no man is infallible, but I'm fairly certain of my diagnosis. Aren't you happy over the prospect of motherhood?"

"Surprised," Jacintha murmured. "I thought I couldn't have children."

"So did your husband, Mrs. Danvers. But you know better now, don't you?"

"Yes, I know better now."

"Being a first pregnancy, there may be a variation of a week or two in the birth date," he continued, pondering a maternity calendar. "But we'll set a tentative mid-July confinement."

Jacintha gazed out of the office window, her mind several miles away, in the hunting lodge at Greystone. Yes, that date would fit.

Misreading her mood, Selby soothed, "There's nothing to fear about childbirth, Mrs. Danvers. It's a perfectly natural occurrence for a healthy woman. I'm sure you'll come through it very well. Give Mr. Danvers the good tidings, and visit me again soon."

Jacintha went home in a trance. Suppose she had told the doctor that her husband couldn't possibly be the father, because they had not been sexually intimate at the time of conception? She could imagine his incredulity.

Of course, there were alternatives. Women spoke of them among themselves, and midwives advertised "sure cures" in the personal columns of the daily journals. Madame Restell, the best known of those practitioners, boasted of a large and elite clientele. The madame lived in a great mansion, entertained lavishly, and rode in elegant equipages, sometimes leading the Sunday afternoon carriage parade in Central Park. Editors called her a vulture, among other things, implied that she was protected from the law by Tammany Hall politicians.

Jacintha shuddered. Abort Earl's child? Destroy the only part of him she might ever have? Never!

She wondered how he would react to the knowledge of her pregnancy. Of course, she could not tell him. He was still with the Army of the Potomac, and was occasionally mentioned in the reports of General Ambrose Burnside's cavalry units. The Union had finally realized what the Confederacy had known all along—the importance of strong cavalry support on the battlefield—and was rapidly increasing its horse soldiers. No, Earl had enough problems —she could not add this one to them.

To compound her misery, Cole had suddenly decided that the time was propitious to launch them in society. He was riding the crest of an unprecedented wave of prosperity in the North. Gold had never been more potent in human relations, and people with enough of it attempted to bribe their way into drawing rooms formerly firmly closed to them. Some succeeded; others did not. But the failures did not discourage Cole Danvers.

His fortune, conservatively estimated at ten million, was impressive enough to bring a few engraved invitations from the charmed circle to Riverview. Jacintha was commanded to attend with him—and then to plan an appropriate Danvers reception. He scoffed at the small guest list she presented to him, and enlarged it considerably. Reading the prominent names, Jacintha voiced her skepticism.

"You're aiming too high, Cole. Some of them won't come. I doubt if they'll even bother to reply. Spare yourself the embarrassment."

He was pompously confident. "They'll be here, all right! Every swell listed has been in one of my Bowery establishments on occasion, some quite recently. They've gambled at my tables, drunk at my bars, flirted with my wenches— yeah, and more than that." He winked significantly, buffing his fingernails on his brocaded vest. "Oh, the gents will come, Puss, along with their fine ladies. Wait and see! Meanwhile, get busy on the details. Hire a caterer, an orchestra, and some prima donna to sing for the fat old frumps. Buy yourself a new gown and wear your jewels. I want the old cocks to see my pretty young pullet and envy me."

Jacintha gave him a sullen, angry glare, for Earl had said this was behind Cole's generosity. "That's how you regard me, isn't it? As one of your possessions!"

"Well, aren't you? Don't you belong to me?"

"I'm not your chattel!"

"No? The law says differently, Mrs. Danvers. A man is lord and master of his property, which includes his wife. Especially his wife."

There was no disputing this. The marital laws, brought to America with the Puritans, had never been substantially amended. They were harsh, medieval, and inflexible, written by men for men. Divorce was practically impossible to obtain, without the husband's consent, and even judicial separation was rare, if contested. But Jacintha insisted defiantly, "You don't own me."

"What's wrong with you lately, woman? You have more frequent fits of tears, tantrums, and the vapors. I thought you were cured of female complaints. Can you be pregnant at long last?"

His directness left her no alternative, and she decided to admit it before the secret revealed itself. She nodded reluctantly, eyes downcast.

A pleased grin spread over Cole's ruddy face. "By God, it's about time! You're sure, sugar? You've seen a doctor?"

"Selby," she answered. "The baby will be born next summer." But she did not specify the month, and Cole was too elated to ask.

"It'll be a boy," he predicted firmly, as if even the Creator would not dare contradict him. "This is great news, Mrs. Danvers, and a real cause for celebration!"

He poured himself a stiff drink, gulped it neat, then grabbed Jacintha and jigged jubilantly about the bedroom. The whirling made her dizzy and nauseous, and she had to rush, retching, to the basin.

"Just don't puke at the party," Cole muttered. "That'd be a helluva mess!"

Jacintha bathed her face with cool water, and then wrung out a washcloth to place on her forehead. "I don't feel like preparing for a party, Cole. Please—can't we wait a while longer?"

"Until your belly starts to swell? That would just be another excuse! Damn it, Jacintha, you're always provoking me! I don't know what you expect from a husband, but I'm sick and tired of pampering you."

"Pampering?" she repeated, astonished. "Is that what you consider your treatment of me? Oh, Cole—sometimes

I think you're insane! You've been obsessed with money most of your life, and now you have this crazy notion of breaking into society!"

"What's wrong with that? If it's crazy, there're lots of lunatics around—whole registers of them! Have you never heard of bluebooks in all your reading?"

"People are usually born into them," Jacintha said.

"They also buy into them!"

Her head throbbed and she began to vomit again. She supported herself by gripping the sides of the washstand. "Pull the bell cord, Cole. I need Lollie."

There were enough unexpected acceptances to convince Jacintha that some of the men did indeed feel beholden to Cole Danvers, or blackmailed by him. But Mrs. Earl Britton, whom he had insisted upon inviting, sent her regrets. Jacintha was relieved, but Cole was bitterly disappointed.

"I thought you said she admired me."

"Maybe she just admires men of your caliber."

Her shrug vexed him. "What does that mean?"

"It means that Mrs. Britton is scorning our reception, Cole. But cheer up—some others almost in her league will attend."

"I especially wanted her here," he said broodingly. "Her name is always in the newspapers. She's a lady of high class, with many friends and much influence. Maybe you didn't word the invitation right. Send her another, delivered by messenger, with a bouquet of flowers."

"I'll do no such thing!" Jacintha refused, tossing the vellum envelope and note into the fireplace and gleefully watching them burn to ashes.

Cole stomped out in a huff, bumping into the housekeeper in the hall and muttering that he wouldn't be back for dinner.

"What's his trouble?" Lollie inquired.

"Obsession," Jacintha replied.

"Is it contagious?"

"Only to similarly afflicted fools."

"He won't be here this evening, Missy."
"That's the best news I've had today, Lollie."

The dismal December weather suited the mood of the city, which was depressed by another disastrous Union defeat, at Fredericksburg, Virginia. The tragic reports had been drifting in for over a week now, darkening the approaching Christmas season. Thousands killed, wounded, missing, captured! General Burnside, alas, was not the victor President Lincoln sought in the east. His replacement was as certain as his predecessors'. There would be no replacements for the victims.

Never had Jacintha felt less like entertaining. She went through the motions mechanically, her spirits only slightly elevated by the holiday decorations. She donated several trees and ornaments to the hospital wards, where she still served six hours a day, and the patients' appreciation of them tugged at her heart. She wrote family greetings for those who were illiterate, or too sick to do so themselves, provided the postage to mail the letters, and wished she could give every homesick boy a personal gift.

Rain fell on the evening of the party and Cole worried that it might keep some guests away. Jacintha hoped for a snowstorm to keep everyone away—but that was fanciful thinking. Most New Yorkers were hardy souls who would venture out even in a blizzard. The rich simply bundled up in furs and traveled by sleigh, if necessary.

"What a doll!" Cole gloated as his wife descended the stairs in a pale blue velvet gown with an overskirt of intricately draped chiffon. Diamond pins fastened the thick dark coils of her hair in place, and the same gems adorned her ears, throat, and wrists. Thus far the only evidence of her pregnancy was a fuller bosom, which merely enhanced her beauty.

Riverview glowed with gas lamps, candles, firelight. A black butler hired for the occasion announced the guests. Meeting Mayor George Opdyke, William Marcy Tweed, and other Tammany Hall sachems, Jacintha wondered if

Cole nurtured political ambitions. To her amazement, some residents of Washington Square, Fifth Avenue, Gramercy Park, and Murray Hill also appeared. The politicians' presence was understandable—elections were coming up, and campaign contributions were always welcome. But what brought the other, more distinguished gentlemen? Did they really frequent Cole's Bowery casinos, dally with his concert saloon entertainers?

Cole was a jolly, gregarious host, shaking hands and clapping people on the shoulder, his naturally florid face flushed with alcohol and complacency—confident that all social barriers had been removed and Riverview would now be inundated with invitations.

Jacintha was a gracious hostess, although she felt detached from the scene. She heard little of the feminine chatter and giggles, the male laughter and braggadocio. The champagne and rich food made her queasy. Some of the men overindulged, held her too tightly while dancing, kissed her too intimately under the mistletoe, and whispered compromising compliments. Jacintha discreetly diverted their lechery—and hoped she could do the same with her husband after their departure.

"Doctor Selby says we must cease this kind of activity until after the baby is born," she lied to Cole that night. "Otherwise I might miscarry."

"That's the trouble with delicate females," he grumbled. "Pregnancy is always a risk to them. We'll stop when you get further along. Seven months or so."

"Before that," Jacintha said firmly.

"Well, not tonight, for Christ's sake! Watching those other fellas dancing and flirting with you made me hot, and I got to put out my fire. Several Wall Street bulls were scenting you. Imagine that, in my own house! And those Tammany bastards are known for chasing petticoats. Did you make any assignations?" He grinned at her indignation. "Just teasing, sweetheart. Hell, your own spouse has trouble lifting your skirts!"

Unable to evade him, Jacintha acquiesced, warning him throughout the ordeal of the possible consequences. "Yeah, yeah," he muttered heedlessly, intent on his own gratification.

"If I have a miscarriage," she cried afterwards, on her way to the bathroom, "it's your fault! Remember that, Cole. *You* caused it. Oh, I think I'm bleeding!"

"Huh? Bleeding?" He heaved himself off the bed and staggered after her, naked and still inebriated. "Well, look and see! Is it blood?" he asked anxiously.

"No, it's just—"

"Semen, that's all! You ought to recognize the stuff by now, Puss. That little rascal is stuck too tightly in there to be dislodged by a little prodding. When King Cole plants a seed, it stays planted."

"Not with rough treatment, Cole! Why must you be such an animal? Why can't you behave like a civilized man?"

"How would you know how a civilized man acts in the hay?" he questioned cagily. "Ever been laid by one?"

"No, of course not!"

"Well, believe me, they're all the same with their pants off and pricks up! Stop blubbering and come to bed. I'm tired as the devil."

"You are the devil," Jacintha muttered.

"A beast with cloven hoofs, eh? Maybe so, although my feet fit fine in boots. And Satan is supposed to have at least one horn, ain't he?" He laughed, pinching her bare buttocks so they hurt. "I'll wake you if I want some more of your pretty little tail. . . ."

As her pregnancy advanced, the hospital authorities restricted Jacintha's nursing duties, and finally the head matron suggested temporary retirement. "Routine precaution," she explained. "We've greatly appreciated your services, Mrs. Danvers, and will be happy to welcome you back after the blessed event. Good luck!"

Jacintha, who had been camouflaging her condition with

larger crinolines and looser garments in order to appear in public, now went into virtual seclusion, venturing out only to visit the doctor. And with little else to do, she concentrated on the captive life in her body. Eventually she must admit the truth, without naming the father, and leave Riverview—if Cole did not kill her first. The least she expected was a severe beating. Fear that the fetus might be harmed or lost as a result prevented her from making a premature confession. Cole was a savage creature, with almost insane rages, and above all else on earth, he wanted a legitimate heir.

It would be a mercy, Jacintha thought morbidly, if she died in childbirth. But, she scolded herself, then Earl's son or daughter would be reared as Cole's. Earl's child would grow up under Cole's evil influence, perhaps with a strumpet for a stepmother. The horrifying prospect forced Jacintha to confide in the only person she could trust.

Lollie listened sympathetically, hearing precisely what she had suspected. "Dear Lord," she sighed. "I do believe you were destined for tragedy, Missy. One day with the major, and this is the result! And he doesn't know yet? You must write to him immediately!"

Jacintha shook her head. "No, Lollie. He'd only worry. A fighting soldier has enough troubles—If he comes back safely . . ."

"And if he doesn't?"

"He will," Jacintha said, with more conviction than she felt. "He must! God couldn't be that cruel to us." She began to rock in her grandmother's chair, her hands clasped prayerfully over her bulging belly. "Perhaps I should go away now, leave this house."

"Where would you go?"

"I don't know. To another city or state. Maybe even to another country. Anywhere would be better than here, I think. One thing is certain. I can't live with Mr. Danvers after the child is born. I won't continue this farce any longer than necessary. Will you go away with me, Lollie?"

"You know I will. But that's in the future. You have to be sensible now. Think of yourself, and the baby. You're grieving too much, not eating or resting properly. All you do is read the papers and pace the floor at night. You worry more about the war than the president and his generals put together."

"I can't help it, Lollie."

"But Mr. Earl wouldn't want you to torture yourself this way, Missy, to risk your health and the child's, too. You're so narrow in the hips. If the infant is large—and the major is a big man—you may have a difficult labor. You'll need your strength. I don't mean to scare you, honey, but you must take better care of yourself. If not, you—"

"May not survive?" Jacintha interrupted, wincing. "I've thought of that too, Lollie, which is why I'm confiding in you. If anything happens to me, I don't want the child to grow up with Mr. Danvers. You must tell Major Britton the truth. And if, God forbid, he is also gone, I want you to take my baby. No, wait, please! Hear me out. I've saved some money from my household and personal allowances, and it's in the estate account in the Britton Bank, along with the proceeds from the sale of Riverview to Mr. Danvers. I'll make a will appointing you executrix and guardian. You'll have the silver, too, and my jewelry—"

"Oh, hush, hush!" Lollie pleaded tearfully. "Don't say any more, Missy. Nothing's going to happen."

"Promise you'll do as I ask, Lollie. You'll raise the child."

"I promise, but please forget it for now. Oh, if only I hadn't gotten rheumatism that day!" she sobbed into her apron.

"Try not to think ill of me or the major," Jacintha entreated. "If you only knew how much I love him!"

"You think I have any doubts, after all these years? I'm not fussing at you, child, or judging either of you, because I believe he loves you deeply too. I just hate to see you suffering so."

Jacintha affected a smile. "The wages of sin, Lollie. But it didn't seem sinful at the time. We were in love. And he was going back to the war."

No, it did not seem wrong. It was still beautiful, a precious memory to sustain her in the harsh months ahead.

PART IV

Chapter 27

SUMMER came late and violently that year. An epic battle was fought in the scorched rocky hills near a small Pennsylvania village—the first significant victory of the Army of the Potomac, now under General George Meade.

The losses at Gettysburg were staggering, and the New England hospitals were overflowing with the wounded survivors. The papers printed the long, stark casualty lists as rapidly and accurately as possible, and Jacintha held her breath while reading the black-bordered columns of surnames under the letter *B*. Part of the Army of the Potomac was still stationed in Washington, and she tried to assure herself that Earl was with these forces. But her fear could not be assuaged, or the demons of doubt exorcised. The Capital was admittedly vulnerable to invasion—indeed, it was the prime target of the Confederacy, as was Richmond that of the Union.

There had been no appreciable rainfall in Manhattan since spring. The few widely scattered showers barely settled the dust. Flies, gnats, and mosquitoes formed a constant menace, and seasonal diseases greatly increased.

Cases of dysentery, typhoid, and other fevers were reported in the crowded Battery and Bowery districts.

Filth and debris, usually washed away by flowing gutters, littered the city streets. Melting asphalt stuck to heels, hoofs, wheels. Greenness faded from the parks and squares. Only well-tended private gardens could flourish in such a drought, and the Riverview handymen were kept busy watering and mulching. The ferries to New Jersey's wooded Elysian Fields and Brooklyn's beaches were packed with people seeking some relief from the heat. Jacintha could only sit and fan herself.

One ominously still morning in July she was dressing for luncheon, striving to be cool in a long sheer smock over her linen maternity hubbard. Her time was near, and she felt clumsy and misshapen, miserable from the heat and her fears for Earl's safety.

Jacintha had just finished brushing and securing her hair in a mesh snood when she was startled by several sharp cracking sounds like the reports of a revolver or rifle. They came from a distance, like echoes, and were soon repeated, too frequently to count. Gun shots?

Cole lay sprawled across the bed in a striped silk nightshirt, snoring in an alcoholic stupor. He had stumbled in at dawn, reeking of liquor and cheap perfume, and Jacintha had no doubt where he had spent the night. Long before his wife had absolutely refused, upon doctor's orders, to accommodate him sexually, his mistress had become a far more exciting replacement.

Jacintha was about to wake him when she was distracted by a commotion in the street—barking dogs, thundering hoofs, a clanging bell, and a shouting male voice.

Moving to a window, she saw a lathered horse clattering on the cobblestones. The elderly rider was curiously garbed in brown canvas breeches, thong-laced shirt, and coonskin cap, and carried a long-barreled pistol, with a Bowie knife stuck in his wide leather belt. A cow-bell was attached to his mount's neck, and he was broadcasting some apparently sensational news to the residents of Greenwich Village.

"God's balls!" Cole swore, rising sluggishly from the bed. "Can't a man get some rest around here? What in hell is happening out there?"

"It's a courier of some sort," Jacintha said as the self-appointed messenger came abreast of Riverview. "He looks like the ghost of Daniel Boone. He's announcing something."

Staggering to the window, Cole elbowed Jacintha aside and leaned out, yelling, "Hey, you! What's all the ruckus? Is the war over?"

"It's jest beginnin', Mister!" declared the former Indian scout and veteran of the Mexican War. "Arm, arm! The Rebels air upon us! They be fightin' in town already! Git yore gun and join 'em!"

"Are you crazy, man?"

"Not crazy enough to be caught in my nightshirt at high noon, with a army of slavers bearin' down on my tail!" he replied, riding on. "To arms, to arms! All citizens harken! The Rebs air here! Harken, harken!"

He mustered a small battalion of volunteers, mostly old men carrying ancient weapons, including Revolutionary War muskets, rusty flintlocks, dueling pistols, and swords. Some were armed with butcher knives, sticks, clubs.

"Mercy," Jacintha murmured, clutching a bedpost for support. "What'll we do?"

Cole was busy dressing. "Leave, of course! Get off this goddamn island before the Rebs sink it. Throw some things in a valise, and we'll hurry to the nearest wharf."

"I'm in no condition to travel, Cole! You know that! Doctor Selby said the baby could come any day now. Besides, where could we go? If the Rebels are already in New York, the escape routes will be blocked. Arm yourself, like the man said, and go fight. Help defend us."

He glanced at her impatiently. "Do you imagine I could stop the Confederate Army and Navy?"

"You could help! Unless you're too cowardly!"

"If it wasn't for your big belly, I'd give you the back of my hand for that! Stop talking and get yourself ready. We'll go north, up the Hudson. I'll buy or steal a boat, if necessary. Maybe we can reach Canada and catch a ship to Europe. I've got money in foreign banks. Hurry, will you?"

"Miss Jacintha!" It was Lollie, hammering frantically on the master suite portal. "Miss Jacintha!"

"Come in, Lollie!"

The housekeeper entered, embarrassed to find them quarreling. "I'm sorry to intrude, but did you hear what the rider said?"

"I reckon the deaf and dead heard him," Cole answered. "New York's been invaded. We'll all be killed or captured if we remain. Pack some clothes for us. We're leaving."

"Leaving? You can't do that, Mr. Cole! Miss Jacintha is about to lie in! She might lose the baby."

"Should she stay and let the Rebs deliver it? Riding in a comfortable carriage to the Greenwich docks won't hurt her. Pregnant women travel across country in oxcarts, and give birth in the wilderness. Now, do as I say, you impertinent old biddy. Move, damn you!"

Jacintha spoke with quiet resolution. "You may do as you wish, Cole, but I'm not leaving this house."

"Oh, yes, you are. I'm going now to order the carriage." Jamming on his hat, he brushed past the glowering women, furious at what he considered sheer female obstinacy.

"He means it, Missy."

"So do I." Jacintha set her jaw defiantly. "He'll have to drag me by the hair."

"Don't tempt him," Lollie advised. "The servants with families request permission to leave."

"Yes, of course. Dismiss them, Lollie. Then come back here, and we'll defy the master together."

"With pleasure," Lollie agreed.

Presently Cole returned, scowling sheepishly, the *Herald* under his arm. "It's not the Rebs, just a riot over the draft. Newsboys are peddling papers in the streets. That loony old bastard ought to have his skull split, stirring up folks with false rumors. Reckon he thought he was Paul Revere. If he comes this route again, I'll harken him all right. I'll shoot his ass off that bony nag!"

"They're rioting in town?" Jacintha asked.

"Yeah. It started at the Third Avenue Enrollment Office, where the names of the first draftees to go under the new Conscription Act were being drawn. That three-hundred-dollar exemption clause seems to be the problem. It says here they're wrecking the draft offices, chopping down telegraph poles, pulling up horsecar and railroad tracks, breaking into gunshops for weapons and ammunition and setting fires. I'm warning you again, Jacintha, it's not safe here. Many folks are leaving, our neighbors among them."

"I've already explained that I can't risk my life and the baby's."

"Be sensible, woman! Your life won't be worth a counterfeit picayune if that mob turns on us."

Jacintha stared at him. "Why should they? We have nothing to do with the draft."

"But we have money and a fine estate! Those renegades hate the rich. I'll pay the male servants to guard Riverview, and I'll hire some extra help at any price. But I'm not taking any chances with a murderous gang of riffraff hopped up on booze and anger. If it's not peaceful by tomorrow, we're leaving."

"Not I," Jacintha reiterated vehemently.

"We'll see about that."

"Yes, we will." She already had a plan. Any attempt to force her would induce labor . . . real or pretended.

Chapter 28

BY midafternoon the situation was out of control, and the city was under a reign of terror.

Conscription had been halted, the lottery wheels and offices destroyed, the recruiting stations closed, and drilling suspended—but the crazed mobs were not appeased. Secure in numbers and their mass anonymity, tasting power and lusting for more, they ran amuck on the streets.

Fifty members of the Invalid Corps were seized and pounded to death with their own weapons. Several of the crippled soldiers were hurled off an East River bluff to the rocky beach below, and huge boulders rolled down on the corpses—proving that there was something more hellish than war.

Negroes were hunted, beaten, tortured, driven from their homes by fire. Some sought shelter in the outlying fields, others hid under the river piers, and a number of black lifeless bodies dangled from trees and lampposts. Negroes had caused the war in the first place, hadn't they?

As night fell, numerous buildings were burning on the Lower East Side. The flames were visible for miles. Explosions from a sacked and burned arsenal formed weird fireworks in the sky and reverberated in the earth like quake tremors.

Cole was atop the roof of Riverview with a pair of binoculars trained on the Bowery. He was concerned about his buildings there: the safes held large sums of money and the bars were well stocked. So far there were no signs of rioting in that ward, which was a stronghold of Tammany Hall. Cole hoped he could depend on the Sheriff's Department to protect it.

Jacintha and Lollie watched the awesome red glare from the cupola, praying that no strong winds would rise and carry sparks to the shingled roofs and frame structures of Greenwich Village. Caravans crowded the streets. Some fleeing citizens trundled loaded pushcarts. Departing passenger vessels, no matter where they were bound, were packed. Should fire threaten Riverview, they would have to leave—but this was the only condition under which Jacintha would consider leaving.

"The city is doomed," Lollie said dolefully. "It'll be rubble and ashes by morning. The firemen couldn't douse all those fires if they drained the Croton Reservoir and pumped the rivers and harbor dry."

Jacintha fanned herself and lifted her damp hair off her neck. The sweltering heat persisted, even at night. "If only it would rain! Are those dark clouds overhead, or just puffs of smoke?"

"I can't tell for sure."

Several low, distant rumbles might have been thunder, but the lightning flashes were obscured by flames. Probably just more gunpowder explosions, Jacintha decided.

"It's nearly ten o'clock, Lollie. We can't do any good up here. Might as well try to sleep."

The patter of rain woke Jacintha. It began falling at midnight—a gentle summer shower that soon developed into a divine deluge. Wind blew cooling mists into the room, so welcome that Jacintha would not close the windows. Cole seemed not to hear anything. She lay gratefully enjoying the godsend, hoping the fires would be extinguished and the raging tempers calmed. She was drifting back into slumber when she heard Lollie tapping softly on the door and whispering her name. She slipped quietly out of bed and donned a voluminous peignoir before stepping into the hall.

"What is it?"

"The laundress is here, asking for you."

"April? At this hour? In this weather?"

"Yes. I heard rapping at the back door, and it was her. She's in the kitchen now, scared half out of her wits. Some rioters were after her and her family.

"Oh, no! Is she hurt?"

"Luckily, she got away. But her sister's husband was hanged and their house burned, and . . . Oh, it's terrible! Can you come down, Missy? She begs to see you."

"Of course. But we must be careful not to wake Mr. Danvers."

April was soaking wet, and shaking all over. When she saw Jacintha, she began to weep, almost irrational in her fright and confusion.

"Oh, Miz Danvers! Thank heaven us got here! They's after us! They burnt our shanty and drove us out. They strung poor May's husband to a rafter and burnt the place over him. The chillen was scattered everywhere like scared chickens. And May, she done in labor—'member I tole you she was due this month? Well, her time done come, and I don't know what to do!"

Jacintha put a comforting hand on her shoulder. "I'm glad you came here, April. Sit down, please. Lollie will fix some coffee and food. Where's your sister and her family?"

"Outside. May weren't sure they was welcome."

"Oh, April, of course they're welcome! Bring them in."

"Oh, no, ma'am! Not in here. May won't come in the house; she about to deliver. Could us please use the cellar, just till the baby am birthed?"

Jacintha wanted to offer a bedchamber but did not dare, not with Cole in the house. "Yes, and we'll help. Don't fix the food now, Lollie; make some preparations. There's a mattress in the basement." She took an oil lamp from the pantry, and some candles and matches.

"I'll do the work, Miz Danvers! I helped May birth all her babies. But you mustn't do nothing. You's about to lay in yourself. All we's askin' is to borry the cellar."

"Better hurry, then," Jacintha urged. "That baby won't wait forever."

April's sister was crouched on the back stoop, trying to shelter her whimpering brood under a slicker and muffle the moans of advanced labor. Her tears were for her murdered husband. She still saw the noose around his neck, and herself on her knees before the wild-eyed lynchers.

They helped her into the basement and onto the linter pad, which Lollie had already protected with newspapers and a canvas sheet.

Old blankets and quilts were spread on the floor for the children, all under the age of twelve, and April ordered them to go to sleep. But even the youngest, a pig-tailed girl of three, was wide awake and full of wonder about the excitement. And when May went into hard labor, making sounds and movements similar to their tortured father's, they feared something terrible was happening to their mother too. April had to silence their wails by threatening to thrash them.

May's travail was a revelation to Jacintha. She knew a little better now what to expect from her own. It would not be easy. May was suffering greatly even though she had experienced childbirth five times before. She tossed, writhed, groaned. Once she emitted an uncontrollable scream, and April quickly clamped a restraining hand over her mouth.

"Don't holler so loud, Sister! You'll wake the master."

"It's all right," Jacintha said consolingly, confident that Cole was in brandied oblivion. "She's in pain, April. Let her yell, if it'll help."

But May suppressed further urges, striving valiantly until the feat was accomplished. Then she lay spent and heaving, tears spilling from her sorrowful eyes. But the crying infant, now cleansed and swaddled in a towel, sent April into another nervous dither.

"Hush, little one, don't you cry!" she soothed, walking the floor with the squirming little bundle. "You is lucky to be alive, so don't go makin' no trouble for these nice, kind ladies. Hush your mouth now, I say."

As if he understood, his crying ceased, and April placed him in his mother's arms.

"Here's number six, honey. What you goin' name him?"

"Abraham," May proudly announced. She gazed up at her smiling benefactress. "If it was a girl child, I'd be giving her your pretty name, ma'am. God bless you and Miss Lollie. April said you were good folks and would help us. And we ain't never goin' to forget it, long as we live."

Jacintha was deeply touched. "We were happy to help, May. You have a fine little son there. His father would be very proud of him and his brave mother. And now, how about some food for everyone?"

But as they approached the stairs to the kitchen, the door burst open. Cole stood in the frame, a crimson robe over his nightshirt, a silver-barreled pistol glinting in his hand.

"What's all this?" he demanded brusquely, his face puffed with sleep and liquor. "I heard a woman shriek and I thought the rioters had come! What are these niggers doing here?"

Jacintha's attempt to explain was interrupted by another angry outburst. "Are you daft, madam? You know what's happening to coons in this town now! You want us to lose our home and maybe our lives for harboring them? Get those darkies out of here!"

"They can't leave yet, Cole!" She indicated the exhausted woman on the mattress. "This is April's sister, and she has just had a child."

"I don't care if she's just had an ape! She'll have to go, and those pickaninnies in the corner, too. They may have been followed. Get out of here, all of you!" he shouted fiercely, brandishing the gun.

"Please, sir, don't shoot!" April pleaded. "We's goin', fast as we can!"

She moved swiftly to rouse the drowsing children. "Wake up, chillen! Rastus, Prunella, Jessie, Chloe, Washington!"

Startled, rubbing sleepy eyes, they stumbled off the pallets, terrified to behold another armed white man. They tried to hide behind their aunt's skirts.

As Lollie assisted May to her feet, Jacintha hurried to wrap the infant in more towels and several small blankets. "I'm so sorry, April. So terribly sorry."

"There, there, Miz Danvers. Ain't no call to be sorry. You and Miss Lollie done helped us over the worst. I reckon we can manage now."

"But May is so weak!"

"No, ma'am. May ain't weak. She's real strong, ain't you, Sister?"

"Strong," May repeated, wobbling on unsteady legs.

"Where will you go?" Jacintha whispered anxiously.

"To the woods and hide," April answered. "The Lord'll protect us, like He do the creatures of the forest. It says so in the Bible, you know."

"In this awful storm? With the children and May' and the baby—"

Her eyes beseeched her glowering husband. Cole shook his leonine head adamantly and motioned the refugees toward the basement door.

"Wait!" Jacintha cried, gathering up blankets from the floor. "Take these, April—you'll need them. Lollie, put some food in a sack—ham, cheese, sausage, bread, cookies. They must eat."

Lollie obeyed, ignoring the master's tense scowl, grateful that he did not forbid her, knowing she would have defied him anyway. But when she brought the provisions, April hesitated to accept them, glancing dubiously at the master for permission.

"Take the stuff," he growled and, relenting a little, yanked a tarpaulin from a shelf on the wall. "This'll help keep the rain off."

"Thank you kindly, sir. God bless all of you."

"Be gone now," Cole ordered impatiently, "before you repay our kindness by bringing tragedy on us. There's a lane behind the stables—use it to get to the woods. And stay out of sight."

"Yes, sir."

"And don't *dare* tell anyone where you've been!"

"No, sir. No, we won't."

"Miz Danvers," ventured April, "do I still have a job?"

"Of course you do, April. Please come back—as soon as you feel safe."

They ventured out into the dark, wet night, April and the two eldest youngsters toting the precious gifts, May bent protectively over her newborn babe. Skulking through the trees to the rear of the property, the pathetic little group disappeared from sight.

"Poor black devils," Cole remarked, feeling a belated pang of conscience. "Under any other conditions, they could have camped here for a while."

"Under any other conditions, they wouldn't need to," Jacintha put in, wincing from a sudden twinge of pain, sharp but fleeting.

Cole took her arm as she faltered on the stairway. "I hope you didn't harm yourself. You should've known better with your own time so near."

"Your concern is touching," she mocked, brushing off his assistance. "I want to have some hot chocolate with Lollie. Go back to bed, Cole. I'm sorry we disturbed you."

He shrugged, yawning. "I still think we should have left, Jacintha. Don't blame me if anything goes wrong now. Blame your own stubborn self!"

The respite provided by the elements was short-lived. Rising with the sun, the mobs embarked eagerly upon another day of crime and violence.

Cole sent one of the hired men out for a paper, and the news was even worse than before.

"Didn't I tell you the wild fools would get wilder! The draft isn't the only issue anymore. These mobs are against the Irish, Catholics, and Jews now. They tried to wreck the Immigration Center, and beat up some people there. They claim the foreigners are taking their jobs, while Americans are fighting the war."

Before noon, one of Cole's burly bartenders delivered an urgent message. "The Puritans have gone to work on Chatham Square, sir, and Miss Roxy says to come quickly."

"Tell her I'm on my way."

Expecting him to make the usual excuses, Jacintha was astonished by his gallant response. Yesterday's coward, cringing at the prospect of a Confederate invasion, was today's fearless adventurer ignoring danger. The longer she lived with Cole, the less she understood him!

"You amaze me, Cole. You wouldn't fight the Rebels to aid your country, but you'll challenge the rioters to protect your property."

"I'm no soldier or marine, trained in military tactics," he explained, arming himself with a cartridge belt and several pistols. "But I know how to deal with hoodlums. I had plenty of practice in my youth. I'll not spill my guts for glory—that's for patriots. But I'll fight like hell to defend what's mine!"

"Your Bowery possessions must mean a great deal to you," Jacintha mused, thinking of Roxy LaFlame. "You don't seem nearly so concerned about your clothing factory and the tannery. I should think the sweatshops would be the primary targets of the exploited and enslaved workers."

"Not when their livelihoods are at stake! However much they may dislike their jobs and employers, they need the wages. Naw, it's the idle rich they hate."

He hesitated only slightly before leaving. "You'll be fairly safe here, I think. I've promised the guards extra bonuses for faithful service. You and Lollie remain inside. Lock the doors and keep some loaded weapons handy, too, just in case. I'll be back as soon as I can. If I can," he added realistically, picking up his Panama hat.

"Good luck."

"Good luck?" A sardonic smile turned up one side of his handlebar mustache. "Does my life mean anything to you?"

She avoided his intent gaze. "As I've told you before, Cole, I don't wish you dead or injured. I don't wish anyone death or injury."

"Thank you, Mrs. Danvers. It's a bone tossed to a hungry dog, but I'm starved enough to appreciate it. Goodbye, Puss. Take care of yourself and make junior wait till Papa can celebrate his birth."

His lips brushed her cheek in a farewell kiss. Then he rushed out to his saddled horse, handing the groom a sheaf of greenbacks before galloping away.

A vague malaise distressed Jacintha throughout the day, increasing toward evening. She attributed it to lack of rest and constant anxiety. A light supper and a soothing wine caudle provided some relief. But physical discomfort awakened her before dawn. She remained in bed, listening to the terrible sounds of the city. Gun shots, explosions, fire alarms, tolling church bells.

Another hot, muggy day to further inflame the frenzied mobs, she thought. Smoke floated over the island like huge black barrage balloons. Soot settled on Village homes and seeped into open windows. The frenzied exodus of terrified citizens continued. Would the holocaust ever end?

As she reached for the bell cord, pain shot through Jacintha's pelvis. She held her breath until it passed, and then tried again.

Up with the birds, Lollie had already prepared breakfast for the men. She answered Jacintha's summons, carrying a tray, but her greeting froze on her lips at the sight of Jacintha's pale, taut face.

"I—I think the baby may come today, Lollie."

"Oh, mercy! I was afraid of that. You strained yourself, helping those poor Negroes the other night."

"No, it's due, that's all."

"I'll send for the doctor. Meanwhile, some nice hot tea will relax you." She sounded cheerful as she filled the cup, but she silently cursed the master for deserting his wife in her crisis. "Drink this, now. And don't worry, dear, everything will be fine."

Like many of his colleagues, however, Dr. Selby was out ministering to riot victims. His office assistant had no idea where the doctor was, or who to recommend in his place. Without informing Jacintha, Lollie sent the coachman to an address in Maiden Lane, where she had recently noticed a physician's shingle.

This trip was successful—but the man Clancy brought back was hardly reassuring. Elderly, unsteady, he was quite the oddest-looking person Lollie had ever seen. His eyes had a peculiar glitter, and the enlarged pupils seemed never to focus properly. His long, gaunt, sallow-complected face twitched about the mouth. His wizened body lurched and jerked, as if afflicted with palsy or St. Vitus's Dance. Careless of dress and habit, he appeared little concerned about anything, least of all the confinement of a strange woman. Doffing his yellowed straw hat, he introduced himself with a snaggled-tooth grin.

"Doctor Jaffet, madam. Where's the patient?"

"This way, Doctor—and please hurry."

He ignored the plea, following slowly, a scuffed leather satchel in his quivering hand. "You can't hurry nature," he said, puffing before he reached the landing.

"This is her first child, Doctor, and she's already having pains!"

"Well, even the Virgin Mary had to endure labor, madam."

Although dismayed by the man's appearance, Jacintha permitted his rough and clumsy examination. She flinched, gritting her teeth and clenching her hands.

"Be careful," Lollie warned, shocked by his manner. She and April, with little medical knowledge, had handled May more compassionately. "She's in pain."

"Naturally, and she'll soon have more. Later contractions will probably be severe."

"Will you sedate her?"

"I don't believe in painless childbirth," he replied airily.

After six hours of crude and torturous midwifery, during which the patient was partially delirious, the fetus was literally yanked from Jacintha's womb with forceps. Drenched in her own sweat and blood, debilitated by prolonged agony, Jacintha wept with relief. Doctor Jaffet dosed her with laudanum. Then, tossing his soiled instruments into his satchel, he requested a fee of fifty dollars in cash.

"You'll receive a bank draft in the mail," Lollie told him. "Will Mrs. Danvers be all right?"

"Barring complications," he equivocated, and made a hasty exit.

While Jacintha slept, Lollie managed to change the bed. Then she bathed and put a clean gown on her. The baby had been tended to and placed in the nursery. He was a vigorous, beautifully formed boy, with his father's fine facial features and his mother's thick dark curls—undoubtedly a Britton.

Twilight found the town luridly aglow again with the work of arsonists, and bullets and ammunition from exploding arsenals continued to rend the torrid summer night. Now in their fifth day of rule, the terrorists showed no signs of abdicating. Nor had the governor's urgent appeals to Washington produced any troops.

An ominous silence had settled over Riverview. While the mistress dozed in drugged oblivion, her strength, her energy, her very life was trickling out, drop by drop.

Lollie looked in on her between chores but did not lift the sheet, reluctant to disturb the apparently tranquil slumber. Not until morning did she realize the true reason for Jacintha's quiet.

She was slowly, silently bleeding to death!

Chapter 29

THE memory of the next twenty-four hours would always be a hideous nightmare for Lollie.

Dr. Selby was still away, somewhere in the embattled city, and another urgent message was dispatched to Jaffet. Lollie worked desperately with Jacintha, employing every means she had ever heard of to stop the hemorrhaging. She forced some ergot down Jacintha's throat. She packed her with cotton, elevated her feet, and placed cold wet cloths on her abdomen. All were helpful to some degree, but none stopped the bleeding entirely.

By the time Jaffet finally arrived, shortly after noon, blood had soaked through the mattress and stained the carpet under the bed. Jacintha's face was as white as the bleached pillowcase.

"High time you came!" Lollie accused him.

He bowed stoically. "My apologies, madam. I was unavoidably detained by an emergency."

"This is an emergency too! Do something, quick! She's bleeding badly!"

"Calm yourself, madam. Hemorrhage is a common complication in protracted labor and instrument delivery. I'll give her some ergot."

"I already gave her some—it doesn't seem to help."

"I'll pack her and apply cold towels."

"I've done all that! It's not enough!"

Jaffet shrugged. His tremors had recently been alleviated by a narcotic. "Well, madam, I don't know why you sent for me. I can't do any more than you have. The situation appears to be under control."

"But it isn't!" Lollie cried, frantic. "That's what I'm trying to tell you! Can't you see? She needs immediate medical attention! You must have treated cases like this before."

"Many times, madam. In my younger days. However, I'm somewhat retired now."

"Well, how did you save those other women?"

"Most of them died," he replied casually. "A uterine hemorrhage that does not cease within twenty-four hours or less is generally fatal. All we can do is wait."

He seated himself comfortably in Cole's easy chair, propping his feet on the ottoman. Removing a newspaper from his wrinkled seersucker jacket, he began to read about the Draft Riots, the accounts of which filled the major journals whose presses were still operating. His reactions to the stories indicated sadistic enjoyment of the gruesome details—a sinister pleasure in the gory and heinous crimes. Once he laughed aloud, then smacked his blanched lips.

Lollie stared at him in horrified astonishment and helpless rage. Was he mad? Had she unwittingly summoned a lunatic? She could imagine what sort of emergency had detained him—an abortion, probably, which he had performed without the benefit of sedation.

"I heard on the way over that some troops from the Army of the Potomac have finally arrived," he remarked casually.

"They should have arrived several days ago."

"Did you read about Colonel H. F. O'Brian, commander of the New York Eleventh Regiment? The rioters made a bloody, mutilated mess of that big Mick. But he was a tough fellow, and took a lot of punishment in the process.

They clubbed and kicked and trampled him before shooting him. And they wouldn't allow a priest to give him the last rites—that voodoo ritual of holy water and anointing oils, you know? Nor would they permit a hearse to remove his corpse to a morgue. They said a handcart or manure wheelbarrow was good enough for the Irish Papist bastard. Oh, I beg your pardon, madam, but that's the description right here in *The New York Herald*. Brave of Mr. Bennett to print such forbidden words—but who's to censor him now?"

He turned the page eagerly. "Well, well! Over on Clarkson Street, near Hudson, they lynched several niggers, then built a bonfire on the scene and danced like ghouls in a macabre play. Ghastly, eh?"

"I don't want to hear any more," Lollie objected, but he continued as though he had not heard.

"No man in military or police uniform is safe, and some authorities are wearing citizens' dress. God help any back-collared minister, skull-capped Jew, or immigrant caught speaking his native tongue."

As the opiate wore off, Jacintha woke and murmured something too incoherent for Lollie to understand. She was dazed, pitifully weak, and growing steadily weaker.

Jaffet rose to observe the patient, and his ghostly visage resembled a skull to Jacintha. She closed her eyes again, certain that Death had come for her. She was too feeble to care.

"She won't last the day," Jaffet predicted. "Too bad her husband isn't here. Is he in the military?"

Lollie nodded, hardly hearing the question. "Oh, Doctor! Can't you think of something?"

"You may as well sit down, madam. Shrieking won't accomplish anything. Death is as natural as life. It's nothing to fear."

Lollie was being pushed beyond endurance. "It's not natural for one so young! She's only twenty-two."

"Madam, my son died before his first birthday—dropped on his head by a clumsy, stupid nanny. My wife was dead before she was thirty. We all die, sooner or later. For some, it's just sooner. I've seen people of all ages, including many children, die. They died like flies in the yellow-fever plague of eighteen twenty-two, and young men are dying by the thousands in battle right now."

Lollie glared at him. "I'm sure human life is no more sacred to you than an insect's."

"Sentiment is of no avail in the medical profession," he drawled, "and few physicians weep at their patients' funerals."

Why, he's out of his mind! Lollie thought, dismayed and suddenly afraid of him. That's why he looks and acts so strangely. He's loony! Oh, sweet Savior! That's all we needed—a mad physician!

In her anxiety, Lollie did not hear the sound of the knocker, until Jaffet announced, "I believe you have a caller, madam."

Lollie sped downstairs. No matter who was at the door, she would beg him to come in and help evict the maniac doctor.

Major Earl Britton stood at the threshold, his uniform dusty and torn in several places, a long scratch across his cheek and a dark bruise on his forehead.

He had been in the Battle of Gettysburg, which was how he happened to be in Pennsylvania when the Secretary of War ordered five regiments from the Army of the Potomac to cope with the Manhattan emergency. Major Britton had arrived early this morning, in command of a battalion composed largely of volunteer New Yorkers, and had been occupied with the insurrection ever since. Overwhelmed by the military might, the insurgents soon surrendered or fled. Gramercy Park and several other squares were transformed into temporary armed camps and stockades, along with the Armory, the Tombs, and other prisons and police stations.

Lollie almost fainted at the sight of him. "Providence must have sent you, Major!"

He smiled slightly. "Uncle Sam sent me, Lollie. I've been here for hours, wrestling with the rioters. I'm a sight, am I not? I didn't get this bashed up at Gettysburg. Lollie, is everything all right?"

Her pent emotions burst in a torrent of tears. "Oh, no! Everything is all wrong! She's sick, sir. Dying—"

"*Jacintha?*"

"Yes, yes! The baby has been born but—"

"*Baby?*"

Lollie nodded, choking on her sobs. "Yes, and now she's dying—"

"Good Lord! Where is she?"

"Upstairs, in the master suite at the end of the hall. Some strange doctor is with her, but he—"

"And Mr. Danvers?"

"He's away. Some trouble on the Bowery."

Earl ran through the foyer and up the stairway.

Jaffet, taking Jacintha's pulse, glanced up at Earl's entrance and assumed the uniformed officer was her husband.

"I'm glad you were able to get here, sir, but I have bad news for you. Your wife is dying."

Earl stared at him for a stunned moment, then swiftly approached the bed, stricken by what he saw. Jacintha was unconscious, her eyes sunk in deep, darkly ringed sockets, her face pallid as a wax lily. She appeared already dead, but he refused to believe he was losing her.

"She can't be dying, Doctor! She can't be!"

"I'm sorry, Major, but she is. Hemorrhage. I managed to ease the flow some, but I can't stop it. Ergot doesn't help, nor does packing." He blithely took credit for the measures Lollie had taken. "I give her another two or three hours."

"Then do something! You *are* a physician, aren't you?"

"I am, sir. Doctor Morris Jaffet. The family physician was unavailable, and I was summoned on emergency. The child, a boy, was born yesterday. The travail exhausted her, and I administered a sedative. She was all right when I left."

"Well, obviously that's not the case now!"

"Sometime during the night she commenced to hemorrhage. It was a long and difficult delivery, and there must have been lacerations of the uterus."

"Must have been? Don't you *know?*"

"Such traumas are hard to detect at the time, Major."

"Can't you repair them by surgery or stypsis?"

"I'm not a surgeon and I have no styptics. Tannic acid might help . . . but I doubt if any could be located in town. The Army has first call on drugs, you know, especially tannin. And with the riots here, what little the pharmacists had in stock was soon dissipated. If the wounds were external, I could apply pressure or do hot-iron cauterization. As it is, these alternatives are unfeasible. What would you suggest, sir? A tourniquet?" His unctuous smile enraged Earl.

"Don't attempt humor, Doctor! It's obvious that you have no real interest in saving this patient."

"Then pray call in another physician, sir. As you have no confidence in me, I do not wish to continue on this case."

"You know it's too late to find anyone else! You'll stay. And you'll do more than talk—even if you do so at gunpoint! Do I make myself clear?"

Jaffet glanced nonchalantly at the holstered pistol. "You don't frighten me, Major. I'm an old man, my health is impaired, my family and fortune gone. At best, I have but a few years left in this world."

"You won't have a few minutes left if you don't help this lady! It was probably your negligence that put her in danger."

"I beg your pardon, sir—but her present straits are more your fault than mine. You were responsible for her pregnancy, not I."

Earl scowled. "You're a disgrace to your profession, Jaffet. You should be barred from practice—if you are not already," he said suspiciously.

"No aspersions on my ability, please. This is unfortunate, but it can't be helped. I've done everything possible. There's nothing left, except blood-letting."

"Blood-letting? My God, man! Are you insane? She's moribund now from loss of blood! You're either a fool or a fiend, or both. You don't really want to save her, do you? You want her to die—you want to watch her die!"

"You misjudge me, Major. Death has no effect whatever on me. I've seen too much of it."

"I don't doubt that." Earl strode to the door and flung it open. "Your services are no longer required, Doctor."

"My fee hasn't been paid."

"What is your fee?"

"One hundred dollars," Jaffet stated, doubling the price originally quoted.

Earl took out his wallet and handed him the bills. "And now please leave!"

"Gladly, sir." Jaffet retrieved his hat and bag. "But you'll need a physician to sign the death certificate."

"She's not going to die!"

"It'll take a miracle to save her."

"Then I'll perform a miracle."

"That's mighty talk, Major. Let me know if you succeed."

"Get out, goddamn you, before I kill you!"

On his way out, Jaffet advised Lollie to prepare a shroud. She rushed back upstairs. "Is she—is she—?" Shaking, Lollie could not speak the dreadful word.

"No," Earl said, frowning gravely. "I ordered Jaffet out. He's demented, either from senility or drugs. The charlatan wanted to bleed her!"

"Oh, I thought he was crazy! I should never have sent for him, but Doctor Selby was out, and—Oh Jesus! Dear Jesus, help us!" She was wringing her hands.

Earl caught her shoulders and shook her gently. "Don't go to pieces, Lollie. There's no time for hysteria. Miss Jacintha's not going to die. We can save her, somehow, but we must work fast."

"Tell me what to do, sir."

"We'll need extra towels, a large syringe, cool water, vinegar, alum, and cotton."

"I'll get them," Lollie called as she rushed out.

Earl was waiting by the bed when she brought the items. His tunic and weapons were off, his shirt sleeves rolled back, and his hands already washed in the bathroom basin.

"Put them on the table," he directed, then explained what she was to do.

Lollie listened carefully, in command of herself now, her faith renewed. She prepared a douche of cool water, vinegar, and alum, while Earl formed a tampon of cotton batting to soak in the solution. Then he pulled the sheet from Jacintha's inert body. Her gown, the linens, the mattress were crimson with warm blood. Fear clutched him like a heavy hand.

He glanced at Lollie. "The old packing must be removed, a sanitary wash administered, and new protection inserted. If you're easily embarrassed, you needn't watch. I think I can manage alone."

"I'll stay, sir, of course."

"Thank you. One mercy—she won't feel any pain. She's completely unconscious now."

Earl worked swiftly, yet cautiously, and Lollie admired his gentleness and skill. If only he had been present during the birth.

"How do you know what to do, sir?"

Earl answered quietly while he worked.

"I've read some medical books, and if that medieval witch doctor had ever read one, he'd have known too. These styptics and astringents have been used for centuries. They are included in the kits of the battlefield medics, along with the Surgeon General's manual."

During the many ministrations, Jacintha remained perfectly motionless, aware of nothing. Her faint pulse was difficult to locate and her lips had a bluish tinge. But at least she was still alive, if barely.

Lollie asked, "What else can we do, sir?"

"We can pray," he answered softly.

"I've been doing that all along, Major." As indeed she had.

"So have I, Lollie. So have I."

Chapter 30

"**W**OULDN'T you like a drink, sir, and some food?" Lollie asked. "You must be tired and hungry—fighting the rioters all day, and now this."

Earl admitted to fatigue but not hunger. "I would like some coffee, however, strong and black, if you care to make it," he said.

"Gladly, sir. I could do with a cup myself."

During her absence, Earl stepped into the adjoining nursery to see the child. He stood by the cradle, remembering, calculating. He thought he knew the time of conception. More important, many of his physical characteristics were visible in the child's—the line of his jaw, the shape of his head, the small flat ears. Both he and Jacintha had dark hair, but the infant had his mother's curls. If ever, during the months past, Earl had doubted the reality of their love, here was the living proof of that love. In those few intimate hours, he had begotten an heir for another man!

Lollie spoke softly from the threshold. "Your coffee, sir."

Brooding, Earl seemed not to hear. His body was tense and the heavy veins of his neck and arms throbbed.

"There's something I must tell you, Major."

But when finally he turned, Lollie knew that he had already figured it out for himself, as she had imagined he would.

"You know, don't you?" she asked. He only nodded, without speaking.

When an hour had passed without the tampon being saturated Earl began to hope. He had seen enough bleeding on the battlefield to realize how much was fatal. He estimated Jacintha's loss to be near the perilous limit; another pint or so would probably kill her.

He remained in constant attendance, intermittently examining Jacintha and listening to her heart. She was still critical, but her condition did not appear to worsen.

Lollie, ever fond of adages, was encouraged. "Where there's life, there's hope, sir."

Earl nodded, afraid to press their luck. "Maybe she senses your presence, sir."

"I hope so, Lollie. I just wish there were some way to give her a transfusion of my own blood."

They kept a long vigil, drinking coffee and bolstering each other's morale with conversation.

Earl was somber and remorseful. "If she dies, I'll never forgive myself, Lollie."

"You mustn't feel that way, sir. Miss Jacintha wouldn't want you to blame yourself. Besides, I think she's going to live! But I'm troubled now about the master. Suppose he walked in here at this very minute?"

"I wish he would," Earl said grimly. "I have an old score to settle with him, and now he has a new one to settle with me. This situation must be resolved. I can't leave her to face him alone, after I'm gone. I'd be wild with worry, expecting him to harm her or the child."

"Do you have a plan?"

"Only the usual solution," he answered. "I'll give him a chance to avenge his honor."

"Honor!" the housekeeper scoffed. "I fear he has little of that, sir."

Earl leaned forward, resting his elbows on his knees and

his chin in his hands. "Nevertheless, I'm the trespasser here, Lollie, and a challenge is in order."

"A duel?" Horror filled Lollie. "Isn't that against the law in this state?"

"Yes, since the Burr-Hamilton incident—but there are ways to circumvent the law."

"Oh, but Miss Jacintha wouldn't approve of that! She considers dueling murder."

"It's hardly worse than war," Earl said musingly. "Men slaughtering and maiming one another in battle, clashing swords and bayonets like nineteenth-century gladiators. Only they have no shields to ward off the Minié balls and artillery volleys. I've often thought it would be more civilized to force the leaders of dissenting nations to settle their disputes and grievances by personal combat, rather than resort to the primitive savagery of massive conflict. War is nothing but bloody insanity!"

Down in the foyer, Lollie heard the heirloom clock striking midnight, and its melodious chimes seemed to echo mournfully through the house. Once the favorite timepiece of Jacintha's grandparents, was it now marking the minutes left on this earth to their beloved granddaughter?

She rose quietly. "I've prepared a guest chamber across the hall, Mr. Earl. You must get some sleep. I'll sit with Miss Jacintha."

"No, you go to bed, Lollie. You need your rest to care for the baby. Please—I want to stay with her."

"I understand, sir. But you could use the trundle. You shouldn't try to stay up all night."

"It wouldn't be the first time," he said. "Don't worry about me, Lollie. Just bring more coffee."

Earl had slept less than four hours in the past thirty-six. His muscles ached. His eyes were bloodshot and swollen, and dark stubble shadowed his face. But worry and a pot of potent black coffee kept him as alert as a sentry. Even had his weary body permitted him to sleep, his anxious mind would not.

He made another examination. Thank God, there was

no evidence of hemorrhage, and her pulse felt stronger. The crisis seemed to have passed, although she was still not out of danger.

His first joyous reward came as the initial gray-pink light of dawn filtered through the east windows. Jacintha opened her eyes and gazed fleetingly at the ceiling before closing them again. By noon she was partially awake, disoriented but apparently remarkably improved. Earl made efforts to rouse her.

"Jacintha! Jacintha!" He waited for signs that she recognized his voice. "Jacintha, it's Earl. Can you speak to me?"

A faint smile dimpled the corners of her mouth, as if she were having a pleasant dream, and finally she murmured, "Earl?"

"Yes, darling, yes!"

"I—I can't see you very well. Come closer."

He dropped to his knees beside the bed, but was afraid of hurting her in his embrace. "I'm right here, Jacintha."

She was still confused, unable to understand what she heard. She had experienced many illusions during death's proximity. Perhaps this was only another hallucination.

"Am I dead?" she whispered.

"No, Jacintha, you're alive! You've been very ill, but you're better now. Lollie is fixing you some broth. And darling, we're the parents of a fine little boy!"

Memory returned in fragments, which she tried to piece together. "Really? The baby is here? It's over, and you—you know?"

"Yes, dearest, I know everything."

"I—I can't believe you're actually here, Earl. I thought I was going away somewhere forever . . ."

His lips brushed hers lightly. "Delirium, darling. I'll tell you all about it later. Lie still now and rest."

But Jacintha had to convince herself by touch, and she lifted a flaccid hand to his face. Earl laid his head gently on her breast—and it was in this position that Lollie found them.

"I've brought the soup, sir. And some gruel, too."

"I'll feed her," Earl said.

The Draft Riots, now believed to have been a Confederate conspiracy to incite anarchy in the Union, had almost succeeded. Similar rebellions were instigated in other large Northern cities. None equaled New York's in violence and destruction, however, or required as much armed intervention to quell it.

The terrible scars would not be soon obliterated: blackened ruins, heaps of rubble, damaged streets, blown-up bridges and docks, hundreds of dead and hundreds of wounded. Funeral processions continued for days, while wreckages were searched for additional victims.

Cole had not returned to Riverview. Nor had he sent any message. Long absences from home were not unusual for him, but the birth of the child had seemed imminent, so Jacintha was puzzled. But she pushed Cole from her thoughts.

Lollie told Earl privately, "I don't think Mr. Danvers stayed in town. He was too anxious to leave when the trouble started. I bet him and that woman went away together."

"What woman?"

"Roxy LaFlame, she calls herself. She's . . . some kind of entertainer in one of his Bowery dens. Miss Jacintha knows about her. She told me Miss LaFlame is close to Mr. Danvers."

"I see." This was the first Earl had heard of Danvers having a mistress.

Without telling either woman, Major Britton authorized and conducted a search of the Danvers properties on Chatham Square. But he could not tell Jacintha what he and his men discovered, until she was stronger.

Doctor Selby soon pronounced her well enough to begin nursing the infant, who had been subsisting on sugar-water with a few drops of brandy, and strained beef-and-barley broth. He was still rosy all over, his tiny face often puckered in plaintive hunger, but Jacintha thought him adorable at all times, the image of his handsome father. She examined his perfect fingers and toes, kissed his cherubic cheeks, fondled his silky curls, and pressed his hungry little mouth lovingly to her breasts. She also rejected the doctor's recommendation that she have a supplementary wet nurse.

"I can recommend a reliable one, Mrs. Danvers."

"No, thank you, Doctor. He's my baby, and I want to feed him myself, if I can."

"Then you must eat lots of nourishing food and take the prescribed tonic," he advised. "In due time, I'll give you a thorough physical examination."

When he had gone, Lollie said, "I've heard that beer helps to make milk."

"Probably an old wives' tale, Lollie—but send one of the men for a keg of it."

Despite the ravages of her ordeal, Jacintha had never seemed lovelier. Earl enjoyed ministering to her and watching her nurse the baby. He supervised her meals and medications. He liked to brush her hair after her bath, twining the damp tendrils about his fingers.

Jacintha smiled at him, feeling stronger every day. "Are you proud of your son, Major?"

"I'm proud of you both," he said huskily. "Words can't express my true feelings, Jacintha."

"I almost died, didn't I? And you saved my life. Lollie told me while you were at headquarters."

"She shouldn't have."

"I insisted, Earl. That stupid, cruel old quack! You came just in time. I owe you my life."

"Just returning a favor, my love. You saved mine once, remember?"

"No, only your arm. Is it all right now?"

"Perfect. Didn't even spoil my aim."

"How long will you be in town?" she asked, after a silence.

"As long as martial law is in effect. A few more weeks, probably, unless there's more rioting."

Jacintha frowned, suddenly voicing what had long worried her. "Why hasn't Cole come home?"

"Concerned about him?"

She glanced toward the nursery. "I'm concerned about a number of things, Earl."

"I know, darling. So am I." There was a tentative pause. "Suppose he never comes back?"

"What do you mean?" she cried, staring at him. "Are you and Lollie keeping something from me? You've been whispering together and you both avoid my questions. What's wrong, Earl? Tell me!" Then, before he could offer a comforting lie, she said, "Cole is dead, isn't he? That's why he hasn't returned. He's dead!"

After some hesitation, Earl decided that knowledge would be preferable to uncertainty. He nodded slowly. "Yes, he's dead."

Jacintha sighed. "I felt it. I had a premonition of his death—and I think he did too. The way he talked and acted before going to the Bowery. How did it happen? Do you know?"

"According to someone who saw it all, thieves were after the safe in his concert saloon. He was shot in the scuffle."

"Poor Cole! Money was so important to him. How ironic that it cost him his life! Who saw it?"

"One of his bouncers."

"And Roxy LaFlame?"

"They died together," Earl said. "Cole was badly wounded but she refused to leave him, even after the rioters set fire to the place. It was reported in the newspapers, which is why we kept them from you."

"Faithful Roxy! She must have loved him greatly, and I think it was mutual. Perhaps Cole's biggest mistake was in not realizing that in time, or thinking that he wanted something else in a wife."

After allowing her time to absorb the news, Earl explained, "The remains have already been interred, Jacintha.

I knew Cole's attorneys, and I asked them to make the arrangements. They will also handle his business affairs until you are well enough for the reading of the will. Cole lost some other Bowery properties, too. The ruins haven't been probed yet, however, and are still guarded against looters."

"He was never happy, Earl. For all his bluff and bluster, and all his success, Cole was miserable. He never got what he really wanted from life."

"Does anyone?" he sighed.

"Probably not."

"I'm sorry if I sound callous, my dear. I just don't feel like eulogizing Cole Danvers." A few days ago Earl had seriously considered killing the man in a challenge, or being killed by him. Some rioters had spared him the trouble, and Earl's only feeling now was relief. "It's over, Jacintha. Let's try to look forward."

"To what? I'm a widowed mother at twenty-two."

Dagger-sharp jealousy stabbed at Earl. "Maybe you miss Cole?"

She shook her head vehemently. "No, but I can't help pitying him, Earl. He longed so desperately for all the wrong things—died for one of them, in fact."

"Well, he doesn't need pity now, Jacintha—or anything else."

"Except prayer," she reflected. "God rest his soul. And Roxy's too."

"Amen," Earl said softly. "I suppose it would be indecent to consider ourselves now, Jacintha, but we must consider our child. Legally he's Cole's offspring and will bear his name, unless I can eventually change it. Death freed you and divorce can free me. It would work no hardship on Laurette, believe me."

"You've spoken to her?"

"Not recently, but I will. The servants said she went to Philadelphia the day before the riots."

"Well, don't go after her, Earl. Rushing her might be the wrong approach."

"Laurette is well aware of the farce our marriage has become. I doubt she'd be much surprised by my request."

"But she may be suspicious," Jacintha argued. "Don't you think she reads the local papers—and knows about Cole?"

"I don't see the connection, Jacintha."

"Oh, Earl! Laurette has been suspicious of you and me since we were guardian and ward. So I don't think it's wise to provoke her prematurely. She might visit Riverview!"

"My God, you're right! Forgive me, Jacintha. You're still recuperating, and you don't want Laurette descending on you!"

He clasped her hand in both of his.

"I'll wait, Jacintha, and do whatever you think best."

His humility moved her deeply. "We love each other, Earl. There must never be any doubt of that for either of us."

"Never," he vowed. "I was half crazy when I thought I might lose you, Jacintha."

"It's always the same for me when you're away fighting, darling. Oh, if only we could be together now as we were that day in the country!"

"If only," he agreed, holding her tenderly.

"What are you thinking, Major?"

"That I have some urgent business at headquarters," he replied, retreating from temptation.

All too soon for Jacintha, martial law was lifted and the troops, including Major Britton's, were dispatched to other missions. When he came to bid her farewell, wearing a new blue tunic with golden oak leaves on the shoulders and a dashing fringed sash, Jacintha remembered the first time she had seen him in uniform.

"How much time do you have?" she inquired tremulously.

"About an hour."

She reached her hands out to him. "I'll write to you every day, Earl. At least we can correspond now."

"Yes."

"I suppose you can't tell me where you're going."

"No."

"But it's a battle zone, isn't it?"

"Jacintha, behave now."

"Sorry," she said sniffing. "Are you sure you're satisfied with the name we decided to give the baby, Earl? Grandpa would be so pleased."

"So am I," he assured her. "One more look at him now, my love, and then I must go. . . ."

Summer passed into fall, and autumn into winter. The war, now in its third devastating year, had become a part of daily life.

One cold, gray November day Jacintha was in the library, writing to Earl, when the maid delivered a calling card on a silver salver. The engraved ivory vellum and narcissus scent were unmistakable. What had brought Laurette to Riverview now? Jacintha concealed the letter under the desk blotter. When her visitor entered, Jacintha was busy arranging a bowl of flowers.

Accustomed to platforms and stages, Laurette made her entrance, wearing a dramatic costume of army-blue wool with gold buttons. The tight jacket, cut in the currently popular military fashion, accentuated her hourglass figure, and she carried a huge muff designed like a haversack. The brim of her matching felt hat was swept up on one side like a cavalry officer's and secured with a jeweled replica of crossed sabers.

Jacintha's greeting was falsely cordial. "Good afternoon, Laurette. How nice to see you again!"

"I've been intending to call for months, Jacintha—ever since I learned of your bereavement. But my civic and social duties keep me occupied, and I also travel rather frequently. I read about your husband's misfortune. It was simply dreadful, and a terrible shock to you, I'm sure. Please accept my belated condolences."

"Thank you," Jacintha murmured. "Won't you sit down? I'll ring for tea."

"Oh, don't bother! I can't stay long—I have to attend a bond rally at Cooper Union. I'm always working for the Cause, you know. Naturally you're still in mourning—but I hope you'll be able to contribute your services again soon. The need grows increasingly urgent."

"I'll try," Jacintha promised, even managing a smile.

Her visitor flounced about the spacious library, appraising the fine furniture and tasteful decoration. "You've renovated Riverview completely, haven't you?"

"Yes, several years ago."

Laurette paused to examine, and covet, a unique ebony cabinet inlaid with ivory, mother-of-pearl, and tortoiseshell. "A rare treasure! Genuine Boulle, isn't it?"

"I was lucky at an auction," Jacintha said modestly.

"Indeed you were! My Boulle pales by comparison. You have excellent taste, my dear. And I must say, Riverview bears no traces of its master's personality. How quickly the dead efface themselves—and how conveniently!"

Jacintha ignored the sarcasm. Even Laurette's compliments were double-edged, and her every remark seemed to be a feeler—a wedge with which she hoped to prize open some secret. Jacintha held herself ready and alert, but how could she outwit a woman so well-practiced in the art of intrigue?

"Since Earl was in town at the time of Mr. Danvers's demise, I trust he paid his respects?"

"I don't know, Laurette. He may have. I was in seclusion, recovering from a difficult confinement. My baby was born during the riots, and my physician forbade visitors."

"How forgetful of me! I believe Cole's obituary did mention a child. A boy, isn't it?"

"Yes. He's four months old now."

"May I see him, please?"

"Of course," Jacintha agreed, praying that he would be asleep, for it was with his eyes open that he was so much his father's son. "Come with me to the nursery. Ronnie is napping now, but I don't think we'll disturb him."

Ronnie was snug in his crib, his adorable pink face framed with dark ringlets, his two tiny fists peeking above the blue bunting. Vigilant Lollie sat in a nearby rocker, knitting bootees. She nodded politely to Mrs. Britton, signaling silence with a finger to her lips, and continued clicking the bone needles. She had not dropped a stitch, though Laurette's presence had taken her by surprise.

Envy glowed in Laurette's green eyes. She had not expected to see quite such a beautiful child, but rather a miniature of Cole Danvers. "He's precious," she whispered.

"Thank you. I'm very proud of him."

"You should be. He's an angel."

"Shh!" Lollie cautioned, motioning again for quiet. Laurette moved away from the crib and held her tongue until she and Jacintha were out of the nursery. "He has your hair," she said on the stairway. "Whose eyes does he have?"

Jacintha had her answer ready. "So far, his eyes seem to be his very own."

"You christened him Ronald—after your grandfather, I presume? Wouldn't Cole have preferred a junior?"

"We never discussed it beforehand," Jacintha replied. "And afterwards—well . . ." She shrugged.

"To quote the Bard, 'what's in a name?' "

"Precisely."

"I know this will sound absurd to you, since I never saw your son before this, but there's something familiar about him. Isn't that odd?"

Jacintha's heart leaped. "Some people think all babies look alike."

"I wish Ronnie had been awake, though. No doubt he's even sweeter with his eyes open. He must be a great comfort to you now."

"My days would be empty without him."

In the foyer Laurette sighed, "Earl has always wanted children, but we were never so blessed. And now, with him in the army . . . Did you know he was wounded in the Battle of Antietam and recuperated here in New York? That he was also in the James Peninsula Campaign and at Gettysburg?" Her feline eyes, now speckled jade and amber, searched Jacintha's face like a prowling cat's.

"Yes, I've read about his regiment's many citations in the war news," she admitted. "I'm glad his battle injuries weren't serious."

"Serious enough! He might have lost an arm. I was frantic when notified—and rushed right home from Philadelphia. He was on the mend by then, however, and had already returned to duty. This terrible war! I wonder if it will ever end. But you need not concern yourself much about anything anymore, do you? I suppose Danvers left you well provided?"

"My financial security is assured, Laurette."

"That's comforting, isn't it? Fortunately I've never had any monetary problems. Nor has Earl. We were born with the proverbial spoon in our mouths—except in my case, it was gold."

The maid was holding the guest's blue silk umbrella.

"I'm sorry to rush off, Jacintha, but I mustn't be late to the bond rally. I'm a key speaker, you see, along with some government dignitaries. I hope we exceed our goal. The War Department is desperate for funds. It could be worse, though, I suppose. I hear the South is bankrupt enough to take people's jewelry. Heaven forbid! Goodbye, dear, and be brave."

"Good luck at the rally," Jacintha said, shaking hands.

And good riddance, she thought as the carriage drove away. But why had Laurette *really* come to Riverview? And why was Jacintha afraid to meet her again?

Chapter 31

IN February of 1864, Earl—now Colonel Britton—received temporary assignment to Washington. But his letters advised Jacintha not to try to visit him. He described the city as a vast armed military camp, always subject to enemy attack.

Undaunted, Jacintha began packing her bags. Lollie tried to dissuade her. "You know what Mr. Earl wrote! You should not risk the trip!"

"I've got to see him, Lollie. Will you take good care of the baby?"

"You know I will—but that's not the point, Missy. What if you can't get transportation to Washington?"

"Stop arguing, Lollie, and help me get ready. I'm going, no matter what!"

After liberally greasing the necessary palms, Jacintha was on her way south. She changed trains in Baltimore, boarding the Washington & Ohio—the only line to the Capital from the north, east, or west.

Camps and supply depots, warehouses, rows of mushroomlike tents and makeshift barracks paralleled the entire route. Soldiers drilled in the village squares, bivouacked on the paths in snow-covered fields, hunched around bonfires while eating from tin utensils.

Long columns of foot and mounted troops, caissons and wagons and ambulances moved along the slushy, rutted roads. They broke down bridges in their paths, churned the streams into muddy bogs, trampled fields into marshes. Maryland's countryside was spoiled, and the natives were resentful. For though the state remained neutral, her slave-holding interests and sympathies lay with the South. Many of the state's young men volunteered to fight with the Confederacy, and the Union had to counteract sabotage actions within Maryland's borders. The transportation system, a prime target, had to be vigilantly protected. Unguarded Northern trains might be ambushed, dynamited, and robbed en route—the principal reasons why Earl had warned Jacintha against coming to Washington.

Fortunately this run was completed safely, and only slightly behind schedule. Arriving in Washington, Jacintha took the first accommodations she could arrange for, sight unseen. As she left the bustling depot behind, she got her first glimpse of the Capitol. The flag waved over the partially finished dome, which had been under construction for twelve years. Indeed, most of the Federal buildings were incomplete. There was something awesome about the great chunks of marble and granite, the stacks of lumber and tiles, the partially erected walls and roofs, the classic Ionic pillars and portals, the broad steps leading nowhere —the foundations of an ambitious metropolis suddenly halted by catastrophe. Perhaps it would never be finished— or perhaps the Rebels would be the architects!

Forts crowned every hilltop. Armored vessels were docked in the Navy Yard and gunboats were anchored in the Potomac. Sentinels guarded all approaches and exits. Uniforms were everywhere. Reconnaissance balloons floated overhead. Traffic was frequently halted on Pennsylvania Avenue while supply caravans and cavalry rumbled over the cobblestones, pounding them to chips and dust. The vaults under the Capitol terraces served as Army bakeries, and military guards patrolled the White House grounds.

Business prospered as never before. Merchants, owners of taverns, saloons, brothels, and casinos, hucksters, and hustlers reaped huge profits. Jacintha had never seen so much sin in the open. No wonder the nation's preachers compared Washington to Rome before its fall.

The Manor House, where Jacintha boarded, was currently the property of an enterprising Yankee widow, and some emancipated slaves were in her employ.

"I'm visiting my husband," Jacintha informed the woman, signing the register accordingly. "I will need someone to take a message to him."

"My son runs errands," she said, beckoning a lad lounging in the improvised lobby. "You'll find stationery, quill, and ink in the desk. Is Colonel Britton in the War Department?"

"The cavalry," Jacintha replied, picking up her key, "on temporary assignment here."

"Well, I'm sure he'll be happy to see you, Mrs. Britton. But you took a chance coming here, you know—especially all the way from New York!"

The youth, also acting as porter, followed her upstairs with the luggage. He waited while Jacintha wrote a note, then sealed and addressed the envelope. "What's your name, son?"

"William, ma'am. Some folks call me Billy Yank, which is better than Johnny Reb, ain't it? I'm gonna enlist soon as I'm old enough, if the war ain't over by then. Ma cries when I say that. She just don't want me to be a hero, I guess."

Jacintha smiled at his youthful naïveté. There were drummer boys his age in the field, and the Army was considering drafting boys of sixteen. "Mothers are like that, Billy—they want to keep their sons safe. Take this to Cavalry Headquarters, please. If Colonel Britton is out, ask that it be delivered to him. Here's a dollar for your trouble."

"Gee, lady! For a eagle, I'd take it to Richmond and give it to old Jeff Davis!" He saluted and marched off whistling "Yankee Doodle," pretending that his bellboy uniform was a real soldier's, and he was on an important mission.

Jacintha was well pleased with her accommodations. While the chambermaid steamed the creases from a petal-pink velvet gown, the guest luxuriated in a warm, scented bath. Earl had not seen Jacintha since last summer, before she was fully recuperated, and she wanted to be especially attractive to him now.

The maid was much impressed by her beauty, expensive wardrobe, and jewelry. "You're much prettier than Kate Chase Sprague," she remarked, helping Jacintha dress. "And Mrs. Lincoln would be even more jealous of you than she is of her."

The feud between the First Lady and the gorgeous young wife of Senator Sprague, former Governor of Rhode Island, was common knowledge—as closely observed by the social columnists as the war was observed by the battlefield correspondents.

Jacintha had read about the brilliant wedding of Kate Chase, daughter of the secretary of the Treasury, in the New York journals. Mrs. Lincoln had declined to attend, even though the President had given the bride away, and she shunned the spectacular entertainments of Washington's now most famous and popular hostess. Journalists surmised that the First Lady bitterly resented Kate's presidential aspirations for her father, Salmon P. Chase, and the use of her elaborate home as a political salon to further her outrageous ambitions.

"Oh, I doubt that," Jacintha said, tucking a pair of pearl combs into her dark curls, where they glistened like iridescent dewdrops. "I suspect many of the stories about the Lincolns are exaggerated, like the caricatures in the newspapers and magazines."

"Maybe. But even the servants say she flies into a jealous rage if he so much as looks at another woman, regardless of her age or condition. And she won't let him open a ball with anyone but her. If she's not on his arm, he must promenade alone—or with another man. Isn't that silly?"

"Absurd," Jacintha agreed. "But I'm sure Mr. Lincoln has far more important matters to occupy him."

Suddenly Jacintha felt sorry for the First Family, having petty gossip about them bandied about. She thanked the chambermaid for her assistance and dismissed her, wanting to be alone when Earl arrived.

Shortly before six o'clock she heard an impatient rapping. Before she could open the door, it was flung open and he ran in, grinning, pausing briefly to admire the lovely vision that so often appeared in his dreams. Then he strode rapidly toward her, incredibly handsome in his dress-uniform, gold-fringed epaulets adorning his shoulders, silver-sheathed sword swinging at his side. Jacintha wanted to meet him halfway, but her legs were suddenly immobilized, and all the warm greetings she had rehearsed, instantly deserted her.

Immediately she was in his strong arms, locked in his embrace, his mouth avidly on hers, aware of nothing but the ecstatic moment. When at last they separated slightly, breathless and trembling, he pretended to admonish her.

"You disobedient little minx! What did I tell you about visiting me?"

"Don't scold me, Earl. I couldn't bear it any longer. I simply had to come!"

"And I've been praying you would, Jacintha."

"Then you're not really angry with me?"

"Furious," he replied with a grin, chucking her under the chin. "As angry as the starving Israelites were when manna fell from heaven." He kissed her again, a deep, lingering kiss. "I'm so glad to see you, darling! You look marvelous, absolutely stunning!"

She smiled. "Thank you, Colonel. I trust you've been well?"

"Well enough. And seeing you, I'm suddenly ten years younger. Tell me everything about my son."

"He's growing faster than I can buy clothes for him, and he resembles you more every day, Daddy. His eyes are exactly the same color as yours now, and he's developing many of your other features too. Lollie swears he'll have your aristocratic nose someday. It's still babyishly tilted, like mine. It's too bad I couldn't bring him along. But you were right about Washington, Earl. It's bedlam!"

His expression abruptly sobered. "The President's advisors believe that invading Washington is the Confederacy's only hope now. We could be attacked at any time."

"There are rumors of peace negotiations in Canada."

"Yes—but the envoys can't agree on the terms, and won't call a truce to discuss them. Wars are always easier to start than to finish."

"America couldn't endure much more, Earl. The country will be destroyed soon."

"It's already fairly well torn up, and putting it back together won't be easy." He smiled. "Don't worry, darling. I don't think Washington will be invaded tonight, except by our own drunken revelers and renegades. It's as wild and bawdy as any frontier town! The provost marshal has his hands full. The guardhouses and compounds are packed. The hospitals treat almost as many barroom brawl wounds as battlefield injuries. A court-martial is always in progress, and the cavalry seems to have more than its share. There's a joke that the Four Horsemen of the Apocalypse are all cavalrymen, not only the rider on the red horse. The men try to find some comedy in this long-running tragedy, and they often fight among themselves, out of frustration."

"Poor boys," Jacintha sighed. "I saw some raw recruits on the train. So young—they still belonged in knee breeches."

"Cannon fodder," Earl mused. "But the South is drafting them even younger, and our Intelligence reports that Richmond is as chaotic as Washington. That's war, Jacintha, and let's try to forget it for now, if possible. How long can you stay?"

"A week—and I want it to be perfect for us, Earl."

"It will be," he promised. "There's an officers' hop at Willard's Hotel this evening—would you like to attend?"

"Oh, yes! But would it be discreet for us?"

"I think so, my love. It's a masked ball, and we'll leave before the midnight unmasking. Your gown is ideal, and I'm already wearing my dress uniform."

"Looking mighty dashing too, Colonel!" She touched the eagle insignia on his broad shoulders. "I've always wanted to go to a masked ball. What luck there's one tonight!"

"They have them quite often," Earl said. "Some of the big brass keep their mistresses or sweethearts here, and it's a convenient way to dance with them in public."

"And do you avail yourself of this convenience?"

"Occasionally."

"I see," she said, after a moment. "Maybe I shouldn't have come without warning. Perhaps you've already promised to escort someone else tonight."

"And if I had?"

She affected nonchalance. "Why, you'd have to do so, naturally. Don't bother about me, Earl. I can read, or—something."

He appeared to consider it. "Sure you don't mind?"

"Not at all," she lied quickly, turning away from him.

Instantly his hands pulled her back, pressing her bare shoulders against his chest. "You little goose! Don't you know I'm teasing you! And you're not fooling me, with your pretense of sophistication. Turn around and let me see your eyes again. I always thought them the most fascinating shade of turquoise!"

"So they're green now! I don't care. I hate every other woman you've ever made love to—and I suppose that's a great many. A harem, maybe. But I loathe them all!"

"I'm pleased," he said, his soothing voice placating her. "But there hasn't been any other woman since—well, that time in the hunting lodge. I swear it, Jacintha. I'd swear it on Ronnie's head."

How could she ever doubt him, doubt the love and devotion in his face? She was ashamed of herself. "I am a goose, Earl—and a pecking one, at that. Forgive me?"

"Just trust me, Jacintha." He held her face between his hands, tilting her chin to fathom the misty blue-green depths of her eyes. "I know what I want—what I've wanted for years. I've had my fill of casual affairs. I crave a permanent bond, and I want you, Jacintha, only you. That's how it is for me now, and will always be."

"Then we are forever," she vowed tearfully.

"Now, now, darling! No tears, please. This is a joyous occasion, remember? A celebration! Where's your cloak? It's freezing outside, and I have a cabbie waiting. We have to find a novelty shop to get some masks."

The prospect excited Jacintha. "Buy me a fancy one, Earl—like the European vizards they wear to masquerades. Oh, I wish we were going in costume, too!"

"We will, soon. The foreign ambassadors have a penchant for costume balls and host them frequently. The French Embassy's are the most spectacular, and I believe they're having one Saturday evening. Maybe the Spragues will throw one of their famous candlelight dances, too—where the lights are so dim that no one can recognize anyone else. Not all the ingenuity in this town is confined to Intelligence operations!"

Chapter 32

FOR a few glorious hours in Willard's grand ballroom, the war and Earl's wife seemed almost nonexistent. The disguised couples might have been masquerading in a brilliant fantasy land where only merriment was real, as a delightful dream sometimes assumes reality.

It was late when they returned to Manor House, silently holding hands in the hansom cab as if afraid of breaking the magic spell.

The night attendant was dozing behind the counter, and Earl and Jacintha slipped quietly up the carpeted staircase, to Jacintha's suite.

Earl unlocked the door and entered first, to light the gas lamps and the fire, already prepared, on the hearth. When the parlor sconces were aglow and the kindling crackling, he helped her out of her ermine-trimmed black velvet cloak.

Radiantly happy, stimulated by champagne, Jacintha bubbled at him. "I had a marvelous time, Earl! You dance divinely, as I knew you would. I could waltz with you forever."

"It's you." He grinned. "I'm a wooden soldier with any other partner."

"How gallant, Colonel, but not quite true! I watched you in the quadrille with that flirt in scarlet grenadine and in the lancers with that slyboots in yellow taffeta—and you weren't the least bit wooden. Outrageous coquettes, flattering you with fluttering lashes and simpering smiles. What were they saying?"

He shrugged. "Who knows? I was too busy watching you and General Forsythe—thinking I might have to challenge him despite his rank. What was the old reprobate trying to do—entice you to his quarters? He lives at the Willard."

"Now whose eyes are green?" she teased coyly. "He wanted me to unmask, was sure we had met before."

"That's the oldest approach in the world! I'm disappointed in the general. I thought he was more advanced in the art of seduction, considering his supposedly myriad female conquests. Would that he were as victorious on the battlefield!"

"Anyway, I still think you're the handsomest officer in the Union Army, and surely the best dancer."

"And you're still prejudiced, Curly Locks."

He had not called her that for a while, and Jacintha became wistful, watching him unbuckle his sword and lay it across a chair. Her flesh tingled and, suddenly, modesty made her as nervous as a bride. The gourmet supper in the Embassy Row restaurant, the vintage wine, romantic music and dancing—the whole evening had been intoxicating. Jacintha suspected that Earl, with his unerring instincts, had intentionally planned the delay, so as to intensify the anticipation. It would have been so easy to take her to bed earlier, aroused as they both were by their first ardent embrace.

"There's some brandy"—she indicated a decanter she'd ordered previously—"if you'd like a nightcap. I won't be long, darling."

Removing a white chiffon-and-lace boudoir ensemble from the armoire, she slipped behind the screen to undress. Earl was pouring a drink when he heard her soft, frustrated curse.

"Damn."

"Having trouble, honey?"

"I can't unhook my gown. Will you lend a hand?"

"Your servant, ma'am." He swallowed some cognac before obliging her, releasing the long row of fasteners skillfully.

"Your facility is remarkable, Colonel."

"I've had some practice."

"In and out of wedlock," she chided. "I thought you didn't perform such husbandly duties at home anymore."

"Well, it's like swimming—you never forget how."

"Or how to make love?"

"I hope not," he said, sweeping the cluster of fragrant curls off her neck and pressing his lips there.

Jacintha's blood surged in a wild thrill, inciting an almost wanton desire. Petticoats and hoops were quickly shed, leaving only frilly pantalettes and corset.

"I think I can manage now, dear."

His breath quickened and passion smoldered in his smoky-gray eyes as he admired the pale swell of her breasts above the tightly laced stays. She fumbled the strings into knots and had to beseech his aid again.

"Why do you torture yourself with whalebone?" he scolded, freeing her of the confining garment. "You don't need to bind yourself, Jacintha. Your waist couldn't be more than eighteen inches."

"It's twenty, since Ronnie."

"You're becoming obese! I shouldn't have allowed you that second pastry."

She crinkled her pert nose at him. "I could have eaten two more, a chocolate mousse, and another parfait."

"Why didn't you?"

"I don't want to look greedy. One hears how gentlemen admire delicate feminine appetites."

"Southern propaganda," he scoffed. "I'm a Yankee."

"Only half," Jacintha corrected, immediately regretting her reminder of his Carolinian ancestry. "I'm sorry, Earl."

"It's all right, Jacintha. I think of my family constantly. I even employed a Pinkerton detective to discover whatever he could about them. Mother and Aunt Evelyn were in Charleston at his last report, but he couldn't learn my brother's whereabouts. I try to convince myself that Larry is still alive—and that he and I have never fought one another. But the South is one great battlefield now, and he might be anywhere. Or nowhere," he added under his breath, reaching for the decanter again.

Jacintha tried to retrieve the playful mood. "The supper was delicious, Earl. The chef there is equal to Delmonico's."

"Armaund's frequently caters to the White House. Would you like to meet the President, Jacintha?"

"Very much! When?"

"There's a reception tomorrow evening."

"And you have an invitation?"

"Anyone is welcome at the public affairs," he said. "Of course, the private functions are necessarily limited to invited guests. Mrs. Lincoln also holds levees. This is a very sociable city, with a wide variety of diversions. Like Nero's Rome, Washington will probably be in the midst of parties, if the Rebels do attack."

Tired of war talk, Earl's attention strayed back to Jacintha and his arms circled her.

"How often I've dreamed of this."

"As have I, my love," she murmured, stroking his face.

The gesture made him conscious of her wedding rings, which he silently removed. He quickly replaced them with the gold signet ring from his own finger. "That's until I can give you the real thing, God willing."

Although it was much too large for her small hand, Jacintha managed to keep the band in place. And in that tender moment, she felt more married to Earl Britton than ever she had to Cole Danvers. She gazed at him eloquently, and then dropped her other hand. Her gossamer white negligee fell to the floor, wispy as a bridal veil, and his urgency could no longer be restrained.

It was Jacintha's first intimacy since childbirth, and somewhat more painful than she had imagined it would be. In the flickering light of the bedside candle, Earl saw her wince. He froze.

"I'm hurting you."

"Not really," she lied. "I'm just a bit tense from lack of exercise."

"From chastity," he surmised. "Oh, Jacintha, you're so fine! How could any man ever be entirely worthy of you? I seduced you at Greystone and—"

"That's not true!"

"Yes, it is. And what you suffered bearing my child—"

Her hand covered his mouth. "Hush, Earl, please. Don't spoil our beautiful reunion! It's sort of like a wedding night for me, and I want to continue. Do you understand?"

He nodded, proceeding cautiously. "You feel like a virgin, and I'll be very careful."

"I love you so much, Earl. I can't tell you how much, but I'll try to show you," she said, arching her body toward his. "Take me, darling, as you did the first time . . ."

Joy and rapture soon obliterated all pain, and repetition was pure ecstasy. Lack of sleep did not exhaust either of them, nor did the interludes of intimate conversation.

"Sip some brandy," he urged, offering her his glass, "and exchange it with me in a kiss."

"We'll spill it."

"And lick it off. Go ahead. It's fun."

She did, and the love ritual was more than enjoyable—it was exciting, stimulating. "Let's do it again."

"What?"

"Share more brandy and make love."

During one long intermission, toward dawn, as the candle burned low, Earl asked, "What was it like with him?"

"I told you at the lodge. Rape, brutal and terrifying. Even the honeymoon was a horror."

"And I was supposed to be your guardian," he lamented.

"But not my guardian angel, darling. My own pride and obstinacy were responsible for that marriage."

"I should have prevented the marriage somehow."

"We were married when you were away, remember?"

He frowned, contemplating the guttering flame. "I could hardly speak when Lollie gave me the news. I walked away from Riverview, telling myself I could never return."

"She told me, Earl. I spent hours crying in the cupola, and I lived in bondage and misery from then until the Draft Riots released me. I couldn't even tell you I was carrying your child."

"I'll make it all up to you, Jacintha, if it takes the rest of my life. Right now, the trouble is that I may receive new orders tomorrow. If so, I'll request a short leave. I have some friends in the War Department, and last week, when my uncle was here—"

"Peter Britton?"

"Yes—for conferences with the Treasury secretary regarding war finances. I sat in on the round table, along with some other Wall Street financiers."

"Your wife promotes bond rallies," Jacintha said unexpectedly, then immediately wished she hadn't.

"So Uncle Peter informed me. Apparently Lincoln's Lady General also fancies herself his exchequer. I understand she has made numerous pledges for the Brittons, but few for the Lancasters—claims her father is doing that through the Jay Cooke Bank in Philadelphia."

"I've purchased some government issues through my legal firm, Earl. I suppose it's a good investment?"

"Only if we win the war," he said. "If not, we'll all be paupers. Would that bother you, Jacintha?"

"Not if we were together, darling. We could start anew somewhere—abroad, or maybe in the western territories." She paused thoughtfully. "Are the civilians being told the truth, Earl? Are we closer to victory or to defeat?"

"Victory, I think. Not, as preachers like Henry Ward Beecher claim, because God is on our side, but because we have more men and better equipment. Might may not make right, but it definitely tips the scales of war."

"But there's still much fighting ahead?"

"I'm afraid so, Jacintha, and I expect to be in it. Grant

will need strong cavalry support in his march on Richmond."

Jacintha grasped his hand desperately, as if feeling the invisible forces that were wrenching them apart. "Have you ever considered resigning your commission, Earl?"

"I imagine every officer has, Jacintha."

"Seriously?"

"Very seriously."

"When?"

"Last July, while I was sitting with you at Riverview. I told myself that, if you recovered, I'd take you and our child to England and never leave you again. I even visualized my family joining us there and all of us living together in the country, safe and happy. Reason returned, however. There's no guarantee of peace or happiness anywhere on earth, and resigning then would have been tantamount to desertion—a sorry legacy indeed for our son! I'm in this war, Jacintha, and there are no honorable alternatives to staying in until the war is over."

"I know, Earl. And you made the right decision—the only one either of us could live with." She laid her head on his chest, moving one hand sensuously over his naked torso, thrilling to his rapid response. "What shall we do about this situation, Colonel?"

"I don't think it requires much deliberation, ma'am." He turned her on her back and buried his face in the rose-scented vale of her breasts. "How sweet and delicious you are—every tender, juicy part of you! I wonder if I'll ever satisfy my insatiable hunger."

"I hope not. At least, not until we're ninety or so."

He smiled, touseling her hair. "It's almost daylight. I'm going to be late for my appointment at the War Department. I'll be lucky if I'm not hospitalized for fatigue. . . ."

Jacintha was in a state of high excitement over her visit to the White House. The formal reception, really too extravagant for wartime, was obviously not the President's choosing. The tallest man in the Red Room, President Lincoln appeared awkward and uncomfortable in evening dress. He moved about considerably, unable to stay still for long. His handshake was warm and his smile friendly, but his eyes were the saddest Jacintha had ever seen. And his mind seemed far away, absorbed in far more serious matters even while he conversed and laughed with his guests.

Mrs. Lincoln's elaborate silver brocade gown and glittering jewels only served to emphasize her short, plump figure and plain face. She was a strange woman—a termagant to her detractors, an enigma even to her friends. Bearing a remarkable physical resemblance to Queen Victoria, she gave herself regal airs. Jacintha noticed that she chatted graciously with some ladies and imperiously ignored others. Off guard, her expression was wary, melancholy, strangely haunted. Was it true, then, that she had never fully recovered from the death of her beloved son, Willie, that she had refused for months afterwards to believe that he was actually dead? Was she now holding séances in an effort to contact his spirit?

"Poor Mrs. Lincoln," Jacintha whispered to Earl as they stood together holding cups of punch. "She seems rather ill."

"Yes," he replied. "Still grieving for their lost boy. So is the President, but he's much stronger than she is."

"I pity them, Earl. So much sorrow. So many heavy burdens to bear."

"Shall we go and meet some of the other guests? The Cabinet members and beribboned diplomats are arriving. And the chief justice of the Supreme Court has just entered."

"I'd rather dance," Jacintha said. "The Marine Band is playing in the Blue Room. Besides, I'm curious to see more of the White House."

Somehow she had expected more grandeur. The Executive Mansion needed renovation. Jacintha was aware of frayed draperies, faded upholstery, worn carpets, stained ceilings, cracked plaster. Was the country so poor, then? She suggested that Britton Bank lend the President some money.

"Why?" Earl asked, amused.

"To repair this house. It might improve Mrs. Lincoln's health and mood."

"Darling, Congress appropriates such funds."

"Well, from all appearances, it's been mighty stingy! Or feathering its own nests. I know you're acquainted with many important senators and congressmen. Ask them to be more generous to the Lincolns, Earl."

"Yes, dear. Just as soon as the war is over. . . ."

Chapter 33

My darling Jacintha,

Spring has come to the Blue Ridge Mountains, and what a glorious season it is here! The snows had barely melted before the pine forests began to glow with brilliant native plants—scarlet azaleas, pink laurel, purple rhododendrons. The valleys are greening, and the meadows are golden with jonquils. Fish abound in the streams and game in the woods. But there are less desirable inhabitants, too. Rebel scouts, guerrillas, deserters, and stragglers keep our boys confined to camp.

You wonder how much longer the war will last. So do the President and his generals. I marvel that it has endured this long, for the enemy seems to have little left with which to fight, except courage and determination.

We have captured troops armed with antiquated weapons, and others with our own new rifles. The men are hungry, ragged, exhausted, ravaged by malnutrition and disease. Many cannot remember when they last ate a full ration or drank a cup of genuine coffee, or slept under a whole blanket. Without medical supplies, they must resort to folk remedies, and their surgeons operate without morphia.

I have seen Rebs wearing bits of cloth and leather tied around blistered, bleeding, frostbitten feet. Napoleon's army could hardly have been in worse straits before Waterloo!

Yet they continue to fight—and even win some important victories! The Union lost over eight thousand men in the fierce engagement at Olustee, Florida. The same General Forrest's troops also stormed and captured Fort Pillow, on the Mississippi River in Tennessee, and massacred every Negro in our garrison there. This savagery against black men signifies desperation, I think, as surely as the South's current conscription of slaves.

Why don't they surrender? Is it gallantry, fanaticism, mulish obstinacy? And whatever it is, can such a dedicated people ever be truly conquered? Physical defeat is one thing; capitulation of the will and spirit, quite another. The enemy may very well be invincible in the latter respect.

Yes, it's true that the War Department has discontinued the practice of exchanging military prisoners —a move regarded as expedient by the High Command. Releasing soldiers to rejoin their former combat units can only serve to prolong the war. But don't worry about its effect on me, should I be captured, because few officers were ever exchanged anyway. Nor do I expect to surrender! I intend to "return with my shield, or on it."

So the civilians are greatly pleased with the President's appointment of General Grant as Supreme Commander of the Federal Armies? His spectacular performance at Chattanooga certainly warranted the promotion. I have no knowledge of his plans to confront Lee, my dear—but undoubtedly many generals will be involved, including Sherman and Sheridan.

What a dull correspondent I am, expounding on military matters! I guess I'm a pragmatist, certainly not a poet. But if you will read between the lines, you will discover all the love that fills my heart and makes my hand falter. Believe this, dearest, as you believe there is a God in heaven.

It's a quiet night—so peaceful one might expect truce bugles to blow shortly. The moon is brilliant and the stars do not appear so distant. Nocturnal birds are singing, crickets chirping, frogs croaking—but the mating calls may also be clever mimicry. Treachery often stalks at night, and we have doubled our patrols.

A breeze rustles the forest, and it's easy to imagine human footsteps. I fancy I hear the roar of the Rapidan River, although it flows miles away. Shall I tell you the loneliest sound on earth, my darling Jacintha? No, not the babble of a wilderness brook, not the hoot of an owl, or the howl of a lone wolf, but the whispering of a pine grove. Night after night I lie on my cot and listen to the wind in these trees—and it is indeed nature's primal wail. It's also fascinating, and makes me feel awesomely lonesome.

What do you do with my letters, love? I like to think you tie them with blue ribbon and file them in a secret cache, to be reread nostalgically.

I cannot save yours, you know. A soldier's personal effects, in case of death, are sent to his next of kin, if possible. So I must reluctantly burn your precious missives. My keen-nosed aide has noticed the periodic incensing of my quarters with your damask rose sachet and, I'm sure, distinguished this delicate fragrance from the heavy narcissus scent of some of my other mail. I do not think I fool him. Perhaps we are not really fooling anyone but ourselves.

There's taps—time to snuff my candle!

> Eternal love and devotion,
> Earl

Jacintha's eyes blurred as she kissed and folded the letter. Then she tied it with blue ribbon and tucked it among the others in a sandalwood chest, which she carefully locked. It seemed an age since Earl had gone to war, a decade since their sweet interlude in Washington. Sometimes she despaired of ever seeing him again. At such times, his letters and his child were her only consolations.

She was a loving, devoted mother, often excusing Lollie in order to tend Ronnie herself. She played with him and his toys, wheeled him in his buggy, rocked him to sleep, singing him lullabies. The slightest cold put her in a state of panic until the doctor reassured her.

"You're spoiling him," Lollie gently scolded. Of course, Jacintha was depriving Lollie of the pleasure of spoiling Ronnie herself!

"Four grandmothers couldn't pamper him more than you do!" Jacintha brushed the dark ringlets from his forehead. "Isn't he beautiful, Lollie? And doesn't he resemble his father more every day?"

"He's the spit and image of him," Lollie agreed, folding a stack of clean diapers into convenient triangles.

"If only Mr. Earl could see him now!"

"You better hope his wife doesn't see him now."

Jacintha frowned, still puzzled about the real reason for Laurette's visit to Riverview. "Do you suppose she suspects the truth?"

"God forbid!" cried Lollie, shaking her head as if to shake away demons.

Jacintha sighed and began to rock again, humming a wistful little tune, rather like the mournful murmur of a wind-blown pine.

As action slackened in the West, it increased in the East. Northern attention focused on three amazing Union generals—Grant advancing on Richmond, Sherman sweeping like wildfire through Georgia, and Sheridan devastating the Shenandoah Valley, whose fertile fields and farms provided food and forage for Robert E. Lee's Army of Virginia.

Military confrontations were so numerous throughout the summer, that newspapers had difficulty reporting them all. But only a few were decisive battles.

Jacintha anxiously awaited the mail, although aware that word from Earl was no assurance of his safety. Many families unwittingly rejoiced over posthumously received messages. The postal system was far behind. Even official notice from the War Department was often long delayed—and Jacintha would not be the one to receive a report from them anyhow.

Earl's December correspondence included a generous draft on Britton Bank and a request that Jacintha purchase gifts for herself, the baby, and Lollie. He suggested a puppy for Ronnie, who was now eighteen months old, walking, and beginning to talk. The nursery already contained a menagerie of stuffed animals, but no live pet. One cold, overcast day, Jacintha bundled Ronnie into a snowsuit and ordered the coachman to drive them to a Broadway pet shop.

The adventure fascinated Ronnie. He enjoyed the cunning cats and dogs, the mischievous monkeys, playful hamsters, and loquacious parrots. But he seemed ready to settle his affections on a honey-colored cocker spaniel. The pup watched Ronnie with appealing brown eyes, licked his hands, and wagged its tail as Ronnie fondled its long, soft, curly ears.

"We have other pups in the kennel," the proprietor was saying when a familiar blue-and-silver carriage halted at the curb and a liveried footman leaped down from the box to assist the occupant.

"Where's the kennel?" Jacintha asked quickly, taking Ronnie's hand.

"Through the rear door, madam."

But it was too late to escape. Laurette had already entered the shop, regal in a sable-trimmed purple velvet cloak and wimpled turban. Spying Jacintha, she removed a leather-gloved hand from her large sable muff.

"So we meet again. How nice. I've been thinking of you lately."

Trapped, Jacintha stammered the first words that came to mind. "Merry Christmas, Laurette."

"Merry Christmas!" Laurette glanced at Ronnie, who was clutching his mother's beaver cape and contemplating his shoes. "Your son? My, how they grow—like the proverbial weed! He's bashful, isn't he?"

"Only with strangers," Jacintha replied, praying that Ronnie would keep his face hidden in her skirts.

"Oh, he can't be that shy! How will he ever get along with the ladies? What's his name again?"

"Ronald, after my maternal grandfather."

"Of course. Look at me, Ronnie! I bet Santa Claus is going to bring you a pretty pet for Christmas—a cute little puppy or kitty or bunny rabbit!"

He peeked at the stranger and smiled—a slow, disarming smile reminiscent of something. Laurette could not immediately identify that something.

"What a handsome boy you are, Ronnie! The handsomest in all New York, I vow."

Another smile provided a full view of his expressive gray eyes under well-defined dark brows—and suddenly Laurette knew why his face was familiar. One of Alicia Britton's most treasured possessions, a miniature painting of her firstborn son at age two, bore such a striking resemblance to this child that Ronnie might have posed for it. Quickly recalling Cole Danvers's coarse features and auburn hair, Laurette asked, "How old is your son now, Jacintha?"

"A year and a half."

"Born during the Draft Riots, wasn't he?"

Jacintha nodded.

"Did your late husband have a chance to see him?"

"No."

"A pity," Laurette said musingly, making some rapid mental calculations. Earl was wounded at Antietam in September of sixty-two and had recuperated in New York during October, during part of which month his wife had been in Philadelphia. October to July . . . a good nine months! It was possible! What else could account for this amazing likeness?

But she would need more than suspicion before she could make any accusations. If only her mother-in-law hadn't taken that miniature with her to South Carolina!

The elderly shopkeeper was growing impatient. He addressed Laurette. "May I help you, madam, while these folks decide?"

Eager to leave, Jacintha made a prompt decision. "We'll take the honey cocker."

"An excellent choice, madam. Fine pedigree. Sired by an English champion descended, I understand, all the way from one of King Charles II's spaniels and—"

"Never mind," Jacintha interrupted. "We don't plan to use him for breeding. Just tell me the price. And we'll need a leash."

"One moment, please," Laurette intervened. "Stud or pet, I can't imagine a pedigree being unimportant to anyone. Why, without one a dog is simply a mongrel, rather like an illegitimate child. Isn't that correct, Mr. Binkle?"

"Absolutely, madam."

"I planned to give General Cutter's young daughter a French poodle for Christmas—but I think she'd prefer that adorable cocker. What are you asking for him, sir?"

Sensing rivalry between the ladies, Binkle hoped to promote a bidding feud and began with a substantial figure. "One hundred dollars. A blue-blooded champion is always expensive, you know."

"Naturally," Laurette agreed, smiling obliquely at Jacintha, determined now to have the dog at any cost. "I'll take him Mr. Binkle. Provided"—she challenged significantly—"this lady has no objection?"

Binkle glanced hopefully at Jacintha.

"None at all," she conceded.

Ronnie, however, objected tearfully when the cocker was taken from him. Tears failing, he protested physically, grabbing at the dog and declaring, "Mine, mine! Don't take!"

"Gracious," Laurette remarked critically. "The little tyke has a nasty temper, hasn't he?"

Jacintha sought to pacify him, suggesting substitutes, all to no avail. Laurette watched imperiously. Binkle beamed with renewed confidence.

Pandemonium reigned. Dogs barked, parrots squawked on their perches, fluttering their wings and rattling leg-chains. Hamsters and squirrels worked their treadmills. A German shepherd snarled behind Laurette, startling her.

"Monster!" she cried, stepping swiftly away. "The noise and stench in this place are unbearable! Hold that cocker for me, sir, and prepare his papers. I'll send someone to fetch him." She handed him her card, bade Jacintha a crisp *adieu*, and flounced out to her coach.

Jacintha and Ronnie left with an aloof black Scotch terrier. The dog seemed to realize that it was second choice and resented it.

"What shall we name him?" she asked, wiping Ronnie's wet cheeks. "Not Scotty or Blackie, but something different. How about MacDonald or Mackintosh? We could call him Mac for short."

Ronnie was silent, still pining for the other puppy and understanding little of what his mother was saying.

"One nice thing about a black pet," Jacintha said placatingly as snowflakes began to swirl, "it's easy to find in the snow. And Mac will look very cute riding on the red sled Santa Claus is going to bring you for Christmas. Why don't you pet him, Ronnie? I think he feels lonesome."

The terrier was curled up on the floorboard, forepaws covering his muzzle. Jacintha put him between them on the seat. But Mac still sulked, and Ronnie ignored him.

"Mean lady," he said, unable to forget.

And vindictive, Jacintha thought. She didn't really want that dog, any more than she wanted the painted doll that Larry Britton won for me at the carnival—but both times she got her willful way!

Jacintha patted Ronnie's mittened hands consolingly. He even brooded like his father, and she wondered how Earl would have handled this matter.

"We'll just have to forget that lady, Ronnie. Santa Claus is coming soon, and there'll be lots of nice presents under the Christmas tree. Won't we have fun opening them? I bet Santa brings Mac a bone to chew, because he's still teething, like you. And we'll dress him up with a red bow around his neck and a Scotch-plaid coat to keep him warm. No more tears now, Ronnie, or else Mommy will cry, too. . . ."

With the fall of Fort Fisher soon after the New Year, the Union gained control of the Cape Fear River and blockaded the last Confederate port. A month later, Jacintha read about the burning of the capital of South Carolina, and worried about Earl's family. Was Earl's regiment fighting in his mother's native state? Was he still all right? She had not heard from him since the December letter.

"I've decided to ask for regular nursing duty," she told Lollie. "Anyone can scrape lint and roll bandages, but there are not nearly enough nurses. The wounded are coming by train and boat. Three hospital ships of coastal casualties are in the harbor now. It seems that one of our men falls for every foot of ground we take! No wonder the President didn't want any celebrations for his second-term inauguration." She paused. "Did we get any mail this morning?"

"Not the kind you're waiting for, honey."

"Why doesn't he write, Lollie? Just a few words!"

"No doubt he's busy."

"I wonder if *she* hears from him. I almost wish we were on friendly enough terms that I could ask."

"Have you seen her since that day in the pet shop?"

"Once, on the street, but we didn't speak. She was with a handsome young man—probably the cousin from Philadelphia who visits her so often."

"I thought every young man was in the service."

"No, not *every* one, Lollie."

Slowly, surely, the Confederacy was crumbling. Grant forced Lee to withdraw from Petersburg early in April, and the evacuation of Richmond began then. The Army of Virginia was the last bulwark of the South—its collapse meant certain defeat. Soon the gray citadel toppled at Appomattox.

News of the armistice brought wild jubilation to the North, New Yorkers sang and danced in the streets. Jacintha wept with joy, relief, gratitude—and rushed home immediately after her hospital shift to hug and kiss Ronnie.

"Daddy's coming home, darling!"

"Daddy?" he repeated curiously.

Lollie shook her head. "You shouldn't tell him that, Missy. He can talk and understand more now—and soon he'll ask questions you can't answer."

Less than a week later they were hanging black crepe on the front door of Riverview, and Jacintha was recalling the White House reception she had attended with Earl.

"Mr. Lincoln had such sad eyes, and Mrs. Lincoln looked haunted. Maybe they had premonitions of this? I hope they get the assassin and hang him higher than Haman! And his conspirators, too, if there were any."

"April came to work crying," Lollie said.

"Her parents were runaway slaves, you know. They escaped their owners, on the underground railroad. She and her sister were born free, but they must have wondered how free they really were, the night May's husband was lynched. And she shouldn't be doing laundry today! Ask her to come and have some tea with us, Lollie. Tell her I insist."

"I figured you'd say that, Missy, and I already invited her. She's in the kitchen."

"Not in the kitchen, Lollie. In the parlor. Tell her I insist on that too."

PART V

Chapter 34

IT was a sadly changed Charleston that Earl arrived in after the war. Under relentless siege from the beginning, the city had suffered greater damage than almost any other in the South, except Atlanta and Savannah. After all, the Union could not forgive Fort Sumter. Fires had ravaged over one hundred and fifty acres of the business district, destroying many famous landmarks, including the cathedrals of St. John and St. Finbar, the first American theater, and Institute Hall, where the Ordinance of Secession had been ratified. And what the flames had spared had fallen under fierce bombardments.

Charleston's beauty and dignity were gone, its antebellum serenity as shattered as its buildings. United States vessels and those surrendered by the Confederacy were anchored in the bay, and blue-clad soldiers patrolled the streets. Negroes wandered aimlessly. Some were contrabands who had arrived with the conquerors, but most were locally freed slaves, now homeless.

Earl had been traveling for days on roads lined with troops and refugees returning to their homes, or what was left of them. They found demolished villages, the countryside plundered, plantations in ruins. Sherman's onslaught on Georgia was tame, compared to the rape of South Carolina, the state many considered responsible for the war.

Worried about what he would find in Charleston, Earl's apprehension increased as he approached the Evanston town house on Legare Street. The chimney pots and part of the roof were shot away. Concussion had broken every window, and the lacy wrought-iron railing of the piazza was weirdly twisted. The courtyard walls were crumbled, and rank weeds smothered the garden. The place appeared abandoned, and Earl did not expect an answer to his knock.

He waited several minutes and was about to leave, when the door creaked open slightly, held by a chain. A turbaned Negress peered at him through the slit, her black eyes warily appraising his uniform. Earl did not recognize her as one of the Evanston servants. Either she had belonged to Larry's wife, or the house was now occupied by strangers.

"Yessuh?"

"I'm Colonel Earl Britton," he explained. "This was the residence of my mother and her sister before the war. Their names are Mrs. Alicia Britton and Miss Evelyn Evanston. Are they living here now?"

The black woman gazed at him skeptically. A Yankee officer claiming to be kin to her mistress?

"There's a Miz Britton here, suh, but she ain't old enough to be your mama. Her name be Miz Lawrence Britton. We calls her Miss Geraldine."

"She's my brother's wife," Earl said, "and I'd like very much to see her."

"I don't know if she in to a Yankee soldier."

"Would you please find out? I've come a long distance to learn the fate of my family—and I must speak with your mistress immediately."

"Well, I see if she receivin', suh."

A long conference had apparently been held before she returned and removed the chain barrier. "Come in, Colonel. Miz Britton in the parlor."

In a severe and shabby black poplin gown, Geraldine appeared even thinner and paler than Earl remembered her, and what little beauty she had possessed, had vanished forever. Her dull blond hair was pulled tightly back from her high forehead into a bun at the nape of her long neck, and her light blue eyes protruded even more prominently in their sunken, dark-ringed sockets. There was no welcoming smile on her colorless mouth, no warmth in her toneless voice. Nor did she invite him to sit down. Indeed, her first words were accusations.

"I should think," she remarked bitterly, "that you would be ashamed to come here in that uniform."

"It's the uniform of my country," Earl answered quietly, "and of yours now too."

"I despise it and hesitate to venture out on the streets, where I see it everywhere!"

"I'm sorry, Geraldine. But the war is over, and I'm not here in an official capacity. I've come about my family."

"You have no family," she informed him abruptly. "Your mother is dead."

Earl closed his eyes briefly. How often had he feared this news? "How did it happen?"

"A stroke, when she was told of her son's death."

Like thunder following lightning, it staggered him. "Larry?" he said hoarsely, clutching the back of a chair for support. "In battle?"

Geraldine nodded, her features immobile. "At St. John's Island, last July. Perhaps you were there?"

"No." Earl raised his bowed head. "Geraldine, I'm so very sorry. Mother, Larry . . . Oh, God, I can't believe it!"

He ventured toward her in sympathy, but she froze him.

"Why not? The Yankees killed them! They killed my son, too!"

Horror piled on horror.

"Your son?" he heard himself whisper.

She stood like a statue, petrified by her grief. "Summer complaint took him nine months ago. Paregoric might have saved him, but your ships had the port blockaded. No medical supplies could get through, so my baby died. As did many other children."

"The ships were not mine, Geraldine; they belonged to the United States government."

"Yankee boats," she insisted inexorably, "and your converted yacht may have been among them. Larry thought he recognized it near these shores once. I will not spare any Yankee this guilt—and you must share the blame. Like it or not, you were—and are—the enemy!"

"I understand your feelings, Geraldine, and realize your suffering. Yours is a double loss—husband and child. But so is mine—mother and brother."

"You fought against your brother, whose death killed your mother! How can you grieve for them? There is no sorrow in any Yankee heart today. Victors do not mourn their victims."

"Some do, Geraldine, more than you imagine. And some conquerors suffer as much as the conquered."

This sparked her anger like dry tinder. "Don't refer to us as the conquered, Colonel! We lost the war but we are not defeated—and never will be. It does not matter what our military leaders did. General Lee surrendered his armies at Appomattox, but he could not surrender the civilians. Only the people themselves can do that, and they have not done so. Our spirit will never die!"

She meant what she said, and Earl was inclined to believe that she was right.

"What about Aunt Evelyn?" he asked.

"She is alive, but not well."

"Where is she?" It seemed that he must extract information from her like a dentist pulling teeth. She volunteered nothing.

"She is upstairs, in her room. I am caring for her."

"That's very generous of you, Geraldine. I'm sure you need help, and I—"

She interrupted harshly. "No, Colonel! I do not want any Yankee assistance."

"I meant financial aid, Geraldine. Naturally, as Larry's widow—"

Again she broke in. "As the widow of a Confederate

hero, I could not accept anything from the enemy. It would make a mockery of all our sacrifices."

Earl tried to reason with her. "You must put aside your prejudices, Geraldine. This is a terrible thing that happened to you, to me, to the entire country. But we can't let it affect the rest of our lives! The North and South must be reconciled. If not, hundreds of thousands of men, including Larry, died for nothing."

"The Confederacy had a cause, Colonel!"

"So did the Union, Geraldine, and it's ridiculous for us to debate the issue now!"

"I shall not betray my friends and neighbors. I'll wear rags and go barefoot, if necessary. I will eat food which I once would not have fed my slaves. But I shall never accept a single Yankee dollar stained with Confederate blood!"

"And that includes Britton money?"

"Was not some of it used to purchase Federal bonds? Oh, we managed to get some Northern journals here, Colonel. Your wife participated in the fund-raising rallies."

"Nevertheless, your husband was a Britton," Earl reminded her, "and you are his beneficiary. I believe he would want you to accept your rightful inheritance, Geraldine. Won't you please reconsider?"

She shook her head adamantly. "No, thank you, Colonel. I would not have deprived the child of his father's estate, but I want no part of it for myself. You may help poor Aunt Evelyn, if you wish. She is old, ill, and helpless, and she is your blood kin."

Earl sighed in resignation. Nowhere on the battlefield had he encountered more defiant resistance than was embodied in this one frail woman.

"Very well, Geraldine. I won't try to force anything on you. May I see my aunt, please?"

"She may not know you, Colonel. Sometimes she . . . well, she's not herself."

"I understand."

"Come with me, then."

Earl followed, silently observing the ruined interior of the once-gracious mansion. The stairway carpet had been virtually shredded by numerous pairs of boots; the mahogany banister had been nicked by sabers and spurs. The furniture showed signs of similar abuse; perhaps some fine wood pieces had been burned for fuel. Food, liquor, tobacco juice, and gun oil stained the upholstery and draperies. Missing pendants from the crystal chandeliers suggested they had been used for target practice. Valuable paintings, silver, and art objects had apparently been sold or stolen.

"If you're wondering about the condition of the house," Geraldine said, "it was used by the Army. Many citizens donated their properties to be used as barracks, bakeries, hospitals, commissaries. We lived at Rosewood until Charleston was evacuated. We also spent some time at my parents' plantation, near Columbia. Somehow my father managed to save it from the Yankee torch, and they are surviving."

"Senator Kenyon always was a persuasive speaker," Earl said in compliment.

"A statesman," she said proudly, "in the tradition of Clay and Calhoun. He was a great asset to this state even before the governor appointed him to the Senate. Of course, there will be nothing but carpetbaggers and their black pawns representing us in Congress now. Pa says there hasn't been a gentleman in the White House since the last Southerner occupied it. Certainly that clod from Illinois did not qualify, and his death was little mourned in Dixie."

Geraldine paused before a splintered door with a cracked Dresden knob. "This is Evelyn's room. Try not to upset her." She tapped lightly. "Aunt Evelyn? You have a visitor. Are you napping?"

"No, dear," a soft voice drawled. "Come in."

Geraldine remained in the hallway while Earl entered and shut the door.

Evelyn sat in her favorite rocker, a pillow at her back, a black shawl over her thin shoulders. Her hair, graying when Earl had last seen her, was now completely white. She had a disoriented look about her.

"Hello, Aunt Evelyn."

She stared at him without recognition. "Yes, General? I hope you haven't come about that dreadful oath of allegiance, for we simply do not intend to take it, though you throw us in the dungeon."

Earl bent down on one knee before her and would have taken her hand, but she refused it.

"Aunt Evelyn, don't you know me? I'm not a general, and I haven't come about the oath. I'm Earl Britton, your sister Alicia's elder son. I'm Larry's brother and your nephew. You must remember me."

She did not understand. But her gentle hazel eyes did not reflect the profound bitterness of Geraldine's, and Earl was grateful. He got to his feet and smiled down at her.

"Forgive my intrusion, Miss Evanston. I don't wish to disturb you and I won't linger. Is there anything I can do for you? Anything at all?"

"Well—" She hesitated, reluctant to proceed with her request, which she would never have made if Geraldine had been present. "I would like some tea, sir. It's very hard to get these days, except on the black market, and terribly high. All food is scarce and dear. But they say the Yankees have plenty of everything, and if you could spare a little tea . . ."

"I'll send a crate of it, ma'am, and more when that's gone. Also some coffee, sugar, salt, spices."

"And some flour to bake a cake? We haven't had any sweets in ever so long!"

"You shall have some soon."

"Thank you kindly, General. I suppose there are some nice Yankees, after all. I must tell my friends that I actually met one. Good day, sir."

"Goodbye, Miss Evanston," Earl replied, shaking the frail hand she now timidly offered.

As he emerged from the chamber, Geraldine inquired, "Did she know you?"

"Not at all. Her mind was wandering."

"It's one of her bad days. But she has good ones, too, when she is quite lucid. Most of the time, however, she seems to live in the past, happy in her fantasies. It's too bad we can't all retreat when reality becomes too terrible."

Earl nodded. "Aunt Evelyn is my responsibility, Geraldine, not yours. Isn't there some nice old-ladies' home where she would be comfortable? She must be considerable trouble to you this way."

"Not really, Colonel. I have a faithful servant to assist me, and I don't mind caring for Evelyn. She's company for me, and happier here than she would be in some strange place, however well they might treat her."

"But you could be with your parents, Geraldine."

"They do not need me as much as Evelyn does. And I think my husband would appreciate my remaining with his aunt. He was very fond of her."

"So am I," Earl said, "and I'll make financial provisions for Aunt Evelyn when I return to New York. I'll supply the means to repair the house and gardens, too. No protests, please, Geraldine! You won't be taking anything from me. It's her home, you know, and she might appreciate some new windowpanes, a solid roof, and food." He placed some greenbacks on the hall table. "I promised her tea, and other things, which I'll send as soon as possible. Meanwhile buy her some fresh fruit, sweets, or anything else she might crave."

Geraldine's smile, sad and retrospective, was the first smile since his arrival. "She's probably planning a tea party right now. She talks about plantation parties and barbecues. And one evening she donned her best formal gown to attend a St. Cecilia Ball—all in her imagination, of course. Sometimes I pretend with her. Pretend that Larry and the baby are still alive and the war never happened . . ." Her voice ebbed as sudden tears filled her eyes.

Earl's compassionate touch on her arm produced instant recoil, as if she felt a patriotic compulsion to remain stoical before the "enemy." It was a common attitude among her class of Southerners.

"Was there much military action in the Low Country?"

"Enough!" she snapped, firing her words like Gatling gun bullets. "Rosewood was sacked and burned by Sherman's desperadoes! Most of the slaves ran away or followed the Union Army. Mr. Digby, the overseer, died fighting the fire."

After a long, solemn pause, Earl asked, "Where are my mother and brother buried?"

"Alicia lies in the family plot in St. Michael's churchyard. Lawrence rests in the Confederate section of Magnolia Cemetery, beside several comrades who fell with him in battle. I felt that this was what he would have wanted."

"Was he in the cavalry?"

"Yes, but he declined a commission. He was proud to serve as just a trooper. Were you in combat in the Carolinas?"

"No, mostly in Virginia."

"That should ease your conscience some, Colonel."

"I was obeying orders, Geraldine."

"I wrote you in care of your wife and sent a box of memorabilia when the mails to the North were resumed. I don't know if it was received. You will find no jewelry. Like most real patriots, Alicia and Evelyn donated many valuable possessions to the Cause. At least the Confederacy benefited from their contributions. The few selfish hoarders who did not donate valuables lost their treasures anyway—their caches were ransacked by the plague of blue locusts that have descended upon us! I wonder if we shall ever be free of them!"

She continued resentfully, "I suppose the terrible crimes committed against us are justified by the idea of the spoils of war going to the victors. But they should be prohibited by law—and certainly helpless women should not be violated."

"Have you been molested?"

"No, but other decent women have, by the undisciplined soldiers. And the Yankee sailors in port are worse than pirates, confiscating the liquor in the taverns and accosting every pretty young maiden in sight. Some have been ravished."

"I've seen it happen on both sides," Earl said. "I've never condoned it under my command and have ordered such culprits severely punished. Unfortunately things sometimes get out of control, and men behave like wild animals."

"Far worse, in some instances, sir."

At the door, Earl put on his hat. "Thank you for receiving me, Geraldine. I hope we meet again under more pleasant circumstances. Goodbye, my dear."

"Goodbye, Colonel."

After paying his respects at both cemeteries, Earl rode his mount along Ashley River Road. The wanton destruction sickened him. The beautiful, enchanting Carolina Low Country was a ravaged, haunted land now. Unable to justify General Sherman's campaign of personal revenge, Earl lost much of his respect for him.

Liberated slaves camped near the ruined and abandoned plantations, scrounging for food in the plundered fields, woods, and swamps. Women and children grubbed in vegetable patches. Earl saw some men trying to chase down a stray hog. Recognizing his uniform, they hailed him for help.

"Afternoon, suh! Would you shoot that mud-slippy devil for us, suh? We ain't got no gun—and we's powerful hungry for some fresh pork barbecue."

Earl obliged, firing his pistol from the saddle, hitting the big boar squarely between the eyes.

They grinned appreciatively, and the first spokesman complimented Earl on his aim. "Fine shot, suh! Lucky you was in Mr. Lincoln's army! When is us goin' git our forty acres and a mule, suh?"

"That'll be decided in Washington," Earl answered, moving on. "You fellows better butcher that animal before some scavenger drags it off."

The arched gate to Rosewood Plantation was broken down, and desolation lay at the end of the long, wide avenue of moss-draped live oaks. The manor was a gutted black shell, its gaunt brick chimneys and charred walls starkly etched against the sinking sun. Demolished levees flooded the rice paddies. The shipping boats were scuttled, storehouses and docks burned. The ancestral burial ground had been trampled by hoofs and boots, gravestones and tombs profaned. Not a single slave cabin remained intact. The magnificent gardens had been maliciously destroyed.

Suddenly Earl remembered, as if from another life, his last visit to Rosewood. During a long, leisurely ride over the lush, sprawling acres, his brother had confided his intentions of becoming a planter. Had it been less than five years ago? The country had gone raving mad in those few violent, rampaging years! What else could explain the insane atrocities, or their terrible consequences? If Larry's death had not killed their mother, this tragic scene surely would have. It was impossible to assess the damage, and the plantation was useless to Aunt Evelyn in this condition. He would arrange to pay the taxes on the land until a buyer could be found.

Earl lingered only a few solemn minutes longer before putting spurs to his mount and galloping back to Charleston—to find whatever transportation to New York he could.

Chapter 35

BY late June Earl was out of uniform and back in his office at Britton Bank. He was four years older and twenty pounds lighter, with some gray in his dark hair, new lines in his tanned face, and two permanent scars. Less visible, however, were the tragic emotional changes wrought by the war—the deaths of his mother, brother, and a nephew he would never see; his aunt's senility; and his sister-in-law's hatred. He could only hope that time would heal Geraldine's wounds. Meanwhile, Larry's share of the Britton estate would be held in trust for her.

Laurette's affected greeting had affronted Earl. Did she imagine that he was ignorant of her behavior during his absence? He shunned her embrace—an indignity to which she reacted with haughty sarcasm. "I suppose you've had a warmer reception elsewhere, for I know that you did not come here directly from the battlefield."

"I went to Charleston, to learn about my family."

"Before visiting your wife?" she inquired angrily. "This is your home, Earl! You should have come to me first, yet I didn't even know you were in New York for over a week."

A cynical smile twisted his mouth. "I thought I'd give you time to send your favorite cousin back to Philadelphia. Aunt Ida Mae said he'd been your houseguest for several months."

"That prattling old biddy and her gorgon daughters thrive on gossip! But Norman Heath is a close relative, after all, and there was nothing improper in his presence here."

"And did General Cutter serve only as your escort for 'proper' civic activities?"

"I needed someone, and both men were kind enough to oblige me on occasion."

"In more ways than one?"

Laurette fumed. "Good Lord! Ralph Cutter is your friend. Are you accusing him of betraying you?"

"A man's friend often has the best opportunity," Earl replied with a negligent shrug.

"You should know, darling. No doubt you've cuckolded your share, including Cole Danvers."

His eyes narrowed. "Who?"

"Oh, come, now, Earl! I'm not that naive. Do you expect me to believe that your relationship with Jacintha has never exceeded wardship?"

"I don't care what you believe, Laurette. I came to ask if you received any mail from Charleston."

"Yes—a letter and package from Geraldine."

"May I have them, please?"

"They're on the desk in the library," she said, trailing after him.

The parcel had been tampered with, and his eyes accused her. "You opened it?"

"Naturally. It was addressed to me."

"It was addressed to *me*, in care of you!"

"Why are you so upset? Was it supposed to contain some secret?"

"It's the principle," he muttered furiously. "But you have none, have you? Your scruples have long since gone the way of your virtue. I presume everything is here and intact?"

"Certainly! I was merely curious, and I'm not a thief. There was nothing of value, anyway. Your mother's hairbrush, a fan, a lace handkerchief, her hymnal, and a few trinkets that belonged to Larry. Sentimental trivia! What did Alicia do with her jewelry?"

"Gave it to the Confederacy."

"How noble! And how pathetic, since her sacrifice was in vain. When I think of those magnificent jewels, especially that fabulous emerald necklace from your father. It should have been your heritage, Earl. She had no right to give it away!"

"It was hers to do with as she pleased, and would never have been yours, in any case, Laurette. I'd have strangled you with it first," he declared bitterly, tucking the package under his arm.

"You're leaving?"

"Yes, I am," he answered evenly.

"But you can't, Earl! What will people say?"

He shrugged and hurried off. Laurette followed him, hurling epithets at his back until he closed the front door between them.

Laurette bore the humiliating situation for a while, resorting to various lies about her husband's war-affected health and recuperation to explain his absence. But the men who dealt with him in business and met him at his clubs and favorite sporting events knew better, and so did their wives. Soon, her pride at stake, Laurette decided to act.

She arrived at his uncle's home late one afternoon, hoping to find Earl there and in a tractable mood. The summer heat steaming off the macadam streets wilted her lettuce-green ensemble slightly, but she still managed to appear reasonably cool and fresh—and her tongue was as crisp as ever. The butler admitted her, saying that the mistress and her daughters were out.

"I'm not here to see *them*," Laurette informed him tartly. "I know my husband is in—that's his carriage at the block."

"Mr. Earl is in the study, madam. Shall I announce you?"

"That's hardly necessary, Milton! I'm his wife, after all."

She brushed past him and continued down the hall, entering the room without knocking. Earl glanced up from the documents he was reading, but he did not rise. It was a deliberate affront, and it infuriated her. "I'm busy," he drawled. "What do you want?"

She closed the door and drew a stabilizing breath. Although it was not as elegant as his Fifth Avenue brownstone residence, Earl was apparently more comfortable in this old gray brick mansion, with its cherry-red shutters and mansard roof. He appeared totally relaxed in the pleasant surroundings, content to remain here. Laurette was direct. "I want to know just how long you intend to play this game."

"It's no game, Laurette." He shuffled the papers in his hands. "I think divorce is the only logical course for us."

"I agree, but not at present."

"Why not?"

"Is Jacintha pregnant again?"

After a shocked pause, he growled, "What the hell are you implying?"

She moved toward him, her hips swaying sensuously under her crinolines. Dramatically, from the depths of her reticule, she produced an ivory-framed miniature painting of a little boy. "Familiar?"

It was familiar, although Earl had not seen it in so long, he had almost forgotten it. Abruptly he rose, demanding, "Where did you get that?"

"Guess!"

"Why, you unscrupulous jade! So you aren't a thief? You must have stolen it from the box of mementos Geraldine sent. It belonged to my mother, and now it's mine." He thrust out his hand. "Give it to me!"

Laurette shook her head, smiling coyly as she dropped it back into her purse. "This little keepsake is more valuable to me now than Alicia's jewels. So don't try to take it from me, Earl. I'll scream for the butler and create a nasty scene. How many years did you trifle with your ward, before adulterously impregnating her?"

Earl scowled at his wife with disgust and contempt. "That's conjecture, Laurette."

"It's fact, and you know it! You'd forgotten about that miniature, hadn't you! Frankly, so had I, until I saw Jacintha's son. What a clever affair you two must have conducted right under Danvers's bulbous nose! I realized you were jealous of Larry when he was courting Miss Howard and you had designs on her yourself. Did you become lovers before or after Larry left? And was her hasty wedding to that old goat an expedience, because she thought she was pregnant by you and needed a name for the brat?"

For a tense moment, as Earl flexed his fists, Laurette feared he would strike her. "I suppose that's a natural assumption for a perfidious bitch like you to make! A slut capable of seducing her husband's brother and committing incest with her first cousin—"

"Might also drag a Confederate hero out of his sacred grave?" she interrupted. "Why not, if I'm so evil? But I don't want to destroy you, Earl. Nor do I want you back in my bed. All I want is a little cooperation. I'm tired of lying about the war's tragic effects on you. It's time we announced your complete recovery with a homecoming celebration."

"Recovery from what?"

"Oh, your many unfortunate afflictions, Colonel. Amnesia, battle fatigue, shell shock, to name a few."

"And you think anyone believes your lies?"

"Not really, but pretense is common in polite society."

She began striding around the room, elaborating her plan. "I'll be very generous. You may continue your affair with Jacintha—discreetly. A weekly night at home will suffice."

"Suppose one of my strange maladies recurs, and I go berserk before company?"

"Unfortunately for you, my dear, that would only prove their existence. The asylums are full of addlepated veterans."

"Get out," Earl commanded brusquely, "before I throw you out!"

She left him, glowering, and met Uncle Peter in the foyer. She cut short his greeting with a curt order. "Have a servant pack Earl's things and deliver them to his proper address, sir. You are losing your star boarder."

Then she swished away in a flurry of ruffled petticoats, her high French heels tapping on the marble floor. She paused at the door, grinning triumphantly. "Please convey my regrets to your wife and daughters, sir. I'm so sorry I missed them."

Peter entered the study, mopping his perspiring brow. "Whew! She's mad."

"Hell hath no fury, et cetera."

"She didn't give the impression of a woman scorned, Nephew. She ordered your gear packed, said you were leaving."

"Yes, in a few days."

"I don't understand, Earl. I thought this separation was permanent."

"So did I, but—" He winced. "Please, Uncle. Don't ask any questions."

"Of course," Peter agreed. "But your aunt and I will miss you. It's been like having a son."

"The feeling is mutual. Now, if you'll excuse me, sir, I'll dress for dinner."

"In this abominable heat? I told Ida Mae I'm dining in my shirtsleeves for the rest of the season. Maybe we can finish our chess game later."

"Sorry, but I have an important engagement. You can work on your next move . . . while I figure out mine."

His uncle nodded. There was a deep feeling between them, and Peter was content to wait until Earl eventually confided in him.

Jacintha and Ronnie were building block structures on the parlor floor. The dog nudged a ball around with his nose, threatening the bric-a-brac. The Persian cat, a new addition to the household, lay on the window seat, flicking her long, fluffy tail. The child had been kept up past his regular bedtime because of his father's visit—a big event to which both looked forward.

"Uncle Earl!" he cried, bounding up and running to meet him, jumping gleefully.

"Hello, Ronnie." Earl scooped him up in his arms. "How's my favorite boy?"

"Love my doggie and kitty." Mac was dancing on his hind legs, nipping playfully at his little master's heels, begging for his usual pat on the head.

"What about me?"

"Love you too." Ronnie hugged him and planted a moist kiss on his clean-shaven cheek. "Love Mommy and Lollie. Love April and Peggy and Job."

"That's nice, Ronnie, and I'm sure everybody loves you too. Guess what Uncle Earl is going to give you when you're a little older?"

"If it's another pet, make it goldfish or a turtle," Jacintha suggested wryly. "Mac is a miniature cyclone, and Prissy is always into mischief. Lollie's knitting basket is her favorite plaything."

"You can keep this pet in the stable," Earl advised.

"Well, don't say any more or he'll expect it tomorrow," Jacintha cautioned, pulling the bell cord. "Kiss Mommy and Uncle Earl good night, Ronnie. It's time for bed."

His small face puckered; his gray eyes clouded. Earl pacified him with a trinket from his pocket and a promise to help tuck him in until Lollie came to take charge.

Leaving the nursery, he told Jacintha, "I brought the phaeton. I thought you might like to go for a drive before dark."

She winked. "Ulterior motives, Mr. Britton?"

"We have to talk, Jacintha."

"I'll get a scarf."

"It's warm outside," he said, taking her arm, "and I'll provide any additional warmth you might need later."

Driving past Washington Square, out of the Village, he related what had happened with Laurette. "I had no choice, darling. You'd understand, if you could see that painting."

Jacintha listened quietly, toying with a lacy flounce. "It sounds like blackmail, Earl. Are you giving in?"

"Temporarily. But it won't interfere with us, Jacintha, because Laurette doesn't really care. All she wants is a graceful exit from our marriage and from Manhattan— more for her family's sake, I think, than her own. Laurette loves them dearly and they dote on her, despite past differences and her defiance of their wishes."

"What wishes?"

"The Lancasters have always coveted a title for their only heir, and probably were disappointed by our marriage. They educated Laurette abroad, traveled with her, and mingled with the peerage. But future kings are usually betrothed in their cradles, and there was no prince available for the princess. Unfortunately the most desirable dukes and lesser noblemen were also taken or promised. Miss Lancaster returned to America, we met, and they settled for the merging of two financial empires. Gold is sovereign in America, you know."

"We're changing the subject, Earl."

"Not entirely. Laurette's mercurial nature can't endure the status quo for long periods. She changes her mind as often as her clothes. We just have to be patient."

"I suppose so." Jacintha was acquainted with his wife's temperament. "Where are we going?" she asked suddenly.

"To the country—but not to an inn. We haven't been to Greystone recently—the manor, I mean."

"I haven't forgotten it, though, and never will."

"I thought I was going to die in the hunting lodge," Earl reflected gravely. "Instead I found a reason to live. Two reasons, actually—you and Ronnie. It may not always seem so, Jacintha, but fate has been kind to us."

For one thing, Cole might still be alive, she thought, shuddering. "Yes, we've been fortunate."

She gazed down the road, trying to visualize their future. Dark shadows interspersed the moonlight filtering through the trees. In the distance, crowning a bluff above Kip's

Bay, she glimpsed the castlelike silhouette of Greystone, which still retained the fairy-tale aspect it had had during her childhood. The family's principal summer residence before Earl's father's death and his mother's return to Charleston, and the scene of many holiday parties, the house now appeared somber and lonely, as if brooding upon mournful memories.

Jacintha was further saddened as Earl lit candles in the central foyer. The enormous rooms, with twenty-foot frescoed ceilings and ornamental columns, resembled the abandoned salons of a palace. Tapestries, murals, ancestral portraits decorated the walls, and she marveled that thieves and vandals had not looted the place. Here and there an armored suit gleamed dully among ancient shields and swords. Cobwebs draped the massive bronze and crystal chandeliers and ornate gold-leaf mirrors. Dust powdered the damask and velvet draperies. The odors of mold and mildew were strong.

"Oh, Earl, how did this happen to Greystone? It seems like a haunted castle now!"

"The curse of vacancy," he said. "No one has lived here for years, and the caretakers were lax during the war. In some respects the manor has outlived its time. But the land has increased in value, and the postwar boom will mean more industry and homes. The city will have to move northward. Greystone will be a part of Ronnie's inheritance," he added, carrying a burning candelabrum toward the great winding stairway. "The master suite, my love, or would you rather sleep in a tower?"

"I did once, when I was nine."

"Ah, yes. The east wing, wasn't it, with the Juliet balcony? My sanctum was in the parapeted north tower."

"I know. I admired your sailing skill the next morning from my mullioned windows, disappointed because I hadn't been invited along."

"But you were, Curly Locks. Your grandfather wouldn't let you go with me because you couldn't swim, but I suspected a different reason. I was a reckless boy, and I loved daredevil stunts. I heard the siren song on the water, and the wilderness call on land. I challenged the sea and wind, rode my steed like a cavalier, and raced my sulky like a Roman charioteer."

"Don't you still?"

"Not since the war," he replied, shaking his head emphatically. "I had my fill of danger in the cavalry charges. I was lucky to survive, certainly luckier than my poor brother," he lamented. "Or the Britton yacht, which was sunk in a naval battle on Chesapeake Bay." His mood brightened as he said, "I plan to replace the *Lorelei* soon, and you shall officiate at the christening ceremony."

Their voices echoed through the corridors, making it seem as though they were not alone. Jacintha shivered. "Do you hear footsteps and breathing?" she murmured.

"Yes, our own." He laughed.

From a window in Earl's rooms, Kip's Bay glimmered below. The lighthouse beacon beamed across the river, on Long Island. Steamers and masted ships were in port. Jacintha felt as if she could pluck a star from the sky, even catch a moonbeam. "Look, Earl! A shooting star. Make a wish, quick!"

He smiled, touseling her hair. "That's a firefly, Curly Locks. And only a fairy godmother could grant my wishes."

"But Greystone is no fantasy, is it? It's real, and we can come here again."

"Frequently, darling. I'll renovate it, hire some help, put in provisions."

"I'd rather enjoy it privately, Earl, whenever we want. We need a haven, and this is ideal. We could bring Ronnie sometimes. He'd love it."

"You're right, as usual. I'll just have the rank growth cleared and some repairs made. This will be our home, a place where we can be together."

His hand moved from her waist to her breast, fondling the already erect nipple and igniting an instant flame that brought their mouths together in a torrid kiss. Spurred by anticipation kindled during the lengthy drive, their desire overwhelmed them. Separating briefly to tear away their garments, they were soon entwined in bed.

Even when desire overwhelmed them, Earl always contrived to vary it, to inject a few surprises, so that it was never predictable. Sometimes the difference was so subtle, Jacintha was aware only of artful nuances in technique. Other times it evoked progressively more frenzy. Now, as her hips rotated rhythmically with his, Earl's thrusts grew more vigorous, and Jacintha, approaching her zenith, closed her eyelids and began to quiver.

"Look at me," he urged, his voice thick, and she obliged. His face was darkly flushed, his gray eyes gleamed in a kind of savage exultation, and his strong white teeth flashed suddenly in a triumphant smile before he found his own violent release. Jacintha realized that he wanted her to witness his passions, and to be as pleased by them as he was by hers. And she was! Indeed, it amplified her own ecstasy, and now she knew why he preferred light to darkness during lovemaking, even if there was only a single flickering candle.

"Why so quiet?" he asked several moments later, as they relaxed in the blissful aftermath, their bodies moist. Later they would towel each other, and Jacintha would savor his bay-rum pungence and Earl, her damask-rose essence, as incense.

"I was just remembering your expression a few minutes ago and wondering how I look when we make love."

Earl smiled. "The same as I, my darling."

"Do I make the same sounds, too?"

"Essentially."

Her fingers traced patterns in the dark damp matted hair on his chest. "I wish we could be together this way more often, Earl. Sex is so wonderful with you. I feel so good afterwards, so healthy and happy."

"Love makes it euphoric, Jacintha. Otherwise it's just sex—and sometimes rather awful."

How well she knew that! "And you've taught me so

much! Life has nothing more beautiful and marvelous to offer a man and woman truly in love. But I want to belong to you completely, with all the bonds that involves. I want our son to have his proper surname, too."

"He will, eventually. I promise you that, Jacintha, with all my heart."

Chapter 36

"IT'S all a mockery," Earl protested as Laurette made preparations for his long-delayed homecoming party, "a sham, and nothing but ridicule can result."

Laurette contemplated her guest list, striking out some names, inserting others. "Conquering heroes deserve to be hailed," she said blithely.

"The war has been over for months—and I'm not a conquering hero."

"You are, compared to most of your Wall Street associates, who stayed in their offices and counted their profits. Your patriotism was so unique, in fact, that I had to support you publicly."

"And became a home-front heroine, playing your spurious role to the hilt."

"I performed some valuable services," she insisted, "and I received many commendations, including several from President Lincoln."

As her plumed quill executed another change on the vellum stationery, Earl remarked cynically, "You act like a queen signing someone's death warrant."

"Well, it's difficult deciding whom to include. We need a

social registry like the Boston Brahmins'. I may make that my next project, with genealogy the primary consideration."

"Better not delve farther back than one generation," Earl advised. "Most family trees have a few wormy branches. You might even discover some flaws in your own. I know damned well mine isn't perfect."

"And it becomes less so every day," she quipped. "What do you think about a military theme for the decoration?"

"No, Laurette! That Yankee Doodle stuff is for Independence Day parades and children's parties."

"Oh? Did you and Jacintha entertain your offspring that way on his birthday? He *was* born in July, wasn't he? About nine months after your sneaky escapade in New York?"

"I was shipped here wounded and barely conscious! If that's an escapade, then I suppose death would have been a folly?"

"Evidently you weren't too incapacitated to chase your pretty little Village pussycat sometime during your recuperation. I have fairly conclusive proof of it, remember?"

Earl scowled. "How long do you intend to keep that miniature, my thieving wife?"

"Until our permanent parting, my conniving spouse, which won't be sorrowful for either of us. I pray for a discreet end to our marriage, but we live in a puritanical society, you know."

She glanced over sharply as he reached for his riding crop. "Going to Riverview? No doubt Jacintha has charms other than musical to soothe your savage breast."

Laurette well knew the power of sex. Her sexuality had reduced Larry to a quivering mouse and put a ring in big, bearish Ralph Cutter's nose. Mutual infatuation had even inspired incest with her dashing young cousin; Norman's blond wavy hair, intense blue eyes, and roguish mustache still excited her, and fear of family discovery added an extra fillip to their intrigue. But she had never been obsessed by love, and she scorned people who allowed it to possess them. Poor idiots! She'd rather be entombed alive than imprisoned in love. . . .

Laurette once more scrutinized the names on the paper, adding one she had never even considered before.

"Watch what you're doing!" Laurette admonished her personal maid, the third one hired in the last six months. "You're spoiling my coiffure."

"Beg pardon, madam. I'll be more careful."

"Indeed you will, or go begging another position! Oh, why did Soubrette leave me? She was a marvel—all French maids are marvels. *You* are a moron."

"Yes, madam."

"I didn't mean that, Becky." Laurette smoothed her hair, ashamed. "No harm done, but do take care. I want to look my best tonight. I believe the master is home, now. You may go, Becky. I'll ring if I need you again."

"Thank you, madam." The servant bowed and backed out of the room, as if in the presence of majesty.

Composing her features and adjusting her décolletage so that it was daringly low, Laurette met her husband at the entrance to his suite. "You're late."

"So?"

"I thought perhaps you weren't coming after all."

He shrugged, opening the door. Laurette followed, rustling in white satin. "Do you like my gown? My jewels will be rubies, sapphires, and diamonds. For the star-spangled effect." She pranced and preened, modeling for him.

"Is that your idea of a patriotic costume? Well, I didn't expect you to dress like Molly Pitcher or Clara Barton. But I wouldn't advise much bending over, not with that cleavage."

"I wish you'd wear your uniform, Colonel."

"No, and don't call me that."

"Why not? Other people will. It's customary."

"The issue is closed, Laurette." He removed his jacket and began unbuttoning his shirt. "Excuse me, please. I have to bathe and shave."

"Go ahead. I've seen you naked before. You used to insist on our sleeping nude together."

"I don't anymore, do I?"

"Not with me."

"Further delay is to your detriment, madam."

She sighed wearily. He was going to be difficult to handle tonight, explosive as dynamite, and she had to beware his short fuse. "Try to be civil, Earl, and remember the purpose of this occasion."

"Ah, yes! Celebrating my homecoming, albeit somewhat belatedly. I saw a convoy of catering wagons, a platoon of extra servants, enough chow for any army, even an enormous cake frosted with stars and stripes. Shall I cut it with my bayonet? Flags and bunting, toy cannons, tin sabers, wooden soldiers. An ice sculptor is painstakingly chiseling a mounted cavalryman as if the statue were a permanent monument. P. T. Barnum couldn't put on a better show, Laurette. But it's all nonsense!"

"Barnum never had a better reason," Laurette declared, blowing him a kiss. "See you in the receiving line, Colonel."

In the marble-pillared foyer, the liveried butler announced the guests, and the host and hostess received them in one of the magnificent twin drawing rooms. Laurette was listening for a particular name, now regretting her impulsive invitation. There had been no response to the RSVP, however. Perhaps the unwanted guest wouldn't come.

Earl stood beside his wife, extending a perfunctory welcome to each new arrival. His attire was formal and dignified, from the black broadcloth swallow-tail suit to the pearl studs in his immaculate white silk shirt. Sensing Laurette's apprehension, he asked in a low tone, "Waiting for anyone in particular?"

"Not really."

His gaze prickled her flesh. "If you dared to invite—"

"I dared," she admitted quickly. "She didn't tell you?"

Anger clouded his face. "This is the vilest thing you've

done in a long time, madam, and you may regret it before the evening is over."

"Oh, don't be a fool! She won't come. Most concubines are afraid of public appearances. And apparently yours keeps some secrets even from her lover. But everyone else is here, I believe. We can begin the festivities."

The orchestra was tuning up for the initial grand march, when once again Gaston's voice rang out, "Jacintha Howard Danvers!"

Unfamiliar to the Britton coterie, the name aroused speculation. As its bearer entered, heads swiveled and people gawked.

Her turquoise velvet gown, less bouffant and more fashionable than Laurette's, confirmed the Paris trend toward smaller hoops and fewer crinolines. The delicate rose-point lace ruffle edging the discreet bodice emphasized her femininity, intriguing the gentlemen far more than the blatantly exposed flesh of other ladies. Her simple gold jewelry seemed more elegant than their flamboyant gems, and her dark natural curls and damask rose scent were delightfully refreshing amid the elaborately coiffed heads and cloyingly perfumed bodies. Instead of an ostrich fan and jeweled reticule, she carried a lace handkerchief and dainty program in her gloved hands.

Laurette appraised her enviously. So young, lovely, and lithe, arresting so much attention. How foolish she had been to invite her! She cast Earl a covert malevolent glance, but he was too absorbed in thought to notice.

"Good evening," Jacintha greeted them, smiling and shaking hands. "Please forgive my tardiness. There were some traffic problems."

"They increase daily"—Earl acknowledged—"along with the population."

"Mostly immigrants and indigent Southerners," Laurette snapped. "It was nice of you to come, dear. But you should have been announced as Mrs. Cole Danvers and worn black or deep purple."

"It has been over two years, Laurette."

"Propriety makes no exceptions for widows, Jacintha. The girlish image is deceiving. After all, you're a mother, not a maiden." She tucked her arm possessively through her husband's, dismissing Jacintha. "Pardon us, please. We must lead the promenade."

"I'll defer that privilege to General Cutter," Earl drawled, faking a limp. "I'm sure he'll gallantly oblige you, madam —considering my war injuries."

Laurette fumed. "Your legs weren't injured!"

"But I have an aversion to marching, which is why I chose the cavalry rather than the infantry."

"But Ralph's wife is here!"

"He has two arms. Borrow one."

Laurette relented. "No, lend Jacintha one of yours." She smiled at her rival. "I don't mind sharing. Do you?"

Jacintha hesitated, gazing at Earl.

"March!" Laurette commanded, startling Jacintha into moving.

During an intermission, while Laurette chatted with some older matrons, widows and wallflowers, one of her dearest friends unwittingly offended her. "Earl has obviously recovered from whatever ailed him these past months. He's looking exceptionally well and handsome now."

"I thought everyone was aware of the unfortunate flareup of his Antietam wounds, Julia. Neither his physical nor emotional condition was the best, which curtailed our social activities. Thank God that's all over now."

"Well, you can be very proud of him, Laurie, and of your contributions on the home front. Some of us, I fear, were lax in that respect."

"Especially some men," Laurette snapped. "Sitting safely in their offices and clubs while others risked their lives."

Julia Weston colored. Her own husband was an eminent attorney, and under forty. "Paul wanted to volunteer but we had three small children, and I became hysterical at the idea of his leaving us."

"I know, Julie, and I wasn't including Paul." Laurette patted her hand comfortingly. "Forgive me, dear. I've been under a strain."

"Hostess jitters," Julia said sympathetically. "I get them myself."

"Really? You never show it. Your parties are always a tremendous success."

"So are yours. That caterer is a marvel. I must engage him for our next affair. But it does exhaust one, this business of entertaining. Why don't you slip upstairs for a respite?"

"I believe I will."

A middle-aged lady was sprawled on the chaise longue in her rooms. A maid and several women were clustered solicitously about her, chattering excitedly, plying fans and wafting vials of smelling salts.

"What happened?" Laurette inquired.

"Oh, just one of Clarissa's spells," someone answered. "She's at that difficult age, you know."

"May I help?"

Mrs. Potter recovered sufficiently to reply, "No, thanks, dear. I'm better now. Run along, ladies."

As they trooped out, Clarissa boosted her bulk from the lounge, her stout bosom heaving above the loosened whaleboned corset, damp cheeks flushed and quivering. "Lord, those dreadful hot flashes! They sneak up on one without the slightest warning! And they're so debilitating. The Creator certainly punished womankind for Eve's sin! As if the menses and pangs of childbirth weren't enough, He cursed us with menopause. It's so unfair."

"Maybe you should rest a bit longer."

"And let my old stud chase the young fillies? That's another way females have been handicapped."

Clarissa waddled off, fanning herself vigorously. Laurette approached the cheval glass, trying to visualize herself ten years hence. Would she be another Mrs. Potter at forty-five? Obese, with multiple chins, sagging breasts, flabby belly and buttocks, gray hair, and wrinkles? No! Ugliness was the result of neglect and overinduglence. DuBarry and Madame de Pompadour had continued to fascinate kings long after their youth had vanished. Vigilance was the secret of eternal beauty. Convinced by her reassuring reflection and her stalwart vanity, Laurette returned to the party like a lioness to her pride.

Servants were sprinkling shaved wax over the dance area. As the music resumed, Laurette engaged in conversation with a social reporter, singling out some prominent guests, including the mayor of New York and several statesmen. Scanning the ballroom, her attention suddenly focused on Earl and Jacintha, and Laurette sensed that others were also observing them. The way he held her, their intimate looks and smiles, suggested a great deal. How dared they carry on that way?

"Who is the lovely lady dancing with Mr. Britton?" the journalist inquired.

Laurette pretended not to hear the question. "Excuse me, please. I must speak with the caterer."

"Of course, madam." The columnist winked at a colleague, who nodded slowly, understanding the situation perfectly.

During the replenishing of the punch bowls, Laurette realized that the lovers had disappeared somewhere. She refilled her glass several times, eyes reconnoitering the various entrances. When they reappeared through the terrace doors, they looked guilty. Jacintha's cheeks were rosy, her lips vivid from apparent romancing. Earl's tie was askew, his hair mussed.

Laurette swallowed more champagne before confronting them. "I trust you two are having fun?"

"It's a marvelous party," Jacintha complimented her.

"Thank you, Mrs. Danvers, but I'd appreciate it if you didn't monopolize all of my husband's time. As host, he should mingle with the guests."

"I had imagined that I was a guest."

"Not a privileged one, my dear!" She surveyed Earl critically, straightening his cravat possessively. "Where were you a while ago?"

"Smoking in the garden," he replied casually. "And now I'd like a drink."

"To quench your thirst, or to dampen your fire? Better get Jacintha one, too, and douse her pantalettes!"

"One more remark like that," Earl warned, "and this silly party will become a sensational spectacle."

Laurette reversed her strategy. "I have no wish to quarrel, Earl, but you are forgetting your manners." Her tone now resembled that of an indulgent mother scolding a thoughtless lad. "You know it's impolite to ignore the wallflowers. Poor Beverly Gaynor and Virginia Colby are about to take root in that corner. Do ask them to dance, Earl. Jacintha will excuse you, I'm sure."

"Certainly," Jacintha agreed, with a smile so warm that Laurette longed to freeze it with a hard, cold slap.

But Earl was beyond intimidation. "You seem to forget, madam, that Jacintha is without an escort, and scarcely acquainted with our other guests. You invited her, and I shall do my best to entertain her."

The orchestra began a romantic Viennese waltz. Earl bowed and offered Jacintha his arm. "May I have the pleasure?" he requested, grinning at his glowering wife as he swept his lovely partner onto the glossy floor.

They whirled through a medley of Strauss selections, while Laurette favored General Cutter and then an elderly gentleman barely able to shuffle his feet. So Earl was deliberately taunting her. She felt an intense urge to retaliate, but common sense restrained her.

At two o'clock she signaled the maestro to conclude the ball. He nodded, tapping his baton on the lectern. Earl's apparent intention to dance the finale with Jacintha outraged Laurette. Enough was enough! Such humiliation was not to be borne graciously.

Lifting her wide skirts, she moved precariously through the crowd, half-running in her sudden frenzy, shoving one couple aside, nearly upsetting another. She had sipped too much champagne on an empty stomach and was fairly intoxicated, unaware of the curious stares and the gasps. The width of the floor appeared enormous, instilling in her a desperate feeling that she could not cross it in time to prevent Earl and Jacintha from dancing that last waltz together. Her green eyes were fierce and glittering, her titian hair escaping its pins, her diadem tilted and bobbing on her head like a mad queen's.

"Oh, God," Jacintha murmured, nudging Earl.

"She's drunk and hysterical," he sighed, motioning to Dr. Stedman, who was already hurrying to the scene.

The perceptive conductor, long acquainted with social melodrama, had become something of a diplomat. He attempted to camouflage the awkwardness by playing louder. Some guests continued to dance. Others stepped aside, astonished by the peculiar antics of the hostess. Laurette was swaying giddily, unable to coordinate her movements, alternately laughing and crying, muttering about an impostor among them, who was about to be arrested for trespassing.

"We shall press charges to the full extent of the law," she screamed before losing her equilibrium completely and sprawling on the floor.

Earl carried her swiftly upstairs, Dr. Stedman close behind, the brass of the orchestra now virtually blaring. Many couples were leaving the floor, talking excitedly.

Twenty minutes later the host returned to apologize, explaining that it was nothing serious, just nervous exhaustion, and that Mrs. Britton was resting comfortably. But many guests, including Jacintha, had already left. Understanding his master's particular concern, the butler apprised him: "Mrs. Danvers asked me to convey her regrets, sir. A storm is brewing, and she was afraid of being marooned."

Earl nodded, as a thunderbolt crashed over the house and lightning flashed at the windows.

"Well, tell the maestro to stop playing, Gaston. The party's over."

Laurette slept for ten hours, waking with a vile headache and only a vague memory of the debacle. Nor did anyone except Earl dare to remind her as she sat glumly in bed nursing a horrible hangover.

"What a travesty!" he remarked, shaking his head incredulously. "I doubt my efforts to explain away your drunken hysteria fooled anyone. Alcohol and jealousy create a combustible combination, Laurette, and you made a goddamn fool of yourself."

She grimaced, wondering if it was really worse than she imagined. "Did anyone hear me accuse you and Jacintha?"

"Of what? You were incoherent, raving about an impostor in our midst. Then you passed out."

"If any paper prints that, I'll sue for libel."

"The gossip mongers will spread the news, without benefit of the press, Laurette."

"What shall I do, Earl? We must repair the damage to our reputation."

"Not *we*, Laurette. Your tippling and temper were responsible. One consolation is that long tongues are often attached to short memories. Some other scandal will soon occupy the gossips."

She nodded, sighing. "Meanwhile, I could go abroad."

"Good idea," he agreed. "That's the standard prescription for exhaustion, isn't it? An ocean voyage. You could sail from Philadelphia on the new luxury liner your father is launching shortly. It's mentioned in today's *Maritime News* that you'll be christening it soon."

Laurette perked up, thinking that Cousin Norman might accompany her on the voyage. Of course!

"I'll start assembling my wardrobe immediately," she decided. "I'll have to wear something special to christen my third namesake."

"May I suggest sackcloth and ashes, with a red letter?"

"Let's not be sanctimonious, dear," she retorted. "A hair

shirt is in order for you too. We could all do a little penance."

"I've been atoning for years, Laurette."

"Poor Saint Earl, victim of self-martyrdom! Why not solve all our troubles by self-immolation?"

"Another impasse," he muttered. "It's like living in a boxed canyon."

"Well, even a cul-de-sac has its advantages, darling. You don't have to wonder where you're going—you know it's the end of the road."

PART VI

Chapter 37

WHILE the South struggled under Reconstruction, the North enjoyed tremendous prosperity. Demand for every type of raw and manufactured product exceeded supply, and companies were hard-pressed to keep up with orders. Industrial stocks boomed, creating millionaires.

Enormous deposits in the Danvers estate accounts expanded Jacintha's fortune beyond comprehension. Like most women in her position, she entrusted her business affairs to lawyers, bankers, and managers. But when labor difficulties in the New England textile industry were reported in the newspapers, she became concerned about the Danvers mills in Lowell, Massachusetts.

Letters to the superintendent brought polite assurances that no such problems existed. Skeptical, Jacintha consulted the Manhattan law firm appointed by her late husband to administer his estate, surprising the senior partner, whom she had met only once previously, when the will was read at Riverview. Her belated interest in Cole's business was puzzling to the attorney.

"Don't trouble yourself, Mrs. Danvers," he advised her. "Everything is under control."

"But I own those mills, Mr. Hickman, and I've read disturbing rumors about the unconscionable working conditions in many textile factories. Perhaps it's time I visited my mills in Lowell and the Boston shoe factory."

"Oh, I wouldn't recommend it, madam," he replied, in an attempt to dissuade her. "You have excellent managers at both concerns, and the employees are treated as well as any others. Surely you have no quarrel with the profits? You are an extremely wealthy lady, Mrs. Danvers." His eyes admired her chic costume, lingering frankly on her face and figure. "Also, if I may be so bold, an exceptionally beautiful one—and so young to be a widow. Are you still mourning your late husband?"

The impertinent inquiry angered Jacintha. "I'm still single, sir, if that's what you mean."

"No offense intended," he apologized, stroking his graying goatee while continuing to leer at her. "It's only natural for a charming young widow to have gentlemen admirers —after a decent interval. Nothing improper in that. Besides, your little son needs a father, don't you agree?"

"We were discussing business, Mr. Hickman."

He nodded, clearing his throat. "Yes . . . well—is there some dissatisfaction with our conduct of your legal affairs, Mrs. Danvers?"

"No, I merely want to learn more about them. I should have done so before."

"That's your prerogative, of course, although most women prefer to leave such things to men."

"I'd like to be knowledgeable about mine," Jacintha insisted. "Please notify the various managers that I plan to be more active in the future, in correspondence and in other ways. I am requesting duplicates of all transactions for my personal files."

"Your personal files, madam?"

"Correct, sir. Mr. Danvers maintained an office in our residence and I shall reactivate it."

"Very well, madam. But you may find such data dull and even confusing. Facts and figures generally baffle the female mind."

His amusement irritated Jacintha. "Not always, Mr. Hickman. Some of us can actually read, write, and comprehend arithmetic."

"And some might handle small inheritances alone. But few could successfully manage a large estate without legal counsel. Nevertheless you shall receive the information you request, Mrs. Danvers. We'll arrange for monthly conferences, if you wish. Naturally, complete quarterly reports will still be furnished. We serve our clients to the best of our ability, ma'am."

Jacintha stood, pulling on her gloves. "Thank you, Mr. Hickman. I'll be in touch. Good day."

But when she related the conversation to Earl that evening, he was inclined to agree with the attorney. "Why involve yourself, Jacintha? That's a reputable law firm, and the Danvers enterprises are running smoothly and profitably, aren't they?"

"Money isn't my concern, Earl. You know about the crisis in the Northern textile mills, don't you? I'm wondering about my mills. The superintendent denies any labor difficulties, but I'm not convinced. Edward Austin was hired by Cole, and I remember *his* business philosophy. Hardly benevolent."

"Ruthless," Earl said.

"I am the owner and I should see for myself how the Danvers mills are operated."

Earl frowned. "I can tell you, Jacintha. Most factories operate under sweatshop conditions, and the textile industry is no exception. You'll find women and children working long hours for paltry pay. The supervisors are invariably male, and some are greedy enough to demand kickbacks in wages, or other favors from the young girls. The workers are mostly immigrants. Many are illiterate and many are ill with chronic diseases. They live largely in dilapidated company housing, perennially indebted to the commissary. Seeing these things would sicken you. So spare yourself. It may be wiser to simply sell to your competitors, who have no qualms about suffering humanity."

"Just pretend all that doesn't exist?"

"I understand your outrage, but I'm trying to protect you. I don't want you hurt, Jacintha."

"Hurt?"

"Reformers often meet with . . . accidents," he explained laconically.

"You mean foul play?"

"Yes."

"But it's a free country, Earl! I have a right to inspect my own premises."

"Certainly, but be sure you hire bodyguards. Labor conflicts can be violent, Jacintha—bloody. In any case, don't go to Lowell alone or without telling me."

She realized that she shouldn't be surprised. She knew that strikes were often murderous affairs. "It all seems so wrong, Earl. Something should be done."

"It is wrong, Jacintha, but not easily remedied. Congressional action would be required, beginning with the abolition of child labor and laws currently favorable to industry. But it took war to abolish slavery, remember? Labor will have to fight for its liberty, too, and it'll probably be a long, complicated, bitter struggle, with much bloodshed. Don't try to crusade alone, Jacintha."

After some restless pacing, Jacintha sat down and pondered the deep-blue carpet as if it were a reflecting pool. "Selling the mills would be the easy way out, and cowardly, wouldn't it?"

"Perhaps," he mused.

She chewed her lower lip contemplatively. "Maybe I should join the women's movement. They care about more than just their own lot. Their goals include compulsory education for every child until the age of sixteen, humane welfare institutions, and decent conditions in industry."

"Noble goals, to be sure, but how much have they accomplished?"

"Not much," Jacintha ruefully admitted. "They have some intelligent and dedicated leaders, but dissension in their own ranks hampers them. They need more efficient organization."

"Like Congress," Earl said sharply, lighting a cigar. "What a mess they're making of Reconstruction. If what I saw on my last trip to Charleston is true of the rest of the South, no wonder Aunt Evelyn tried to jump from a window."

Jacintha gasped in dismay. "You didn't tell me that. Poor soul! Her mental state must be deteriorating."

"On the contrary, I think she's improving, and Geraldine agrees. Aunt Evelyn recognized me this time, and spoke rationally. She's escaping less into senile fantasy now, and she was probably trying to get away from reality. Defeat is harder on the old, you know."

"Are you and Geraldine on better terms now?"

"Better, but not friendly. She can't forget the color of the uniform I wore and won't accept any part of her rightful inheritance. Eventually, perhaps . . ." Earl shrugged. "Right now I'm more concerned about our status. It's a dilemma that would torment the devil himself, I think."

"The agony of adultery," she murmured.

"Not really adultery, everything considered. There's more to marriage than the vows and ring, darling. Surely you realized that with Cole."

"Yes, and I'm not recanting now, Earl. God forgive me, but his death was a great relief, a release from bondage." She laid her head on his strong shoulder. "How long do you think Laurette will stay in Europe?"

"As long as it amuses her," he answered wryly. "With her family's connections in London and the European capitals, that could be a year or more."

"The foreign correspondents say the *Laurette III* is honored in the major ports, as if American ambassadors were aboard. In the *Tribune*, Kate Field writes of glamorous presentations at court and regal entertainments at palaces."

"Gold always works magic. The Lancaster shipping empire is second to none in the world, and the family is prestigious and politically powerful. Laurette's male traveling companion is a poor relation—a mere peasant by comparison."

"Is Norman Heath really her blood kin?"

"They're first cousins," Earl said. "Their mothers are sisters, which makes it rather convenient for them to travel together without arousing suspicion. I don't know exactly when their incestuous relationship began—possibly in adolescence. But it's not the worst of Laurette's trangressions—one of them nearly killed me."

"Larry?" she asked perceptively.

He was tensely silent.

"It's all right, Earl. I suspected that she was responsible for his sudden departure, though at the time I blamed you."

"Seducing my own brother," he said reflectively, wincing at the memory. "God, how I hated her for that! But more for its effect on Larry than on me. He was tormented by what he'd done. Neither of us could speak of it to the other. I only pray that he didn't die with that weighing on him."

Jacintha held him comfortingly, stroking his back, trying to soften the pain. "You must forget it, Earl."

"How, Jacintha? Tell me how! In a way, it caused both his death and Mother's. Larry might not have gone South if it hadn't happened, and Mother might have come North."

"But it did happen, Earl, and nothing can change that. Regard it as destiny."

"You may be right," he said wearily.

"Certainly destiny brought you and me together. But now some perverse force seems to be working against us, and I worry every time we make love. What if the precautions fail?"

"They may not be necessary."

His body jerked as if he had unexpectedly been stabbed. "Is that a medical opinion?"

"No, but there were childbirth complications, you know. Jaffet was hardly a qualified physician."

"Goddamn charlatan! I still feel like killing him. But weren't Doctor Selby's examinations later on reassuring?"

"Well . . . I suppose so."

"Let me take you to a specialist."

"In due time, darling. We can't test any gynecological assumption now, anyway. I'm supposed to be widow, remember?"

"How could I not remember?" he asked bitterly.

As daylight faded from the sky, the sun's last rays struck brilliant facets on the diamond-paned windows, enhancing the castlelike aspects of Greystone's lofty tower. A pair of pigeons were romancing on the parapet, billing and cooing. Winged shadows appeared on the glass, and Jacintha heard the plaintive cries of sea gulls. Soon twilight would bathe the gray stone in ethereal hues of lavender, violet, and deep purple before velvet darkness encompassed their sanctuary.

"Evening is so lovely here," she remarked as Earl was lighting the lamps and candles. "I used to pretend that Greystone was the only estate on the island—a real castle —and the surrounding rivers were moats. Childhood imagination is a wondrous thing, isn't it?"

"A divine gift."

"Ronnie is beginning to pretend that you are his father," Jacintha said timidly.

"I am."

"But he doesn't know that, Earl."

"He will eventually."

"Is it too early to go to bed?" she asked, digressing, suddenly needing reassurance.

"It's never too early, or too late, to make love." Earl grinned. He parted her silk negligee and nuzzled his face between her warm, fragrant breasts. "Each time it seems more intoxicating, and I'm more eager."

He slipped the gossamer garment off her shoulders as she released the tasseled cord of his robe and pressed her bare bosom to his hard chest. There was no concealing his spontaneous arousal or denying her desire for him.

They lay back on the bed, and Jacintha's arms bound him for a few possessive moments. Sometimes this physical contact seemed the only real thing in their lives. Oh, the thrilling reality of vital flesh and pounding hearts!

He did not take her immediately. His hands and mouth

toyed with her tensely expectant body, while he rode his own impulses with a curbed bit. Kisses stifled her voice. Gradually, tentatively, his inquisitive fingers and tongue explored secret regions, venturing more deeply and boldly than ever before. A different experience, this, unique in its voluptuous raptures. Jacintha achieved a wild and glorious climax before his mouth returned to hers.

"Did you like that, my love?"

"Yes," she murmured shyly. "Is it wrong?"

"How could it be wrong if we both enjoy it?"

"But is it—" she hesitated, abashed by her wild abandon, "—is it nice?"

Her naïveté made him smile reassuringly. "Nice? It's beautiful, Jacintha, and perfectly natural."

"Beautiful," she agreed, craving more.

His face loomed over hers, his voice teasing. "Feel wanton?"

There was so much to experience, and Jacintha knew that they would never tire of experimenting together. Reaching out, she pulled him to her.

Chapter 38

JACINTHA'S impulsive decision to travel alone, ignoring Earl's warnings, precipitated a lovers' quarrel on the eve of her departure.

"Damn it, Jacintha!" he swore in exasperation. "I told you I can't leave town now. Uncle Peter is at home, recovering from a stroke, and the bank is busier than ever. Please, Jacintha, wait until I can go to Lowell with you. You shouldn't travel alone."

"Unchaperoned? Darling, I'm a widow, not a maiden! And I promise to telegraph you if anything goes wrong. . . ."

She would heed no further argument and Earl was forced to satisfy himself with accompanying her to the train depot the following morning.

The textile industry of Massachusetts was centered in Lowell, the state's second largest city, often called the Manchester of America. Long buildings, sheds, and warehouses lined the banks of the Merrimac River, and the social distinctions between the mill owners and mill workers were rigid.

Despite what she had read or heard about working conditions, Jacintha was shocked by their reality. The much-advertised "Lowell Offering" of the 1830s had regressed dismally in the past thirty years, until not even its false image remained. Sturdy young girls had been recruited from New England farms and villages, lured by promises of good wages; supervised dormitories; free time for Sunday worship, holidays, and recreation. Many, realizing the lies involved, had returned to their homes, often disgraced. But replacements came from the thousands of hopeful immigrants landing daily on America's eastern shores.

As Cole had once told Jacintha, entire families frequently worked together in the textile mills, existing in poverty and squalor even when they combined their meager wages. The machines were as efficient as modern technology and skilled mechanics could make them, but the operators labored under severe handicaps—dim lighting, poor ventilation, thick dust, abominable heat in summer and numbing cold in winter. Lung ailments were rampant, and Jacintha heard hacking coughs, gasping, and expectoration all around her. She estimated that at least half of the employees were afflicted with some form of chronic lung disease.

Too, long hours and monotony contributed to accidents. Nudging by conscientious comrades prevented some. Falling asleep on the job was cause for dismissal. Most appalling to Jacintha were the numerous children with rheumy eyes and runny noses, constantly sniffling as they labored. Illness and poor nutrition had already stunted the growth of some and disfigured their bodies. They resembled hunchbacked gnomes. They raised timid hands to overseers in order to be excused to perform natural functions, and Jacintha suspected that permission was denied if requested too often.

The superintendent bragged about the high level of production. "Never an idle hand. We're always ahead of schedule."

Jacintha wanted to remark that Simon Legree ran his plantation in a similar fashion, except that he had a frequently employed whip. Edward Austin's scourge was invisible, but equally fearsome.

He paused for compliments, puzzled when they were not forthcoming. "Had I been told about your visit, Mrs. Danvers, a better reception could have been prepared."

Did he mean a better picture presented? Fewer sleepy youngsters on the job, more coolers of fresh water available, some open windows, less filth?

"Impromptu inspections are usually more accurate reflections of reality, I think, Mr. Austin. You see, I've read about the strife in the textile industry, and I was curious about my own mills. Am I to assume that this operation is the same as our competitors'?"

"It's standard," he replied. "And any labor complaints can be blamed on the new cotton mills rising in the South. Future competition will be so keen below the Mason-Dixon Line that some New England mills may be forced into bankruptcy. Starving Southerners are willing to work longer hours for less pay than the smallest Northern companies offer. Many factories are already considering moving South. Why, we may even be hard-pressed to attract immigrants here!"

"Couldn't we survive without them?"

"Not very well. So labor leaders figure now is the time to strike. Trade unions disbanded during the war are being reactivated. We'll have to fight to protect free enterprise." He addressed his assistant curtly. "Isn't that correct, Mr. Holden?"

Brian Holden hesitated, his reluctant nod qualifying and even denying his superior's statement. Still in his twenties, Brian's mill career had begun in childhood, before his parents had left England. After some years in the Danvers mills, his father, a mechanic, had died of a massive lung hemorrhage, while his pregnant wife and young son watched in helpless horror. Several months later the weak and grieving widow perished in childbirth, leaving a sickly infant daughter for her teenage boy and a kindly neighbor to raise. Ellen Holden, now sixteen and pretty in her wraithlike frailty, worked in the dyeing rooms. She had learned the trade from an immigrant British calico printer who had taken a fancy to her before his untimely death of an anil dye disease.

Jacintha realized that Holden had been coached about what to tell her, and he surely knew that his and his sister's livelihoods depended on his discretion. She wondered what revelations Brian might provide under different circumstances, and she decided to gain his confidence.

She paused to talk with some of the girls, most of whom avoided direct facial confrontations while answering her inquiries.

"It's fine here, ma'am," one replied with an Italian accent, her dark eyes downcast.

"I like it here," another said, minding her loom. Her butter-colored braids suggested Dutch or German ancestry.

"They treat us well," a French-Canadian spindle operator added, crossing her fingers under her apron. "We've got no complaints, and it's good pay, too."

A pert Irish redhead volunteered, "They promised to build us a social hall and allow more time for recreation." She sighed wistfully.

Jacintha, brushing lint from her clothes, exchanged covert glances with Brian Holden, whose honest gray eyes told her the girls were lying, because they had no alternative. A complaint in the superintendent's presence could result in not just dismissal but blacklisting at other mills.

"No labor problems here," Austin boasted. "Just one big happy family! Those union renegades won't have any luck stirring up trouble here. You can return to New York with complete confidence. But first, please honor my wife and me with a visit to our home. She is most anxious to meet you."

"Thank you, sir. And you and Mrs. Austin must be my dinner guests at the hotel."

"We'd be delighted." He smiled in acceptance, turning again to his assistant. "Mrs. Danvers might find the dyeing rooms of interest, Holden. Show them to her, and introduce your sister." He bowed to Jacintha. "Your pardon, madam. I'm due at an important sales meeting. We are receiving many new orders."

"I understand, sir."

Austin left smiling, entirely confident that Brian Holden would cooperate.

For a while it seemed he would do exactly that. He escorted Jacintha through an entire block of buildings and sheds, guiding her safely away from the humming machines, explaining the various operations knowledgeably and courteously. But as they progressed, Holden realized that this was not merely a routine inspection. Mrs. Danvers had traveled a considerable distance, and her interest seemed more than selfish.

"Is this your first tour of a textile mill?" he inquired as they entered the dyeing rooms.

"Yes, and I'm curious about all the procedures, although I realize it would require years to learn them. Is there a training program?"

"A brief basic course," he replied. "That's why most operators remain with the same machine, in the same position, for years."

"How monotonous! Doesn't it stifle workers' enthusiasm?"

"Yes. But management has its reasons."

That needed no clarification. Broad experience was apt to promote dissatisfaction with tedious jobs.

Jacintha indicated the huge wooden tubs of bright liquids. "I presume these are the color vats. What is the process?"

"It's long and tedious," Holden said, "but I'll try to cover the important points."

She listened attentively as he briefed her on the most common sizing materials, starches, and tarrangeic gum, and their application to the numerous intaglioed rolling machines, which transformed plain cloth into multicolored bolts. The hand-printed fabrics were especially fascinating, requiring a skillful artisan to produce wonderful designs and brilliant hues on the intricately carved wood blocks.

Brian's sister was exceptionally adept at the craft. As Jacintha admired her work and complimented her on it, Ellen graciously thanked her, adding, "If you prefer any particular pattern, Mrs. Danvers, the mold can be reserved exclusively for you, or destroyed to make sure that the pattern is yours alone. I could also design one to your specifications."

"Aren't you kind! They're all so lovely, Ellen, I can't decide. I'd appreciate your excellent taste in helping me."

"I'd be honored, Mrs. Danvers."

"Your sister is perfectly charming," Jacintha told Brian Holden later, "but she doesn't seem very well. She should have a thorough medical examination."

"The mill physician says she's in fine health," he replied ruefully. "That's his diagnosis of all employees . . . regardless of their condition. I know Ellen is very ill, Mrs. Danvers, and I'm afraid she has the same lung disease that killed my father. There is a terribly high rate of consumption in all the textile mills."

"Take Ellen to Boston to consult a respiratory specialist, and forward the bills to the Danvers estate."

Brian paused, choosing words carefully.

"And what of the others, madam? The ten-year-old boy who hobbles on a stick because his foot was mangled and he can't afford crutches, and the little girl who spits up blood in violent coughing spasms, and the asthmatics who gasp for air with every breath, and the expectant mothers who will probably miscarry or deliver stillborn or malformed infants—shall I take them all to Boston specialists and bill your late husband's estate?"

Jacintha was embarrassed. "I'm sorry, Mr. Holden. I just wanted to help. I didn't think. I'll speak with Mr. Austin and the company doctor. There must be remedies taken for everyone here."

He couldn't tell her that any such suggestions would be ignored. He caught her looking at his leg and explained his slight limp.

"The game leg is a childhood affliction from a mysterious disease that often kills, cripples, or paralyzes. Because the leg exempted me from military service, Mr. Danvers suggested my being promoted from overseer to assistant superintendent. The war also gave my sister a chance to learn a skill usually practiced only by men."

Jacintha wanted to spend more time in the mills, with Brian Holden as her educator, but she was also curious about the workers' homes. His hesitancy when she mentioned it suggested that he had received orders from Mr. Austin about that too.

"Lowell is a mill town, Mrs. Danvers, and no better or worse than others, I suppose. Visionaries and their advocates may dream of utopias, but they are only fantasies."

"Things *must* change eventually, Mr. Holden. Nothing stays the same forever. Civilization must either progress or perish."

Glancing at her shyly, he ventured, "You are a rare person to concern yourself about us."

"I didn't always have wealth, Mr. Holden. I used to be quite poor."

After a short silence, during which Brian Holden absorbed this information, Jacintha urged, "Tell me more about your family."

"It's a familiar story. Like many other immigrants, my parents had heard of great opportunities in America. It took years to scrape together the money for passage, but they finally managed. We took a boat that landed in Boston, because most of the textile mills are in Massachusetts."

When he felt that she was listening intently, he went on. "Well, good mechanics are always in demand, and Father had no difficulty finding employment. But the wages and working conditions were no improvement over Manchester's. Mother and I had to take employment in the mills too. I lost an older brother who died from fever and flux on the trip, and he was buried at sea." He paused, reluctant to continue lest the truth seem like a bid for sympathy. "They later considered returning to England, but could never save the fare. Besides, my father was already consumptive and my mother expecting. She survived him only by a few months, orphaning me and the baby. That's about all, Mrs. Danvers."

Impressed by this sensitive, intelligent young man, Jacintha invited him to escort her back to her lodgings. "I'll be in town a few more days, sir. We can resume this discourse tomorrow. Right now I'd like to rest and write some letters."

"At your service, Mrs. Danvers," he said, assisting her into the carriage provided by Mr. Austin. "Perhaps you'll permit me to show you some of our more pleasant sights? We do have some."

"That would be very nice," Jacintha agreed. "I enjoyed the steamboat voyages on the rivers from Boston. This is such a beautiful state. So many streams and waterfalls!"

"Which provide power for the factories and mills. Good for industry, but bad for nature."

Cole would have considered this remark idiotic. "Were you acquainted with Mr. Danvers?" she asked.

"Not very well. He spent most of his spare time here with Mr. Austin."

Birds of a feather, Jacintha thought as they reached her destination. "Please don't bother getting down, Mr. Holden. I'll see you in the morning, about nine?"

"Certainly." He tipped his hat, clucking to the horses. Driving away, he could feel his curiosity growing. Meeting Mrs. Danvers had inspired him, brightened his life, and for that, Brian would always be grateful.

Chapter 39

BRIAN HOLDEN was early for their appointment the next morning. Jacintha was in the hotel dining room when he arrived, spruced up in a dark suit, a clean white shirt, and neat cravat. What a nice-looking young man! she thought as the waiter directed him to her table.

"Good morning, Mrs. Danvers," he greeted her cheerily, admiring her radiant beauty and lovely costume.

"Good morning to you, sir! Will you join me? They serve a tasty buffet here."

"No, thank you. Ellen fixed breakfast for me at home before dawn. Her shift starts at seven, and tardiness is penalized."

"No exceptions?"

"It's a rare excuse that qualifies."

"I understand. But you are not on duty now, so sit down and have a cup of coffee, at least."

He eagerly accepted, and she finished her meal. He creamed and sweetened his coffee, which he usually drank plain, nervous that she might glance up from her plate and catch his enchanted gaze. He had never known a lady so glowingly fresh and lovely.

Between sips of tea, Jacintha inquired, "Does Ellen ever work at night?"

"Only in emergencies. Artificial light can distort a textile printer's vision. Then the colors might not be true. Ellen's an artist in her field," he said proudly, "and could easily go to another mill. But she stays because of me. She works on the most expensive cloth, while printers of lesser ability handle the cheaper goods."

"What is her salary?"

"Five dollars a week. She works six days, twelve hours each."

"Shocking!" Jacintha declared.

"I agree, ma'am. Men with half her skill earn several times as much."

"Then raise Ellen's salary to compensate."

His grave expression told Jacintha that she had erred. "The superintendent reserves that authority for himself, Mrs. Danvers. And I'm sure he won't like your idea."

Jacintha could not conceal her exasperation. "Mr. Austin discriminates against women?"

"It's general policy," he said.

"Well, it's unfair! Your sister should be paid for her services."

"Unfortunately it does not work that way, Mrs. Danvers. Ellen is actually training men who will eventually earn more money than she does. They'll work shorter hours and have opportunities for promotion. My prayer is that she will find a good husband soon and leave the mills."

She picked up her reticule and put on gloves in a determined manner. "I'm ready to leave now."

Holden proudly escorted her through the lobby, striving to control his limp. Outside he assisted her into the company buggy, basking in her smile, as bright and warming as the sunshine of the summer day. But her request to see the infirmary made him anxious again, despite her reassurances.

"This will have no effect on your or Ellen's employment," she promised. "If it does you need only contact me.

I'll leave my address. Send a letter or telegram. Or come directly to New York, expenses paid."

"There is no infirmary," he said as they left the Merrimac Inn, "only a staff physician with a private practice."

"Not even a trained nurse on duty?"

"The mill hands give one another first aid in accidents and other emergencies," Holden explained.

"And the plans for leisure facilities?"

His silence was eloquent.

"What about the drawings posted on the walls?"

"They've been there for years, and are replaced with new ones when they fade. Fantasies to encourage gullible girls, who expect them to eventually materialize."

"And they shall," Jacintha said determinedly, "along with a clinic! These will take precedence over mill expansion—and over remodeling of the executive offices."

"Noble intentions, Mrs. Danvers, but none of this will be easy. Move cautiously or your competitors will consider you a zealot."

"Was Mr. Danvers a hard taskmaster, Brian?"

"Like all the others," he answered honestly. "Business is business."

"His family were immigrants, too, working in mills and sweatshops. Brutalization hardens some people, instead of making them compassionate. Apparently this happened to Mr. Danvers."

Brian drew rein by the Merrimac River, on a knoll near a panoramic view. "Look at the water, ma'am! It was once clear and pure, tumbling down from Pawtucket Falls. Now there are poisonous dyes, sewage, and other waste matter. Industrialists seem to think that God created water only for their benefit."

Jacintha watched the snaking slime of varicolored liquids. The stench was so bad that she covered her nose and mouth. "It's criminal, Brian," she said angrily as they drove away. She then reminded him that she wished to see where the workers lived.

The company housing projects were just like metropolitan slums, with dilapidated tenements and old boarding-houses, where six or more girls shared a single small dormitory, as crowded as charity wards. Families of eight and ten occupied pitiful shacks that had no sanitary facilities whatever. Drinking, cooking, and bathwater was obtained from community pumps or rain barrels, and filthy privies crawling with vermin interspersed the area. Jacintha marveled that epidemics did not wipe out the population.

But these horrors, Brian explained, obstinately squaring his jaw, were not on his tour. He was supposed to show only the comfortable residential sections inhabited by supervisory personnel and local businessmen, before proceeding to the mill owners' mansions.

"Would you care to go inside one of the Danvers properties?" he inquired. "Proprietors are privileged to enter at any time, you know."

Proprietors, Jacintha told herself, abashed. Dear heaven! She owned some of these wretched hovels!

She shook her head vehemently. "No, I can imagine the interiors, Brian."

"There's a commemorative plaque on one place."

"For what reason?"

"To mark the house in which the Danvers family once lived," he explained. "Mr. Danvers commissioned it before his death, and a ceremony accompanied the mounting. It's supposed to show the workers that it's possible to accomplish the seemingly impossible. He always mentioned it on his visits."

More as self-praise, Jacintha thought, than as inspiration to others. "I've seen enough here, Brian. Too much."

"Well, Royalty Row is next on the itinerary. The palaces of the mill kings, Lowell's ruling aristocracy."

And palaces they were, as grand as any Jacintha had ever seen. Some were bizarre in their architecture, some beautiful; all epitomized wealth and power. The landscaped grounds were equal to private parks, and summer gardens created gorgeous splashes of color.

"They all have lots of servants," Brian said. "They entertain lavishly and travel a great deal. Their children are either tutored or attend private schools, mingling only with their class. Who says America has no caste system?"

"Americans tend to beguile themselves, Brian, and a peerage of sorts exists in our society, whether we recognize it or not."

"You know," Brian said carefully, "that labor activities are not exactly secret now. The pot is beginning to boil. It may spill over, possibly explode into violence. There's no reason to suppose your mills won't be involved, Mrs. Danvers."

Jacintha frowned, chewing her lower lip. "Somehow I never think of them as *my* mills, Brian."

"But they are, ma'am."

"Yes . . . they are.

"Have you considered where you would stand if trouble develops?"

He answered without hesitation. "I would resign my position and support the workers. Lead them, if necessary."

"What about your sister?"

"Ellen would go with me."

"I thought you would say that, Brian."

"I'm sorry, but it's how I feel."

"Don't apologize for honesty, Brian. From my observations, labor's grievances are justified, and evidently you don't believe things can be changed through reason."

"You can't debate a one-sided issue, ma'am."

He was right. The mill owners recognized only one viewpoint—their own. But, as Earl had warned her, compassion and outrage would not alter the status quo. Reforms did not often result from bleeding hearts; often bodies had to bleed as well.

"What you say is true," Jacintha said. "But please don't consider leaving the Danvers mills. I need you, Brian. More important, the workers need you."

"Thank you kindly, ma'am. But I was assigned to escort you, not convert you. Perhaps you would prefer to dispense with dour business for a while—take a leisurely drive in the country?"

"I would indeed."

It was pleasant and relaxing to travel along the rural lanes through sunlit woods and meadows of wild flowers, crossing rustic covered bridges, once splashing directly into a shallow brook fringed with ferns and cattails, Jacintha and Brian chatting like friends on an outing. The pond of rippling blue water amid white-trunked birches and weeping willows suggested the peace and serenity of *Walden* to Brian. Here he confided his dreams to Jacintha, as he had to no other person except his sister, inquiring anxiously, "Does it sound like the ravings of a mad dreamer?"

"The idylls of a poet," she said softly. "Is that your ambition, to settle here? Wouldn't it be rather lonely?"

"Oh, I won't be a total hermit! I'll bring Ellen with me. Sunshine and fresh air might restore her health. And I'd be fulfilling the deathbed promise I made to Mother if I could really take care of Ellen."

Jacintha struggled with emotions threatening to overwhelm her. "Then do it, Brian! Pursue your dreams. Ellen is blessed in having you."

Worry began to shadow his mood. "Nevertheless, some evil people are critical and suspicious. Already we've heard vicious gossip insinuating that there is more than a sibling relationship between us. Lies, of course! We care deeply for each other, and I feel a definite responsibility for Ellen —but that's the full extent of it." His eyes rested on the pond and instantly he was visualizing the cabin he would build on its banks. "So why haven't I taken a wife? Well, the mill girls have dreams, too. They fancy the princely sons of the mill kings and prosperous merchants, not a bloke with a twisted leg and sickly sister."

"Surely they can't all be so foolish, Brian? The right one for you just hasn't come along yet."

"And when she does," he said, shrugging skeptically, "I'll have to work to support her and a family. Life in the woods will remain a fantasy forever."

"Not necessarily." Jacintha wanted to offer him a loan to construct his dwelling immediately, but she feared she might offend his pride. Another way must be found to help him and his sister.

The sun was sinking as they returned to town, and the Merrimac River, stained with scarlet and crimson dyes, seemed to be flowing blood. An awesome sight, it chilled Jacintha and prompted her to ask, "Do you think the labor strikes are imminent, Brian?"

"Maybe, maybe not. Naturally the mill owners have informers in the labor organizations and keep abreast of the situation. But a boil can fester only so long before it bursts. Prevention lies in lancing it before it reaches that stage, and management is the only physician in this case."

Jacintha understood. The superintendent was in complete charge of labor, and Ed Austin was a cold-blooded bastard. Something would have to be done about him. Meanwhile, she hoped there was time to make plans.

"I'll be leaving tomorrow, Brian."

His keen disappointment was obvious. "So soon? Have I offended you somehow?"

"Of course not. Quite the contrary, Brian. It's just that . . . I have a little boy in New York, and I miss him terribly. He is my primary concern, which probably makes me less of a businesswoman."

"Just more of a woman," he said complimentarily.

"Those poor blind mill girls! Can't they see that a knight in shining armor walks among them?"

"Limps," he corrected ruefully.

"Oh, Brian, it's not a deformity! Why, it's scarcely noticeable." She handed him a card containing her name and home address, which he slipped into his breast pocket.

"Mr. Austin will be curious about your sudden departure, Mrs. Danvers."

"I think he'll be relieved, Brian."

"May I take you to the landing tomorrow?"

"On one condition—that you stop addressing me so formally and have dinner with me this evening."

"That's two conditions."

"So it is." She smiled, offering her hand. "Well, are we agreed, Brian?"

"We're agreed, Jacintha."

Chapter 40

A S soon as she was back in New York, Jacintha ordered the estate lawyers to retire Edward Austin as superintendent of the Danvers mills and replace him with Brian Holden. Mr. Hickman's reluctance infuriated her, implying a personal interest in the matter.

"I regard that as a mistake, Mrs. Danvers, and would be remiss in my duties if I did not tell you so. I've met Brian Holden. He's too young and inexperienced for such a big responsibility. Austin is older, wiser, and far better qualified for the position. He has held it over twenty years, after all."

"Long enough. He should retire," Jacintha said, unswayed. "I'm confident that Mr. Holden will prove his ability."

"To whose satisfaction, madam?"

"Everyone's."

"And if he fails to fulfill these expectations?"

"I'm not concerned about his failure, sir, only that he may not accept. He has other aspirations."

Hickman snorted, curling his lip contemptuously. "What higher goal could a poor cripple have than to be superintendent of a major textile mill?"

His attitude paralleled his late client's in many respects, reason enough for Cole to have engaged his firm's legal services. "Not everyone thinks of achievement in the same terms, Mr. Hickman. Some have other ideals."

"March to a different drummer? Such nincompoops usually fall behind in the march of progress and get left by the wayside. If your profits suffer under this game-legged idealist, don't blame me."

Jacintha was silent, wondering what court action was required to break a will or change administrators. Earl would know, and she would discuss it with him later. She had already sent a message to Britton Bank, and expected him to call that evening.

He did not wait that long. His phaeton was standing in the driveway when she returned, and they rushed swiftly into each other's arms. Ronnie tugged at her skirts and his trousers, vying for attention, until Lollie whisked him off to the nursery, explaining, "Uncle Earl played with you enough for one day, Master Ronnie. Leave him and Mommy alone now."

Earl was so relieved to have Jacintha home safely that desire overrode restraint and, for the first time, he made love to her at Riverview.

"Shame on you," she gently admonished as he ushered her upstairs to the master chamber. "What will the servants think?"

"That we're in love and couldn't wait any longer," he replied in the same gentle tone. "Is that wrong, Jacintha? And does it really matter what other people think?"

"No," she murmured, answering both questions with reciprocal hugs and kisses.

"I missed you, darling! But I ought to spank you for leaving without protection. I worried that something might happen to you."

"Well, nothing happened, dear. But I did learn a lot. And I made some important decisions."

"Tell me later," he urged. "It's been torture without you."

Urgency propelled them into bed, and it was twilight

before love was gratified enough to allow for conversation. Jacintha lighted the bedside candle and fluffed the eiderdown pillows against the velvet-padded headboard while Earl poured drinks for them. Like the candle, the after-love drink was a ritual with them, increasing the enchantment. Admiring his magnificent torso as he approached, Jacintha patted the empty space beside her, smilingly inviting him, wishing he could always share this bed with her.

"Why the secretive smile, Mona Lisa?"

"I was just thinking that you'll need a robe, if we intend to make a habit of this."

"Do we?"

"What?"

"Intend to make a habit of it."

"If you wish."

"Yes, but not in this same bed."

"It didn't seem to inhibit you a while ago."

"But it might in the future, unless I'm master of this house."

"You are, in spirit."

"But not in reality, Jacintha."

"I'll have this suite completely redecorated," she promised, sipping her Madeira, the radiant glow of his lovemaking still apparent upon her roseate flesh, her sensitive skin still tingling from his touch. "Would that help?"

"Some." He nodded. "Now tell me what you found in Lowell."

"You were right about the mills, Earl. The conditions of the employees are abominable! The superintendent is a greedy, uncaring brute, concerned only with profits and his own welfare. But his assistant is a decent human being, and I'm hoping to put him in charge. The estate attorney advised against it. Earl, is there any way I can break Cole's will?"

"Not without sufficient legal cause, Jacintha—fraud, mismanagement, collusion, or theft of funds—and I doubt there's any such evidence. That firm has a respectable reputation, and courts tend to adhere to the deceased client's stipulations. Some wills contain irrevocable clauses forbidding the beneficiaries to resort to litigation, actually denying them any say-so. Fortunately Cole did not place those restrictions on you—perhaps because he never imagined you would want to make changes. So you have some leeway."

"Even if Mr. Hickman opposes my plans?"

"According to the document, he can only advise, not dictate to you, Jacintha. And since the firm is receiving a lucrative administrative fee, I doubt that Hickman would jeopardize it in court."

"Then I *can* offer Brian Holden the position! And I can change management in the Boston factory, too! Shorter hours and a living wage are imperative. Discrimination against females should also be eliminated, along with child labor. Oh, there's so much to be done, one scarcely knows where or how to begin! It's a national problem—a national disgrace, really."

"I'm glad you realize that, Jacintha," Earl declared with obvious relief. "I was afraid you might try to tackle the monumental task entirely alone." His face lit up as he changed the subject. "I have some good news for you. Laurette is returning in September."

She tensed, frowning. "How is that 'good' news?"

"Hear me out, darling. A member of the British peerage, Lord Percival Compton, is arriving with her. From what I've read about the old boy in London and Paris gossip columns, he has a penchant for handsome young men— and is likely more interested in Cousin Norman than in my spouse. But he's also a wastrel who has squandered his family fortune and run up mountainous debts. He has little now except his title to trade on. Well, the Lancasters have always fancied English titles. If Compton is prospecting for gold, and I suspect he is, he may have discovered one of the richest lodes in America."

"But Laurette is married!"

"Divorce to marry into nobility is not so abhorrent to society," Earl said. "Indeed, it's relatively common among the aristocracy. All Philadelphia will be vying to entertain his Lordship."

"Are they landing in Philadelphia?"

"Yes, thank God. I've been requested to welcome the ship."

"Will you?"

His brow creased as he worried about Jacintha's reaction. "Probably."

This was almost more than they had dared hope for.

"I'm praying that Laurette and Compton can make a match. Maybe they'll arrange a marriage of convenience and take Cousin Norman back to England with them. What a *ménage à trois* that would be! Both Lord and Lady Compton in love with the same American adonis."

"That sounds awfully complicated."

"It's quite simple, actually, and not as rare as some people imagine. I'll explain it to you sometime, my precious innocent, but not right now." His mouth sought hers, and his knowing hands stroked her under the scented linen sheet, kindling the familiar fire. "Oh, Jacintha, maybe at long last we can have a life together! Man and wife, with our child, and others to come . . ."

Mute with love, overwhelmed by new possibilities, Jacintha clung to him desperately, straining toward the ultimate rapture only he could provide.

Chapter 41

EARL'S participation in the welcoming ceremonies was brief and perfunctory, consisting of handshakes and a few words, after which he became more of an observer. His newly finished yacht, which he had insisted that Jacintha christen with her name, was moored in the Philadelphia harbor. Though a sleek, seaworthy vessel, the *Jacintha* was eclipsed in terms of size and grandeur by the *Laurette III*. This floating palace, comparable to the best of the Cunard luxury liners, had undoubtedly caught his Lordship's eye in the Thames Pool. Parchment replicas of his bronze coat of arms had been previously shipped to the Lancasters and were now nailed to staffs hoisted by the crowd on the pier. The Union Jack waved beside the Stars and Stripes, a red carpet was spread before the gangway, and flower petals were showered on the happy trio debarking the ship. To Earl's amusement, Norman was in the center, linking arms with the couple, each of whom was obviously courting his affections.

Apprised of the romance between his wife and Lord Compton, Earl telegraphed his attorney, Henry Fields, who came posthaste from New York. Unable to persuade a solicitor to accompany him to the United States sans retainer, Compton was represented by Morris Trevaine, one of the Lancasters' lawyers. Discussions regarding the divorce, the marriage contract, and the dowry demanded by his Lordship continued for a week in the Lancaster library.

Meanwhile Laurette and Norman amused themselves riding in their new English saddles, driving in the country, strolling in the family gardens and the public park along the Schuylkill River while Mrs. Lancaster and the caterer planned a grand ball for the spectacular announcement.

Compton had a long list of demands, which Mr. Trevaine was to draw up for him in a formal document. Earl could scarcely believe that Robert Lancaster would agree to the extortion merely to acquire a tarnished title for his daughter. Indeed, the Philadelphian's subservience to an English lord, in the very city where the Declaration of Independence had been conceived, disgusted Earl. Glancing over the clauses in fine print, he read the high points aloud.

50,000 pounds British sterling upon signature of the marriage contract.

The *Laurette III*, or a new Lancaster ship built to Compton's specifications.

Payment of all bills for repairs, renovations, and maintenance of Compton Hall and other Compton properties.

Purchase of twenty-four thoroughbred mares and eight blooded stallions to add to Compton's stables.

Six custom-designed carriages, open and closed, and four racing vehicles.

Settlement of all of Compton's outstanding debts, including gambling wagers.

10,000 pounds for replenishment of his wine cellars.

10,000 pounds on account to his tailors.

10,000 pounds annually for domestic staffs.

10,000 pounds annually for holiday travels.

20,000 pounds annually for entertainment.

40,000 pounds annually for personal and miscellaneous expenses, and the same amount again for his wife.

Shaking his head incredulously, Earl shoved the list across the library table to his father-in-law. "How much of this outrageous ransom am I expected to finance?"

"None," Mr. Lancaster replied, ignoring his counsel's advice. "We are arranging my daughter's dowry, Earl. You refused one when she married you, but it is customary in these circumstances. Indeed, a dowry is often mandatory with royalty. I do not find Lord Compton's stipulations unreasonable."

In Lancaster's place, Earl knew he would have destroyed the paper, possibly even crammed it down Compton's greedy throat. Didn't the old gentleman realize that he was bartering his daughter to a dissolute rake and degenerate who much preferred the young man out with her now?

"Well, sir, if it pleases you, I surely have no objections," he conceded. "But I insist that my attorney and I have sufficient time to study the divorce petition and recommend changes if any are appropriate."

"Certainly, my boy. We have no wish to defraud you or to hurt you, Earl. It's just that Mrs. Lancaster and I want our daughter to be happy. And we believe she will be, once all this is settled. It's fairly evident, I think, that your marriage was a misalliance. Unfortunately it's too late for an annulment, so divorce is the only alternative."

"I agree," Earl said quickly.

"As a gentleman, you will—I assume—admit full responsibility for the action?" Trevaine inquired nervously. "We all realize that accusations of infidelity have little effect on a man's reputation."

Earl's stoical nod masked his intense relief at the prospect of freedom.

When his Lordship joined them, dipping snuff, he

drawled, "Naturally my legal fees are to be included in the marriage contract."

"Naturally," Lancaster agreed, bowing his head. He was sixty-six, with steel-gray hair and beard, one of the wealthiest men in America, a distinguished citizen in his state, and prominent, along with his sedate and attractive wife, in social affairs. Earl could not imagine the reprobate nobleman contributing anything at all to the Lancasters, except eternal demands.

"Shall we leave the business details to the counselors, gentlemen, and take a respite for brandy and tobacco?"

When the cognac was served by a black butler and the Havana cigars offered, Lord Compton raised his snifter in a congenial salute. "I should like to propose a toast: to a happy future for everyone."

"I'll drink to that," Earl said.

The cousins returned at dusk. As they entered the dining room for dinner, holding hands, laughing, teasing each other like children at play, Compton's odd eyes smoldered with jealousy. He was not jealous over Laurette. Was her father too staid, or perhaps too benighted, to see what was going on? Earl wondered what his father-in-law really thought of all this. Percival pouted over the rack of lamb with mint sauce, the artichoke hearts and asparagus in Hollandaise, the delicious ice cream dessert baked in a crisp meringue crust, and sipped the superb imported wine as if it were cooking spirits.

Mrs. Lancaster, still in awe of their noble guest, sensed his displeasure and worried that the family had somehow failed to provide proper hospitality. Peering at him over the floral centerpiece and flickering candles in silver holders, she remarked conversationally, "Your Lordship will surely want to see some of our local tourist attractions, and Laurette is a knowledgeable guide."

His response was patently sarcastic. "I doubt a true Englishman would enjoy your Revolutionary War monuments, madam—your Independence Hall and cracked Liberty Bell, or whatever. But the countryside and waterways might be of interest. I fancy traveling in one of those paddlewheel steamers I noticed in harbor. We don't use them in England, you know."

"We shall arrange a private excursion on a Lancaster model," his host promised. "There are many in our fleet, including one which accommodated Charles Dickens on his last visit to the United States. He was our houseguest while in this city, and graciously signed his works for us."

The nobleman was not impressed by information about a commoner author whom he did not especially admire. "I'm not an avid fan of Mr. Dickens, although I've read the accounts of his American travels. Some of them are hardly flattering."

"His journals reflect his own opinions," Earl interjected, "to which he has every right. They might have been more valuable references, however, had he better restrained his personal prejudices."

"Touché! But you can't quarrel with his depiction of your New York slums as the worst in the world," Compton persisted, more out of perversity than in defense of Dickens.

"Really? I thought Hogarth awarded that dubious distinction to London's slums."

His in-laws silently thanked him, while Laurette squirmed nervously, afraid of an argument between her patriotic husband and cynical fiancé, who quite obviously detested each other. "We'll skip the Revolutionary relics, as well as those of the War of Eighteen-twelve," she said decisively.

Earl affected nonchalance. "How diplomatic, since his Lordship is certainly aware that Lancaster vessels fought the British in both conflicts."

Norman, feeling left out of the conversation, suggested that Lord Compton might like to visit "our most famous Civil War battlefield, which is only a short distance away."

"Gettysburg, where your fellow men slaughtered one another like mad butchers crazed by summer heat? It's a cemetery now, isn't it? I find nothing inspirational in ground hallowed by gore."

"The English have spilled their share of blood, foreign and domestic, over all the earth," Earl reminded him.

"True, but I don't make pilgrimages to the scenes, sir. Furthermore, although we remained neutral in your War Between the States, the Queen was sympathetic to the South."

"In more ways than one," Earl said gravely. "The Crown's furtive favoring of the Confederacy helped to prolong the war and cost us all more lives."

"Mr. Britton lost his brother in the war," Laurette hastily explained. "Ironically, they fought on opposite sides. His mother, also dead now, was a Southerner."

"I see." Percival shrugged his narrow shoulders negligently, aware that their feud was personal, having nothing to do with international policy. "Actually I paid little heed to your internal squabble, and I couldn't abide that boorish clod, Lincoln. I consider his successor an absolute ass. And your Congress is a political arena comparable in intrigue to the Roman Forum, though without its statesmanship."

"Matched only by your Houses of Parliament," Earl retorted.

"Ah, but you can't fault our prime minister!"

Mrs. Lancaster tinkled the silver bell that signaled the meal's end and the men their freedom to pursue debate elsewhere. She was astonished that an innocent suggestion on her part had triggered it.

Curious to know if the negotiations had been completed, Laurette hesitated to inquire. A lady was not supposed to concern herself with such matters.

Nor would Earl ever tell her at what price she had been sold to nobility. And since only the formality of divorce remained before the formal betrothal, the parting couple was properly separated at night—Laurette slept in her dainty girlhood chamber; Earl, in comfortable guest quarters down the hall. Lord Compton and his valet occupied an elegant suite on the third floor of the mansion. Cousin Norman was placed in an attic dormer befitting his poor-relation status. The only child of Martha Lancaster's widowed sister, Philippa Heath, mother and son had been sponging off their affluent kin for years.

Norman had never done a day's honest labor with his hands and very little with his head, despite a good education and several proffered opportunities in the Lancaster enterprises. His one experience in an office, where he assumed undue importance, as a Lancaster relative, created such havoc among the other employees that his uncle decided it was better to retire him with a regular allowance. Mr. Lancaster was as pleased as Lord Compton that nephew Norman would soon be sailing to England—to remain there permanently, he hoped.

Ascending the stairs at bedtime, Laurette remarked to her husband, "I noticed your new yacht lying offshore. Rather confident in naming it, weren't you? Are Jacintha and the boy aboard, by any chance?"

"Certainly not."

"Then the maiden voyage took place in other waters?"

"I'm tired, Laurette. That was quite a lengthy conference in the library today."

"But amicable, I trust?"

"Oh, yes. Everything was resolved to his Lordship's satisfaction. Your father is very generous. And compliant."

"Why not?" she asked. "I'm his only heir, after all, and he loves me dearly. Far more than you ever did."

"That's ancient history," Earl said, walking swiftly down the corridor to his room.

"Good night," Laurette called, but there was no answer.

Chapter 42

THE Lancaster reception for Percival, Lord Compton, was Philadelphia's social event of the season. Every chandelier, wall sconce, and candelabrum blazed in the stately red brick Georgian Colonial mansion in Fairmont Park. Ornamental lanterns glowed along the tree-lined driveway. Torches were reflected in the pools and fountains of the landscaped grounds. The October evening was ideal for the dashing formal capes of the gentlemen and the regal furs of the ladies.

The honored guest, a latter-day Beau Brummell in courtly attire, occasioned some amused and even cynical male comments.

"A strange breed, that old boy."

"Too much lace and ruffles on his sissy shirt, and a perfumed hanky tucked in his sleeve, no less!"

"The way he struts and swishes in those fancy opera pumps, I'm sure he's good at pirouettes. La-dee-da!"

"A fop, and she *had* a real man."

In England, thinly disguised satires in the press hinted at Compton's drug addiction, bizarre habits, and perversions. He was the subject of a banned biography comparing him to the Marquis de Sade, and a recent play depicted him as the most depraved nobleman in the British Empire since the notorious Fourth Duke of Queensbury. Persona non grata at the Court of St. James, he was not yet ostracized in the more liberal European palaces. He frequented the Tuileries, and even boasted of having propositioned Louis Napoleon's favorite mistress on his last sojourn in Paris.

Overhearing this remark, Earl cornered him and questioned him skeptically, "When was this?"

"Oh, rather recently, old chap! The Comtesse de Castiologne is the reigning beauty of Europe's aristocracy, you know. Few men can resist her charms, though they risk the guillotine for pursuing her. The emperor is extremely jealous of the gorgeous creature, and the empress would probably like to poison her."

"You don't fear irate husbands?"

"I'm a formidable swordsman, sir. Also handy with dueling pistols, a bow and arrow, and other weapons."

"It must be embarrassing, though, not to be received by your own queen."

"I make no apologies to anyone for my way of life, sir. Furthermore, I expect to be reinstated in Her Majesty's good graces, eventually, when I am ready to recant. Perhaps at seventy or so. Many sins are pardoned in old age, but I haven't reached that stage yet. I'm only fifty."

He appeared much older. Tall and exceedingly slim, his pallid skin was stretched transparently over his delicate facial bone structure. His long acquiline nose had snuff-tinged nostrils, and his thin-lipped mouth wore a perpetual smirk. To Earl he personified the decadence into which some men sank out of boredom and frustration, indulging every whim, wasting their inheritance.

Lord Compton had received a number of marriage offers, but mostly from elderly dowagers, homely of face and figure, with children to share in their estates. Although an American commoner, Laurette Britton was the first reasonably young, attractive, childless, and affluent prospect he had met in recent years. And despite his homosexual preferences, he felt capable of consummating a marriage. Nor was he oblivious of the romantic attraction between Laurette and her handsome cousin. The thought of the trio under one roof conjured erotic fantasies. He knew of certain aphrodisiacs to release inhibitions and had become familiar with their use.

His eyes followed Norman, who was dancing with a pretty young girl, and Earl goaded him, "They make a charming couple, don't they? Unfortunately Norman is too poor to be considered a good match for Miss Doris Chalmers. Her people are very rich."

"Not richer than the Lancasters?"

"No, the Lancasters have no peers in wealth."

"You consider me a mercenary bastard, don't you?"

Earl shrugged, smiling laconically. Then he excused himself and walked over to Laurette, who had been watching them. "Methinks his Lordship has more than a casual interest in Cousin Norman, or hadn't you noticed?"

In a Worth gown of pale green velvet and rose-point lace, bedecked in her finest jewels, including a diamond-and-emerald tiara on her titian tresses, she might already have been Lady Compton. "He regards Norman as a younger brother," she said, steadying her champagne glass with both hands.

"You can't believe that, Laurette. His admiration is far from fraternal—it's lustful."

"You have an evil mind, Earl."

"Not compared to Compton's, my dear. Surely you're not oblivious of that lecher's motives?"

"He's a complex man maligned by his enemies. But even if what they say about him is true, it's no novelty abroad. Many aristocrats flirt with both sexes simultaneously, and one hears strange tales at every gathering. How different the Old World is from the New!"

"Give us time, Laurette. They've had a few thousand years more to reach their present state of decay. But we're doing our damnedest to catch up. All that aside, how do you feel about his Lordship personally? The truth, please, if it's in you."

"Are you jealous?"

"Curious."

"Well, I'm quite fond of him. I realize that he's eccentric and possibly wicked, but he's also fascinating. I thoroughly enjoyed our stay at his Mayfair residence in London and his country estate in Sussex. Compton Hall has been a part of his family for centuries. The manor is in the Tudor style, with ninety rooms and several banquet halls. The battlements are still intact, and the moat is now a charming canal with several gondolas imported from Venice. The furnishings and art are priceless. There are many beautiful gardens, a large forest and game preserve, stables and kennels, and even an aviary of exotic birds. A great many servants, of course. Tenant farmers work the land and live in quaint thatched-roof cottages. We're going to host fox hunts and lavish entertainments, and people will vie for invitations."

"In that case, maybe the dowry should be increased."

"What are you implying?"

"Didn't you read the marriage contract before signing it?"

"In part. Father has no complaints, and I resent your vile insinuations. I'm hardly an old hag, Earl!"

"No, indeed. But Percival is quite a *bon vivant*, with extravagant tastes, and he's accustomed to indulging himself."

"That's one of the privileges of nobility, and I hope he isn't disappointed in this little soiree. We tried to meet his expectations."

"It's somewhat puzzling to see Philadelphia's elite groveling to him as if he were the Prince of Wales. He's only an insolvent nobleman, in disfavor with his sovereign and besieged by creditors."

"Must you harp on his finances?" Laurette demanded angrily. "He may be pressed, but he's not impoverished! Nor does he seek only security in our marriage. I think we'll have most interesting relations."

"Undoubtedly," Earl agreed. "You have my best wishes, Laurette."

"Do you mean that?"

"Sincerely."

"Will you attend the wedding?"

"No, but I'll send an appropriate gift."

"Odd, isn't it, how things developed? If Jacintha hadn't attended your homecoming party and I hadn't created that ridiculous scene . . . well, I might not have gone abroad, and none of this would have happened. Then again, it might. Destiny has a way of arranging these meetings."

"And retributions."

"Try not to be nasty, Earl, although I fear you don't know any other way of being. I wonder what fate has in store for Cousin Norman? He's such a dear."

"A clairvoyant might predict his imminent involvement in an unusual triangle," Earl said, tongue in cheek.

"Oh, I suppose he'll do his share of wenching. Most men do, single or not." But she knew what he was referring to.

"How do you think he'll react to your new spouse?"

Pretense could not disguise her worry. "Percy has invited him to live with us. Norman is rather dependent, you know, with little future in America. And he does like England. Actually, he and Percy have much in common."

"In addition to debts?"

"There you are, being mean again!" Laurette cried furiously. "Why can't we have a civil conversation, Earl? His Lordship hasn't tried to beguile me or present a false image of himself. He's an honest person with few illusions about himself—and rather handsome for his years, don't you agree?"

With his narcotic pallor and peculiar hooded eyes, Earl thought Compton resembled a corpse in baronial shroud and ribbons. But he lacked the heart to further antagonize her. "Definitely, my dear, and your union should prove to be a unique experience. You'll notify me, I presume, when the final arrangements have been completed?"

Humor restored, Laurette winked archly. "I think you really are jealous."

"The eternal coquette," he replied mockingly. "Vanity, thy name is Laurette."

"Still anxious for your freedom, darling?"

"Well, now that you've found a replacement, why delay?"

Her laughter teased him, and she tapped a provocative finger on his satin lapel, flicking the white carnation boutonniere flirtatiously. "That's not very subtle, sir. I must confess that absence has made you appear more attractive to me, and some ladies here must be wondering what attracts me to Lord Compton besides his title. Shall we mull it over further in bed tonight?" She had not lost any of her audacity!

"I wouldn't want to crowd Cousin Norman," Earl drawled. "I suspect he'll be sneaking down from the garret again later, as he did last night."

Tempted to toss her champagne into his face, Laurette barely restrained herself. "Why, you despicable wretch! Still spying on me!"

"Don't flatter yourself, Laurette. I couldn't sleep and was going to the library for a book. Norman was scratching at your door like a tomcat following a scent, so eager to get in, he didn't see me. Your secret is safe, my cunning hypocrite."

Quivering with mortification, Laurette spilled some of her champagne on the carpet. "It'll be a pleasure to be rid of you, Earl! Neither I nor my family will feel the slightest regret."

"They approve of his Lordship?"

"Why not? I couldn't make a worse mistake with him than I did with you. The devil himself would be an improvement!"

Compton was maneuvering across the crowded ballroom, resembling a specter amid the more wholesome figures, including some hardy descendants of William Penn's Quaker colonists.

Sensing that he had interrupted a quarrel, Percy sought to mend it. "I presume the Brittons have reached an amicable understanding?"

"Quite some time ago," Earl replied. "It has just taken longer than we expected to implement it. I must admit, you were the necessary catalyst."

Compton regarded this as a compliment. "Then you don't anticipate any legal obstacles?"

"None from me, I assure you."

"Good. I dislike messy involvements. In this case, more for the lady's sake than mine, however." Opening a jeweled snuffbox, he applied a pinch of tobacco dust to each stained nostril and inhaled appreciatively. "I must say, you Americans are more civilized than I imagined."

"Only some of us, your Lordship. There are still many savages at large, and even a few cannibals."

"Not in New England, surely?"

Earl grinned at his wife, who, unlike Percy, had not missed the allusion. "You explain it, dear. I can't bear to disillusion him."

"My husband relishes jests," Laurette said, fuming under her serene façade.

Percy said with a sour grimace, "Then he should come to the Court of St. James. The dour queen is much in need of a court jester." Offering Laurette his arm, he bowed gallantly. "I believe this is our dance, milady."

"So it is, milord."

They danced well together, for Laurette had the toes of a ballerina, and his Lordship possessed equal grace.

Absorbed, Earl was unaware of Norman's approach until his morose remark: "It seems, at long last, that the Lancasters are about to acquire a title in the family. They would like the wedding to take place here, but Compton insists on having it in England. He claims it's a great occasion when a lord takes a lady, and must be celebrated in grand style, at Compton Hall. Do you think Laurette will be happy, Earl?"

"Do you?"

"For a while, yes. Like a child with a new toy, Laurie can usually be temporarily amused. But it rarely lasts. I believe the unsavory rumors about his Lordship. Their marriage won't be just a holiday which his wife can abandon at will. How long can she endure it when she knows his true character?"

Earl pitied Norman, despite his certain knowledge that the younger man had incestuously cuckolded him. "Laurette is not naive, Cousin."'

Norman drank from his crystal goblet, wiping his golden mustache with a linen kerchief. "Oh, I'm sure she's aware of some facts, Earl. But awareness and true acceptance are two different matters. Laurette is accustomed to being the center of attention, and she craves it like food and drink."

"People adjust to the situation at hand," Earl consoled him. "Human nature is amazingly flexible, Norman. I learned that in the war. When there's no alternative, one endures things that would otherwise seem impossible. Incidentally, how did you avoid conscription?"

"My health," Norman explained, embarrassed. "I have jaundice from a chronic liver ailment. Some sort of fever in my youth, for which my physician furnished an affidavit. I'm considered cured now, although I still suffer periodic attacks."

"Will you be sailing to England with the Lancasters?"

"I'm looking forward to it," Norman replied.

"Bon voyage," Earl wished him, then turned and left him standing there.

Chapter 43

ONCE set into motion, the legal machinery functioned with amazing speed to remove the impediments to Laurette's marriage. An uncontested decree was quietly granted, and there were no critical social repercussions. A flurry of fabulous prenuptial entertainments preceded the departure of the now-formally engaged couple and their loyal entourage for the official ceremonies at Compton Hall.

Earl did not remain for the departure, but Jacintha read about it in the Philadelphia and New York journals. Laurette had requested the restoration of her maiden name, signifying total and permanent dissociation from her former spouse, to both Earl's and Jacintha's relief.

"Well, Mr. Britton, you look as pleased as if you had accomplished the coup of the century!" she greeted him on his return to Manhattan.

"That's precisely how I feel!" he said, swinging her jubilantly off her feet and bestowing a triumphant kiss on her mouth before setting her down again. "The former Mrs. Britton, once again Miss Lancaster, will soon become Lady Compton, and a British subject. All arrangements were made to accommodate his Lordship's stipulations."

Jacintha pinched herself. "I can hardly believe it! Tell me I'm not dreaming, Earl."

"You're wide awake, Curly Locks, and it's happily true. The convoy is on the high seas now, and I understand the wedding will be the grandest and most flamboyant since the Prince of Wales took a princess. Some members of the Royal Family may even attend, as well as European royalty. It should be quite a spectacle!"

Hearing Earl's voice, Ronnie ran into the parlor, his pet yapping at his heels. "See, Mac, I told you Uncle Earl was here!"

The "uncle" designation had always chagrined Earl, but now he knew that he could change it soon. The prospect induced a happy smile as he knelt to cuddle the child. "How would you like a father, Ronnie?"

"A real daddy for always?"

"Yes, every day, for keeps."

"Fine, if it was you, sir."

"It will be me, son. Your mother and I are going to be married, which means we will be living together. I won't be just a visiting uncle much longer."

Ronnie's bright gray eyes beamed; his sturdy legs jumped for joy. "Oh, good, I can't wait! You hear that, Mac? We're gonna have a daddy!"

The dog barked its approval, and Jacintha joined the rejoicing circle on the floor. "I knew you would be pleased, Ronnie, and so will Mommy. But now Uncle Earl and I must make plans, so go to your room and play."

"Yes, ma'am. I guess it's grown-up talk, Mac, and we're not supposed to listen. Come on, let's race upstairs!"

His parents gazed fondly after him, their thoughts mingling. Earl spoke first. "Perhaps we should tell him the truth, Jacintha?"

"We will, when he's old enough to understand. I don't think he would understand now. Oh, I hope we can give him brothers and sisters!"

Joy could not banish the persistent imp pricking at her conscience. "What were the grounds for the divorce?"

Earl hesitated, reluctant to disturb her. "The usual one:

adultery on my part, but no corespondent was named. Although the petition is a matter of public record, Jacintha, it won't affect you or Ronnie."

"And so my image is untainted—a respectable widow living quietly with her child? Our affair is a well-guarded secret? Nobody is aware of my late husband's notorious fleshpots, or that he was cremated in a harlot's arms? You don't think Laurette ever confided any of these things to her female friends?" she asked skeptically. "You honestly believe that bitter, vindictive witch never betrayed us?"

"Discretion was to her advantage, Jacintha. I could have thrown stones of reprisal at her glass house, and incest is far more serious than infidelity. Besides, her inordinate pride was at stake. She is an enigma I never fully understood, and I'm sure she often puzzled herself. I'd like to forget her now, and concentrate on us."

Jacintha acquiesced and sat down on the love seat. "Where will we live?"

"Wherever you wish," he said. "I know how much you love Riverview and how you sacrificed for it."

"What about your own residence?"

"It's just a house, Jacintha, and holds no fond memories for me. I've often wanted to escape it. We can keep Greystone for a country place, or build another somewhere. Long Island, Connecticut—we can decide later."

Her fingers traced the delicately carved pattern of the rosewood-framed heirloom. She sighed. "I had some very bad news while you were gone."

He was lighting a cigar, and stopped puffing, dismay on his face. "How so?"

"Brian Holden, the young assistant superintendent I told you about, is unable to assume management of the textile mill. His sister has consumption, and the prognosis is poor. Holden wants to care for her in the country. He wrote me in detail, expressing humble appreciation and regret, and requesting a leave of absence. You may read the letter, if you like," Jacintha offered, removing the correspondence from the desk.

Earl was deeply impressed by its sincerity, and by the sacrifice the young man was prepared to make on his sister's behalf. He could understand Jacintha's admiration for Brian Holden, and her confidence in him. "He must be quite a fine man, Jacintha. Let us hope Ellen will improve, and you won't be deprived of his services for long."

"Meanwhile there's still Edward Austin and the same labor problems," she lamented.

Earl paced before the fireplace, his grim countenance profiled by the blazing logs. "Restraints can be placed on him through the estate attorneys, Jacintha. He'll have to adhere to them or find himself replaced. Would you like me to go with you to the law firm? I think I can convince Mr. Hickman of what must be done."

"Please do, Earl! My conscience would never rest otherwise. Ellen Holden is sixteen and probably doomed to an early grave. And there are hundreds, thousands more like her in the industry, some even younger. I see them in my sleep. It haunts me," she said ponderously. "I wonder what to do, how to help—and while I search for answers, people sicken and die. When we discussed it before, you said only legislation could alleviate such an abominable situation. Perhaps you could persuade some of your influential friends in Congress to work on measures?"

Earl paused, puffing thoughtfully on his cigar for a few moments before tossing the cheroot into the flames. "Unfortunately Congress is currently bogged down in a morass of Reconstruction bills, and I doubt if Jesus Christ and the apostles would be heeded on other issues now."

"What about the President?"

"Andrew Johnson is facing threats of impeachment. The kind of influence he needs in the House and Senate can't come from the working class, because they have no power anywhere."

"It's the children's plight that grieves me most, Earl. Their emaciated little bodies, pale, gaunt faces, tragic eyes never leave me. I visualize Ronnie in their place and wonder how their mothers can *bear* it."

"Most have no choice, except to starve."

Her chin quivered. "It's a crime against humanity!"

"I agree—and God should have forbidden child labor in the Commandments. But even so, it would have been ignored . . . just like His others. Poverty and injustice are rampant everywhere, Jacintha, and children are the principal victims. In every city slum young boys steal, and even kill to survive. Little girls turn to prostitution, and some are sold into white slavery by their own ruthless or desperate relatives. Is it more horrible to hire them out in sweatshops, where they frequently work beside their parents, or their brothers and sisters?" He frowned. "How does society weigh evil against evil, balance wrong against wrong? Wise men have pondered these questions for ages, without finding answers."

"Perhaps wise women could help to resolve them."

"Perhaps," he allowed.

"Some are trying, you know."

"Yes. Do you want to join them?"

"I'd like to work for children's rights."

"And did you imagine I'd object?"

"Not really, although many men do disapprove of the women's movement and consider it a threat. I attended a meeting at Cooper Union while you were in Philadelphia, and several bruised wives testified to being beaten by irate husbands merely for broaching the suffrage subject in their homes."

"Well, fear not, darling. I don't believe in beating my wives."

"Seriously, Earl, the speakers talked about many horrors —the deplorable conditions of the insane asylums, hospital charity wards, orphanages, and prisons. They organized committees of volunteers. I think it only fair to tell you that I offered my help."

"You have my blessings, Jacintha. I certainly wouldn't deprive you—and I'll try to twist some politicians' arms, although I can't guarantee results."

"Oh, Earl, I do love you! And I promise my dedication

to this won't interfere with our marriage. Other wives and mothers manage; so can I. I met many of the leaders, including Miss Anthony and Mrs. Stanton. Some of the ladies have large families, and others were obviously pregnant."

"I wish you were," Earl said, pulling her to her feet and kissing her passionatcly.

She wagged an admonitory finger. "Not until we're married, dear."

"That'll be soon." His eyes focused on her luscious pink mouth again. "Any ideas about the honeymoon?"

"A few. You?"

"A Caribbean cruise might be nice." He had considered Europe, but feared encountering Lord and Lady Compton.

"Marvelous!" Jacintha cried. "If we put into Charleston, maybe I could meet Aunt Evelyn and—and Larry's wife."

"Widow," Earl corrected. "We'll see."

"Can we take Ronnie and Lollie along?"

"Wouldn't sail without them! What kind of wedding would you like, my love?"

"It doesn't matter, as long as it's legal."

But it did matter, more than she would admit. If only she could have the ceremony of her girlhood dreams and come to him pure and innocent! If only she could somehow vanquish those terrible years with Cole!

"Cold, darling? You're shivering." His arm around her, he guided her gently to the hearth. "Is this better?"

Her head bobbed against his chest as she struggled to control her emotions. "Much."

"Marital jitters, Jacintha? You're not having second thoughts about marrying me, are you?"

"Oh, my dearest, of course not! The tremors had nothing whatever to do with us—you and me. Some ominous shadows from the past just suddenly appeared."

An understanding nod revealed a similar confrontation in Earl's mind. "Are they gone now?"

"Yes—I hope forever."

"If they return, we'll dispel them together."

Burning love warmed her more than the wood fire as he embraced and kissed her again. Their bodies seemed to weld, becoming more inseparable with each tender word and gesture. "I already have the ring," he whispered, nibbling her ear. "A plain gold band, because you said you like them best. It's inscribed, too."

"Tell me the inscription."

"Not until I place it on your finger."

"I'll never remove it," Jacintha promised, "and I want your ring to be inscribed with the same words."

"What words?"

"True love, eternal love."

"You're psychic!"

"Snoopy," she confessed. "While you were busy a while ago, I picked your pocket. The engraving orders are printed on the jeweler's invoice."

He laughed, tweaking a springy curl. "I know, slyboots. I felt your eyes reading it behind my back."

"I'm sorry."

"For snooping?"

She grinned sheepishly. "For getting caught. But don't worry, I won't make a habit of rifling your pockets."

"You wouldn't find anything that didn't belong in them," he assured her. "Oh, Jacintha, what a treasure you are, more precious than gold!" But abruptly his mood sobered. "I'd better go now."

"Do you want to?"

"I never want to leave you, Jacintha—you know that. But since the wedding is so close now, you might prefer to wait for the blessing."

"Blessing—from a minister?"

He nodded. "There's a little church around the corner of East Twenty-ninth Street, in Murray Hill. The pastor is rather broad-minded about human errors, including divorce. We could say our vows before him."

"Oh, yes, Earl! When?"

"I'll speak with him today."

Never had he seen such radiance on her face, such shimmering brilliance in those beloved turquoise eyes. He

stared, mesmerized and enchanted, wondering if any portrait painter, however great, could do her justice. Who
could ever capture that particular expression on canvas?
"How beautiful you are," he said softly, deeply moved.
"Your eyes gleam like stained-glass windows illuminated
by the sun."

"Rain will cloud them if you say any more," she warned,
maneuvering him toward the door. "Hurry now, and bring
me the good news. There's so much to do!"

After kissing and waving him off, she lifted her skirts
and rushed upstairs to the nursery, calling, "Lollie, come
quickly! I need your help!"

"Is something wrong?"

"No, no! God's in His heaven, and all's right with the
world. I have to find my mother's wedding ensemble."

"It's stored in the attic, Missy. But you—you can't wear
it to wed Mr. Earl!"

"Why not?"

"You know why not."

"Is it against the law?"

"You're a widow, not a virgin bride."

"Lollie, I've seen pregnant girls in bridal regalia. Mr.
Britton knows a minister who'll marry us in church, and
I want to wear my mother's clothes, if they fit."

They climbed to the attic, where Lollie found the trunk
and Jacintha opened it. Tissue paper and pomanders protected the now-ivoried lace gown and fingertip veil attached
to a dainty seed-pearl crown. There was a cameo brooch to
adorn the modestly high neckline, as well as ivory silk
gloves and a small monogramed prayerbook.

"Not quite white any longer," Jacintha remarked, observing the revered articles, "but everything necessary is here,
even a frilly blue garter. And the lace hanky was probably
borrowed. I think the costume will do nicely, don't you?"

"You'll look as lovely as your mother," the housekeeper
agreed, vividly remembering Madeline Hartford on her
special day. "I can still see her poised at the top of the
stairway, like an angel about to float down on a cloud."

Jacintha tried to visualize the image in Lollie's mind and

thought she succeeded. "I'm not flouting convention much, you know. My first marriage was largely a sham. I never loved Cole Danvers, and I don't believe he ever truly loved me. There was someone else before and after me, and they died in each other's arms. Certainly what happened between us in bed was never an act of love, only enforced marital rights, more like rape." Jacintha clutched the cherished garments to her breast, trembling at the memory. "I was terrified that first night! I wanted to die, and I was afraid he might actually kill me."

She wept in Lollie's comforting arms, as she had so many times since childhood, and was soothed by the motherly voice. "Hush, baby, don't cry. You can't meet your prince with red, swollen eyes. Didn't I always tell you he'd come someday?"

"I wanted him when I was nine; now I'm twenty-six and he's in his late thirties."

"Just the right age for you, Princess. And he's just the right man. Shall we try the gown now, in case it needs some alterations? You'll have to wear fewer petticoats and a narrow crinoline—broad hoops weren't in style then."

"I want you and Ronnie there, Lollie, and so does Mr. Earl. Afterwards we're sailing to the Caribbean on his new yacht. All of us, including the pets. And how different this voyage will be from that horrible one on the steamboat to New Orleans! Oh, Lollie, I'm so happy!"

"Well, stand still! How can I do anything with you dancing up and down? I might stick a pin in you."

"Go ahead. I wouldn't feel it."

"Probably not, child. That's the magic of happiness."

"And love," Jacintha added wistfully, "which is the most powerful magic of all!"

Lollie fastened the final hook of the molded basque, which enhanced Jacintha's slender figure as if it had been designed just for her. Reverently she adjusted the exquisite Chantilly lace-and-tulle veil on the gleaming black curls. Standing back for a critical survey, Lollie clasped her hands before her in tearful admiration.

"A vision! Your dear mother should see you now, child. Your proud father and grandparents too."

"Maybe they can, Lollie. It would be a miracle, but I'm beginning to believe in miracles now."

"Me too," Lollie sniffed, taking a kerchief from her apron pocket. "And so will Mr. Earl when you walk down the aisle, Missy. So will the princely groom when he beholds his enchanting bride!"